The BORROWED Souls

Global Endeavor PUBLISHING

The BORROWED Souls

A NOVEL

PAUL B KOHLER

Edited by Amy Maddox
Cover design by Paul B. Kohler
Cover image by Sergiy Trofimov
(used and modified with permission)
Interior design and layout by Paul B. Kohler

ISBN-13: 978-1-940740-14-0
ISBN-10: 1-940740-14-2

www.paul-kohler.net

Give feedback on the book at:
info@paul-kohler.net
Twitter: @PaulBKohler
Facebook: facebook.com/Paul.B.Kohler.Author

Printed in the United States of America

First Edition

FOR ALICIA

BOOK 1

The SOUL COLLECTOR

Chapter 1

Everything was a blur, and I had to force my eyes to focus on the hand touching my shoulder. With effort, the watch on his wrist became clear. It read 1:45. My eyes followed up his arm, to his shoulder, and finally to the person the hand belonged to. The face was covered by several days of growth, and he had crystal-clear eyes.

"Hey, buddy. Last stop," he said, standing above me.

It took me a few moments to realize what was going on. Was this ... heaven? Or was it hell? I tried to stand up but slumped back again.

"Easy now. Had a few too many tonight?" asked the driver.

"Uh, I . . ." is all I could form in my mouth.

"Don't worry, buddy. I've been there before. You know I'm supposed to call the police when I find a drunk on my bus, but you look harmless enough. Let's get you out to the bench and you can take your time waking up." The driver pulled me up and led me down the aisle of the bus. He helped me down the steps and over to the bench.

Bidding me farewell, the bus driver climbed back in and drove off. I glanced around but nothing looked familiar. To say I was feeling a bit disoriented would be an understatement. As I sat on the cold steel bench, I tried to piece together what might have happened to me. I looked at my watch: 1:53 a.m. Where had the time gone? All I could surmise was that I was extremely late getting home from work and that Cyndi was probably worried.

Despite my throbbing head and the strong desire to curl up on the bus-stop bench to take an extended nap, I forced myself up and began to stagger down the block. As I neared the corner, I looked at the street signs. Neither of the cross streets sounded familiar. I looked in all four directions, wondering which direction home was, and chose the one that looked the most promising.

As I slowly stumbled along the vacant sidewalk, my mind began to retrace my evening. For the life of me, I couldn't even remember even getting on the bus. The last thing I could remember was leaving some café after work. I tried to remember who I was with and kept coming up blank. I must have been with Cyndi. But every time I thought of my wife, I began to feel anger creep into my head. Where was the anger coming from?

After another block of foreign surroundings, I realized I wasn't alone. With my head clearing more by the minute, I slyly glanced back over my shoulder and noticed a man. He was older, dressed in a tan suit with a white fedora. He followed me, keeping pace about a half block behind. Looking forward again I mumbled, "Cyndi, where the hell am I?"

Speaking her name jarred something loose in my head, and the memories from the past twenty-four hours began to resurface. A feeling of loss and despair rushed in, but I could not pinpoint the reason behind it. I felt my pulse rise, anxiety shot to the surface, and my pace quickened. I looked back at the man following me, and he also increased his pace. Not wanting to discover his intentions, I turned the corner, and, once out of sight, I sprinted to the nearest alley.

Ducking into the darkness of the backstreet, I stood in the shadows until the man passed by. He never did. I waited several minutes before I decided to move, and just as I stepped away from the dingy brick wall, a voice came from behind me.

"Feeling a little lost, Mr. Duffy?" The voice was little more than a harsh murmur, but the echo in the alley was thunderous.

I spun around, and the man was standing calmly in the alley. Next to the brightness of his hat, the color of his skin paled in comparison. His eyes were deep and sorrowful as he looked upon me with determination.

"Come again?" I asked.

2

"It's completely understandable. Riding the M-5 for six hours nonstop would certainly cause bewilderment for anyone," said the mysterious man.

Dumbfounded, I stared at the man. He was a stranger to me, but there was something about him that seemed familiar. "I'm sorry, have we met? You seem to know me by name and know where I was tonight."

"We've not been formally introduced, but rest assured, I'm not here to harm you. What do you remember from last night?" he asked.

"I tell ya', not much. I woke up on the bus, and all I can remember is leaving a café sometime after work. The rest of my day is a blur," I replied, rubbing my temples to soothe an ever-present headache.

"I sometimes find that starting at the beginning of the day is best. Shall we have a seat and begin?" asked the man as he led me across a dimly-lit street to a park bench that I hadn't noticed before stepping into the alley. As unusual as the situation was, it seemed like the right thing to do at the time, so I didn't protest.

"Now then, Mr. Duffy. What was the first thing this morning that you can recall?" asked the man.

"Wait up. Seeing as you know me, maybe you should at least tell me who you are," I stated, hoping to glean as much information about the stranger as I could.

"Come now, Mr. Duffy. You know who I am."

"Sorry, but I really don't. You seem familiar, but I don't remember ever meeting you."

"Oh, that is quite correct. We've not been formally introduced."

"Then what do I call you?"

"Whatever you wish," he said smiling.

"I don't understand. Haven't you got a name?"

"I do, but it doesn't matter what you call me."

We sat on the park bench for several moments in silence; all the while I was racking my brain as to why the last twenty-plus hours were missing from my memory.

"As I mentioned, it might help starting from the moment you woke this morning, or yesterday morning, rather."

The stranger held his closed hand toward me, and when he opened it, there was a large gold coin in his open palm. "Take this coin, Mr. Duffy. Take it and turn it over in your hands. Examine the two faces of the coin, and try to focus on the moment you woke."

I took the coin and did as he asked. The coin was quite old, the surfaces worn nearly smooth. I could just barely make out the words, "In God We Trust," but nothing more. I turned the coin over, and as I did, my morning came flooding back to me.

Chapter 1.5

I rolled over and glanced at the time: 6:43 shone in amber on the nightstand. I reached over and clicked off the alarm. Isn't it strange how one day you can set your alarm and wake up moments before it goes off, but another day you forget and you wake an hour late?

Not wanting to get up, I rolled onto my back, staring at the ceiling. Why did life have to be so demanding? Couldn't I just lie in bed and waste the day away? As I lay in silent contemplation, Cyndi began to stir. I looked over. Her eyes were closed tightly against the rays of morning sunshine beginning to peek through the drapes. I often wished I could be as content with my life as she was with hers. Rarely did anything faze her happy persona.

I reached over and touched the soft skin of her cheek. I could still smell traces of her perfume. The scent was intoxicating. Even after fifteen years of marriage, everything about her made my heart race.

"I love you," I whispered.

"Hrmm?" she mumbled, still in the grasp of sleep.

"I love you, baby," I repeated.

She smiled, eyes still closed. "Me too. You better get up or you'll be late again."

Cyndi was the exemplification of punctuality. I still don't know why she married me. I was late to my own wedding.

"I know. I was just lying here thinking about . . ."

"About what?" she asked, sliding her head over to rest on my chest.

"Work. Life. You. Take your pick," I said as I stroked her hair.

"I'm happy I'm in there somewhere," she replied as she opened her eyes for the first time. Even having just woken, her eyes sparkled brightly.

"What are your plans for today? Want to have lunch?"

She glanced at the clock before answering. Faint frown lines developed between her eyes and she said, "I can't today. I am volunteering at the Redevelopment Foundation. Remember?"

I did remember but was still hopeful. "Oh right. The foundation. When will you be done?"

"The donation center is open until five, so I should be home around the same as you." She sat up, pushing the covers away. She stretched and tilted her head to the side, her eyes wincing slightly.

"Does it still hurt?" I asked. Cyndi had fallen while rollerblading in the park a few weeks back, and ever since had had neck and backaches.

"Yeah. I was hoping I didn't need to fill the prescription again, but—"

"If it still hurts, fill it. You don't have to take them all."

"Yeah, I suppose. Would you mind picking it up for me today? I'll call it in to the pharmacy near your office."

"Sure thing. Need anything else while I'm there?" I asked, rolling out of bed and reaching for the ceiling in a giant stretch.

"I don't think so. But if something comes to mind, I'll call your office before you leave. Getting off at your regular time?"

"Yeah, probably. Unless Pearlman asks me to stay late for something."

"Just let me know either way," Cyndi said as she lay back onto her pillow, closing her eyes.

Why can't I go back to bed? I asked myself. I shuffled off to shave and shower. Forty minutes later I was dressed and in the kitchen finishing my breakfast. Cyndi sauntered in and sipped from my coffee.

"Don't forget my prescription. I put the slip in your briefcase," she said before vanishing again to shower.

Chapter 2

Feeling beads of sweat slide down my forehead, I used my free hand to wipe them away. I opened my eyes and realized I was still sitting on the park bench next to the stranger. I jumped to my feet, dropping the coin to the ground.

"What the hell just happened? What's going on?" I demanded as I turned to look at the man still sitting casually on the bench. "It was like I was there in my bedroom this morning."

"I assure you, Mr. Duffy, nothing 'is going on'. I'm just here to help you. Think of the coin as a hypnotic device that clears your mind of the unnecessary clutter that slows us all down from time to time." He smiled as he leaned over, picked up the coin, and held it out to me once again.

I sat down and reluctantly took the coin from him. I didn't even have the coin fully turned over in my hand when I was snapped back to my apartment.

Chapter 2.5

After finishing my coffee, I grabbed my briefcase and headed for the elevator. A glance at the clock on the way out told me that I was going to be late. That's all I needed. Punching the elevator call button three times for good measure, I waited a few moments before the familiar ding sounded and the doors parted.

Happiness enveloped me; the eight-foot by eight-foot metal car was empty. Pushing the button for the parking level, the doors closed and the elevator began to drop. My happiness quickly evaporated as the elevator stopped at floor twenty-three. On came Ms. Eastman. "Good morning, Jack," she said, smiling up at me from her four-foot-tall frame.

"Morning, Ms. Eastman." Hoping to avoid an uncomfortable conversation with the building's gossip queen, I pulled Cyndi's prescription from my briefcase and began to read. Thankfully, the elevator doors opened once again a few floors down and on came three more people. Unfortunately, the elevator stopped at nearly every other floor the rest of the way down. After stopping at the lobby to unload most of the passengers, the car dropped two floors farther, letting me and a few others off in the garage.

I climbed behind the wheel of my aging sedan and turned the engine over. After a few cranks, it roared to life. The problem was that the familiar rumble was accompanied by a new knocking sound. I knew it was time for a service, but as the morning was moving along, my mood was drifting swiftly in the wrong direction. The service would have to wait till the weekend.

Unfortunately, I left too late to avoid morning traffic. And although I pulled right into the middle of it, the flow of cars wasn't terrible. I would have been able to make it to work somewhat close to on time if it wasn't for the old woman driving two cars ahead who ran the red light.

The Lincoln Town Car—a yacht on wheels—plowed into the side of a subcompact heading across her path. Three other cars collided in the intersection as well, bringing traffic to a sudden and unavoidable halt. Yep. I was going to be late for work.

Surprisingly, the emergency vehicles arrived on the scene quickly and were able to restore the morning commute to its natural flow in short order. Short order meaning thirty minutes. Once beyond the bottleneck at the scene of the accident, traffic picked up pace. I was able to pull into my office's parking garage only an hour later than normal.

Chapter 3

I lurched forward uncontrollably, gulping air in an effort to catch my breath. I looked at the stranger, and he only smiled at me knowingly.

"It sounds like the makings for a bad day, Mr. Duffy," he chuckled. "A very bad day. How were your emotions at that point?"

"Honestly, I don't really know. Just now, I started to feel my anxiety increase, but I'm not sure if that's related to the events from earlier or to how I'm experiencing everything again."

"That's understandable and quite expected. Are you ready to continue?"

"Maybe, but—" I paused, thinking of the right way to say what I was thinking. "Why am I doing this? Can't I just call my wife and have her come get me? To tell the truth, it's a little bizarre sitting on a park bench in the early morning, talking to a stranger trying to figure out what happened to my last twenty hours. I still don't know your name," I prompted, hoping to glean more information from the old man.

"Ah yes," he replied, looking at me with a sideways glance. "My given name is Wilson, Wilson Oliver. But I haven't been called that in quite some time. And while you certainly could try to call your wife, where would you have her pick you up from?" asked Wilson as he looked about the vacant park. "Furthermore, what would you tell her about your . . . condition? Honestly, Mr. Duffy, I think it best that we find out what happened to you and your day before going any further with contacting your wife."

Strangely enough, what the old man was telling me sounded logical. I simply nodded and then once again flipped the coin over between my fingers.

Chapter 3.5

After a short ride up the elevator, I was sitting behind my faux mahogany desk ready to dive into my day. There were a few voice messages, each one from my boss, Mr. Pearlman. Listening to each message in succession, Pearlman's voice grew more irate, yet it was still not far from his normal communication level.

After listening to his final message, all I wanted to do was lock my office door and hide until the end of the day. I knew that wasn't going to be an option when Gwen, Pearlman's personal assistant, walked in.

"Good morning, Mr. Duffy. Mr. Pearlman needs to see you right away. Shall I tell him you're on your way up?" she asked, sounding friendly despite working for the asshat of the department.

Even though he was originally in a middle management position below my own, Julio Pearlman was promoted to department chief six months ago. Now he's my freakin' boss. Please, just kill me.

"Uh, yeah. I'll be up in a few minutes. Let me get settled in, it's been a crazy morning."

"Sure thing, Mr. Duffy. I'll tell him you are on your way up," Gwen said, changing my words.

Not being too eager to meet with the man, I took my time sorting my desk to start the day. After several minutes of mindlessly pushing piles of paper from one side of the desk to the other, I took a deep breath and headed for the elevator. As the elevator was mindless of my impending agony, the ride up was mercilessly short and the doors opened directly into Pearlman's lobby. I stepped out and headed toward his office. As I was about to knock, Gwen opened the door and glided out of the office, leaving the door open.

Having known Pearlman since before his promotion, I'd never seen him smile. Not once. Even now he looked particularly unhappy. It was as if he was making a concerted effort to sneer at me. I knew this meeting wasn't going to go well.

"Mr. Duffy, how nice of you to make it in today. You know you're more than an hour late this morning?" Pearlman started off. I stood in silence for a moment, contemplating the best reason to give for my late arrival.

"Well? What do you have to say for yourself? Why were you late? Again, I might add."

"There was—"

"I don't want to hear your excuses!" Pearlman barked. "You're a substandard employee doing a substandard job. If I had my way, you would have been let go a long time ago. And frankly, I'm trying to find a reason why my predecessor even hired you in the first place. This morning's irresponsible action only illustrates my point. Do you think you belong up here with all the other hard-working people of the company?"

Wishing for a rock to either crawl under or crack over Pearlman's head, my tongue was frozen to the roof of my mouth. I couldn't speak to save my life. And honestly, I'm not sure words would have benefited me in any way. Thankfully, Pearlman paused his chastisement long enough to catch his breath.

"I hope you realize, Mr. Duffy, that you are by no means irreplaceable. Your employment here at the company makes no difference to me or to anyone else for that matter. So I believe the choice is yours. You're either here at your desk on time, or you can find another job. Do I make myself clear?"

I decided to stay silent. I knew it would be pointless to argue. Since my morning was deteriorating rapidly, I took the high road. Besides, if I were to point out that the last time I was late was because the parking garage was locked, it would only prolonged the lecture.

13

Once Pearlman realized that I wasn't going to give him the rope to hang me with, he barked loudly, "Get out!"

I happily obliged and retreated past Gwen's desk and back down the elevator to my office. I unceremoniously deleted Pearlman's voice messages before digging into my work.

While my PC booted up, I pulled the latest spreadsheet from the mergers and acquisitions project folder and laid it out next to the keyboard. Although an entire team was working on the merger, it was my responsibility to quantify this particular acquisition with hard numbers. Really, it was just busywork, as all the data had been assembled by others. I just needed to find the correct solution to a few key points and send it up the ladder for approval.

The task at hand was to review sales numbers from the target company over the past decade and compare their reaction to world events, religious activities, and technological advancements in the stated period. Even though the work was tedious, I tried my best to stay on task. But I knew that even after spending days on end evaluating the data, it would all end up stuffed in some file folder, never to be seen again. Busywork or not, my professional pride prevented me from treating it as such. The entire report hinged on this one final solution, and despite the speed and accuracy of the modern-day computer, it could not calculate that outcome without the required data.

The morning passed quietly as I stared at various flow charts and spreadsheets. As I switched back and forth between two key charts, I could sense a rhythm in the numbers that I had failed to notice before. As I homed in on a certain string, the answer would dance off the screen, causing me to flip to another document. The drifting of numbers was maddening, but I knew I was close. I stuck with it. I also knew that I couldn't force it, because heading down that rabbit hole was a CLM that I couldn't afford to take.

Pushing the thought of Career Limiting Moves out of my mind, I caught sight of something on the third spreadsheet. Could it be? I quickly shot back to the original document and then back to the modified version. Yes! There it was. The solution was coming into focus. I initiated a few test computations, and although I was certain it would come back green, my pulse rose slightly. As I intently watched the screen for the solution to appear, I was startled by the sound the phone. Jumping slightly, my hand twitched on the mouse just enough to click the cancel button on the screen.

"God dammit!" I yelled. The computation was gone. The elusive solution was now a whisper in the wind, and I knew I would have to try to retrace the path again.

Chapter 4

"How unfortunate, the timing of that phone call. And you lost all your work up to that point," said Wilson.

"Hmm. It looks like I did," I replied, as I thought about what I had just recited to him. "It's weird. I don't remember any of this stuff happening to me, but as I go through the memories and tell them aloud, I know they are my memories. Why is that? I mean, why are they foreign to me until I tell them out loud?"

Wilson nodded his head as he listened to my question. He sat silent for a few moments before replying. "I am certain the memories are all there inside your head, but there must have been a critical event that caused you to block them from your conscious mind."

"What kind of critical event are we talking about?" I asked.

"Oh, it could be anything from a pet dying to witnessing something disturbing. It quite often varies from person to person, depending on how intense their personal life is. Let's continue," said Wilson as he glanced at his watch.

Chapter 4.5

The phone rang again and again. In my disgust, I snatched up the receiver and barked, "Duffy."

"Mr. Pearlman needs to see you right away," Gwen said on the other end of the line.

"Can it wait until after lunch? I'm at a critical—"

"I'm sorry, Jack, but he said immediately," Gwen said before disconnecting the line.

"I'll be right up!" I said sarcastically to the dial tone in my ear. I began to wonder what he needed me for. I looked at my watch. I had been staring at my computer screen, unmoving, for three straight hours. A distraction might have been welcome, but Pearlman was not what I had in mind.

As I stepped off the elevator, Gwen nodded in the direction of Pearlman's door as she buzzed me in. This was twice in the same morning that I'd had to stand in front of his unsmiling gaze.

"I need you to run over to that Thai place I like. Get me an order of red curry chicken, an order of pad Thai shrimp, and four spring rolls," Pearlman ordered.

I was again speechless in front of this despicable man. I was about to protest, but he spoke before I could get a word out.

"Listen, Duffy. I know you were probably just wasting your time in your office, and my secretary has more important things to do. Just don't mess this up, and I might consider forgetting about your tardiness this morning. Well? Get moving."

I did the only thing I could do right then without getting fired:

I nodded and turned on my heel. As I passed by Gwen's desk, I could have sworn I saw a smirk on her face.

I stopped in my office long enough to jot down Pearlman's order and grab my car keys. Although I could have walked the dozen or so blocks to the Thai place, I felt driving would be quicker. Besides, it was hot out, and I didn't feel like sweating through my last white shirt of the week.

The elevator was quick, and although my car started up relatively easy, my breath quickened when the engine died a moment later. I turned the key again, and after a hint of protest, the engine fired again and away I went.

The lunch hour traffic was expectedly slow, but to my delight, I was able to park right in front of the restaurant. I considered leaving the engine running while I ran into The Catcher in the Thai, but I removed the key out of habit. I double-checked my pocket for the lunch order. Two pats on my breast pocket and I headed into the crowded restaurant.

The air inside reeked of rancid cooking oil laced with a hint of old seafood. The line at the to-go counter was eight souls deep. As it inched forward every five minutes or so, I shuffled my feet and contemplated my project. As much as I hated my job, I constantly dwelled on it. Maybe that was why I hated it so much: because of its silent demand on my attention. Having been passed over for promotion twice in three years, I sometimes wondered if it was worth staying with the company. I was obviously going nowhere, but at least I got a paycheck every other week.

I was so deep in thought, the Hispanic woman behind the counter had to say it again: "Can I take your order?"

I pulled the sheet of paper from my pocket and relayed the order. Her pleasant smile never wavering, she entered the lunch order into the decrepit system and repeated it back to me precisely. I swiped my company credit card and gave the nice woman a twenty-five percent tip. Compliments of Mr. Pearlman, I thought to myself. She handed me a ticket number, and I stepped aside for others to place their order.

As I stood along the wall of the narrow restaurant, I contemplated the irony of a Hispanic woman working at a Thai restaurant in New York. "Only in America," I mumbled. Nobody around me noticed. The patrons were all self-involved with their smart phones.

It wasn't long before they called my order, and as I stepped forward to check that the contents of the Styrofoam containers matched my receipt, the Hispanic woman watched attentively. I nodded at her when I found everything in order. She smiled and nodded her head low.

Once back to the car, I was greeted by an offensive yellow parking ticket tucked haphazardly under the blade of my windshield wiper. By this point in my day, I concluded that the world was in fact out to get me. Thankfully, the car started on the first attempt, and the trip back to the office was unremarkable. Total round-trip for Pinhead Pearlman took just under an hour.

Back up to the sixteenth floor, I stalked right by Gwen and into Pearlman's office. He looked up as I unceremoniously dropped the food on his desk, pulled the receipt stapled to the bag, and read it aloud.

"One order red curry chicken. One order pad Thai shrimp. Four spring rolls." Pearlman looked up from the receipt and scowled profusely in my general direction. "I said curry beef, not chicken." His scowl turned to disgust as he pulled the food containers from the paper bag. "I suppose I can choke it down. Now if you're done bothering me, why don't you get back to work. Isn't your lunch hour just about over?"

The aroma of the food reminded me I had not had lunch myself. I was famished. With my lunch hour wasted on a fool's errand, I hoped I had a snack stashed away in my desk.

"Yes, that sounds about right," I replied. Before leaving Pearlman's office, I pulled the charge receipt from my breast pocket and dropped it on his desk, directly next to the red curry chicken. Smiling, I turned and walked out of his office. Gwen stood poised outside his office, waiting for my exit. As soon as I passed her desk, she slipped in, closing the door behind her.

Chapter 5

"What an incredible douche bag!" I said aloud. "I can't believe he made me his errand boy again."

"This Mr. Pearlman is not a candidate for boss of the year," said Wilson.

"Far from it. He is underqualified and overpaid. He is your run-of-the-mill brownnoser and only got the position because he knows the right people—"

"A baboon could do his job better," Wilson said.

Shocked that Wilson said the exact words I was going to say next, I looked over at the old man. He was still sitting in a casual manner, but the lines between his eyes had deepened, and if I didn't know any better, I would have thought I noticed a bit of compassion in his eyes.

"You are a peculiar man, Wilson. What gives?" I asked.

Wilson whistled softly. "Oh, I've been doing this for more than sixty years."

"And what exactly is it that you've been doing for more than sixty years?"

"I guess you could say I lend an ear to those in need," Wilson said, deftly avoiding the question.

"OK, but how have you been at this for sixty years? You don't look a day over sixty-five. How does that work?"

Wilson fidgeted with the shiny cuff links holding his sleeves tight to his wrists. "That's a whole other matter. One which we have no time to discuss. Please, Mr. Duffy, continue."

Wishing for more information from the old man, but also wanting to get through the rest of the day, I quickly flipped the coin over.

Chapter 5.5

"Pearlman did it again, didn't he?" came a voice from behind me.

Before turning to see who it belonged to, I slid the last of my dollar bills into the vending machine and punched E9, launching the spiral delivery system into motion. The kerplunk echoed throughout the tiny break room, and I pulled out the last candy bar in the machine.

"Hey, Alan. Yeah, Pearlman got me again," I replied before tearing open the plastic wrapper and biting off half the candy bar.

"I'd tell you about lessons learned, but I'm sure you don't want to hear it."

"Here's the thing, Alan: I wrote down the order before I left. He's just a crazy bastard," I replied. "I got him in the end though. I charged it to the company and left the receipt, along with the handwritten food order, on his desk."

"Great! That's one for the peasants. How'd he take it?" Alan asked.

Swallowing the last of my candy bar, I shook my head. "Not sure. I left before he noticed. I thought it best to get out before he realized what had happened."

Alan fell in to stride with me as we walked back to our offices. Alan's office was across the hall from mine.

"Why didn't he just send Gwen?" Alan wondered. "You can't tell me she was too busy typing memos or something."

"No, she was swamped, according to Pearlman. Hell, he even had me get her lunch too."

"Seriously? What did you do to piss that man off? Ever since he got Nelson's job, he's made you his personal bitch. Why don't you stand up for yourself?" Alan asked as we paused outside our office doors.

"I know I should, but I just didn't feel like getting fired today. Besides, he's the department head, and he has his nose buried so far up the VP's ass, he probably knows Snyder's eating habits personally."

"You know he's going to keep doing it until you break."

"Yeah, I think that's what he wants. He's been looking for a reason to get rid of me since day one. You know as well as I do that Pearlman does what Pearlman wants. Isn't that obvious by the string of hot secretaries he's had in the short time he's been here?"

"You really think so?" he asked.

"How many other execs take their secretaries—I mean personal assistants—out to lunch four days a week and then are conveniently busy the rest of the afternoon?" I asked, raising my eyebrows.

"But he's married. I met his wife at the holiday party. They seemed happy together, and she wasn't terrible to look at herself," Alan stated.

"No need to tell me, I was there too," I agreed. "But because you left early, you missed all the action."

"Dammit! How am I just learning about this?" Alan asked.

"I meant to tell you afterward, but it must have slipped my mind."

"Well? What happened?"

"After you left, the two slowly drifted apart, consuming more champagne than should have been possible. Near the end of the night, his wife was flirting with the head of advertising, and Pearlman was trying to fit his head through the neck of his secretary's blouse. It would have fit, too, if it weren't for her still being in it."

Alan whistled quietly. "Seriously, how did none of this make it to the water cooler?"

"Don't you remember that memo that went out after the party?"

"'The dos and don'ts of sex jokes in the workplace'?"

"No, the other one. It came from Snyder himself."

"Ah yes. 'What happens at company parties stays at company parties.'"

"Yep. My guess is Pearlman persuaded Snyder to cover his ass with that one."

"Pathetic."

"I concur. I wholeheartedly concur."

"Tell me, Jack, why didn't you try for the position when Nelson left? You've got a master's degree, and if you ask me, you're the sharpest person on the floor."

"When Nelson was run out of the company, I had no idea the position was open until Pearlman was announced as the new head. Trust me, buddy, I would have given it my best effort if I had been given the opportunity." I shook my head, wondering just how long I would be Pearlman's bitch. Hell, I was even Pearlman's secretary's bitch.

"Listen, Alan, I've got to get back to work. I'm about to crack this code, and I would like to leave here today having accomplished something," I said as I turned in to my office.

"Sure thing. Grab a coffee tomorrow? My treat," Alan offered generously. It was a pity offering, but it felt genuine just the same.

"Always take a freebie. Thanks."

Alan returned to his office as I sat behind my desk.

Flipping on the monitor, I began to review the spreadsheets displayed on the screen. I spent the next fifteen minutes trying to reimmerse myself into my project. However, all I could think about was Pearlman and his bastard ways. As I tried to focus on the equations, my mind reviewed, word by word, the conversation with Alan. What he said made sense. I was the brightest man on the floor. And now that I thought about it, I was the only one around here with a master's degree. I didn't even think Pearlman had one. I began to wonder if that was his motivation to drive me from the company. Feeling my blood begin to boil, I scoured the thoughts from my mind.

I returned to the original document on my screen, reading the text and scanning the data for the hundredth time. Flipping from document to document, reading and scanning, I felt like my afternoon was going to be a lost cause. I tried my best to recreate my solution, but all I saw was scrambled gibberish. I sat reviewing the lines of data on the spreadsheet that I felt would produce the elusive solution, hands hovering over the keyboard, ready to input the key as soon as it blossomed in my mind.

On my third pass, something deep in my cerebral cortex twitched. I blinked and read the last line again. Could it be? Could I have stumbled across it again? I quickly jotted down the quadrant address on a piece of scratch paper and returned my hands to the keyboard. I blinked fast and felt my heart quicken. I was almost there. I scanned the passage once more, and just as I was about to identify the solution without running any computations, the phone rang.

Snapped back to reality, the solution fluttered away. The phone rang again, and as I contemplated picking it up to tell the caller to go to hell, I calmly pressed the do-not-disturb button on the phone's base and shut down my computer. Had I known how shitty the rest of my day would be, I would have stayed at my desk.

With my office now silent, I grabbed my briefcase and headed for the door. I momentarily popped my head into Alan's office.

"Hey, Alan. I'm heading out—taking the afternoon off as PTO."

"Everything OK?" Alan inquired.

"Yeah, I'm fine. Just need to clear my mind. I'll see you in the morning. If Pinhead comes looking for me, tell him you haven't seen me."

"Will do," Alan said, nodding in compliance.

As I stood waiting for the elevator, I reached into the side pocket of my briefcase to fish out my car keys and found Cyndi's prescription.

"Damn," I mumbled. I had completely forgotten that I promised to pick it up. I glanced at my watch, and as much as I wanted to just get home and forget about the day, it was only a hair past 1:00. I had plenty of time to swing by the pharmacy on the way home.

Minutes later, I was down in the parking garage. I slid the keys into the ignition and turned it over. Nothing happened. I switched it back to off and tried again. Nothing. No dash lights illuminated, no dome light came on. The car was completely dead.

"Shit!" I yelled. I felt like punching the dash. I tilted my head back and began to breathe slowly. It had been months since I last visited my therapist, but I recalled some of the tips he taught me to calm myself in moments of great anxiety. Seeing as my whole fucking day was the poster child for all things stress inducing, I practiced a few.

First, I slowed my breathing to better control my heart rate. Next, I focused on something pleasant: Cyndi, my happy place. I closed my eyes, envisioning her beautiful face in my mind. Finally, I counted backward from twenty, skipping every other number.

"Twenty, eighteen, sixteen, fourteen, twelve, ten, eight, six, four, two, zero," I said aloud, breathing deeply in between each number. Surprisingly, I felt much calmer than the moment before. I no longer wanted to junk punch my car or light a match, toss it in the gas tank, and walk away.

I popped open the glove box, found my roadside assistance number, and dialed it on my cell phone. I explained the situation to the man on the other end of the call, who seemed to think it just needed a jump. He dispatched a driver and said it would be no more than thirty minutes.

Hanging up, I contemplated walking the dozen blocks to the pharmacy but decided against it. As my luck was going, I would get mugged halfway there and miss the tow-truck driver completely. I might even get run over on the way back, I mused. No, no. I waited, sitting on the hood of my car instead. Besides, it was still sweltering out, and walking nearly a mile on the concrete paths of the city didn't remotely appeal to me.

Nearly an hour later, my wait was rewarded by a balding tow-truck driver smelling of stale cigars and burnt motor oil.

"Darn good to meetcha'," he said, pumping my hand a little too aggressively. "What seems to be the problem?"

"Darn thing won't start. I think the battery might be dead, but it just ran a few hours ago," I explained to the overweight man as he popped the hood.

"Well, let's take a look-see," he said as he leaned in near the engine, scrutinizing every part of the grease-covered compartment. "Wanna jump in and give it a try?"

I hopped behind the wheel and turned over the ignition.

Nothing happened.

"Go ahead, try and start it," the driver said again.

I turned the ignition back to off and then forward again. Nothing.

"Are you turning the key all the way over?" he asked impatiently.

"I am. I tried it several times just as you asked," I replied, nearing the end of my patience.

"OK, hold on a sec," he said as he jiggled some hoses and wires along the side of the engine compartment. As he did so, I could see sparks fly from under the hood, and the dome light came to life.

"Give it a go," he hollered, still bent over under the hood.

I turned the key to start, and the engine roared to life. "Hurray!" I called out in excitement.

"Looks like you've got a frayed wire leading to the starter. I got 'er fixed for now, but it'll need replacin' soon," said the driver, wiping his hands on a dirty rag hanging out of his side pocket.

"I'll get on that this weekend. What do I owe you?" I asked as I shut the hood.

"Eh, the normal cost for a jump is ninety-five. I really only charge for jumps or tows, but I gotta call this in. Let those that make more than me decide," he said as he climbed into his tow truck.

After several more minutes discussing things on his CB, he popped out with his clipboard in hand.

"Looks like they want me to charge you for the jump anyway. I tried to argue with 'em that it really wasn't a jump, but I lost that battle. You got cash or do you wanna put it on a card?"

"I suppose it makes sense. Here, put it on this," I said, handing him my personal credit card.

"Give me a sec. I'll call it in." He once again disappeared into the cab of his truck only to reappear moments later. "There seems to be a problem with your card here. Got another to try?"

I didn't have the time or the patience for another problem today. "What kind of problem? The card should be paid up and have plenty of room on it."

"Don't know. They jus' said it was declined," he replied,

standing close enough that I could smell what could either be rotten eggs or incredibly offensive body odor.

"OK, give this one a try. I know it's good," I said, handing him my corporate card. With the awful day I was having, it was the least Pearlman could do for me. Either that or I'd be fired for abusing company resources.

Five minutes later, the driver returned with a slip for me to sign and a copy of the invoice. I thanked him again, but he wordlessly climbed back into his truck and sped away.

I jumped into the car and blasted the AC before pulling out into the afternoon traffic. I turned up Eighth Avenue and headed toward the pharmacy. Thankfully, traffic was far less hectic than it was that morning or at lunch. I contemplated leaving early every day, just to avoid the traffic. I chuckled at the far-fetched notion, knowing good and well it would never happen.

Ten minutes later I pulled into the parking lot of the pharmacy and found the last parking space available. I left the engine running as I went in to pick up Cyndi's prescription, thinking I would need to call for a jump again otherwise.

Once inside, I fully understood why the lot was full. There was a line at the pharmacist's counter much longer than the line for Pearlman's lunch. I moved to the back of the line and waited. The line moved at a snail's pace, and if I hadn't left work early, I would not have stayed. But as it was only 2:45, I had plenty of time.

Thankfully, another pharmacist opened a second register and half the people in line moved to equalize the wait. The pregnant woman behind me nearly plowed me over to get into the other lane. I graciously stepped aside. Who am I kidding? I let her over there so she would stop bumping into me with her enormous belly. Seriously, don't people know what personal bubbles are these days?

With the line reduced by half, I progressed to the counter in no time at all. I handed the prescription over and he entered a few things into the computer. A moment later, he handed it back to me and looked at me quizzically.

"Uh, I need to see your ID before I can fill this," he stated.

I slid my driver's license across the counter. The clerk compared it to his screen.

"Hmm. I don't think I can give you this," he said with a confused look.

"Excuse me? You can't give it to me why?" I asked, trying to hold in my rapidly-approaching anger.

"Yeah, the prescription is for oxycodone with acetaminophen. That's a narcotic, and I'm only supposed to give it to the person on the prescription. Your license says you are Jack Duffy, and the prescription's for Cyndi Duffy."

"Ah, I see. Cyndi is my wife. I'm picking it up for her," I replied as calmly as possible. I could feel my anger inching ever closer to the surface.

"Like I said, you're not Cyndi, so I can't give this to you."

"But she's my wife. See, look at my license. We even have the same address. I don't see what the problem is here. I've picked up prescriptions for her in the past."

"The problem? How do I know these pills will even make it to her after I give them to you?" the clerk asked.

"Listen, Clint," I stated, reading his name tag, "I've had very bad day. If you don't find a grown-up back there that can help you out with this, I am going to get pissed. In fact, I might even become irate. NOW FIX THIS!" I yelled, attracting the attention of everyone in line as well as the pharmacist at the other counter.

Clint jumped and took a step back as I barked my orders. He moved to the other pharmacist and the two whispered momentarily. He then disappeared in the stacks of medicines behind them. Moments later, he returned and slid a puffy white envelope across the counter to me along with my driver's license.

"Great. What do I owe you?" I asked, relieved not to be thrown out for making a scene.

"Your insurance covers medication copays," he replied, then he looked at the person behind me. "Next?"

I know I shouldn't have, but I gave Clint the finger as I turned and walked out. It's the little things that help the day move along.

When I stepped back outside, it was getting hotter. I looked at my watch and saw that is was now past three. With any luck, I would make it home by three-thirty, two hours before I normally got home. With that amount of time, I should be able to get in a nap and then maybe cook dinner for Cyndi before she got home.

Chapter 6

After a few minutes of silence, I looked over to the old man. In addition to the frown lines between his eyes, his eyebrows were now furrowed with concern.

"Is there something you're not telling me? You seem to know me, and the recounting of my day hasn't really . . ."

"Has not been a surprise to me," Wilson said, finishing my sentence.

"How are you doing that?" I asked, slightly annoyed that he seemed to be reading my thoughts.

"I am reading your thoughts, Mr. Duffy. It sort of comes with the territory of what I do. I can't read all your thoughts, and not everyone has thoughts that are understandable to me." He quickly straightened his face and smiled. "It's nothing to worry about just yet, Mr. Duffy. I think a bit more recitation and everything will become clear. Please continue."

Without having a better alternative, I flipped the coin.

Chapter 6.5

Fifteen minutes later I pulled into my parking garage. I was happy with myself for making great time despite the heavy traffic. I grabbed my briefcase and jacket and made for the elevator. The ride up was uneventful. I slipped my key into the lock and opened the door.

When I walked in, the first thing I noticed was that the living room lights were on. Cyndi was usually meticulous about conserving energy and almost always walked around the apartment in the dark. Despite my frequent reminders of her own clumsiness, she still did it nightly.

Thinking nothing more of it, I headed to the kitchen for something to drink. That's when I noted the second oddity. Cyndi had left her shoes lying in the middle of the floor, and I spotted a few used plates left on the kitchen counter. My lovely wife must have come home early. Her back pain must have been more severe than she had let on that morning.

Not wanting to wake her, I tiptoed down the hall and slowly opened the bedroom door. Within seconds I heard the noises.

Curious, I pushed the door fully ajar. The shades were drawn; the room dark. Despite the dimness, I could see Cyndi in bed, but she certainly wasn't sleeping. In the shadowy glare from the hallway behind me, I could make out an additional body. I stepped to the side, allowing more of the light to spill across the bed. I could see the shape of not one but two people entwined, covered by the thin bed sheet. The actions I witnessed fully aligned with the sounds emanating from the bed. They were fucking.

My knees began to weaken beneath me. Frozen and unable to move, all I could do was watch in horror. There I was, standing in the doorway of my bedroom, watching my wife having sex with another man. My chest began to tighten. My breathing quickened. I was horrified, but I couldn't move.

I finally forced my legs to move. I slowly backed out into the hallway, pulling the door to its original position. I retraced my steps through the apartment and back out into the corridor. I left the front door open, not caring whether Cyndi knew I had been home or not.

Chapter 7

I had no words to describe what I was feeling. The old man cleared his throat, but I paid him no attention. All I could think about was what I had just witnessed—for the second time. Sadness turned to anger. I could feel my soul moving inside me, and I had to do something or else I felt like I would explode. I stood and walked to the edge of the dirt path near the park. From where I stood, I could see the sky grow a shade lighter. Dawn was approaching, and here I was, standing in an unknown park, speaking to a strange man about the most fucked up day I've ever had. Cyndi and I used to love sunrises. How ironic, I thought.

"Did you know?" I asked the old man, who was now sitting straight up. It was as if he had prepared himself for an onslaught of questions.

"I cannot say what I knew exactly. The answer to you would prove confusing at best," he replied, making zero sense to me.

"Was that the event that caused my memory block?" I asked, taking a seat next to him.

"That might have something to do with it, but according to my calculations," he paused to look at his watch again, "you are still missing an hour or so before getting on that fateful bus ride."

I nodded. I had assumed as much. Coin in hand, I continued my trip down memory lane.

Chapter 7.5

Delirious, I made my way back to the elevator and gently pressed the call button. I stood there, waiting, my mind in a fog. As the elevator dinged, there was a cry coming from the direction of my apartment. It was Cyndi, now dressed in a robe, standing just outside our apartment door. The doors parted, and I casually stepped in to the elevator. I pressed the button for the lobby, and as I turned around I could hear running footsteps. Cyndi came into view at the precise moment the elevator doors closed her face off from me - forever.

The elevator made its descent to the first floor in less than a minute. I walked out into the penetrating heat and turned right down the sidewalk. I was numb, and had no particular destination in mind. I just needed to walk away.

The sidewalks were beginning to fill with the daily workforce leaving for the evening. The farther I walked, the more crowded the sidewalks became. Having no real plan, I decided I would step off the concrete path of civilization and have a seat.

A block later, I came upon a little bistro with a small outdoor courtyard. I moved through the entry and out onto the terrace. I sat along the outside railing, and a waiter brought me a menu and a glass of water.

Despite the cover on the patio, the heat was nearly unbearable. Moving to a table inside never crossed my mind. I just sat in the silence, wondering why this day was destined to be so disastrous. There was nothing left for fate to deface.

I sipped from the glass of water, feeling its cool tingle as it passed my lips. I looked around the patio and realized I was alone. My soul was just as alone. I wondered what I should be feeling. Hate? Fear? Anger? I felt them all but none at the same time. I felt like crying but couldn't find the energy. I thought about calling my therapist but dismissed the thought. I knew what he would tell me: it was all going to be OK. How on earth was it going to be OK? My wife, the center of my world, had just cheated on me. My job was horrendous. My entire life seemed to be in a tailspin heading for a fiery crash.

I suddenly realized that throughout the last thirty minutes, I had been carrying my briefcase. Why hadn't I set it down in the apartment when I walked in? I sat it on the ground next to my chair and saw Cyndi's prescription. I pulled it from the side pocket and laid it on the table in front of me. I took another sip of water and began to read the label.

I scanned through the generic warnings and precautions. Toward the end of the label, it mentioned that the side effects could be numbness and drowsiness. That sounded about right. I tore open the sealed envelope and popped the lid off the bottle. I emptied a handful of pills onto the table in front of me and contemplated my future.

What exactly did my future hold? I no longer had a wife that loved me. Hell, did she ever love me? I had a boss that would be happy to see me thrown out onto the street. I had no kids, thankfully. Both my parents had passed away years ago. I had nothing left at all. I knew right then that nobody would ever miss me. I took another drink.

Having dealt with depression for many years, I was no stranger to the thought of suicide. Hell, I think everyone thinks about the what-ifs of suicide at least once in their life. I just happened to have thought about it many times over the years. Through countless sessions with my therapist, we concluded that the depression stemmed from mass bullying throughout primary school. The feeling of hatred was still strong toward the people that caused me so much pain. At that moment, random neurons in my brain connected two events in my live, separated by nearly 20 years. Pearlman was the coalescence of all the bullies of my youth.

And there I sat, contemplating my future, my mortality. Whether or not to take my own life. I looked from pill to pill. I knew how easy it would be to end all the pain and suffering. Just a handful of pills and a quick gulp of clean, cool water would be so easy.

I reached up and wiped a bead of sweat from my brow and glanced around once more. I tried to think of a single reason not to take the pills, but nothing came to mind. All that I could think about was seeing my wife move rhythmically with another man.

Chapter 8

"Please, God, no!" I said, barely containing my growing anxiety. "Please tell me," I begged.

"You were supposed to wait for me on the bus," he said.

"Why's that?" I said turning fully in Wilson's direction.

The old man held his hand out, producing an amber-colored prescription bottle out of thin air. He gave the bottle a shake, rattling the remaining Percocet pills inside.

"Who are you?" I asked, afraid I already knew the answer to the question.

"You already know who I am," he replied.

"All right then. Why are you here?"

"I think you know the answer to that question as well."

I nodded my head in agreement. Although yesterday was an absolutely horrific day, now I wasn't entirely sure I wanted to die. A terrible job and a cheating wife were no reasons to end a life, and all it took was a kind stranger and a bus ride to figure that out.

"Did I really take all those pills?" I asked, looking down at the coin still in my hand.

"Why not find out for yourself? You've come this far, but I wouldn't think less of you for not wanting to see your final moments."

Before I had a chance to decide, my subconscious mind made the choice for me. I turned the coin for the final time."

Chapter 8.5

As a tear rolled down my cheek, I reached for a pill and placed it on my tongue. I instinctively swallowed it without water. A moment later, I took two more. I sat there waiting for something to keep me from taking the whole pile, but nothing did. I scooped the remaining pills from the table and tossed them back all at once. I washed them down with the last of my water.

Not wanting to cause a scene at the quaint little restaurant, I slid the pill bottle into my pocket and left the patio through the side exit. Back on the sidewalk, I meandered aimlessly for few blocks before coming to a bus stop. With no motivation to proceed, I sat on the bench.

Leaning back, I wondered how long the pills would take and how it would happen. Having never used pain medications, I was unsure what the effects would be. All I felt was anxiety.

As the moments passed, I thought about what I had witnessed. Seeing Cyndi with another man was an absolute betrayal that I would have never imagined. Not for the first time, I asked myself how she could do it. Had our love for each other meant nothing to her?

I tried to figure out where our relationship might have gone wrong, but thinking back to our last fight some six months previous, nothing stood out. That last fight was over something stupid, like leaving dishes unrinsed in the sink. It wasn't really the dishes that the fight was about, but it certainly was the igniter. The fight carried on for several days, and every little idiosyncrasy fueled the argument. Finally, after I was tired of being mad at her for being mad at me, I apologized, and all was better. So I thought. Could that have been the reason? Could that have made her look at me differently? Surely not, I mused.

I felt so alone.

Moments later, I noticed my breathing begin to change. It felt as if I could not get enough air in my lungs. I tried to take in larger breaths, but just as soon as I inhaled, I involuntarily let the breath out. My accelerated breathing caused my heart to beat faster. I didn't notice it right away, but once my hand began to twitch, I knew it was from the pills. I leaned my head back and tried to relax, but the combination of the traffic noise and the overdose of pills prevented me from doing so.

Then, out of nowhere, it felt like my stomach flipped a somersault. I quickly leaned forward, and as I did, I knew I was going to puke. I looked up and down the street for a garbage can, but none were in sight. With no other alternative, I stood up and staggered to the curb. Leaning over, I threw up what little food I had eaten through the day. I spat out the languishing bile in my mouth and tried to stand up. A sudden dizzy spell took over, and I nearly collapsed backward. I reached out and grabbed the signpost to steady myself. I felt the time was near. I figured it would be quick, but I had no idea that the pills would affect me so soon.

As I stood there, a man walking by stopped next to me and asked "You doing OK, man?"

Although confusion was setting in, I heard the man's words and nodded. When I looked into the man's eyes, I saw worry and concern.

He patted me on the shoulder and continued down the sidewalk. For a brief moment, I wondered if I had made the wrong choice by taking the pills.

A moment later, a city bus pulled to a stop right in front of me. It took me a moment to realize that I was still standing at the bus stop. I instinctively pulled my bus pass from my wallet and climbed aboard. In typical fashion, the first several rows of the bus were filled, so I moved to the very last row and slumped down. The bus lurched ahead, and I felt as if I had left my stomach back at the stop. I leaned forward, feeling like I was going to puke again, but it was just dry heaves. There was nothing left in my stomach.

I looked around at the other passengers on the bus. They were all on their time schedule. Most were just getting off work and heading home, while others were heading in the other direction. For me, time had no meaning. Unlike those around me, I had no pressing matters. I knew the end was near. The pungent odors of sweat and unwashed bodies drifted about the cramped vehicle, but I was unfazed. Nothing bothered me. I leaned back and smiled. For the first time all day, I felt contentment.

As moments passed for me, hours passed for the others in the world. I drifted in and out of consciousness, waiting for the end to take me. It wasn't until the jostle that my eyes opened.

Chapter 9

"So, am I dead then? Is that why you're here?"

"Well, yes and no. I'll explain." He pulled a white handkerchief from his breast pocket and dabbed it across his forehead. "You see, much like yourself, I was late today. Actually, I need to correct that. I was with you earlier, but it wasn't at the proper time, so I left you to take care of another matter. When I returned to you, you had in fact died but had miraculously come back to life."

"If I'm alive, then why are you still here? I can go now, right? I got a second chance?" I eagerly suggested.

"It's not like that, Mr. Duffy." He paused and slid the refolded handkerchief back into his outer pocket. "You did die. And as soon as you took those pills, you set a number of other events in motion. So, per my orders, I need to take your soul. You see, I'm a soul collector."

"But you said I miraculously came back to life. Doesn't that mean I am, in fact, a miracle myself?"

"In all the years of doing this job, Mr. Duffy, I have only witnessed a similar event one other time."

"And what happened then?" I asked.

Wilson looked down to the ground. "What happened then doesn't matter now. What does matter is I need to turn in a soul, and yours is the one that needs collecting."

We sat in silence, both of us staring at anything but each other. I thought about getting up and running. At his age, it would be no contest.

"Yes, you could run, Mr. Duffy, but it would be pointless," Wilson stated matter-of-factly.

"How'd you . . . never mind."

"I know more than you could ever imagine, Mr. Duffy. I know things sometimes before they occur."

"If that's the case, how'd you miss me dying? Wouldn't you have foreseen that as well?"

"Excellent point. With my advanced age, it appears that I might be losing my edge. You see, time passes slower for me than it does for the living. Much slower. For every one of my hours, eight of yours passes. That's why I thought that I would have been able to collect another soul and still have time to get back to you. The other soul had fallen from a building at a construction site near here. Poor fellow. He left a loving wife and three children behind."

"Oh," is all I could think of to say in response. I thought this process would be different.

"Different in which way?" asked Wilson.

"Well, I guess I never thought someone like you would age at all. Granted, I never really thought about what happens after death in the first place. Earlier you said it was too late for second chances and something about other events set in motion. Any chance we could stop them?"

"Here's how it works. Society has a specific number of souls in use, with new souls being generated as demand sees fit. Those new souls are developed at an established rate that was predetermined a millennia ago. Once a person dies, their soul is recycled into a new birth. You've heard the term 'old-soul'? Well, that just means the soul has been through many lives. There are far more old souls than there are new souls in the world."

"I find all this extremely interesting, Wilson, but how does me coming back to life affect any of this?"

"Every time a person dies, a new birth is in line to accept their soul. Your soul has been claimed, and the birth is imminent. As all the new souls have been claimed to date, your soul needs to be moved along within a reasonable time frame."

"And my soul is the only one available? People die all the time. You can't tell me that there aren't other souls that can be put into place."

"I understand your apprehension, Mr. Duffy, but those other souls are being placed into their assigned births all the time. Tomorrow's quota might be—will be—completely different than it was for today." Wilson paused a moment. "Listen, Mr. Duffy. I need a soul to turn in, and I cannot understand your sudden resistance. After all, you did in fact attempt to end your life. Even if I could let you live, your life would never be the same. The fact that your wife committed adultery would not change. Can you honestly tell me you would happily take her back just to avoid moving on to the afterlife?"

"I guess I really didn't think about that. Isn't there a way to go back a few days earlier?"

"I'm not a miracle worker. I'm not a time traveler. I'm here only to collect your soul."

Hearing the finality of Wilson's words, I had never felt more alone. I began to cry.

After several moments of silence, Wilson spoke. "Suppose I had an alternative—"

"Name it," I replied quickly, wiping the tears from my cheeks. "I'll take whatever you've got to offer."

"Slow down, Mr. Duffy. You might not like what I have to offer. It most certainly will not give you the life you've become accustomed to."

"I'm listening."

"You see, I have been doing this for sixty-one years now, and when I became a soul collector, I was fifty-seven."

"Wait, what? How is that possible?"

"I died when I was fifty-seven. I had a heart attack and was brought back to life. I was dead for several minutes, and because there happened to be no more new souls available at the time, a used soul needed to be collected. The soul collector at the time of my death had been doing her job for quite some time. I also didn't want to cease to exist, so we turned in her soul instead. In other words, she retired."

"OK, I think I get that, but the math doesn't make sense."

"It's the eight-to-one ratio that is probably throwing you off. Think of it like this: I continued to age at the same rate as everyone else, but I lived eight times longer. If I hadn't become a soul collector, I would be sixty-six, although I would have been that age more than fifty years ago."

I started to comprehend the difference in time as Wilson explained it. That's when it hit me.

"So, just like that? You're ready to retire?" I asked.

"It's not as spontaneous as it appears, Mr. Duffy. Like I said, I've been at this for sixty-one years. I'm getting tired. I've been contemplating moving on for many years, and I think I'm finally ready." He looked at me as if sizing me up. "You see, I've been on the lookout for someone to take over for me. That person is you."

"What happens next for me?"

Wilson held both of his hands out, palms up. As I looked at them, a small wooden box appeared on each hand. A name was carved on the lid of each box. One box had my name, Jack Duffy. On the other box, Wilson Oliver was carved. The box with Wilson's name was much older than my box.

"If you take over being a soul collector, you will take both of these boxes. The box with your name will be yours to keep until you feel it's time to retire. At your current age of thirty-five, you would almost certainly be able to live into the twenty-fourth century."

"Done! Let's do this," I replied excitedly.

"Not so fast, Mr. Duffy. There are consequences. You would not be able to talk to anyone from your previous life again. The only conversations permitted would be with the dead or dying, much like I am speaking to you now. Trust me when I tell you that it gets quite lonely."

"Wilson, I've lived the last five years of my life in relative solitude. Besides my wife, who just cheated on me, I had no real friends. I don't see a big difference."

Wilson nodded in agreement. "I knew that was going to be your response. Once you take these boxes from me, you cannot go back. You will be a soul collector from now until you turn in your soul. This is just prolonging the inevitable."

"I get it. I'm in till I retire. I can do this," I replied.

"OK then, Mr. Duffy. Take the two boxes from my hands. Once you possess them, open the box with my name on it and hold it open toward me."

"Wait. What happens to you?"

"I'm retiring, boy. Haven't you been paying attention?"

"Yes, I get that. But will you just cease to exist? What about your body?"

"I will become an unknown death in the current year, and you will capture my soul in this box. You will then turn in that soul and get another empty box. You will continue to fill boxes with collected souls until you retire."

"OK, but how do I collect souls? Will there be some sort of training?"

Wilson laughed out loud. "You ask too many questions. Once you take the boxes, all will become clear."

I took a deep breath as I reached for the boxes in Wilson's hands. Just before I slid them from his hands, I paused. Our eyes met, and I could have sworn I saw a twinkle in his. I held my hands next to his, palms up. Wilson rotated his hands on to mine, transferring the boxes to me simultaneously. He lifted his hands in the air, and now it was his turn to lean back to relax. I turned the boxes over in my hands, examining each of them individually. I thought about sliding my box into my pocket, but before I could, it vanished. Startled, I looked up at Wilson.

"Things will be much different for you from now on, Mr. Duffy. You will have, shall we call it, practical magic at your disposal from this point forward."

"Cool."

"Now if you would, open my box and hold it out in front of me."

"What? That's it? You pawn off the boxes on me and you're out of here?" I asked, astounded. I wondered if I had just made yet another bad choice.

"There's nothing left to say. I've lived my life—both in reality and in the afterlife. What would you have me say or do that would make a difference?"

"Well, for purely selfish reasons, can you give me any tips? Do I eat, and if so how often? How about sleep? And when does happy hour start?"

Wilson laughed. "Sorry, there's no happy hour, Mr. Duffy. The only tip I will give you will be the same advice that my predecessor gave me." He paused as he placed his hat atop his head. He sat straight up, looking at me eye to eye.

"Forgiveness is a virtue that needs to be nourished. Resentment only leads to disappointment."

"That's it? That's your sage advice? I was hoping—"

Wilson continued, "And listen to Hauser. He is wise well beyond his years."

I nodded silently, not because I had no words, but because I couldn't breathe. I wasn't choking or gasping for breath, but there was no air in my lungs to speak.

"Now, if you please. Open the box and I'll be on my way," Wilson said with his own last breath.

I did as Wilson requested. I opened the box and looked inside before turning it toward him. The inside of the box was just as plain as the outside but without any signs of wear. I turned the box around and held it open toward Wilson. "What now?" I asked, suddenly able to speak.

Wilson closed his eyes and began to sing a song. The words sounded familiar, but I couldn't place it. As he sang, I began to notice a wisp of smoke or fog leaving his mouth. It lifted out and away from his lips. Once the trail of smoke was completely out of him, his voice ceased, and the paleness of his skin dulled as he slumped back against the bench. The cloud began to move through the air in the direction of the wooden box. Once it completely entered the box, the lid closed on its own and instantly vanished. In its place, another box appeared. The new box looked just like my box, but the name was different.

The name on the box was Cyndi Duffy.

Book 2

Regretful Absolution

Chapter 1

The silence of the approaching dawn was upon me, and the impact from my foolish choices was deafening. Lost and disoriented, I could almost hear the voice screaming out instructions for what to do next. The only problem: Wilson was dead and he could no longer speak. He sat next to me, slightly slumped to the side, but not enough to tumble off the park bench.I looked into his hollow, lifeless eyes and wondered what I had gotten myself into.

While Wilson's fixed gaze continued to stare into the ether, I took in my immediate surroundings. The sun was on the rise, and a faint mist hung low to the ground. It seemed like only moments earlier that I was awakened from my suicidal sleep, before heading out into the deserted streets of the city. Now here I was, sitting next to a soulless body, and for all intents and purposes, I was no longer a living, breathing man, either.

Do I have to breathe now? I wondered. Now that I am a soul collector? Breathing is such an absentminded act that you normally don't pay much attention to—unless you can't do it, that is. I straightened my back and focused on the rhythmic action of air moving in and out of my lungs. After a particularly deep breath, I stopped breathing. I wasn't exactly holding my last breath, I just ceased to take another. As I sat listening to the early morning sounds of the city, I began to feel my lungs burn. They were being starved for air. Beads of sweat quickly formed at my temples, and I felt the *whump-whump* of my heartbeat in my ears. Finally, when I didn't think I could take any more, I felt a hard slap on my back and I inhaled sharply. I spun around, but there was no one there. I looked at Wilson, certain that he wasn't capable of raising his lifeless arm to smack air into my lings.

Concluding that my mind must still be coming off the drugs I took earlier, I took several more breaths of fresh air and focused my attention on the box in my hand. It was made of wood and was about the size of an old Rubik's Cube. An intricate pattern covered the box, and appeared to be hand carved. The box wasn't worn or scratched. It looked brand-new. I opened it and looked at the interior, which was void of the ornate whittling present on the outside. Closing the box again, I read the name engraved on the top.

Cyndi Duffy.

Reading her name sent chills up and down my spine, and I wondered where she was. If my new job, as Wilson explained, was to collect souls, then I needed to find Cyndi, my wife, and collect hers. I closed my eyes and tried to envision her face in my mind. Strangely, I could not pull her likeness into focus.

"Wilson, a little help here would be nice," I said aloud, but Wilson's frozen gaze didn't falter. I followed his line of sight and noticed that he was staring directly at a billboard: *The Dodson Apartment Center—40 stories of high-end living is closer than you think. Just 12 blocks south, in midtown.*

"Well, then. Thanks, Wilson. Had I been paying attention during our little talk earlier, I could've figured things out all on my own." I stood and looked around to get my bearings. The sun was on the rise and recognition began to set in. I really was just a few blocks from home. I smiled wryly at myself. The pills from yesterday must have caused some serious disorientation, severely impairing my senses. Now confident about my location and where I needed to go, I headed for home.

Chapter 2

I walked in silence for several blocks, wondering what I would say to Cyndi when I walked into our apartment. "Hi, honey. I need you to spit your soul into this box, you cheating whore." No, I didn't think that'd quite do the trick. Perhaps a more subdued approach would be more appropriate. "Excuse me, but would you mind not saying a word while I perform a soulectomy on your sorry ass?" Again, no.

As various scenarios of the inevitable confrontation ran through my mind, I absentmindedly crossed 49th against the light. A taxi sped by me, nearly hitting me. I stopped in my tracks mere seconds before getting blasted by the hustling driver. I quickly jumped back onto the curb and waited for the light to change. After a few moments, the white walker light shone brightly, and I once again moved into the street.

Stepping onto the curb at the other side of the street, my mind reeled at the sudden realization. If I was going to collect Cyndi's soul, she had to be close to death. After my brief discussion earlier with Wilson about how soul collection worked, I knew it was too late for Cyndi. But despite her cheating ways, I was still apprehensive about her impending death. My mind bounced from one tragic thought to another about what could have happened to her. Maybe it was just an accident, and she was hit by a speeding taxi, just like the one that almost hit me. Or maybe she'd felt bad about her actions and decided to take her own life, similar to my own actions yesterday.

As I crossed 43rd, halfway back to the apartment, I slowed my pace. Various dreadful thoughts of what could have happened to Cyndi continued to course through my mind. I realized that if she was on death's bed, she might not even be at home. She was probably laid up in some hospital bed. Or worse, she could be lying face down in some dark and dingy alley, unable to move. Panic seeped into my soul, but I didn't know what to do or where to go. My mind cycled through all the options in front of me, and I flashed back to when she had fallen in the park a few weeks ago. She had elected to go to County General for help. Just as the thought of the hospital pulled up in my mind, my vision suddenly faded to black and I felt as if I was being hoisted above a crowd and carried through the air by the random hands of strangers. I tried to open my eyes and look around, but it was useless. Darkness prevailed. The rush stopped as quickly as it had begun, and my vision swiftly returned. Once I was able to focus again, I doubled over and involuntary puked. When nothing came out, I gather that there was most likely nothing was left to vacate from my stomach. It was just dry heaves, most likely caused from whatever that ... feeling was. I looked around and discovered that I had mysteriously transported onto the seventh floor of the hospital.

I stood in front of the bank of elevators, alone. Straight ahead was a vacant reception station. To my left and to my right, long corridors led to various unknown rooms. I stepped up to the reception desk and waited. After what felt like an eternity, I realized that either the station was unattended at this hour or the receptionist was running errands somewhere else in the hospital. I decided to explore the floor on my own, figuring that I had been brought here for a reason—meaning Cyndi was probably near.

Turning around, I noticed a sign on the wall. Arrows indicated that rooms 701 through 718 were to the left, and ICU/CCU was to the right.

"ICU it is," I said aloud and headed down the corridor.

As I moved through the vacant hallway, I came upon a pair of glass doors leading into the intensive care unit. Gripping the handle on the left, I pulled, but the door did not budge. I tried the handle on the right but was met with the same result. I leaned close to the glass door and peered in as far as my eyes could see. The corridor veered to the right, disappearing out of sight. I looked around for some sort of communication device and found a small buzzer button. I pressed it and waited. Moments later, the door buzzed back and I heard an audible click at the door handle. I pushed through and walked down the hall.

The first room I came to was empty. Across the hall was another room—also empty. But another pair of doors further down the hallway looked promising. Each of the doors had medical clipboards hanging on hooks right outside. As I approached, I could read the names on the top sheets of the clipboards. Dewayne Mitchell and Leonard Stewart. I continued to walk down the hall, reading names off of charts. As I turned the corner, I saw what appeared to be a central nurse's station at the hub of several additional rooms. There was one attendant present, and he had his back toward me. I continued to move along the right-hand side, reading names on the charts as I went. Finally, as I was about to walk into the attendant's view, I saw Cyndi's name. I stepped into her room and pulled the curtain closed.

I took a deep breath, then turned to look at my wife. She lay unconscious, with multiple tubes and wires attached to various parts of her body. As I moved to her bedside, I noticed her face was bruised and battered. Almost as if she'd been beaten to a pulp. Both of her legs and one of her arms were wrapped in some kind of soft cast that prevented movement. Her left arm was also bruised. The rhythmic *beep-beep* from the machine next to her bed was all that could be heard.

Not knowing the proper procedure, I pulled the wooden box from my pocket and placed it on her chest. I opened the box and stepped back. Nothing happened. I leaned in and gently touched the side of her cheek.

"Oh, baby, what happened to you?" I asked.

She remained silent.

Fighting back tears, I attempted to open her mouth, thinking that her soul likely needed a clear pathway to vacate her body. As I pulled apart her lips, I noticed that her jaw had been wired shut. Blood and mucus coated her teeth, and the sight of it made me cringe.

Frustrated, I grabbed the box and snapped it shut before shoving it into my pocket. As I did so, my hand brushed against the coin that Wilson had used to bring back my memories.

I slipped the coin from my pocket as I lowered myself into the chair next to her bed. I rubbed the coin thoughtfully, contemplating my options. In order for the soul to release from its host, did I need to relive something from the host's past?

"What do you think, Cyn? Care to take a trip down memory lane?" I asked.

She didn't answer, of course. I figured it was probably best that way. I'm not sure I wanted to hear her pleas of protest, not wanting me to experience something that would not shine a flattering light on her.

"Here goes nothing," I said as I turned the coin over inside my hand, just like I had done numerous times with Wilson by my side. Nothing happened.

"Dammit," I exclaimed. I sprang from the chair and paced about the room, wondering what it was that I needed to do. I walked back and forth at the foot of her bed, thinking as I fumbled with the coin.

It struck me that it was Cyndi that needed to turn the coin in order to activate her memories. I moved back to her side and placed the coin in her hand. Without touching it myself, I used her fingers to flip the coin over in the palm of her hand. Darkness enveloped me as I vanished from the hospital room.

Chapter 2.5

Cyndi Duffy was engrossed in a dream when the first flashes of light fell upon her closed eyes. She squeezed them tight, determined to thwart the advance of day. With the dream so close to becoming fully lucid, she didn't want to move an inch for fear of losing the warmth of Kevin's touch.

The early morning dream had been the third in as many days, and even though they were really just fantasy delusions, she still felt guilty for having them. She knew that she should at least be dreaming about Jack instead of Kevin. But it had been years since Jack had given her butterflies like Kevin gave her now, imaginary or otherwise.

Eager to stay in the moment, she welcomed Kevin's gentle touch as he began to caress her body. She moaned softly as his hands worked their way over her breast and down across her abdomen. She lost track of Kevin's hands though when he leaned in and kissed her. The moment his lips touched hers, passion tugged at all of her senses. She longed for his body to melt deep inside of hers, when she heard him say something. Confused, she wondered how he could be talking when his lips were firmly planted on her own. She tried to ask "What?" but all that came out was "Hrmm?"

The voice, louder now and obviously not coming from Kevin, said, "I love you, baby." Cyndi's mind snapped out of her mildly erotic dream and into the early morning reality of her own life. She recognized Jack's voice at once and began to stir. Without opening her eyes, for fear that he would sense her betrayal, she murmured, "Me too. You better get up or you'll be late again."

Hoping that the dream would only pause long enough for her husband to get started on his day, Cyndi lay silently without moving.

Jack broke her comfortable silence "I know. I was just lying here thinking about . . ."

It quickly became obvious to Cyndi that Jack wasn't ready to get out of bed just yet. She figured that she might as well soothe his soul for a few minutes before he got ready for work. It was the least she could do, considering what she was just about to do. Albeit in a delusional fantasy.

"About what?" she asked, sliding her head over to rest on his chest. She lay motionless as he formed his response.

Lying on his back, Jack began to stroke Cyndi's hair as if he were petting a cat. "My project. Life. You. Take your pick."

As Jack spoke, Cyndi knew that there was more to his response than met the eye. It had been several months since his depression had surfaced, and she'd thought that he had finally gotten control of it. Not wanting to let him focus on the troubles at work anymore than he already was, she tried to steer their conversation in a lighter direction. "I'm happy I'm in there somewhere."

Surrendering to the morning light, she opened her eyes slightly and stared up at the ceiling. She didn't focus on anything in particular, but just laid in place while her eyes adjusted to the morning brightness.

"What are your plans for today? Want to have lunch?" Jack asked.

Accepting the fact that her dream was indeed lost, she looked at the alarm clock before answering. "I can't today. I'm volunteering at the Redevelopment Foundation, remember?"

The Redevelopment Foundation was the one thing that Cyndi was passionate about. Jack's income was enough for them to live comfortably without her having to take a job, and in the beginning, that was all that she wanted. To stay home and be a loving housewife. She'd enjoyed filling her days with making their home a happy one. For the first few years, that was enough. Then, once they discovered their challenges of starting a family, Cyndi quickly became bored of being Suzy Homemaker. The foundation alleviated that apathy, if only for once a week. Seeing Kevin on a weekly basis was just a perk. She forced the remains of her dream from her mind, and knew that she had some difficult decisions ahead.

After several minutes, Jack finally responded. "Oh right. The foundation. When will you be done?"

"The donation center is open until five, so I should be home around the same time as you," Cyndi said as she sat up and stretched. She winced at the pain that shot up her spine. It had been two weeks since the shameful accident, and she wasn't sure how much longer she could keep the truth from Jack.

"Does it still hurt?" he asked, a look of concern crossing his face.

Seeing his expression made it that much more difficult for Cyndi to lie. She had to either come clean with Jack or stop things with Kevin, completely. "Yeah. I was hoping I didn't need to fill the prescription again, but—"

"If it hurts, fill it. You don't have to take them all," Jack said, the sound of concern thick in his voice.

After several more minutes of mundane conversation, Cyndi was happy to have solitude once again, as Jack finally got out of bed and into the shower. She rolled over and tried to reenter sleep.

Chapter 3

I removed the coin from Cyndi's hand and leapt from her bedside. "Why didn't you tell me?" I asked.

I looked at her, expecting to find a dispassionate countenance on her face. Instead, she wore frown lines between her eyes—almost as if she was in misery. I looked around for her medical chart in hopes of determining whether she was on any pain medication. Unfortunately, it was nowhere in sight. I suddenly remembered seeing it hanging just outside the door in the nurses' station. Not wanting to explain my presence in the ICU ward, I opted to check the label on her bedside IV instead of going for her chart.

As I moved toward the medical contraption positioned on the opposite side of Cyndi's bed, I heard footsteps right outside her room. The curtain was still closed, and I figured I had only seconds to get out of sight before somebody walked in. I burst toward the bathroom and latched the door behind me with only seconds to spare. Once inside the small tiled room, I discovered that it was a shared toilet with the adjacent room, and its door was wide open. Panic enveloped me as I inched toward the open door and peered into the adjoining room. My fear was quickly abated upon finding the room empty.

I moved back to Cyndi's common door and waited, listening intently to the sounds that trickled in from her room. I could hear muffled voices, but nothing discernible. As I leaned against the closed door, my mind replayed Cyndi's morning, clouding my thoughts. I decided that some fresh air was in order.

Hoping to get out of ICU unnoticed, I walked into the adjoining room and out into the wide open corridor. As I looked about the nurses' station, it was clear that a shift change had taken place, as there were three new nurses milling about behind the counter. To my surprise, nobody paid me any attention. Seeing a second exit just to the right, I took my chances and walked right past the counter and through the door. Without turning to look back, I continued my march and headed for the exit stairway. Moments later, I stepped out into the morning sun. Mindlessly, I moved out into the burgeoning crowd of pedestrians and quickly fell in with the flow of foot traffic.

As I walked silently among the morning crowd, I wondered what I was going to do. I knew I had to collect Cyndi's soul, but when was it going to come out? Did I have to experience her entire day, leading up to whatever accident had happened to her? I wasn't sure I had it in me to experience the fornication from her point of view. Just seeing the few moments of her internal thoughts from yesterday morning was enough to make my blood boil.

As I moved through the streets of the city, the ebb and flow of the pedestrian crowd took me along the edge of City Park. Looking out across the vast acreage of green grass and flowering beds, fond memories began to surface in my mind, and I slowed my pace. I felt the people around me become agitated, so I began to make my way to the edge of the crowd.

"Excuse me," I said. "Pardon me." I repeated the niceties several times, without a single comment in return. I realized then that there really were some rude people in the city. Had I been one of them before, I wondered.

As I neared the edge of the crowd, I inadvertently bumped into another person.

"Forgive me," he said as he continued walking away from me. Despite his reluctance to slow down, he at least exercised common courtesy.

Finally making it to the edge of the city herd, I sidled up to a metal rail at the edge of the park and stared out onto the massive lawn. "What the hell am I doing?" I asked.

Slowly, I looked around the park until I noticed a small footbridge a few hundred feet from where I was standing. I remembered crossing that bridge on the numerous walks that Cyndi and I used to take. Without any other reason to return to that bridge but for memory's sake, I decided to cross it and follow the path for a while.

I stepped back into the flow of pedestrians until I reached the access point, moving through the crowd at my own pace. As I neared the break in the metal railing surrounding the park, I realized that nobody on the sidewalk was paying any attention to me whatsoever. I stopped directly in the middle of the moving crowd, and not a single person bumped into me or stepped around me. It was like I wasn't even there, and the people somehow just avoided me entirely. That's when I remembered something that Wilson had said while sitting on his park bench.

He'd said, "There are consequences. You would not be able to talk to anyone from your previous life again. The only conversations permitted would be with the dead or dying, much like I am speaking to you now."

Curious, I turned to face the oncoming flow of pedestrians head on. As a particularly attractive young woman approached me directly, I screamed, "Can anyone see me?" at the top of my lungs. Not a single reaction from anyone in the crowd. I was invisible to the world around me. I began walking against the flow of the crowd, and not a single person bumped into me or stopped because of me being there. Everyone just ... avoided me, almost instinctively. That's when the sudden realization hit me: the person who had acknowledged me not five minutes earlier was the only one who could see me.

I stretched my neck above the crowd in hopes of catching a glimpse of the stranger, although I probably couldn't have picked him out of a two-person lineup. I should have been disturbed about the entire crowd not acknowledging me, but it was the one stranger that did that really shook me up.

I rushed through the crowd to where I thought I remembered bumping into him, but he wasn't there. Then I remembered he'd been walking in the other direction. Maybe if I ran in that direction I could find him again.

I began pushing my way back through the crowd, wishing I could talk to someone, anyone, that could help me complete my job. If Wilson could have only stuck around for a little while . . .

Suddenly, I vanished from the crowded sidewalk and reappeared next to Wilson's dead body.

Chapter 4

"What the hell?" I said. Again, my stomach felt a little queasy, but I didn't retch this time.

Wilson's body continued to sit and stare at the faded billboard, his eyes beginning to develop a white fog. Freaked out by his bizarre, zombie-like eyes, I dropped my hand over his line of sight and tried to force them closed. But rigor mortis had set in and they were fixed open. I had a crazy idea to put sunglasses on him. Unfortunately, I didn't have a pair with me, so I began to check Wilson's pockets. In the first pocket I searched, I found a vintage pair of horn-rimmed shades and slid them onto his face. I leaned back and smiled. "When you're cool, Wilson, the sun never stops shining."

Satisfied with my attempt at lightening the mood, I sat down next to the dead body. "What's going on, Wilson? I thought I was making progress this morning, but when I tried to take Cyndi's soul, nothing happened. I opened the box and struggled to get her mouth open, but zilch. Does she need to be awake? Does she need to say something? What?" I leaned back and tried to figure out what I might have missed, but I couldn't focus on any one thing. So many thoughts were galloping through my mind. "And another thing. I seem to keep mysteriously beaming, or whatever it's called, from place to place," I said. I leaned back and looked up into the cloudless sky.

There was no response. The only sounds present were those echoing through the bustling city streets. That, and the sound of an approaching car.

I looked up the street and caught site of a police cruiser approaching slowly from the left. "Shit," I said in a low voice.

Before I could get up from the bench, the cop car stopped directly in front of our park bench and the passenger window rolled down.

"Hey, buddy. Wake up. It's time to move along now." Wilson didn't respond. I laughed.

"Hey. I said it's time go!" the cop yelled from his cruiser. Moments later he got out of the passenger seat and slowly approached the park bench, his hand on his holster.

"What do you think this is? Let's get a move on before I haul you in." The cop stopped directly in front of Wilson, leaned down, and shook his lifeless shoulder. "Hey, buddy, are you all right?"

Wilson's body drooped.

"Hey, hold yourself up now," the cop said, but it was too late. Wilson's body continued to slide to the right, nearly rolling off the edge of the bench. The cop touched Wilson's neck, most likely searching for a pulse.

"Hey, Pete," he said to his partner still seated behind the wheel of the cruiser. "I think we've got a dead one here. His body is cold, and I can't find a pulse. You better call for a bus. I'll see if he has an ID."

The cop began to turn out Wilson's pockets, starting with his back pockets first, but Wilson didn't have a billfold. Next he checked the front pockets of Wilson's trousers, and again he came up empty. Finally he opened up Wilson's suit jacket and pulled a rosary from the inside pocket. After examining it for a few moments, the cop placed it in Wilson's shirt pocket.

"He's got nothin', Pete. No ID, no wallet. He's a John Doe," the cop said as he returned to the cruiser. He leaned into the open door window to converse with his partner.

As he did so, I looked back at Wilson and could see the rosary slightly visible over the edge of his pocket. I knew then it might be more beneficial to me than it would be to the cops or the morgue. I reached over and tried to remove it from his pocket, but it was stuck. It actually felt like it was cemented in place. I looked back at the cop car, and both officers were staring in my direction. I tried again, but the rosary was still firmly in place. I wondered if while the cops looked at Wilson's body, it somehow prevented me from taking the rosary from his pocket.

I stood up and stepped behind the park bench. As I did so, the cops turned their attention to something on the dash of their cruiser. At that moment, I quickly reached into Wilson's pocket and pulled the rosary out effortlessly. It'd been quite some time since I'd practiced any form of religion, but I recognized the rosary as a Chaplet of Divine Mercy, just like the one my grandmother had. I slipped it in my pocket and walked away.

"Good-bye, Wilson. I hope you have a peaceful afterlife," I said as I walked directly in front of the idling car. The cops paid me no attention.

As I crossed the street, I tried to figure out how it was that I could travel in jumps, or whatever it was. I thought back to the sidewalk in front of the park where I had just been, recalling what it was that I was thinking of at the time, and then I vanished once again.

Chapter 5

"Shit!" I said as I appeared on that very same sidewalk near the park entrance. At least the nausea wasn't accompanying the travel jolt any more.

Once I regained my bearings, I again looked around for the guy who had bumped into me earlier. I knew it was a long shot to find that one person in a city full of millions of active people, but I knew I wasn't imagining things. Or was I? Did he really bump into me?

Concluding that the guy was long gone by now, I decided to see if I could hone the transport thing a little more. I figured it was controlled somehow by my thoughts. When I traveled to Cyndi's hospital earlier and then when I was beamed back to where Wilson was, I had been thinking about them individually just before I jumped. Then, just now, I was thinking about being right here in front of the park entrance, and poof.

I wondered . . . I thought of a new place, somewhere that I hadn't yet visited by the mystical transportation technique. Then, I vanished.

When I rematerialized, I stood in front of my own apartment. The door was open, but a wide strip of yellow crime scene tape crossed the opening. I ducked under the tape and walked in. Nothing appeared to have been disturbed in the past thirty-plus hours. Cyndi's heels were still on the kitchen floor, and the dirty dishes still sat in the sink. I moved farther into the apartment and down the hall.

As I approached the bedroom, visions of the previous day came flooding back. I pushed the detestable act from my mind and walked in. The curtains were now drawn, and there was a lab technician analyzing the room. He was taking samples from the bed and nightstand. This must have been the crime scene, I surmised. I wondered if Cyndi had been beaten. I wanted to ask the tech, but I knew he couldn't see or hear me.

I moved past him and into the bathroom, looking up at the mirror in an attempt to see my own reflection. I could in fact see myself, but only faintly, like I was an apparition. I was transparent, as was everything that was on me. I looked at my business suit and noticed that the lapels were stained with vomit. If I were to change, I wondered, would my new clothes be translucent as well?

I darted from the bathroom and into the closet. I quickly flipped through the stack of hats on the top shelf and grabbed my favorite Yankees ball cap before returning to the mirror. The hat was just as transparent as the rest of me. I took the hat off and it remained transparent, but as soon as I placed it on the vanity, it became solid once again. Curious, I reached over and picked up the hand towel from the counter, and as I did so, it blinked into transparency in the reflection.

"Cool."

I tossed the hand towel back on the vanity and headed back into the closet. Although nobody could see me, I could see myself, and I didn't want to walk around wearing barf-stained clothing for the rest of eternity. As I browsed through my clothes, I realized that my choices were rather mundane. I thought of what Wilson had worn when we met and wondered if that was what he had been wearing when he became a soul collector or if it was a style that he'd adopted along the way. Either way, I felt I needed a new look. But until I could arrange some alone time in a menswear store, I'd have to choose something from my own collection.

After nearly twenty minutes of cycling through my entire wardrobe, I picked out a simple black suite with a white shirt. And although wearing ties made me feel staunch and uptight, I donned a thin black tie today, in honor of the multitude of ties that Cyndi had given me over the years. A smile crossed my face as I remembered her gifting me a tie for every year that we'd been together. The smile quickly vanished though as I wondered if all those years were filled with lies.

Once I was redressed, I reentered the bedroom. The crime scene examiner was finished processing the bed and had moved on to the dresser. As I walked past him, I said, "You're gonna to have a blast once you get to the bath and the closet." I smiled at my own sarcasm as I walked out into the living room.

Looking around, most likely for the last time, I began to wonder where I would sleep. Would I have a place to live? If I was to live life at an eighth the pace as everyone else, I'd certainly be around for quite some time. Would I even need to sleep? Would I eat?

I shook the many questions from my head and focused on the importance of the now. I needed to finish figuring out how the transportation thing worked. From what I'd gathered, all I had to do was think of a place and envision myself there. To try this out, I thought about one of my favorite vacation spots in the world—Hampton Court in England. I then envisioned myself standing in the middle of the king's throne room. Within seconds, I was whisked off to the sixteenth-century palace. After walking around for a few moments—unseen by anyone, naturally—I thought about Wilson's bench and envisioned myself there. Once again I appeared at the lonesome park bench within seconds.

"I think I've got this," I said, but Wilson was no longer on the bench. The area had been cleared and the body most likely was off to the city morgue. Oddly, even though I barely knew the guy, I had a sudden feeling of sadness for the old man. Here he was, a soul collector for what, nearly sixty years? And now he was gone, not missed or mourned by anyone. I wondered who would miss me once I was discovered gone.

Not wanting to go down that depression-riddled rabbit hole, I decided I needed to face the challenges in front of me. I thought about Cyndi's bedside chair and then I was there.

Chapter
6

Standing next to the bed, looking down at her beaten and bruised flesh, remorse flushed over me once again. I sat in the chair and wove her lifeless hand into my own.

"Where did we go wrong?" I asked. "Was it something I did or didn't do?"

I caressed her hand, trying to will her to answer my questions. It felt like a wasted effort. I slipped her box from my pocket once again, hoping that I had endured enough of Cyndi's final day to earn her soul.

I placed the box upon her chest and opened it. Nothing happened. I slid my finger between her lips in a halfhearted attempt to free her soul, but it was no use. Resigned to the fact that I had to finish reliving her day, I swapped the box for the coin from my pocket and placed it in her open palm.

Chapter
6.5

Walking down the busy sidewalk, Cyndi headed toward the foundation. From the moment she had woken up and heard Jack's thoughtful words, her mind had gradually escaped the dreamlike state that clearly distorted her feelings for Kevin, and masked those that she had for Jack. Deep down, she knew that their fling had run its course, and it wasn't good for her mental state to continue on with it. No, she had to end it. She knew that if she didn't do it now, she might begin to develop stronger feelings for him, while pushing Jack further away. Deep down, she loved Jack, always had. But there was just something missing when it came to her feelings for Jack that she couldn't quite put her finger on. Was that a reason to leave him? After so many happy years? She didn't know. She was confused.

Walking the fifteen blocks gave her time to reflect on their marriage, as well as what life would be like if she chose Kevin instead. Looking back to when she and Jack first began dating, she remembered having the same irresistible feelings for Jack as she had for Kevin right now. From the very beginning, Jack was her life, her world. Then, things changed.

Sometime after learning of their infertility, they started to drift apart. She had accepted that it was nobody's fault, but her desire to have children had remained strong. Adoption was brought up numerous times, but nothing ever came of it. It was all just talk. She knew, or she felt she knew, that Jack was scared. Scared of the adoption process and what it might mean to his bottom line.

Meaning the exorbitant expense of raising a child who inherently wasn't their own was emotionally problematic.

Cyndi pushed the thoughts from her mind as she passed through the double entry doors into the Redevelopment Foundation's headquarters. As she passed the various donation tables set up, her eyes scanned the room for familiar faces, one face in particular. When she found no sign of Kevin, she dropped her purse and sweater off in the locker room before returning to the donation center.

"Oh, good morning, Cyndi," Stan, the center's administrator said. "It's very good of you to come in today."

"It's my pleasure, Stan. Where would you like me today?"

"Why don't you help Beth out at the children's table. Wednesdays are usually busy with infant clothing donations, and Beth is the only one at that station," he said.

"Sounds good," Cyndi said. Before she headed to her assignment though, she asked, "But doesn't Kevin usually help Beth?"

"Yes, but he's running an errand for me right now. As soon as he returns, I'll decide whether to put him in a different station or move you somewhere else."

Cyndi wasn't sure if she should be elated or disappointed that Kevin wasn't there. She had rehearsed in her mind how she would approach him about ending their relationship. Was this really a relationship, she wondered.

After thirty minutes of accepting various children's items, Cyndi couldn't wait for Kevin to return, if only to relieve her from this particular station. With each piece of infant clothing that passed through her hands, she was constantly reminded that she might never hold her own child. And with each creak of the entry door, Cyndi's eyes darted up to see if Kevin was coming in to release her from her misery. As the absolution never came, she tried to focus on something else. With a lull in donation activity, Cyndi closed the lid of a filled box and told Beth that she would take it to the back. Beth nodded and continued to sort through the remaining garments on the table.

The box wasn't particularly heavy, but with her injured

shoulder, any abnormal weight caused discomfort. As she headed into the back room, moving slowly so as not to trip, she lifted the box above her head and slid it to the top of the processing pile.

As she dropped her arms back to her side, she could feel and hear her shoulder pop.

"Oww," she moaned.

"You know, you should have asked for help with that," a voice boomed from behind her.

Cyndi turned and smiled at Kevin's presence. Gently massaging her shoulder, she said, "It's okay, I can manage."

"Still hurt?"

"Yeah. A little."

"What did the doctor say?"

"He said not to lift boxes over my head," Cyndi giggled.

Kevin smiled, but concern tightened his brow. "Seriously though, are you going to be okay?"

"Yeah, Jack is picking up a refill for my medication. I think another week of those pills should fix me up."

"Speaking of Jack, has he—"

"No, he still thinks I fell at the park. He has no idea."

"For what it's worth, Cyndi, I never meant to hurt you. That Kama Sutra book really puts our bodies into perilous positions. But I have to say, that was the best sex I've ever had."

Chapter 7

I pulled the coin from Cyndi's hand. Shocked and overwhelmed at what I just witnessed, I stepped away from her bedside.

"Are you serious?" I asked loudly. "Your injury came from having sex with Kevin?"

Cyndi's unconscious soul did not reply.

As I paced next to her unresponsive body, I finally noticed the nurse attending to the tubes and wires connected to Cyndi's body.

"I wouldn't bother, nurse. This woman is a cheating whore, and I'm here to collect her soul," I said, standing right next to her.

The nurse didn't react to my voice. She just continued cleaning and adjusting Cyndi's life support. Moments later, another person walked in and approached the bedside.

"Any status change?" he asked.

"No, Doctor. The patient remains unconscious."

The doctor flipped open Cyndi's medical chart and reviewed several pages, starting from the last page forward. "Next of kin?"

"Not that I'm aware of, Doctor. According to the sergeant on duty, her husband can't be found."

The doctor nodded as he jotted some notes in her chart.

"What's the prognosis, Doctor? Do you think she'll make it?" asked the nurse.

The doctor paused momentarily. I moved closer to be sure I heard every word.

"Unfortunately her fall was quite severe. Aside from the multiple fractures to both of her legs and her right arm, it's the damage to her brain that will most likely take her life. But there's no way of knowing at this point. She needs to fight."

"How far was the fall?" asked the nurse.

The doctor flipped through the chart looking for the information, but it wasn't present. "I'm not exactly sure, but from what I understand she lived on the twenty-fifth floor and her body was found at the base of the stairwell on the first floor."

"My God, how could she even survive that kind of fall?"

"Perhaps her guardian angel was looking out for her. Unfortunately that angel can only do so much. The damage is just too severe," the doctor said making his final notes. "Nurse, see if you can track down any other relatives that can be notified. It would be such a shame if she passed without any family present."

"Will do, Doctor," said the nurse before they both walked out of the room.

With the medical staff gone, I stood and stared at Cyndi's lifeless body. This emotional roller coaster was killing me. I returned to the chair next to her bed, once again taking her hand in mine.

"Well, klutz. It looks like you really fucked things up this time," I said caressing her skin. "I really should be several levels beyond pissed right now, but for some reason I only have pity for you. Pity for us."

I wished the dreadful ordeal were over, but I knew it wouldn't be until I finished what I had come here to do. I slipped the coin back into her hand, clenching my teeth at what I might experience next.

Chapter 7.5

The elevator doors closed, and Cyndi pressed the button for 25.

"Listen, Kevin, I really do appreciate everything you've done for me. You've been a rock for me for so long, especially when I needed someone the most."

"But—"

"I think that what we've had has been wonderful, but I think it needs to end."

Before Kevin could reply, the elevator dinged and the doors parted, revealing the twenty-fifth floor corridor. Cyndi stepped out and led the way to her apartment door.

"Then why'd you invite me to your apartment?" Kevin asked.

"Because I wanted to talk to you about this in private. Sure, I could've just blown you off at the donation station, but I felt I owed you more than that," Cyndi said. "Besides, I figured we could have lunch together one last time."

"So you want to cut everything out, not just the sex?"

"Don't you think it would be better that way? If we go on being friends, our own animalistic desires might take over."

"You really are an animal sometimes," Kevin joked.

Cyndi snickered. "Would you be serious, please?"

"I am. Cyndi, you are the most wonderful woman that I've ever been with."

Cyndi blushed. "That'll be enough of that, Mister. Do you want a sandwich?"

"Yeah, sure. What do you have?"

Cyndi opened the refrigerator door. "Well, we have turkey. We have roast beef, or we have peanut butter and jelly."

"What kind of jelly?" Kevin asked, imitating a little boy's face.

"It's raspberry, you goof."

"If that's the case, then I'll take the roast beef, please."

As Cyndi made them both sandwiches, Kevin moved about the living room, looking at the various family pictures of Cyndi and Jack.

"Tell me, why are you really breaking things off with me?" he asked.

"It's complicated."

"Uncomplicate it."

Cyndi slipped off her heels on the kitchen floor before carrying their lunch plates to the table.

"Thank you. This looks delicious."

Cyndi nodded. "I've always imagined having a big family. I thought that family would consist of myself, Jack, and two or three kids. After we found out that we couldn't have children, I tried my best to reenvision our future together. It was difficult. We've talked about other alternatives, but . . . Then I met you."

Kevin glanced up at her sorrowful face, winked, and then took another bite of his sandwich.

"You see, you were a distraction."

"Ouch."

"A wonderful distraction." Cyndi smiled. "But recently I've discovered that I still love Jack. I do, with all my heart. And I know he loves me. Regardless of the fruitless curveball that has been thrown at us, we're gonna make it through this."

Kevin finished his sandwich and placed his plate in the sink.

"And you're sure?" he asked

"Yes, I'm sure. Despite Jack's flaws, I truly believe he's my soul mate," Cyndi said, wiping tears from her eyes.

"Well, I'm thankful to have been your distraction, even if just for a little while. You are beautiful woman, and all I can say is, it was fun while it lasted."

Cyndi's appetite was lost, and she emptied her plate in the garbage.

"Thank you, Kevin. You have no idea how difficult this has

been," she said, her tears flowing rapidly.

"Hey, hey. Come here," Kevin said pulling her into his arms. "It'll be all right."

Cyndi sobbed into Kevin's shoulder, her body shaking in his arms.

Kevin stroked the back of her hair as her emotions flowed freely. He leaned down and kissed the top of her head.

Cyndi lifted her head and looked into his eyes.

"What do you say? One more romp for old times' sake?" Kevin asked before kissing her gently on her lips.

Silently, Cyndi led Kevin into the bedroom.

Chapter 8

"Oh, hell no," I said, pulling the coin from her hand. "I've already witnessed that once, I'm not going to relive it again."

I leaned back and thought about what I'd just witnessed. Part of me wanted to hug and kiss Cyndi for all the love that she had for me, while the other part wanted to sob like a baby at her betrayal. Right after punching Kevin in the face, obviously.

Wondering how exactly I could fast-forward past that unforgettable scene, I fumbled with the coin between my fingers.

"Why me, Wilson? Why was I selected to collect her soul?"
I sensed movement behind me, but when I stood and turned, there was nobody there. I walked to the door and pulled the curtain open. There were two nurses behind the station, but nobody else was around. Figuring I was imagining things, I returned to Cyndi's bedside and slipped the coin into her hand.

Chapter 8.5

I appeared in the hallway of my apartment building, but I was alone. This should be Cyndi's personal reflection and not my own. As I stood there trying to figure out what I did differently, I saw a shadowy figure walk out of my apartment door directly toward me. As the shadowy figure got closer, I realized that it was me walking toward ... me. I could not make out any discernible characteristics, but I knew it was me. It was as if a camera lens was unfocused on the man walking toward me.

I'd expected the apparition to walk around me, but he stepped through me. My chest tightened and I caught my breath. A sudden chill shot through my body, from the top of my head to the soles of my feet. I turned and watched my blurry apparition press the elevator call button and wait.

As my shadowed self stepped into the elevator, Cyndi's scream echoed through the hallway. I turned in the direction of my apartment door just as Cyndi blasted through me, giving me the same sensation of chills I had experienced seconds before . . .

"Oh God!" Cyndi screamed, standing in front of the apartment door. Then she ran as fast as she could to catch the elevator door from closing. Unfortunately she was only seconds shy from stopping Jack long enough to explain what he'd just seen. Tears streamed from her eyes as she watched the elevator readout count backward: 24 . . . 23 . . . 22 . . .

Just then Kevin walked into the hallway, barefoot and only

wearing his trousers.

"Hey, are you okay? You didn't say anything when you ran out of the apartment," Kevin said.

"Get out! Just leave. You've made of mess of everything," yelled Cyndi.

Without waiting for another word from Kevin, Cyndi ran around the corner and burst into the stairwell. She hoped that the elevator would stop at least a few floors on its way down, that she might be able to get downstairs before Jack.

The stairwell was brightly illuminated, light reflecting off the stark white walls. The stairs were hard concrete with a worn steel guardrail at the center. Cyndi leaned over and could see all the way down to the first level. She was relieved to see that nobody else was in the stairwell to impede her race to the bottom.

She took the steps two at a time, moving slowly at first, establishing a rhythm in her stride. After passing the twentieth floor, she felt confident enough to increase her speed to three steps at a time. The breeze formed by her speed began to tug at the tails of her bathrobe. She ignored the fluttering, and remained focused on getting to the bottom before Jack.

At the eighteenth floor, she grabbed the railing tight and swung her body around, throwing herself farther down the stairs. But her robe caught on the end of the handrail, launching her over the edge of the metal guardrail.

The echoes of Cyndi's scream went unheard as she fell through the center of the stairwell. She lashed out multiple times to catch a handhold along the way down, but as her plummeting body picked up speed, each grasp of her hand launched her in the opposite direction, knocking her legs and body against the numerous guardrails all the way down.

Around the fifth floor, her calf slapped hard against the guardrail, slowing her speed down greatly, but snapping her leg bone at the same time. She screamed in pain. Moments later, her naked body slammed onto the floor at the base of the stairwell, the edge of her jaw driving into the bottom stair tread.

Chapter 9

Breathless, I opened my eyes, which were blurry with tears. I was back in the hospital room, Cyndi at my side. I tried to keep my emotions in check, but I sobbed softly as I held Cyndi's hand, wishing for the pain to be over. Wishing for it all to be over.

I wiped the tears away and suddenly felt Cyndi squeeze my hand. I blinked my vision clear and gazed into her eyes. She was staring back at me, blinking through tears of her own. She tried to speak, but her jaw would not move.

"Hold on a minute, baby. This might hurt," I said as I leaned close to her.

I gently parted her lips and looked inside her left cheek. I found where the wires were twisted together, then slowly unfastened them, partially freeing her lower jaw.

"Shh. Don't try to speak yet. I have to do the other side."

Tears streaked down the side of her face as she nodded.

Repeating the procedure on her right cheek, I tossed the bloody wire to the side, allowing her jaw to move freely. As I sat on the edge of her bed, her eyes squinted tightly, most likely fighting back the pain.

Cyndi moaned as she opened her mouth as far as she could.

"You don't have to speak, baby. You don't have to say anything," I said, wishing her pain away.

She opened her wet eyes, her stare piercing into mine. "M'm. Sus ssorrry."

"Cyn, I've thought about what you did to me, and I am upset.

But I . . ." I dropped my head down and rested my forehead on the edge of her bed. "I just wish you would have said something. I could have changed. Whatever it was, I would have moved mountains for you. Cyn, I love you, and I . . . I forgive you."

Tears flowed freely from my eyes. I was surprised with myself at how quickly I was able to forgive ... for something that I had only witnessed just yesterday. I wiped my eyes on the bed linens, then looked into her hopeless gaze. Her eyes were as wet as mine, and I knew the time was imminent.

Moments later, the strength of her stare faded as she stared off into the distance. Her clutch on my hand went flaccid, and her head lolled back into her pillow. A wisp of smoke began to slip past her bruised and battered face.

Wishing I had more time to share some last minute words with her, but I was caught off guard. I quickly pulled her box out of my pocket and opened it in the palm of my hand.

Her soul drifted freely through the air, sliding in and out of my own body before entering the box. As the last bit of smoke entered, the box closed before it vanished. In its place a new box materialized.

I slid the box into my pocket before leaning in and kissing Cyndi. I kissed her forehead and then her nose. Then I kissed her lips for the last time.

Tears rolled off my cheeks and dropped onto her face, streaking across her bruised skin.

"I love you," I said, and wished to be someplace else. A second later I vanished from her bedside.

Chapter 10

I appeared on the sidewalk in front of Engineers Gate, which led into the park. I looked around and wondered what had brought me to that exact point.

I stood fixed on the sidewalk and pondered. Cyndi had been my soul mate, there was no question. I wondered how I would continue on without her to talk to every day. My heart ached deeply at the loss of her life. The loss of my wife – my partner – my life. It felt like a part of me was ripped from my being, leaving a gaping hole, void of purpose.

Compartmentalizing those thoughts, I rotated slowly, taking in my surroundings in all directions. My eyes fixated on a grand Art Deco church that sat directly across the street. Without a second thought, I crossed over and entered through one of the double entry doors. According to a small sign on the wall, the doors led into a vestibule under the west gallery. Beyond, three arches led into the nave. I stepped through the arches and into the voluminous chamber. Aisles were situated between internal buttresses that rose with arches to near-full height. I somehow knew that I was in the right place.

Slowly, I walked up the center aisle to the front of the nave. To my relief, the church was practically empty. I needed solitude right then. Or was it something else that I desired? Solitude—the act of being alone—was not quite the same as no one being able to see me. If I was in a crowd, I was not alone. Lonely, perhaps, but not truly alone. It's a fine distinction.

I pulled the rosary beads from my shirt pocket and held them in my hand as I kneeled in the first pew. I bowed my head and attempted to pray. My only problem: I had no idea how to pray.

The last time I had been to church was with my grandmother when I was six or seven. Although my father was Catholic, my mother was something completely different. I honestly cannot remember what her religious preference was. All I could remember was her constant disagreement with my grandmother about how I should be raised. I think my mother kept me out of church just to spite my grandmother. Thinking back to their bitter feud that lasted until death, I think it worked.

I closed my eyes and tried to think of the words to say. Nothing remotely religious come to mind. I shook my head.

"Well, Wilson. I think I've done it. I've collected her soul," I said as I opened my eyes and focused on the crucifix directly in front of me.

"I have to say, this is all pretty eye-opening. I only wish I could have met you before I took all those pills. I wish I would've known what I was throwing away," I said as I absentmindedly rubbed the beads between my fingers.

"Wilson, I don't know the right words to say, but I'd like to pray for you and your soul. I wish you a pleasant afterlife, if that's what you call it."

Despite my best intentions, I could not stop thinking about Cyndi. Seeing her fall so horrifically made my own soul ache. She didn't deserve to suffer such pain and agony.

"And if it isn't too much trouble, could you look out for my wife's soul coming your way? Despite her indiscretions, I think—no, I know—she has a good soul and deserves only the best. Please, Wilson, do what you can to ease her pain."

Leaning forward off my haunches, I sat on the wooden bench and continued to stare at the crucifix. As I slipped Wilson's rosary beads back into my pocket, I pulled out the new box that replaced Cyndi's. With my mind in such a haze, I only fumbled with the box, not focusing on the name for the next soul.

"So who's the next victim?" came a voice from behind me.

I nearly jumped out of my skin. I turned to see a man. The very man that had bumped into me earlier. "You. You can talk to me?"

"That I can. And you can talk to me. It's funny how conversation work," he said as he moved into my row.

"But, I tried to find you after you—"

"I know. I wasn't expecting you to bump into me. I was only supposed to observe your first official collection," he said as he looked around the church.

"So you know what I am?" I asked.

"Of course. I'm one as well. Hell, I trained most of the collectors in the last century."

I scratched my temple. "But you don't look that old."

"Thanks! I need to hear that every fifty years or so. I'm Hauser."

"Hauser? Wilson mentioned you."

"Did he? I hope it was all good things," Hauser said, smiling.

"He said that you were wise well beyond your years, or something to that effect."

"Well, I'm not sure about that," Hauser said, blushing modestly.

We sat in silence for a few moments. Hauser continued to look around the church while I was trying to calm my mind. I had a million questions but didn't want to blurt them all out at once.

"Did you find this place all on your own?" asked Hauser.

"Well, I . . . sort of felt like it would do after what I just went through. I needed someplace to say a few words."

Hauser nodded as he turned to look at me. "I think it's peculiar that you chose this church over all the other churches in the city."

I shrugged. "It's not *that* out of the ordinary. I popped onto the sidewalk just across the street. I just happened to notice it sitting here is all. What makes that peculiar?"

"The Church of Heavenly Rest has a history, you know."

"I'm sure it does. It's just another church to me," I said, trying not to sound too insensitive.

"Oh, it's not just an ordinary church. Cyndi never mentioned it to you?"

An explosion of knowledge burst inside my head. "Right. The Redevelopment Foundation. That's here?"

Hauser nodded. "Yep. It's out back."

"I had no idea. Cyndi would talk about this place a lot, but I've never been here."

"The aberrant nature of this location doesn't stop there either," Hauser smiled.

"How so?"

"You see, Cyndi was also baptized here. Many years before the two of you met. You sure she never mentioned this place?"

I was flabbergasted. "No, not a word. We really didn't discuss religion much. We agreed to believe in each other," I said, thinking about that decision all those years ago. "Maybe that was a mistake."

"Ah, that's water under the bridge now. Don't beat yourself up about it."

Silence came over us once again. I wished I could heed Hauser's advice, but my mind continued to fumble through what I'd just learned. After several minutes of thought, I spoke.

"So, you could only observe? How much were you around?" I asked, thinking back through the day, and my fumbling about with the transport jump thing.

Hauser's eyes shifted away from me and then back quickly. "I, uh ... was in and out a number of times, just staying in the shadows as best I could."

I nodded and tried to envision just where he could have been at in each of the situations where I thought I felt someone's presence.

"Were you there when Wilson passed?" I asked, remembering getting hit on the back while sitting on the bench.

"Unfortunately, I just missed Wilson's departure. I would have loved to see the ol' chap once more before he gave up the ghost," Hauser said. "No, I first showed up just shortly after."

"Uh huh. I thought so. That was you that smacked the air into my lungs."

Hauser smiled. "Yep. You caught me. Considering you immediate history with trying to end your life, I didn't need you giving it all a second try right after Wilson gave you his soul."

"What? I wasn't trying to kill myself. I was just ... checking something," I said, slightly embarrassed for my personal experimentation of life after death. "I wanted to see if I needed to breathe. You know ... After I died and all. If you hadn't smacked me right then, you would have seen me take a breath just seconds later."

"Heh. Sorry 'bout that, then. I just didn't want you to get any idea's is all."

"Trust me, Hauser. I wish I could go back and undo all that I did in that café. Suicide was not the solution, and now everything I knew or had is lost."

Hauser bobbed his head as he studied the crucifix in front of us.

We sat in uncomfortable silence for several more minutes before I spoke again.

"And you couldn't have helped me out with the collection. Just observe?"

"Oh, I could have helped. Would have, too, if you couldn't pick things up on your own. I just wanted to see what you were made of." Hauser whistled quietly. "Let me tell you, you move to the front of the class, bub. What lousy luck for you to have to go through what you just did. Your own wife? If there was a bar that served our kind, I'd buy you a drink."

"Thanks, I guess."

"Don't mention it. So, who's up next? Have you looked?"

"What? Oh yeah." I flipped the box around until the name was readable.

"It's Abigail Whitaker," I said, looking at Hauser.

He nodded his head knowingly but remained silent.

"What? Are you not telling me something? Do you recognize the name?" I asked.

"As a matter of fact, I do. I was actually hoping that would be the name that popped up for you next."

BOOK 3

ETERNAL DEVOTION

Chapter 1

The pungent aroma of smoky peat filled my nose as I leaned in close to the half-filled glass of scotch. I'd only been dead for a short while, but the longing to slowly sip at the wonderfully woody spirit was overpowering. I wondered if I'd ever drink the golden nectar again.

To think of myself as dead is a little disingenuous, as I really am alive. I just can't talk or interact with the living, only the dying. So it goes.

I stepped away from the edge of the bar as Jake, the proprietor, slid the lowball tumbler toward his customer—a well-dressed businessman most likely stopping off for a cocktail after a long day at the office. Prior to a few weeks ago, I too stopped at Jake's for a drink from time to time, just to release the built-up demons of a hard week at work. And until recently, Jake's was a relatively quiet little hole-in-the-wall that gave me the solitude I craved. The fact that it was located directly across the street from my apartment was just a bonus. Now, everything's changed. With all the news coverage, Jake's has transformed into a hotspot for fans of all things mysterious and captivating, hoping to catch a glimpse of the portrayed dastardly man on the run. Me.

Looking up at the television behind the bar, I wished I could hear the broadcast. But as the place was rather packed on this particular Thursday afternoon, I couldn't very well turn up the volume on my own. Not with all these people around, watching. I had to stand there, reading the text scroll across the bottom of the screen.

"The woman that mysteriously fell more than twenty flights of stairs two weeks ago has died. Cynthia Duffy, the wife of Jack Duffy, succumbed to her injuries shortly after being discovered. The exact cause of her fall has not been determined at this time, but police continue to investigate the scene. Jack Duffy, her husband of fifteen years, has not been seen or heard from since the day of the accident. Police are reluctant to declare if foul play was a factor in the accident. The couple had no children, and no other family members could be reached. For more details on this tragic incident, our on-the-spot correspondent, Addison Madera, is live at the scene."

"Thank you, Claire. I'm at the Dodson Apartment building, where Jack and Cynthia Duffy lived for more than eight years before Cynthia's life came to a tragic end almost two weeks ago. She was found unconscious at the base of the exit stairwell by another building tenant, who dialed 911. When emergency services arrived on the scene, Cynthia's husband was nowhere to be found, and their apartment was riddled in mystery. Their apartment door was left wide open, but nothing appeared to have be taken. After speaking to several of the Duffys' neighbors, all of whom declined to come on camera, a resident from the floor below spoke candidly with us. Beatrice Eastman said that she knew the couple well, and that for as far back as she could recall, the Duffys were relatively quiet people, generally keeping to themselves. Ms. Eastman went on to say that despite their reserved nature, they would be greatly missed."

"Such a tragedy. Addison, do the police have any leads on the whereabouts of the husband?"

"Yes, it is. Very heartbreaking. I spoke with the police chief just thirty minutes ago, and she said that they are actively looking for Jack Duffy for questioning. She said that at this time, he is in fact a suspect, but they are also looking into other leads as well. Namely, an acquaintance of Cynthia's, a man named Kevin Roberts. The police chief said that Mr. Roberts has already been interviewed once, and although he is not in custody, he remains at the precinct."

"Very compelling. Did the police chief disclose anything about why Roberts was being questioned?"

"Not at this time. She said it was too early to speculate, and that they would know more soon."

"Okay, then. Thank you, Addison.

"If you have information on the whereabouts of Jack Duffy, you are asked to call our tip line at 210-555-9076 with any information. We'll continue to monitor the situation and update you with any breaking news on the story."

Shaking my head in disgust at the nonsense of the news report, I refocused my attention to the bottle of scotch nearly at my fingertips.

"Please, Jake. Just pour me one drink. After the hell I've been through these last few weeks." My pleas to be served were drowned out by the dull murmurs throughout the bar.

Frustrated and confused, I blasted my way through the crowded bar for the exit. Even though I was basically invisible, I hadn't quite grasped the concept of still occupying space. As I trudged through the crowd, I did so without touching a single soul. It was as if I were Moses and the sea parted for me. I'll have to ask Hauser about that when I next see him, I mused.

Stepping out into the late evening, I wondered what I should do. I had a job to do—to collect the next soul. But in order to do that, I'd have to return to the hospital. Something I was not quite ready to do just yet. I could try to clear my name, but what use would that do? I struggled with the inability to talk to anyone; to even attempt to explain the truth was futile. Unless they were about to die, I would be wasting my time. No, my efforts were better off spent doing something else. But what? I thought about my apartment and how there might be something there that could occupy my time. A second later, I vanished from the sidewalk.

Chapter 2

I appeared on the twenty-fifth floor of my apartment building, at the center of the elevator lobby. I looked around. The corridor was empty. The hallway leading toward my apartment, however, had been cordoned off with multiple strips of yellow police tape.

I ducked under the tape and walked up to my apartment door, but didn't enter immediately. The door was open, and I could hear several voices echoing from inside.

"Aren't they done in there yet?" I questioned.

Stepping across the threshold and into my apartment, I encountered several plainclothes detectives. I knew they were police by the familiar brass shields dangling on chains around their necks and by the IPO-CSI emblazoned on their ball caps. There were two in the living room and one in the kitchen. As I walked through the entryway and deeper into my apartment, I could hear more voices coming from the master bedroom. It appeared that they were skimming through every belonging that Cyndi and I had. Talk about an invasion of privacy.

I knew instantly that whatever I was there for would be difficult to do with all of these people around. Based on the moment that I first tried to take Wilson's rosary, I knew I wouldn't be able to touch a thing as long as somebody else was in the room with me. Walking down the hallway and past the master bedroom, I stepped into my study. Surprisingly, there was nobody inside. There had been, however, recent activity in the room. All of my prized book collection had been boxed up, as well as all of my sports memorabilia. It was obvious that the police were looking for something, most likely searching for a clue as to my whereabouts. But how is boxing up all of my stuff going to tell them anything?

I moved around my desk and sat in my chair. I looked across the desktop and noticed that it was also void of all of my personal belongings. I quickly opened all the drawers and found each of them empty as well. Frustrated, I slammed the last drawer shut, misjudging my force. It shut so hard that the only thing present on top of the desk, a Tiffany-style lamp, nearly fell off the edge. I leaned back and wondered if the noise would bring in a visitor. Within moments, one of the detectives walked in, a baffled look plastered on his face. I laughed out loud. He walked around the desk and peered at the empty space in front of my chair. The cop couldn't see me right in front of him. He circled back around the desk, grabbed a packed box of my stuff, and carried it out into the apartment.

"Hey, bring that back," I yelled.

Again, I knew it was useless with all these people around, but there had to be something I could be doing. This was my stuff, and I wasn't going to idly sit around while they continued to crate up all of my things.

"This should freak them out plenty," I chuckled. I moved to the stack of boxes and began to unpack them, placing the items back in their original locations as best as my memory served.

After freely unpacking two boxes, the third box in the stack became frozen in place. I quickly realized that I was no longer alone and turned to find a female detective staring right through me at all the books that I'd just unpacked.

"Would you be a dear and bring me a few more boxes so I can continue living my life?" I said sarcastically.

"Hey, Franklin. Come in here for a second?" she called out to one of the other detectives. She stood motionless, perplexed. Within moments Franklin, the same guy who had just been in here, stepped back into my now overly crowded study.

"What can I do for you, Detective?" he asked.

"Didn't I . . . ask you to box up everything in this office?" she asked.

Franklin glanced at the bookshelves that once again hosted a number of my personal effects. He nodded. "Yeah. Simmons and I both were in here a few hours ago and everything should've been . . . wow, that's weird."

"Weird? Explain."

"Sorry, Detective, but it's just . . . we had everything boxed up in here. I swear. I was just in here a few minutes ago, and—"

"Does this look like everything is boxed up?" The detective interrupted him and motioned to the bookshelves.

"Um, no. I'll, um, get it done right away," Franklin said, clearly embarrassed.

"And make it quick. Transport is supposed to be here within the hour, and all this needs to get to the crime lab ASAP."

Hearing that, the gravity of the situation really hit home. I was about to lose everything I've ever owned, and there wasn't a damn thing I could do about it.

Determined to at least slow them down, I darted from room to room, looking for any unoccupied space. Stepping into the master closet, I found all of my clothes had been boxed, along with all of my hats. As fast as I could, I rehung everything I could that had hangers. I took the box of hats and just dumped them on the floor. As I stepped back into the master bedroom, the smile on my face vanished. Two movers were hauling out our bedroom furniture.

I ran past them and into the living room and found that half of the furniture had already been taken out of the apartment. As soon as the two guys carrying the mattress walked out the front door, I found myself alone. I grabbed as many boxes as I could, ran them back into the bedroom, and scattered their contents across the bedroom floor.

"You know, you should be careful with that stuff," a voice came from behind me. Startled and caught off guard, I turned so fast I nearly lost my balance. Hauser was leaning against the wall, picking at the cuticles on his left hand.

"What . . . what are you doing here?" I asked.

"I should ask you the same. Don't you have a job to do?"

"I, uh, I'll get there. I just want to . . . find something in here," I stammered.

"You know, Jack, all of these things, these possessions, they don't mean a thing. They're all items that were once yours and Cyndi's, but not anymore."

"Then what's going to happen to them? Neither of us have any family," I said.

"Does it matter, Jack? Does it really matter what's gonna happen to any of it? It'll all probably be donated after it sits in some police storage warehouse for ten years. And that's something that neither you nor I can control."

"But it's my stuff," I pleaded.

"And now it's not. I hate to be so direct about this, but the moment you died, you lost everything. You lost your right to possess. You lost your right to live." Hauser paused. "Listen, buddy, I know where you're coming from. I've been there many times before. You can do this."

"I don't understand. How is it that you've been *here* many times? Didn't you become a collector something like two hundred years ago?"

"Yeah, I only personally went through this once, and it was more than two hundred years ago. Obviously things were different back then. But I still experienced the loss that you are experiencing now. Through the years though, through all of the trainings that I've done, I experienced this same thing over and over again, albeit secondhand through my trainees. I've had to walk their feelings through to the other side, just like I am with you right now. And let me tell you, buddy, you have it easy. When I made the transition, my trainer was a complete asshole. He used the tough love approach. And trust me, you would much prefer me than him."

"Your trainer, is he still around?" I asked.

Hauser paced around the room almost as if he were looking for an exit. "Yes and no. He still exists, but he's no longer a trainer. But enough about him and me. This is about you, and letting go."

I nodded. "Isn't there anything, just one single item, that I can keep? You know, as some kind of memento?"

Hauser shook his head and walked toward the door. "Sorry, bub. No bueno."

"But Wilson had the coin. How was he able to keep that after he died?"

"Well, that doesn't really count. And I think you know why."

"No, please enlighten me," I said, beginning to feel frustration build.

"The coin, along with many other items, are tools of the trade. They each do something special in the aid of soul collecting. With more experience, you will be able to gain more items as you go along."

I knew the coin was able to bring back certain memories of the person's past, but what did the rosary do, I wondered. "So, nothing of my own, not even an—"

"Nothing," Hauser said with finality and walked out of the bedroom.

Before I could follow him, the female detective stepped into the room. The shocked look on her face was severely comical.

"Franklin!" she yelled.

As much as I wanted to hang back and watch Franklin fumble with an excuse, I wanted to—no, I needed to—continue the conversation with Hauser, so I followed him into the living room.

"Listen, Jack. I understand what you're going through. Trust me, I get it. But the more you come back here, to your old life, the more difficult this transition is going to be for you. What you need to do right now is to think of a different place and jump there. You mustn't come back here again. Ever. It'll do you no good. Besides, within a week or two, this place will be cleared out completely. There'll be nothing here for you to come back to."

Feeling defeated, I nodded slightly. "It's just so difficult, you know?"

"I do. But each of us handles this transition differently," Hauser said as he glanced at his pocket watch. "Back in my day, this part of the transition was fairly easy for me. My background and heritage was—how should I say this?—different from your own. We put far less value in personal possessions than the world does today. To give up everything that I owned . . . let's just say I didn't give it a second thought."

"Then how can you relate to my difficulty here?" I asked.

"It's the vices that I struggled with," Hauser said. He looked at me and smiled as he patted at his shirt pocket, looking for something. He continued to pat down his body, into his pants pockets, until he found what he was looking for. He slipped out a pack of gum and put a piece into his mouth. "It's the vices that will kill you, let me tell you. Listen, Jack, regardless of how different our situations were, I know one thing: you'll make it. You'll just have to trust yourself and let go."

"Just like that?"

"Yep, just like that."

"Where should we go? I'm not sure I'm ready to collect the soul yet."

"There's no rush. The soul will be there whenever you're ready, granted that you don't take too long. Just pick a place. Make it your new home base, per se."

"Home base?"

"Yeah, kind of like a security blanket. It'll be your place to go that will always be there whenever you need to get away from it all, or to just be alone."

I paced around the living room, thinking about various places that I could jump to. Most of them had some trace of Cyndi's memory. I dismissed those and moved on to the next place in my mind. After a few moments of pondering, I knew right where I would be going.

I smiled at Hauser and vanished from the room.

Chapter 3

When I appeared next to the bench, I momentarily expected to see Wilson staring off into the ether, but that was just wishful thinking.

I sat down and wondered if Hauser would follow me directly or if he would give me time to truly find my own place. I had my answer the moment I leaned back and crossed my leg, as Hauser materialized right next to me. He sat in a mimicking fashion. I looked at him, noting his state of complete relaxation, and wondered how he could be so cavalier about what we do. As I continued to stare, he noticed me.

"What?" he asked.

"It's nothing," I lied. It didn't feel right questioning his logic, seeing as he was going to be my trainer for the foreseeable future. "How is it that you knew where I would go?"

"Oh, it's not that difficult. I knew you wouldn't go to your place of employment, because I've already seen that video. You've already been to the bar, and you just left your apartment so . . ."

"Am I that predictable?" I asked.

Hauser chuckled. "Nah, kid. I had help."

Hauser withdrew an antique monocle tucked into his shirt. It was attached to a lengthy bronze chain slung around his neck.

"This little gizmo helps me track other soul collectors as they jump from place to place. Every time you vanish from one place and materialize in another, you leave a faint trail, invisible to the naked eye. If I put this up to my eye, I can follow along. But only if I catch the scent quickly enough," Hauser explained.

"Is that how you knew I was at Jake's?" I asked.

"Yeah, sort of. I've been following you around all week, and knew you'd turn up there sooner or later. I was already there when you popped in."

"What, you've been following me?" I asked, feeling a little violated.

"But of course. You're the new kid on the block, and it's kind of my job to keep you in line," Hauser said. "So why this place? Is it because of Wilson?"

I looked at the advertisement for my apartment building plastered on the billboard across the street and pondered that very question. "I don't know. I guess it's probably something to do with him. It's funny, I only knew the guy for thirty minutes, but I feel so connected to him. I can't explain it."

"Wilson will be missed, that's for sure. He had a . . . a way of talking to people that made them feel special." Hauser paused. "And for the record, I'm not at all knocking your choice of this here park bench as your *special* place. You should see mine," Hauser chuckled.

"Okay, I'm intrigued. What is your place, or where is it?"

"Nuh-uh, compadre. Like I said, you're the new kid, and not too many people know where my secret hideout is," he said with a wink.

I nodded, even more interested to find out where it is that he goes.

Several minutes passed as we sat in silence. I had a million questions for Hauser, but I didn't want to flood him with them all at once. Before I had a chance to ask one, Hauser spoke.

"So listen, sport. We both know that it's been a few weeks since you got your last box. I think it's about time you stop ignoring your responsibilities."

"I'm not ignoring them. It's just that I need some time, you know."

"And that's fine, some of the past collectors needed more time than you to get started, and some much less. But you have to realize that when you agreed to become a soul collector, you agreed to maintain the stream of soul boxes that come to you.

There is only so much time before any one individual box can go before it needs to be filled," Hauser said.

"How much time do I have?" I asked.

Hauser shrugged his shoulders. "You know, each soul is a little different. I've seen soul boxes fill nearly instantaneously, and I've seen some go along for months without being filled."

"How do you know that my current box isn't one of those? One of the long-term jobs?"

"Ahh, you got me there. But unless you at least attempt the collection, we'll never know, now will we? Besides, the members of the Sentinel will not remain patient forever."

"The Sentinel? Is that like God's minions or something?" I asked jokingly.

"Nah, it's got nothing to do with God. He's around, but he's got more important things to deal with. Let's just say the Sentinel are our employers and leave it at that," Hauser said with finality, his eyes darting around as he shivered slightly.

As I contemplated this new bit of cryptic information, Hauser pulled out a pocket watch that was quite peculiar. Its face had no numbers. Instead, I could see faint images around its perimeter. After a moment of looking at it, he clicked it closed, returned it to his pocket, and stood up.

"Listen, kid, I'm going to cut you a little slack, but not too much. I know you're full of questions, and we'll get to all of them in good time. But for now, do me a favor. Go visit your intended mark. For all we know, she's ripe for the picking."

I stood up to follow Hauser and asked, "But aren't you going with me?"

"I've got someplace I need to be right now, but I'll meet up with you at the hospital shortly. I'll only be a few minutes—a half hour tops," he said before vanishing.

Instinctively I looked at my wrist for the time and realized for the hundredth time that I'd forgotten to put on a watch. I looked up into the sky to see where the sun was, hoping it would give me a clue as to the time of day. In the small park nestled at the center of the city, the buildings prevented me from seeing the sun directly. My best guess was that it was midafternoon by the warm temperature around me.

I withdrew the box from my pocket and read the name aloud—"Abigail Whitaker"—but nothing happened. I didn't beam to her hospital bedside. Convinced that something was wrong, I shook the box and tried it again. "Abigail Whitaker." Nothing.

Still holding the box, I sat back on the park bench and thought through some of Hauser's words. Actually, only two words were occupying my mind. *The Sentinel.* Who were they, and why did Hauser clam up when I asked about them? If I didn't know any better, I'd think Hauser was a little afraid of them. I wondered if Wilson had ever met any of the Sentinel himself or if Hauser was the only one that had any dealings with them. Like a go-between guy.

Then there were other oddities that piqued my curiosity. The monocle and his pocket watch. I wondered how many of these kind of special items existed for the soul collector's job. Personally, I had two. I was familiar with the function of the coin, but I still didn't know what the rosary did, or if it even had an ability.

The longer I sat on the bench, contemplating the ever-increasing list of questions, the more I knew that if I wasn't at the hospital when Hauser got through with whatever it was he was doing, things would not look good for me. I did my best to push everything from my mind and only think about the hospital where Abigail Whitaker lay dying. A moment later I disappeared from the park bench.

Chapter 4

When I arrived at the hospital, I didn't land in Abigail's room. I instead landed on the first floor, near the bank of elevators. Sure, I could have just as easily popped right into her room, or at least to her same floor, but coming into the hospital as I did was a calculated effort. I needed to ease myself back in.

It wasn't until I was standing in front of the elevator doors that I realized that taking the lift would not be an option. Not with the slew of people milling about the hospital. I walked around the corner and found the stairway access, and thankfully no one was around.

As the clang of the door echoed through the stairway, I began my assent to the seventh floor. With each step, my mind continued to dwell on what had prevented me from coming back to the hospital. The memory of Cyndi. It had been almost two weeks ago that I had last seen my wife alive. Now here I was, back in the same building, heading up to the same floor where she'd died.

The inevitable nature of my new job would most certainly bring me back to this hospital many times, and that inevitability was not lost on me. But knowing that still didn't make it easier.

I continued to trudge up the steps, holding my head down, watching my feet rhythmically climb, step by step, trying to think of anything but Cyndi. As I rounded the corner at the fifth floor landing, I ran into another person.

"Hey now, watch where you're going," Hauser said.

I nearly jumped out of my skin.

"Jesus, Hauser. What the hell are you doing here?" I asked, my pulse racing.

"Waiting for you, naturally. I, too, often take the stairs. Keeps the energy level up," he said, falling into stride next to me. "Wouldn't you agree?"

I nodded, and we climbed the remaining two flights of stairs in awkward silence. It seemed like with every additional interaction with Hauser, I was more puzzled. I wondered, was I the one that was strange, or was he?

As we reached the seventh floor, Hauser inched the door open and peeked through the crack. A moment later, he fully opened the door and stepped through.

"All clear, buddy," he said.

I followed him through and into the empty corridor. He moved at such a quick pace, it took effort for me to keep up with him.

"Hey, what's the rush?" I asked. "Do you know something that I don't?"

"No sir. I'm just a firm believer in a diligent work habit," he said as he rounded the corner and headed for the ICU ward. As he stepped up to the secured doors, he reached over and pressed the call button multiple times to the tune of *Shave and a Haircut.* When he finished, he glanced over at me and winked.

"Enjoying yourself?" I asked.

"If you've been doing this job as long as I have, kid, you'd try to make every moment enjoyable too. Otherwise, you might just go crazy."

Within seconds, a buzzer sounded, and Hauser pulled the door open and stepped through. As we walked through the outskirts of the ICU, my eyes darted to the room where Cyndi had been. Common sense told me she was long since gone, but instinct prevailed.

"Are you telling me that you've not been back up here since?" Hauser asked.

"Yeah, about that . . . I've been meaning to . . ."

"You know, Jack, I'm sure you could pop over to the morgue and see your wife once more, but you'd only be visiting a shell of her former self."

Until Hauser uttered those words, the thought had never crossed my mind. To actually go see her? As I thought about the possibility, I quickly realized that seeing her battered and broken body again would be too much.

"You're not actually thinking about it, are you?" asked Hauser.

"Um, no. Honestly, I never thought that they would keep her body this long."

"Your situation is unique, Jack. Because you're not around to claim her body, and she had no family, right? She'll probably remain in the morgue's freezer until the investigation is complete. After that, I'm sure—"

"Okay, stop. I really don't need to know what happens to the unclaimed bodies."

"But you could probably see Wilson while you're there . . ."

Ignoring his banter, I stepped around Hauser and walked right up to Abigail's room. I took a breath and stepped inside.

Chapter 5

Walking into the room instantly brought memories of Cyndi to the forefront, but I promptly blocked them. I moved to Abigail's bedside and looked down at her unconscious body. Her conditions so closely mimicked Cyndi's when I'd first found her: multiple tubes penetrating her arms and neck, along with a tube that was through her open mouth. Pity enveloped me, and I began to wonder what I'd gotten myself into when I agreed to take over as a soul collector. I could only hope that the job would get easier with each new dying person I encountered.

"So . . . do I remove the air tube?" I asked, trying to make sense of the situation.

Hauser stepped beside me. "The medical term is that she has been intubated. It's a little tricky, but her soul can be retrieved without removing the tube."

"Then, what? Do I whistle for her soul? Like I'm calling a Labrador retriever?" I asked, my words dripping with sarcasm.

Hauser ignored my derision and said, "No, I don't think that'll be necessary today. Besides, there's really more to it than just sucking her soul out. The soul needs to be cleansed properly before it is sent on to its next borrower."

"Cleansed? Wilson didn't tell me anything about cleansing anything. What about his soul, or the soul I took from Cyndi? I didn't—"

"I took care of both of those collections, after the requisition had been put in for their new placements."

Listening to Hauser speak with such lack of emotion nearly made my head spin. "All right. Where do I begin?" I asked, trying to sound eager even though I had no idea what it all meant.

"It's hard to explain, really. As you recall with Wilson and Cyndi, their soul vacated the vessel—their bodies—in the form of a stream of smoke. As soon as it enters the transportation chamber—the wood box—the cleanse can begin."

"That doesn't sound too difficult. What's involved with the actual cleansing?" I pressed.

"That's where it gets a little tricky. The soul can become a little agitated once placed in the box—"

"Agitated?"

"Maybe 'agitated' isn't the right word here. Maybe 'unbalanced' is a better term, and not all souls react the same way. Some souls are much gentler and handle the process better than others."

"Really. What about the old saying 'walk into the light'? Wouldn't that be easier here?"

"Ha. You can thank Hollywood for that one, although the old process was quite similar."

Feeling more confused and overwhelmed by the minute, I pressed. "And?"

"Back in the day, there was no wood box to carry the soul from borrower to borrower. When a borrower passed on, the soul would slip from one dead body to the life of another, without incident. The job of the soul collector was nonexistent. That all changed a few hundred years ago."

"How so?" I asked, becoming more intrigued, to the point that I almost forgot about the task at hand. Hauser, on the other hand, had not. He nodded his head in Abigail's direction.

I followed his gaze and saw Abigail's eyes staring back at me. I instinctively smiled and rapidly tried to think of something to say. Before anything came to mind, Hauser spoke.

"I'm sorry, Mrs. Whitaker. Did we wake you?"

Abigail nodded her head slightly, although it was barely perceptible.

"I do apologize. My colleague and I were just making rounds, and we thought we'd stop in to see how you were feeling. Are you in any pain?" Hauser asked.

Abigail closed her eyes momentarily and then gently shook her head side to side.

"That's good. Good."

I remained silent as Hauser and the old woman had a brief one-sided conversation. Abigail's consciousness only lasted a few moments before she drifted away once again.

"It's clear that she can see us," I said as I slid the box from my pocket.

"Put it away, Jack. She's not quite ready yet. She'll let us know."

"How can you tell?" I asked.

"Experience, mostly. I've done this so many times that I've learned to recognize the signs." Hauser stepped away to the far side of the room, motioning me to follow.

"You see, Jack, some souls need coaxing, and Abigail's may need just that."

"Is that like what Wilson did for me and what I did for Cyndi? Do I have to relive some day of their life with them?"

"Maybe yes, other times no. And sometimes a little outside influence is necessary. With experience you'll learn to recognize the appropriate time as well."

"What kind of outside influence do you mean?" I asked, really feeling the information overload.

"Take Mrs. Whitaker, for example. She's been involved in an auto accident—"

"Are you sure?" I asked, shooting a quick glance at Abigail. I could see no physical injuries. "Besides her age, she looks fine to me."

"When I'm not training new collectors like you, I collect souls myself. As a matter of fact, just a few weeks ago, when you decided to go all splitsville with your life, I was collecting a number of souls from a horrific auto accident upstate. It was a multicar pileup on the freeway, and most of those with severe injuries succumbed to death quite rapidly. Abigail and her husband were involved, but only in a minor fashion. Abigail's husband was driving the car. He swerved to avoid the accident and ended up in a ditch. Abigail here was wearing her seatbelt, but her husband wasn't."

"Did you already collect his soul, then?" I asked.

"No, not yet. As a matter of fact, he's here at the hospital, but he's in much better shape than Abigail is. Because Abigail had her seatbelt on, she did not lurch forward as her husband did when their car stopped at the bottom of that ditch. She would've been fine had she not had a heart attack right after the accident."

"Oh my. And you knew all this for the last few weeks and didn't say anything to me?"

"Yes, that's right. I knew that you would need time to adjust, otherwise I would've pushed you harder."

"And what about her husband? I'm confused. You said that he did not have a seatbelt on and, what? What about his injuries?"

"He has a few bumps and bruises, but he should be fine," Hauser said quietly. "Listen, let's . . . get out of here for a while. I think we'll have plenty of time on this one. Let's head to the Bronx and do a little fishing."

"Are you being sarcastic or do I need a fishing pole?"

Hauser only smiled before he vanished from the room. I chuckled and thought about the last time I was in the Bronx before vanishing as well.

Chapter 6

Moments later I arrived on a nondescript block, shadowed in uncertainty. Hauser was standing on the opposite side of the street, staring into a dark alley. As I walked up to him, I began to hear rowdy voices emanating from the alleyway.

"So we're not really going fishing, are we?" I asked.

"Well, sort of. You're in training, kid. Over the years I've taken almost all of the new trainees to locations just like this."

"To the ghetto? Is this an exercise in proving that we made the right choice—to no longer live in a crime-riddled world?"

"Not so much. Not all new soul collectors tried to kill themselves. That's just you, my friend."

I looked around for a proverbial rock to crawl under. When none could be found, I asked, "Then why?"

"Coming to a place like this, especially at a time like right now, will give you some invaluable hands-on experience with some quick soul collecting. You see, there are more than a hundred street gangs in the Bronx. And recently, the truce between two of the major gangs has come to an end, and a battle is imminent. It'll be almost like shooting fish in a barrel."

"But the name on my box is Abigail. How am I to get another box without filling this one first? Is that not how it works?"

"For the most part, yes. Until you've gained enough experience, you'll only be allowed one box at a time. After your twenty-fifth collected soul, you'll have the ability to collect a random soul that's near your proximity. I've had that ability for more than a century now, and for these training exercises, you've been granted that same ability. Temporarily, that is."

"So we just stand here and wait for them to kill each other? What if nothing happens?"

"Yep, we just wait. And trust me, it'll happen. I've been in and out of this neighborhood a dozen times over the last week, and the tension between these two gangs continues to heighten."

As if on cue, the sound of a gunshot echoed about, and I instinctively flinched at the report.

"See? What did I tell ya?" Hauser said with a smile before stepping into the alley.

Following a few steps behind, I began to feel a burning sensation on the palm of my hand. I held it up to see what was causing the irritation, and as I did, a new box materialized. A new name was neatly carved in the wooden lid: Alfonso Dorn.

"Hey, I've got a new box," I called out to Hauser, "but I don't see any dead bodies yet."

"Give it time, kid. I think this is going to be a big night for you. I've already received four boxes. All we have to do is wait."

Hauser and I stepped out of the narrow alleyway and into a large open area where two other alleys met. From our position we could see more than a dozen gang members along the perimeter. At the center of the open area, four young men faced each other. It appeared to be two members from each of the gang factions arguing about whose rights to the turf were being disrespected. Hauser ambled over to the edge of a brick wall and sat on a stack of crates.

"Take a load off, kid. We don't know how long this argument will last before it comes to blows, or even better, until the heavy weapons come out."

I sat down next to Hauser and noticed he did in fact have four boxes in his hands. He set them on the surface between us before sliding a stick of gum from his pocket and into his mouth.

"While we wait for the unfortunate outcome of the brawl, let's talk a little more about the cleanse," Hauser said.

My gaze had been intently focused on the gang activity when Hauser mentioned it. With my interest instantly piqued, I turned to face him.

110

"So, the cleanse. Every soul has a memory, or memories. Depending on how old the soul is, and how long it has been borrowed, will determine its level of toxicity."

"Toxicity? Is it lethal?" I asked.

"Not exactly. Toxicity is a kind of . . . term to explain its current state. Our job, as part of being a soul collector, is to clean or eradicate those memories from the soul."

"Just like that? The cleanse will eliminate all memories from the associated soul?"

"Well, not *all* of the memories. Obviously with new souls there are no associated memories present. But most of the souls in population right now are old souls. The older the soul, the more residual memories remain," Hauser said. "Our best guess is that the cleanse removes about eighty percent of the memories present at the time of death."

"Wow. A guess? And only eighty percent?"

"Hey, it's not exactly a science, kid. Before we started doing the cleansing, as you can imagine, there were souls floating around with so much past life information running through their minds, the mental institutions all over the world were severely overpopulated, all because the soul borrowers couldn't differentiate from the memories of their own and those of past borrowers. The Sentinel feels that twenty percent is an acceptable amount of residual memories, and that they add character to the new recipient."

"Interesting. I guess that makes sense. I can remember having dreams when I was young that were of people and situations that I have never before encountered. I guess that those kind of dreams are triggered from past memories of the previous soul owner?"

"Quite possibly, but most dreams are delusions fabricated by your own personal experiences. I'm no dream specialist, but think of it like this: you can dream about a black cat without ever seeing one in person. If you've seen a white cat, and you know what the color black looks like, your mind can fabricate a black cat in a dream. That's the simplistic explanation, obviously."

I nodded as I processed Hauser's information. What he was saying did make sense, and who was I to question its full meaning?

"All right. I think I understand the reasoning and the outcome, but what about the process?"

"Take your newest box. Do you notice anything peculiar about it?" Hauser asked.

I looked at the box and turned it over multiple times, examining each of the surfaces for something—anything—peculiar.

"Can I have a hint? This one looks the same as all the other ones," I said as I held out the box for him to look at.

Hauser didn't even glance at the box. "Look closely along the front edge, where it meets the top. You see that?"

I looked where he indicated, and sure enough, I saw an oval-shaped hole right along the leading edge.

"Huh. How'd I miss that?"

"That, my friend, is the extrication portal."

I opened the box, looked at the inside surface behind the portal, and found a dozen smaller holes around that same area.

"Do all of these smaller ones lead to the larger one?" I asked.

"You're very astute, Jack. I've had to practically draw a picture for the last three students in your position."

Feeling somewhat proud of my inquisitive nature, I asked, "But what's it for?"

"Oh, come now, Jack. You're so close. Care to take a guess?

I closed the box and again looked at the orifice on the outside corner. The hole was about a quarter inch diameter and almost certainly had something to do with the smoke associated with the soul.

"Does the wisp of smoke have to go through it?" I asked. "It looks pretty small to make it through, though."

"Oh, you're so close," Hauser chuckled. "Get ready for your mind to be blown."

Hauser's timing was uncanny. Within seconds of his statement, a full-on brawl erupted in front of us. At first the fight consisted of kicks and punches, but before long knives and clubs were brought out. One unfortunate gang member took a bat across the side of his head, the force jerking his neck sideways with an audible crack.

"There's one," Hauser said, holding all four of his open boxes in his hands. I quickly fumbled with my box, opened it, and waited for the familiar soul cloud to exit the body. As it began to seep from the lips of the dead kid, a loud *pop-pop-pop* echoed through the arena. Two more gang members dropped to the ground, and the fight stopped almost instantly.

"Is it over?" I asked. "Didn't you get four boxes?"

Before Hauser could answer, tinted vapors left the latest fallen victims and found their way into two of Hauser's boxes. As I watched this, I noticed that the first victim's soul had entered my box, which closed on its own.

Once Hauser's boxes closed, he took one of them, placed the hole to his lips, and inhaled sharply. Seconds later, the box disappeared and was replaced with another. He looked at me, nodding at the box in my own hand.

Nervously, I brought the box up to my mouth and placed my lips around the hole, just as Hauser had. I inhaled deeply. An acrid taste filled my mouth and I began to cough uncontrollably, similar to the first time I'd smoked pot.

"Slow down, sport. Take smaller breaths if it helps," he said as he patted me on the back.

"That . . . is absolutely disgusting," I said. "I have to do this with every soul?"

Before Hauser could answer, my box disappeared and was replaced with another.

"Yep. Doesn't get any better than this," Hauser said with a bit too much enthusiasm.

"But the taste, do you get used to it?" I asked.

"Well, it's interesting. Each soul that we cleanse really has a different flavor. As far as I can tell, the more sorrowful or disturbing the soul's memories are, the more acidic the flavor. The more pure or innocent the memories are, the sweeter the taste. Sometimes you have to take the good with the bad."

I sat next to Hauser, the rank taste still lingering in my mouth, and hoped that it would not last.

As I contemplated the unpleasant flavor, the fight resumed— a melee of swinging knives and clubs, along with more gunfire. The fight continued for another ten minutes, filling a total of nine boxes—three of my own and six for Hauser. With each cleanse, the flavor did in fact vary. The last soul collected and cleansed was practically tasteless. I noticed it came from a teen so young that I doubted he was even old enough to drive.

After some time, the surviving gang members fled in opposite directions, leaving the dead bodies lying haphazardly around the open alleyway. In the end I was left with only Abigail's soul box. Even though the whole ordeal had lasted less than thirty minutes, I felt thoroughly exhausted. I slumped back against the wall, thankful that it was over.

"Not bad, kid," Hauser said. "The tiredness that you're experiencing is directly associated with the soul cleansing that you just performed. It's normally not this bad, but seeing as you did in fact just cleanse three souls, the effects are much stronger."

"Do you . . . ever get used to it?"

"Heavens no. And you don't want to. It's like a necessary evil of the job, you know?"

I did, associating it with the dreaded paperwork that accompanied many of the tasks of my former job before I . . . left.

"Why don't you take it easy for a while? I've got some things to do, and I'll pop in on Abigail from time to time to check on her progression. If something comes up before you see her again, I'll come find you."

I nodded, and before I could say anything, Hauser vanished.

I sat, languishing on the dilapidated wooden crates for another ten minutes before I thought of my park bench and vanished myself.

Chapter 7

As I sat on my familiar park bench, my mind reeled from the horrific butchery that I'd just witnessed. Granted, they were a bunch of drug-dealing gang thugs, but still, they were lives lost, foolishly. I was also somewhat disturbed by Hauser's eagerness for the carnage to take place. I suppose that after witnessing so much death in the span of his life, he must have somehow desensitized his emotions.

Fully aware of the level of exhaustion I was experiencing, I twisted my body to the side and leaned back on the park bench. Gazing up at the stars, I tried to remember the last time I'd actually slept. I mentally walked through my previous several weeks and realized that I hadn't slept a wink since the morning of Cyndi's death.

"How can that be?" I asked aloud.

Somehow, since that fateful moment on this very bench all those weeks ago, I hadn't experienced tiredness. Come to think of it, I hadn't eaten or drunk anything either. Did I need to eat or drink? Or sleep? I didn't seem to have any ill effects from not doing any of it.

As I lay there, my mind hashing through the last hour of my life, my vision began to cloud over. I was drifting off to sleep, and I couldn't do a thing to stop it.

A loud explosion nearly jarred my wisdom teeth loose. I opened my eyes and saw that I was lying on my bed, my skin drenched with sweat. I looked to Cyndi's side of the bed, which was eerily vacant.

Swinging my feet to the floor, I stood and quickly donned a pair of shorts before walking out into the hallway. It was the middle of the night, and everything was dark except for a glow emanating from my study. Ever so quietly, I tiptoed to the open door and peered inside. There, on top of my desk, sat Cyndi with her back toward me. She was naked. Facing her was a tall, dark-haired man, thrusting his naked body into the loins of my wife. Rage overtook me, and I charged into the room.

"What the hell is going on?" I screamed. When Cyndi turned to look at me, her face was covered in black soot. She smiled, baring her polished white teeth at me. She laughed wildly as her canines dripped red droplets of blood to the ground. Repulsed by her grotesque appearance, I darted from the room.

As I stepped into the hallway, light began to shine from all directions. I walked down the hall, and as I stepped into what I expected to be my living room, it turned into the aisle of the Church of Heavenly Rest. The interior of the church was lit only by candlelight, and every pew was full of parishioners. At the front of the church, a bright source of light began to shine down on an open casket. I was drawn toward it as if by a tractor beam. The closer I got, the deeper the fear settled in my soul. I knew it would be Cyndi. I prayed that it would be the old Cyndi and not the one the one with horrific, demon-like face that I had just seen.

As I neared the casket, Cyndi's face came into view. It was, thankfully, her old, beautiful self. She wore a cream-toned blouse with a lilac-colored ribbon pinned to her chest. Her complexion was as clear as ever, and she wore light-pink lipstick, her favorite. Wanting to hold her one last time, I reached down and gently stroked the back of her hand. The instant my flesh touched hers, her eyes opened, her eyeballs solid black. She smiled and hissed before gripping me with such force that I felt a bone crack in my hand. She pulled herself upright and stared out at the crowd behind me. She nodded her head and then cackled like a witch on Halloween. From behind, I heard the parishioners begin to chant, "Burn, burn, burn."

I yanked my hand from her grip and recoiled away from her.

As I neared the edge of the pulpit, her casket burst into flames. Staring out at the parishioners, I finally recognized them as the gang members who had just fought in the ghetto. Before I could react, the entire front row pulled out various sized pistols and shotguns and pointed them at me. In unison, each of them pulled the hammers back and fired them.

I lurched, falling off the park bench.

"So, Jack. Was it a frightening dream?" Hauser asked, sitting on the bench.

"Uh, how'd you know?"

"Lucky guess," he said, winking at me.

I rolled onto my knees and pulled myself up off the ground before sitting next to Hauser.

"The dream was . . . surreal, I guess," I admitted.

"Well, buddy, all I can say is that you'll learn. Like I did so many years ago."

I rubbed the sleep from my eyes and noticed that the sun had come up. "What? I'll learn?"

"Yep. The moment you became a soul collector, your ability to have fluffy, feel-good dreams ceased to exist. Almost every collector that I've known stopped sleeping completely just to avoid the wicked nightmares. It's just not worth it," Hauser explained. "And to answer your other question, no, you don't really have to sleep."

"How'd you—"

"I just know. Jack, you are my twenty-fourth trainee. Trust me, I've heard every question imaginable. The question of whether we have to sleep, to drink, to eat—they've all come up dozens of times."

"If we don't have to sleep, then why was I so tired after—"

"Because, Jack, you just ingested the memories of three vigilante gang members, and that certainly takes it out of a person. Don't get me wrong, Jack. You can sleep, but you will no doubt experience some of the most horrific dreams you could ever imagine. Do you want to talk about what you dreamed just now?"

The image of Cyndi's horrific demon face came to mind, and I knew that I wanted to forget it ever existed. "No, I think I'll keep it to myself."

"Suit yourself. Just remember, I'm a good listener too," Hauser offered.

"You say I don't have to sleep anymore, but how do I get any rest? I really felt totally and completely exhausted earlier."

"Did Wilson explain how we live, us soul collectors?"

"Sort of. Do you mean living eight times as long?"

"Yeah. That's it. Sleep is kind of the same. If you rest yourself completely for an hour, you will feel like you've slept for eight."

"Seriously?"

"As serious as taking half a bottle of Percocet," Hauser said with a wry grin.

"Ouch. That hurts."

"Sorry. Too soon? My bad."

Somehow I sensed Hauser wasn't trying to be mean but was in fact trying to lighten the mood. I was almost certain that he knew just how ugly of a dream I'd had and wanted to soothe my soul as best he could.

"What about eating and drinking?" I asked. "I honestly can't remember the last time I ate a thing."

"What goes in must come out, remember that."

I chuckled. "So what you're saying is I can eat, but then I'd have to . . . relieve myself sometime down the road?"

"Yep. And just remember, not all restrooms will be vacant," Hauser said. "Kind of makes it hard to take care of business that way."

"Yeah, but it would be worth it for just one more slice of New York pizza, or the occasional snifter of brandy."

"Whoa, now. Let's not get ahead of ourselves, shall we? The effects of alcohol on our type is quite a bit different. Use your imagination, but the same eight-to-one ratio comes into play."

"So, projectile vomiting after a half a beer?"

"Something like that. Listen, Jack. Without going into too much detail about my past, I've had to make some severe lifestyle changes. For starters, I haven't slept in almost a century; the horrific nightmares of my past were just too much. I gave up booze shortly after I became a collector; it just wasn't worth it for me. The hangovers were immensely worse." Hauser paused and fished a stick of gum out of his pocket, slipped it past his lips, and began to chew. "Let me ask you, Jack, did you smoke? Cigarettes or cigars?"

"Nah, not really. I had an occasional cigar while out with the guys, but as for cigarettes, I never got the attraction. Why?"

"That's good, kid. Smoking was one of the hardest habits to break. I've been a soul collector for more than two centuries, and I gave up smoking about the same time I gave up drinking, but I still have the craving for a cigarette."

As I began to put things together, the chewing gum began to make sense.

"Wow, I had no idea. More than two centuries?"

"Yep. I go way back."

"Tell me, how did you become a collector, if you don't mind sharing."

Hauser pulled his pocket watch out, looked at the face, and returned it to his pocket before answering. "Perhaps another time, sport. I think it's about time we made a visit to Abigail, wouldn't you say?"

Despite my mind being on overload, I had to agree. As much as I wanted to hear more about Hauser and his past, I needed to get Abigail out of her misery. I reflected on my sudden care for the old woman in the hospital. Just a few hours ago I couldn't have cared less about her and her life. I attributed the deeper sense of caring to recent events.

"Yep," I said, mocking Hauser's standard reply. "Lead the way." A moment later we both vanished from the park bench.

Chapter 8

Hauser and I appeared in Abigail's hospital room at nearly the same moment. As I looked around the room, I noticed that we were not alone. There was an elderly gentleman sitting in a wheelchair alongside Abigail's bed. I assumed that it was her husband, as he was dressed in a hospital gown and had one of those plastic patient ID bracelets strapped around his wrist. I looked at Hauser for guidance, but he just shrugged his shoulders.

"Really?" I asked.

"Jack, my friend, I believe you are going to be in for quite an experience. A rare occurrence indeed," Hauser said.

I glanced at the elderly couple to see if I could tell what Hauser was talking about, but nothing stood out. When I turned to Hauser for an explanation, he was gone. He'd just disappeared.

"Shit," I exclaimed aloud. Thankfully the husband was unable to hear me, and Abigail was unconscious.

As I stepped up to the side of Abigail's bed, I wondered if I could collect a soul while another living person was in the room. I slipped my hand into my pocket and touched Abigail's box. But before I could withdraw it, Abigail's husband began to speak.

"Hello, my darling. Can you hear me?" he said. "It's me. It's me, Raymond, your husband. The doctors tell me that you're in some rough shape, and they're not sure if you'll wake up again. I told them, my dear, that you are a tough woman, and that if there's any way possible, you will make it back to me. You see, you have to. Make it back to me, that is, because I haven't told you that I love you today. Abby, darling, I love you. And I'm sorry I haven't made it to you sooner. Between my own injuries and your condition here in the ICU, they haven't allowed me in until just now."

At that point, Raymond pulled himself up from his wheelchair and gently kissed Abigail on her forehead. Slumping back into his seat, he continued to speak.

"Abby, my sweet, I hope you can hear my words, because I need you to hear them. I need you to know just how much you mean to me and how much of a pleasure it has been to be married to you for sixty-three years. I want you to know that I've been proud to have called you my wife every single day." Raymond paused briefly to wipe the tears from his eyes and adjust his posture.

"Do you remember, darling, the day we met? I do. I've relived that day hundreds of times in my mind through the years. I was so thankful that you agreed to dance with me. Do you remember? I had just transferred from Osborne and I think it was maybe my second week at Madison. I had no friends, just a few people that agreed to tolerate me hanging around with them. I don't know if I ever told you this, but each and every one of those boys had something of a crush on you. And let me tell you, they were fit to be tied when I up and asked you to dance. I can't imagine what my life would be like today if you hadn't said yes all those years ago."

Raymond inched his wheelchair closer to Abigail's bedside and adjusted her bedsheet enough so that he could touch her. With her hand free from under the covers, he slipped his own hand into hers. As I stood right next to the bed, I could see her hand close tightly in his.

"Oh, darling. My God, you can hear me. Abby, I love you with all my heart. You are an angel sent from heaven. My angel," Raymond said, sobbing freely.

As I stood next to the couple, I fought back tears of my own. Suddenly I noticed Abigail's eyes slide open. She glanced first at Raymond, smiling gently, then she turned her gaze toward me. With a movement so barely distinguishable, she bobbed her head up and down as she looked into my eyes. Her gaze told me that she was ready. A moment later her stare drifted up and to the right, and her mouth fell open.

Despite the intubation tube between her lips, her soul gently slipped past it and into the air. I was prepared, and slipped the box from my pocket, opening it in one swift motion. Abigail's soul did not hesitate long before it entered the box completely. As the box closed, I brought it to my lips and inhaled slowly. The taste of Abigail's soul was sweet, so sweet I swear that I have never tasted anything sweeter.

I pulled the box from my lips and then it vanished. In its place, a new box appeared in my hand. Without thinking, I read the name aloud.

"Raymond Whitaker."

Chapter 9

"NO!" Raymond cried as the device at the side of Abigail's bed began to blare warning sounds intermixed with a flat, dull tone.

I reached over and silenced the machine. When I returned my gaze to Raymond, I found his flooded eyes staring back at me.

"Oh my God, is that it?" he asked.

"I'm so sorry for your loss, Mr. Whitaker, but I'm afraid so. I assure you, your wife did not suffer long."

"Oh, God. Oh, God, no. No. Please, no. Please, isn't there anything you can do?" he begged.

All I knew was that it was her time to go. I wasn't sure what I could tell him that would ease his pain. In addition to having no real knowledge of her medical condition, I was hesitant to say much of anything at this point.

"I . . . apologize. But her age was quite a factor in her condition," I said, hoping I didn't sound like a complete idiot. "The doctors here are the best in the region, and I assure you that if there was anything—"

"Wait, you're not a doctor?" Raymond asked, drying his eyes on his shirt sleeve. "Come to think of it, I didn't even hear you enter. When did you come in?"

Oh shit, I thought. Neither Wilson nor Hauser had told me what to do in a situation like this. Do I lie? Do I tell that I am a doctor after all? Or do I tell him I'm, what? A nurse? A priest? Think!

"No, I am not a doctor. I'm a . . . a counselor here, to lend an ear to those who have lost a loved one. And I apologize for not announcing my entrance. I am sometimes too quiet for my own good."

"So that's it? The doctors won't try to bring her back?" Raymond asked.

Being somewhat familiar with how hospitals operate, I quickly recognized the red medical tag around Abigail's wrist.

"I'm sorry, Mr. Whitaker, but your wife must have authorized a DNR. I'm sure that there was a valid reason for her to do so."

Raymond slouched back in his wheelchair, looking defeated. "I . . . guess I remember them talking to me about something . . ." he mumbled.

"It's okay, Mr. Whitaker. You may have been unaware of the situation, due to your own condition."

"Abby and I talked about this just a few months ago. At our age we both agreed that we would not be a burden on one another, if something . . . happened. But never in my worst nightmare would I have imagined that it would be her going first." Raymond began to cry again as he held her hand tightly. "Oh, Abby. What will I do now? How can I go on without you?"

"If you don't mind my asking, how long were you and Mrs. Whitaker married?" I asked. Even though I had just heard his loving declaration, I figured a little extra coaxing for his soul couldn't hurt.

"Abby and I were high school sweethearts. We met in our junior year, 1950, I think, and were married the year after we graduated. That was sixty-three years ago. Sixty-three wonderful years."

"Abigail sounds like a wonderful woman. How was it that you two met?" I asked, already knowing the answer.

Raymond sat up in his chair and beamed. "Back in the day, Abigail was quite a stunner. All the boys in school constantly fell over themselves after her. I remember the day we met like it was yesterday."

"I'd love to experience that day with you, if you would allow me to?" I asked.

"I . . . I don't understand. How can you experience it with me? It was so long ago," Raymond said.

I slid a chair up beside him and sat down. "Well, Mr. Whitaker, I have this coin, you see, that is mildly hypnotic. If you would allow me, I could take you back and relive that day one more time before—"

"Oh, yes! Please, yes. I would love to see her again, the way I saw her for the first time," Raymond said eagerly.

I slipped the coin from my pocket and placed it in the palm of Raymond's hand.

"Mr. Whitaker, I need you to focus on that day. That first day that you and Abigail met. When you have that vision firmly in your mind, I need you to turn the coin over."

"That's it? No dangling pocket watch to follow with my eyes?" Raymond asked.

I chuckled. "No, not quite. This coin is . . . somewhat different than the traditional hypnosis techniques," I said, hoping that my words were believable.

Raymond closed his eyes tightly as he brought forth the memory. He held his hand close to his chest, squeezing the coin as he did so. A moment later, he turned the coin over.

Chapter 9.5

Raymond's final class of the morning came to an end when the bell rang. Lunch hour was up next, and the activity in the hallways would be frantic, with everyone wanting to drop their books off at their lockers before heading to the cafeteria. That wasn't on Raymond's agenda, however. He was halfway through his third week of classes at the new school, and he'd only made a friend or two. Acquaintances, really, and both of them had basketball practice over their lunch hour. Raymond, however, had an irrational, potentially life-changing destination in mind.

Raymond heedlessly strolled through the cavernous hallways, waiting for the bustling crowds to funnel into the cafeteria.

As Raymond turned the corner that led to the school exit, he practically ran headfirst into another straggling student. A girl.

"I, uh . . . s-s-s-s-sorry," Raymond said as he tried to step around her.

Raymond wasn't surprised that the other students stayed away from him like they did. He knew it was because of his stuttering. Raymond had experienced random moments of stuttering all through school, but until just a month ago, the occurrences were few and far between. His parents attributed the reduction in his word stumbling to his comfort level with his peers. Now, with his dad taking a new job and moving the family across the river and into New Jersey, the stuttering had returned in full force.

"That's quite all right, Raymond, is it?" the girl said.

"Y-y-yes, that's right. My n-n-name is Raymond Whitaker," he said, blushing at the chance meeting with arguably the prettiest girl that he had ever seen.

"You're new here, right?" she asked, discreetly blocking Raymond's path.

As butterflies and nerves battled it out in his gut, Raymond nodded, shifting his weight from foot to foot.

"Well, on behalf of everyone here at Madison High, I officially welcome you to the home of the Bobcats," she said, thrusting her hand toward him. "Hi, I'm Abigail. Abigail Caldwell, but all my friends call me Abby."

"I . . . I, uh, kn-know who y-you are," Raymond said. "We've had a f-few classes together."

"Oh, right. You have Mr. Daniels for biology?"

"Y-yes, and we have history together t-t-too," Raymond said, speaking as slowly as possible to minimize his stuttering.

"Oh, please. Don't remind me. I detest history. I completely forgot to do my homework last night, and—"

"I can h-help you out, if you'd like," Raymond eagerly offered, changing his plans on the fly.

"Sincerely? You would do that? That would be so cool. Are you heading to lunch now?" Abigail asked.

"Y-yes, I, um, just after I . . . I drop my books off at my locker."

"Great, how about we sit together and go over the history lesson?"

Raymond's tongue felt as thick as a slug and twice as sticky. Did the most popular girl in school just agree to have lunch with him?

"That would be n-n-nice, but won't your friends be expecting you at their lunch t-table?"

"Yeah, sure, but they'll understand. Besides, it's not every day that you make a new friend," Abigail said. She slipped her arm through Raymond's as she steered him to his locker.

As Raymond opened his locker, Abigail leaned against the wall next to him and waited patiently. After Raymond stuffed every one of his schoolbooks back inside, he slipped out his history textbook and the associated notes before closing the door.

"Wow, do you always carry all your books around with you?" Abigail asked. "Or are you trying to get a workout while in the school hallways?"

"I, uh, was um . . ." Raymond began, trying to come up with an excuse that wouldn't let on to his plans for self-destruction.

Abigail giggled. "It's okay, Raymond, really. I'm just teasing. Ready?"

"Sure," Raymond said before turning and heading toward the cafeteria.

"So, what was your previous school like? Did you have a lot of friends?" Abigail asked.

Raymond focused on each word before speaking, hoping that he could speak clearly. "It was . . . v-very similar to Madison. The school was in upstate New York, and folks were p-pretty friendly there, too. As for friends, I had a few. Most of them I'd gone to school with since the f-first grade."

"Oh, how unfortunate. I would be a complete mess if I had to start over in a new school with no friends. Why did your family move here to New Jersey?"

"It was because of my dad. H-h-he got a new job at RCA, and they're based here, so they transferred the whole f-family."

"But couldn't you and your mother have stayed in New York and just have your dad travel for work?"

Raymond shrugged. "You would think, but he insisted the whole f-f-family come. It's all right though. I got a b-bigger bedroom with the move."

"See? That's the spirit. I like people that look at the brighter side of things."

Raymond could have sworn that he felt his heart increase in size at the kindness that Abigail was showing him. It was the first time since being in the new town that his confidence began to return. With his newfound internal strength, he decided to throw caution to the wind.

"Abigail?"

"Please, Raymond. You can call me Abby."

"I'd like that, Abby. Are you planning on going to the dance this Friday?"

"You sly," Abby said, tugging on Raymond's arm gently. "Why

yes, Raymond. I was planning to go with a bunch of my girlfriends. How about you?"

"I . . . I haven't decided yet," Raymond said.

"Well, I think you should. Maybe we'll see each other there," Abby said as they turned the corner into the cafeteria.

Raymond smiled all the way through the lunch line and until they sat at a table, history books scattered in front of them.

Chapter 10

Raymond let the coin slip from his hand and drop to the floor, pulling us back to Abigail's bedside. We couldn't have been gone for more than a few minutes, but it seemed to me that Raymond had aged several years in that amount of time. His eyes had sunk in slightly, his flesh had faded to grey, and his posture drooped considerably. If I didn't know any better, I would've thought he was already deteriorating, even though he hadn't passed on yet.

"Thank you, Raymond, for sharing that wonderful moment with me," I said.

"It's hard to imagine how one day can truly define a person," Raymond said. "That was my one day. Abby saved my life with her pure kindness," Raymond said.

"How so?" I asked.

"What you didn't see in that memory was the depth of my despair. At that point of the day, I had decided that I had had enough of my youthful obscurity. I was sixteen, and the world didn't even know I existed. My father was a workaholic, my mother an alcoholic. My sister . . . well, she just existed in her own little world, and to hell with everyone else. Having transferred midway through my junior year of high school left me friendless and completely isolated. Depression wasn't really a thing back then, and there were very few people that knew how to deal with it. So that afternoon, I was going to take matters into my own hands."

"Oh no, Raymond. Please tell me you weren't going to—"

"I don't know what I would've done, but I did know that I was going

130

to go home for lunch that d-day and, and n-never come back. I w-was going t-to run away or . . . who knows, I may have ended up killing myself too. God knows the thought crossed my mind so many times."

The room fell silent. Several moments passed as I tried to find the right words to say, but I couldn't piece together anything worth a shit. Was this fate's way of throwing life in my face? Was this God's plan to show me that if I hadn't taken those pills, Cyndi may have been my very own form of Abigail? Assuming we could have made it past her infidelity.

"I . . . I'm not sure what to say, Raymond. I think you're right, Abigail may very well have been your guardian angel."

"That's exactly what she was. After that day, Abby became my best friend. I did go to that dance that Friday night, and we danced all night long. Much to the chagrin of all the other boys in my class. Several months later, Abby became more than just my friend. I was convinced that she was my soulmate. Abigail Caldwell was my first and only true love," Raymond said as he slumped sideways in his wheelchair.

Raymond's strength was clearly draining rapidly. I knew his death was imminent, and I wondered if I should tell him anything about who I really was.

Before I could make a decision, Raymond leaned forward and tried to pull himself upright. His first attempt was a failure, his frail body falling back into his wheelchair. On his second attempt, he was able to use the guardrail on the side of the bed to assist him in standing. Once up, he shuffled his feet closer to Abigail's bedside before he stopped. I knew what he was going to do, and there was nothing I could do to help. It was like a train wreck about to happen, and all I could do was watch.

He took several deep breaths before he lifted his leg up, sliding it on the edge of the bed. With his right hand, he reached across Abigail's body and gripped the far handrail. In his awkward three-point stance, Raymond pushed off the ground with his left foot, while pulling himself up with his right hand.

Once fully on the bed, Raymond adjusted his position around his dead wife, their two bodies unified. He began to weep.

"Oh, Abby. Why have you left me? I'm not strong enough to live this life without you." Raymond said ignoring the tears streaking down his cheek. "God, why couldn't you have taken me and let my wife live? She had the kindest soul. You could've taken me and spared her life. She could have continued on to spread so much joy—the joy that she has given me for so many years. Why her?"

As I witnessed Raymond declaring his love for his wife and pleading to his God, I knew the moment was imminent. I slipped my hand into my pocket and gripped the wooden box in preparation.

"Raymond, there is—" I said, beginning to tell him why I was really there, when I was interrupted by the sound of a man clearing his throat.

I turned toward the sound and saw Hauser standing at the foot of the bed. He was dressed like a doctor, complete with a stethoscope slung around his neck. As he and I looked at each other, his eyes piercing, he shook his head discreetly. Understanding, I nodded and released my grip on the wooden box. I looked back at Raymond as he laid his head on his wife's shoulder and began to shudder from his uncontrollable sobs.

Until that moment, I don't think that I had ever witnessed true love so completely. Selfishly, I envied his love for Abigail. I only wished that the love Cyndi and I had had was just as true, before . . .

As I contemplated my horrific life choices, Raymond's shuddering began to subside and his breathing began to slow. His eyes closed, and for a moment he looked like he was in total peace.

I glanced back at Hauser, who motioned for me to open the box. I quickly retrieved the box from my pocket and opened it, placing it on the edge of the bed. A few moments later, Raymond's lips parted and his soul shot from his open mouth directly into the box, nearly tumbling it off the bed.

Chapter 11

The sudden burst of Raymond's soul made me jump. Startled, I stared across the bed at the box sitting on the edge. From behind me, I heard a faint chuckle. Turning, I saw Hauser quickly cover his mouth, silencing his outburst.

"You insensitive prick," I said without thinking. "How can you think this tender, touching moment is funny?"

"Relax, Jack. I wasn't laughing at the couple. I was laughing at you. You jumped nearly a foot in the air," he said, laughing even louder.

"Oh, shut up," I said, fighting back my own internal laughter.

"I have to say, Jack, your training will certainly go down in infamy. First you have to collect your own wife's soul, and then this—such a beautiful display of love and dedication."

"Don't forget to mention that crazy gang fight that you dragged me to. That was pretty epic, you have to admit."

"You know it, kid. It's all going in my report for sure."

"So I'm being graded on this?" I asked.

"Well, sort of. The Sentinel"—Hauser's voice lowered—"they like to keep tabs on pretty much everything."

I began to wonder if there was something more to our employers that Hauser wasn't telling me. I made a mental note to bring it up later.

"I have to ask. When did you know that I would be collecting both of their souls? You did know, right?"

"Yeah, I kind of knew. The moment we walked back in and

saw the husband sitting next to the bed, I could see a . . . faint aura around him. It's nothing scientific by any means, but it's just something that I've learned to sense through the years. I'm sure, with enough experience of your own, you'll be able to pick up on certain things along the way as well."

"So, including Wilson, I've now bagged seven souls. How am I doing?" I asked. "How am I *really* doing?"

"All in all, Jack, I think you're right on par with the majority of my training candidates. There's a few things that you could work on, but I think you have what it takes."

"Wow, you make it sound like I'm auditioning for a job. Am I?"

"I'm not gonna lie to you, buddy. It's true. Not everybody is cut out for this job. You are ahead of the curve, but don't get cocky."

I smiled before looking at Raymond and Abigail one last time. Satisfied that this was a job well done, I began to move toward the door.

"Um, aren't we forgetting something?" Hauser asked.

I stopped and turned back toward the hospital bed where Raymond's soul box was sitting.

"Oh, shit," I exclaimed. I first grabbed the coin from the floor and slipped it into my pocket. Then I went for the box. Picking it up, I placed my lips around the extrication portal and inhaled deeply. The taste of Raymond's soul reminded me of clover honey, with a hint of cinnamon. Once the flavor was gone, the box disappeared and was again replaced with a new one. Turning it over, I looked for the name of my next assignment but was slightly confused when there was none carved on the lid.

"Huh. It looks like I got a dud. There's nothing on the box," I said as I turned it toward Hauser.

Hauser leaned closely, scrutinizing every detail of the ornate wooden box. "Well, that's not good."

"So, you've seen a blank box before?"

Hauser whistled softly. "I have to say, Jack. I'm at a bit of a loss for words right now."

"You? At a loss?" I chuckled and turned the box around in my hand to get a better look myself. As I did so, I began to see the faint outline of a name form right in front of me. "Wait a minute. I think there might be something here."

Hauser stepped close and we both watched intently as a name etched into the box lid. As the moments passed, the name engraved deeper into the wood and started to became legible.

"Noah Clayton," I read aloud.

As the name left my mouth, Hauser yanked the pocket watch from his trousers so quickly I expected the chain to snap.

"So? What does your watch say about Noah, here?" I asked, assuming his watch with no numbers was closely related to the soul collecting business.

Frown lines formed at the edges of Hauser's eyes as he intently studied the images on his watch. "I . . . have to go," Hauser said as he snapped his watch shut.

"But what about my training?"

"Uh, you're doing fine, sport. This Noah Clayton seems like an ordinary mark. I'm going to let you take the lead on this one for a while. Can you handle that?"

"Well, sure. I can't imagine it could be any worse than what I've already had to deal with. Is there something the matter?" I asked, concerned with Hauser's sudden behavior change.

"Oh, it's probably nothing. It's . . ." Hauser paused and took one last glance at the box in my hand. "I have to go. Promise me, Jack, that you stay on task with this one. No more returning to your old apartment?"

"Yeah, sure. You have my word. These last few days have really opened my eyes about what we do. Although I have deep regrets, I understand now that my past is unchangeable."

Hauser patted me firmly on the back. "That's really great to hear, Jack. I was hoping that at the end of the day you would have in fact learned something."

"That I have," I said, feeling a tug on my emotions, knowing the thoughts of Cyndi would continue to drift further from my own reality.

"Well then, what say you and I get out of here. You've got a soul to collect and I have . . . somewhere to be."

Hauser smiled at me, then vanished. I looked once more at Raymond and Abigail, their bodies woven together in an eternal stillness, before I vanished myself.

BOOK 4

The ROSARY

Chapter 1

The giant metropolis growled faintly as I stalked my prey. In a city occupied by millions of people, only one person mattered—the one that was about to die. Noah Clayton's fate was sealed the moment I received his wooden box, and there wasn't a damn thing he could do about it. I'd been following my mark around for weeks, and I somehow felt the moment of my reward was nearly upon me.

The sun had just gone down and I'd tracked Noah to a rather seedy part of town. The neighborhood was not his normal stomping ground, and I knew of no reason for him to be there. But as I was relatively new to this job, who was I to reason why?

As we walked down Forty-Second, an old neon sign blinked sporadically above the entrance to an alley. ENTER HERE glowed in dark amber, and an arrow pointed into the alley. Noah stopped and looked around. Besides me, whom he couldn't see even if I'd been standing right in front of him, he was alone. Without hesitation, he walked directly toward the obscure alley and disappeared into the darkness.

As I recalled my last visit to a location such as this, visions of the horrific gang fight flooded my mind. I was certain that now was the time—the time for Noah to die. I slipped my hand into my pocket, touching the wooden box assuredly. Good, I was prepared.

I chased after Noah, entering the alley without delay. When I stepped into the shadows, the stench of rotting flash invaded my nose. Something was dead down there, and I suddenly had an uneasy feeling about everything. I caught up to Noah and fell into stride next to him.

"Hey, buddy, do you know what you're really doing down here?" I asked. He ignored me.

Noah continued moving forward, slowly, his eyes on a solitary door midway down the alley. His final destination, I assumed. Along the sides of the alley, garbage was scattered around the overflowing dumpsters. I noticed a rat scurry along the edge of the wall, looking for a hiding place. It amazed me that a squalid place like this could exist just moments away from a lively civilization.

My thoughts were interrupted when Noah stepped up to the door and rapped loudly. Bang. Bang. Bang.

After several minutes, the door cracked open slightly and a vertically challenged man peered out from just below the door handle.

"What do you want?" The dwarf asked.

Noah quickly looked up and down the alley before replying. "I'm . . . looking for . . . McGuire," Noah said.

The dwarf looked sternly at Noah, sizing him up before responding. "He's occupied. Come back later," he said, then slammed the door.

Noah clenched his fists and tilted his head from side to side, cracking his neck in the process. He reached out and banged on the door again.

"Let me in. McGuire is expecting me," Noah protested.

Besides the faint buzz emanating from the neon sign at the alley entrance, silence enveloped us. As we waited, I questioned whether the dwarf would return at all. I racked my brain for a reason why Noah would be here. Was he involved in something sinister? Before my mind could form an answer, the door opened abruptly. Just inside the standard-sized doorframe stood a behemoth man who looked severely agitated. He ducked through the opening and into the alley.

"My little friend said McGuire is busy," said the beast of a man.

"My name is . . . Clayton. My friend Leonard sent me," Noah said.

The large man's brow rose considerably at hearing Leonard's name. He ducked back inside and said something to the dwarf. A

140

second later the little man wobbled down the dingy hallway and disappeared around the corner.

"Stay here," the beast said as he closed the door.

"Last chance, Noah. Let's get out of here," I said, not terribly eager to find out who McGuire was. Strangely, Noah still couldn't hear me. Perhaps his death was not as imminent as I'd expected.

Suddenly I heard what I thought were footfalls on the pavement behind me. I spun around to see who was there but found no one. When I turned back to face Noah, another man stood on the opposite side of him. He wore a silk blue suit and a matching bowler hat. He stared straight ahead, as if waiting for McGuire as well. I looked at Noah. He didn't react to the man's presence.

"Hey," I said, testing the new man's ability to see or hear me.

"Hey, yourself," he said stiffly, and turned in my direction.

I wasn't expecting a response from the man, but now that I had his attention, my curiosity piqued.

"You can hear me?" I asked.

"You'd be surprised at how many people can see and hear you, that are not about to die," he said, stepping directly in front of Noah. "I've actually been keeping tabs on you, Jack."

"Keeping tabs on me?" I asked. "Why?"

"Ah, anytime Hauser gets a new recruit, I kind of . . . pop in to see what all the hubbub's about. And I have to tell you, I think Hauser's way off his game lately."

"I don't follow."

"Like I said, I've been watching you, and I'm a little surprised at your ineptitude," he said.

"You don't even know me, what gives you the right to judge—"

"I've seen many a soul collector in my time, and you have to be the worst. Is this really the way you want to handle this collection?" he asked, nodding to Noah, who was oblivious to our conversation.

"I think I'm doing just fine," I stated firmly.

"So that must be the way Hauser's telling you to do things these days. If this was my mark, I'd have had this soul collected weeks ago."

Before I could respond, the behemoth opened the door and motioned for Noah to enter. Noah stepped forward, passing directly through the man in the blue suit. At that moment, I realized that he was not any normal person whatsoever.

"Well it's a good thing that this isn't your soul to collect," I said as I followed Noah through the door. A moment later, beast man shut the door and bolted it behind us. He slipped past us and led us down the corridor to where it veered to the right. As we turned the corner, I noticed several smaller doors spaced evenly along a much longer hallway. The enormity of the man leading us gave him great strides so that Noah and I had to practically run to keep up with him. When we reached the end of the hallway, he stopped and knocked on the last door. Before a response came, a voice echoed from behind me.

"Hey now, don't you walk away from me. Don't you know who I am?"

I turned and found the man in blue right on my heels. I looked him square in the face. "No, as a matter of fact I don't know who you are. I've never seen you in my life."

"Ah, I'm Enoch. Enoch Gant," he said, lifting his chin into the air slightly. "How is it that nobody's told you about me?"

"It must have slipped everyone's mind," I replied. "So who are you, then? Are you here to help with my training, or are you just another soul collector?"

Enoch blinked slowly and shrugged his shoulders. He stepped past me and right up to Noah's side. "That's neither here nor there. What I can tell you is that you're going about this collection all wrong."

"Care to enlighten me?" I asked.

"Well, I would've ended Noah's life much sooner than now. You know, move things on a bit faster."

"Do you mean you would've killed him just to get your next soul box sooner?"

"Sometimes, Jack, you have to advance the protocol in order to keep the flow of soul boxes moving. And sometimes that means taking matters into your own hands."

Shocked, I said, "That doesn't quite sound like appropriate procedure for a soul collector. And strangely, Hauser has never mentioned anything about it. Neither had Wilson, for that matter."

"Well, that's because Wilson and Hauser are a bunch of pansy-ass wimps. Let me tell ya', I've been around for a lot longer than those two yahoos, and if you want to rise to the top, you'll have to actually take a life every once in a while," Enoch said calmly.

The sound of the door opening grabbed our attention. Beast man stepped to the side and Noah walked through the door. Enoch and I followed close behind. Once we were inside, the door closed, and the three of us stood in front of a wildly attractive woman wearing a white pencil skirt and platform heels.

"I'm McGuire. Who's asking?"

McGuire wasn't a *he* after all, I thought.

"I . . . I'm Noah. My friend—"

McGuire cut Noah off as her phone rang. She stepped around the desk and picked up the receiver. "Go," she said to the caller.

"You know, you can do it right now," Enoch said.

"Do what? Actually kill Noah right here? You're crazy. Just leave me alone and let me do my job, at my own pace."

As I stepped away from Enoch out of utter repulsion, I wished with all my might that Hauser would appear. He was always popping in when he was least expected, and this would be a particularly opportune moment.

"Well, if you're not man enough to do the job right, I might as well help you out. And trust me, you'll thank me later."

Enoch stepped toward Noah and suddenly produced a sawed-off shotgun from his inside his jacket. He raised the barrel of the gun to the back of Noah's head, pulled back the hammer, and released the trigger. The enormous chamber explosion reverberated in my eardrums and startled me awake.

Chapter 2

"You know, Jack. I think you're really onto something here. This park bench is much nicer than my own place," Hauser said as he sat next to me and, flipping through a magazine. "I see you've decided not to heed my warning about sleeping,"

"I, uh . . . what?" I asked, straightening myself up on the bench and tussling my hair to the side. "Well, it's been a long three weeks. I've been following that guy around and he just won't die. Kinda wears a person out."

Hauser nodded his head. "You're preaching to the choir, buddy. I've had countless jobs just like your guy." Hauser closed the magazine and focused his attention on me. "So, you give in to sleep just like that?"

"It's not like I planned on it. I've been following Noah around for nearly every moment that he's been awake. And most nights, too. I just sit in the corner of his room while he sleeps. You know, in case he dies before he wakes. So I decided to take a break here. As soon as the sun went down and the lights dimmed, it was out of my control."

"Listen, Jack. You *can* control it. You *need* to control it. What was this latest dream about?" Hauser pressed.

"Yeah, this one was a little bit . . . different."

"Different how?"

"Well, different from the last couple of dreams," I confessed.

"Couple of dreams? Jesus, Jack. How often have you been sleeping?"

"No, it's not like that. This is maybe my third or fourth nap. The first one was more of a nightmare than anything else. It was about Cyndi."

"And the other ones?"

"Well, they kind of jump around. I am myself in all of the dreams, and Cyndi was there at the beginning. But then the dreams kind of took on a life of their own, drifting around the city, but not exactly. It's strange. It's *this* city but it's just . . ."

"It's different. I've heard that. Anything else?"

"With this last one, I was able to speak to somebody in the dream. I was following Noah around, and I tried to talk to him. And it was just like it is here in real life—he couldn't hear me. Then all of a sudden this other guy walks up and starts talking to me, questioning me about how I do my job and why don't I speed things up."

Hauser's head cocked to the side. "Describe him."

"Well, he was . . . middle-aged, maybe? He wore a blue suit and a matching hat. He had no visible hair."

"He was bald?" Hauser asked.

"From what I could tell. He did have his hat on the whole time." I paused, trying to remember the dream more clearly. "Strange. I don't recall seeing any eyebrows or eyelashes on the guy, either. Should I be worried? It's just some apparition created by my mind, right?"

Hauser shrugged and sat up straight. "Mmm. What else did he say?" His eyes were penetrating, as if staring into my own soul.

"That's where it got weird. He told me that I needed to hurry up so that I could get to the next soul. He seemed to know everything about what we do. It was as if he was a soul collector himself."

Hauser nodded his head as his eyes scanned the surrounding park. "Is that it? Did he say anything else?"

"Yeah, he said that sometimes we have to take things into our own hands. Hauser, he wanted me to kill my mark."

Hauser gasped before standing abruptly.

"Hauser? It was just a dream. Right?" I asked, hoping that it really was nothing more than just my mind playing tricks on me.

Hauser ignored my question and started to pace around my

park bench. "Did the man tell you his name?"

"Enoch Gant."

Hauser stopped pacing and stood directly in front of me. "Listen, Jack. You have to promise me that you will refrain from sleeping until I tell you otherwise. Do you understand me?"

In the short few months that I'd known Hauser, I'd never seen him so riled. Especially over something as innocuous as resting. "Yeah, sure," I muttered, wondering what was really going on.

"Now, fill me in on your current collection. You say you've been with him nonstop?"

"Yeah, pretty much. From what I can tell, Noah is as healthy as an ox. He's young, married, and has two kids. He has a good job over on Griffin Street, earning enough so that his wife can be a stay-at-home mom," I said, fully realizing that Noah was living my life, or the life I had wanted with Cyndi. Only better. "Honestly, I think this box is a mistake. There's nothing remotely wrong with this guy. He's happy, he's healthy, and he has no vices to speak of."

"Come now, Jack. Do I need to draw it out for you?" Hauser asked, returning to the bench next to me.

"I think I know what you're going to say."

"Not everybody needs to be old or have some kind of disease in order for them to die. Accident, murder"—Hauser paused—"and, well, suicide. All of those could be a factor here."

I squinched my eyes tight at hearing his latest rationale.

"Listen, champ. You're just gonna have to keep with it. Keep following your target. Stay with him, and death will come. I wish there was more I could say to make this easier for you."

I opened my eyes and nodded, staring straight ahead. "Yeah. Okay."

Hauser stood. "Anything else before I take off?"

"Now that you mention it, do you mind if I borrow your monocle for a moment? Will that help me see the exact moment Noah dies?"

Hauser smiled. "Well, the monocle isn't really used in that way. It has a completely other purpose. There are, however, other items that are useful in our profession. But at this moment, you do not have access to any of them. You'll have to just stick with it. Do it old school. Think of it as paying your dues." Hauser winked. "You'll earn your first apparatus soon enough."

"Other items?" I asked, my interest piqued.

"Not quite yet, compadre. In due time," Hauser said. "And one more thing. I know you've been spending a lot of time with him, getting to know his life, his habits, his family. Just try to keep everything in perspective. Don't get too close. It'll just make the collection that much more difficult in the end."

I shrugged, disappointed at the lack of information. Before I could form another question, Hauser disappeared.

"No, no. It's okay. I'll just chat with you later," I said sarcastically before I jumped back to Noah's apartment.

Chapter 3

When I popped into the Claytons' apartment, I landed in their bedroom. Noah and his wife were still fast asleep. The alarm clock on the nightstand shone 5:47 in vivid red numerals.

"Any chance you want to wake up and die?" I asked. Not surprisingly, there was no response.

I made my way to the corner of the bedroom where I'd spent far too many mind-numbingly boring nights, waiting. I leaned back into the intersection of the two walls and slid my back down until my butt was firmly resting on the floor, my legs crossed beneath me, Lotus style. As I settled in for the early morning, I thought back to what Hauser had said. *There are other items useful in our profession.* I wondered, besides the coin, what else there was that might help me. Wilson must have had something else, something more that he'd earned along the way.

I remembered the rosary and pulled it out. While I fumbled with it, I began to hear stirrings from the bed next to me. Initially ignoring the sounds, I continued my inspection of the beaded crucifix. After a few moments of review, I dismissed its magical potential and thought about what else Wilson might have had. The only other thing he'd had with him was his sunglasses. Panic overwhelmed me at the thought of me haphazardly placing them on the dead man's face just as an attempt to add humor to the situation. What if that pair of sunglasses allowed me to see something in the future? What if they somehow enhanced the wearer's perception in some magical way?

"Crap," I yelled. How could I have been so oblivious to even the most remote possibility? I thought about what Hauser had said, that Wilson's body might very well remain in the coroner's freezer until they determined who he was or until somebody claimed him as a long-lost relative twice removed. Knowing good and well that that event would never happen, I wondered just how long an unidentified body would continue to take up space in the city morgue. I made a mental note to ask Hauser about it.

As these thoughts coursed through my mind, I was interrupted by voices from the bed.

"Hey, baby. Are you awake?" asked Ashley, Noah's wife.

Noah rolled over onto his back, and Ashley slid her body next to his, spooning his side with her feminine curves.

I slipped the rosary back into my breast pocket and focused completely on the couple. Was this the moment? Could Noah be having chest pains? An aneurysm? A fatal bout of halitosis?

Ashley caressed Noah's chest for a few moments before speaking again. "What do you want to do today?

"Hrmm rmm," Noah shrugged, not putting any more effort into the morning conversation than was necessary. "You?" he asked.

Ashley's hand continued to weave in and out of Noah's chest hairs, inching lower down his abdomen with each pass. "It's up to you, Babe. You worked hard all week. It's the weekend, and you deserve a little fun."

Before Noah could say another word, Ashley's hand disappeared beneath the bedsheets, causing Noah to moan slightly.

"Are you serious?" I asked. "First I have to wait for you to die, and now you are going to make love to your wife right in front of me?"

Noah didn't answer my sarcasm but instead leaned into Ashley and kissed her passionately. The kiss only lasted a moment though, as Ashley slid herself beneath the sheets, causing more moaning from Noah.

"Nope. I'm outta here," I grumbled before disappearing from the bedroom corner.

Having improved on my ability to jump from place to place, I popped into Noah's living room, just on the other side of their bedroom wall. I wasn't a stranger to watching the occasional porn video, but that was back when I had the ability to release with Cyndi. Now that I was forever in detached solitude, I didn't need to get all dressed up with no place to go, so to speak.

As I paced around the apartment, I hoped that their impromptu act of love making would be quick so that I might be able to move on with my job. I was discovering that the more I followed Noah and his family around, the more I liked the guy. He was a good husband, and he was living it right. I knew now what Hauser meant about becoming too attached, and my only hope was that it wasn't too late.

Moving into the kitchen, I noticed 6:12 a.m. glowing on the microwave's digital readout. "How long am I going to have to wait?" I asked. To my surprise I heard a whimper from just down the hall. In the otherwise silent house, it sounded like a trapped animal calling out for attention. Quietly, I crept down the hall toward the sound. Just past the powder room I came to a closed door. As I stood just outside, I listened intently at the noise. The whimpering came and went, and even though I'd never been around puppies growing up, I recognized the sound instantly.

After following Noah around for so many weeks, I knew the dog was a new addition. Deciding that it was far too early for anyone else to be awake, I stepped into the room to see the puppy for myself. The room was dark, but the early sunrise cast in just enough light, revealing the compact laundry room.

Closing the door behind me, I turned and looked around for the source of the crying. In just a few moments, I found the crate that the pooch was penned up in. As I leaned in close to the wire-framed cage door, I found two dark eyes looking back at me. They belonged to what looked like a beagle puppy, and strangely, I sensed that the dog could see me.

"Hey, buddy," I said. "You're new around here, aren't you?"

As soon as I muttered those words, the puppy began to bark and yelp. It was clear that he was aware of my presence and he was not happy, either about being locked up or about seeing a strange person just outside his cage.

"Hush, now. It'll be all right," I said as I quickly unlatched the cage door, freeing the black-and-brown spotted puppy.

The moment he was out of the cage, he rushed between my legs and began to scratch at the door that led to the rest of the apartment.

"Come here, you little shit," I hollered, but the dog ignored me. I wondered if I was initially mistaken and he actually couldn't see me after all.

I stepped back, flipped on the light switch, and fully took in my surroundings. I noticed that the puppy was in fact a beagle. And now that I could see him more clearly, he looked to be maybe a few months old.

"Come here, pup," I said as I knelt down in the middle of the room. I remained still for several minutes before the he turned and looked in my direction. "Come on," I said as I patted my leg.

Like a bolt of lightning, the puppy shot forward and tried to jump up and nip at my face, barking and howling the whole while.

"Hush, now. You're gonna wake the family," I said, hoping it wasn't already too late. I grabbed him, shuttled him back into his sleeping crate, and relatched the door. The howling didn't subside though, and I knew it would only be a matter of moments before someone would come barging in to check on the little guy.

I stood up quickly and leaped for the light switch. No sooner had I done so I heard the floor creak just outside in the hallway. I sprang back from the door just as Katie, Noah's daughter, burst into the room, followed closely by Tim, Noah's son.

I wasn't sure how our bodies would interact in such close quarters, so I froze. After a quick moment, I changed my stance. I didn't want to cause the two kids to accidentally bump into an invisible being, so I climbed up on the countertop next to the washer. I sat there and watched the kids kneel close to the pet cage, slipping their fingers through the wire-framed door, touching the puppy's soft fur coat.

"Do you think we should let him out?" Tim asked anxiously.

Katie, being a few years older than Timmy, nodded thoughtfully. "I think we can, but just for a minute. We don't want to wake Mom and Dad."

With a flick of the metal latch, the door sprang wide and

puppy sprang from the cage once again. Once out, he bolted toward the door. Luckily, Katie was able to kick it shut just seconds before he could make it out of the room.

The puppy stopped and barked a few times, then howled loudly. Being in such a confined space, the echo in the room was grating.

"Hush!" Tim screamed, but the puppy continued to shriek. Katie sat on the floor and began to pet him, from the top of his head to the tip of his tail. Within moments, the puppy's howling began to subside as he was placated by the attention. Just when I thought it was going to be okay, the puppy looked up at me sitting on the counter and it started all over again. He began his yip-like barks at first, running to the base of the cabinets and trying to jump up, before the full-on howling continued. Thankfully, the kids couldn't see me. I figured the only way I could possibly calm the ruckus was to remove myself from the situation. I vanished and a moment later popped back into the living room, where I was alone once again.

"Shit," I mumbled. "That complicates things." By now the sunrise was nearly complete, and the rays of light that came through the window were strong. I sat down on the faded leather sofa and contemplated my predicament. The noise from the yelping dog down the hall was subsiding, but I knew it would only start up again once they let him out into the rest of the apartment. How was I going to continue to follow Noah around if that little dog raised hell every time I was around?

No sooner had the thought crossed my mind than the bedroom door clicked open and Noah stepped out. He had donned his bathrobe and wore a look of complete displeasure on his face. He headed straight for the laundry room, to the source of the early morning distraction. A moment later Ashley sauntered out and into the kitchen. Within minutes she had begun to make breakfast.

The glorious smell of coffee filled the air, and I had a moment of a craving so uncontrollable that I almost stood up and walked right into the kitchen to pour myself a cup. But like most people in the world, coffee makes me poop, so I forced the desire from my mind. Instead, I tried to figure out what it was about that dog the seemed . . . off. In the past month or so, hadn't I been around other animals? Hadn't they all ignored me like every other person that I'd come into contact with?

As I shuffled through the last four weeks' activities in my mind, I was slow to notice Noah come back into the living room. He was carrying the puppy and was trailed by his two kids. Before I could react, the dog started to howl almost instantly. It was clear that they were going to take the pup for a walk. Noah stopped in his bedroom first to dress. Unfortunately, he failed to close the door all the way, and the dog nosed his way out, back into the living room.

YELP YELP YELP!

Before I could stand, he was jumping up on my legs, trying to get onto my lap. I looked at the kids, who just stood in the center of the room, watching the dog.

"Kids, don't let him get on the couch. If we want to keep him, he's going to have to be trained," Ashley said, coming into the living room. She walked up to where I was sitting and bent down to pick up the puppy. Before she could get ahold of him, he bolted out of her grasp and began to circle the coffee table, barking and yipping as if playing a game.

Normally I would have found the scene quite comical, but at the moment I needed to think. And to do so I needed some quiet. Noah was in his room, dressing, and the kitchen was relatively open to the rest of the flat. I decided to just jump to another, unoccupied room of the apartment and go from there. Katie's room was the first to come to mind, and a second later I was standing at the foot of her bed.

"Ah, finally. Peace and quiet," I said as I sat at on a wooden trunk in the corner of her room.

"*Squawk.* Peace and quiet," came a scratchy voice from the adjacent wall. I nearly jumped out of my skin, but I saw no one.

"Hello? Who's there?" I asked as I moved to the center of the room for a better look. Upon further investigation, I was certain I was alone. There was nobody else in the room but me.

"Hello. Who's there. *Squawk,*" came the voice from beneath a sheet on the dresser.

I moved toward the sheet and lifted the edge slightly. As I

peeked underneath, I saw a colorful bird perched on a wooden bar at the middle of the birdcage. The bird locked its beady eyes onto mine and bobbed its head a few times before speaking again.

"Who's there?" it said, stepping sideways along the bar.

"Are you kidding me?" I asked. Was I suddenly doomed to a nearly impossible job?

"Who's kidding. *Squawk!*" said the bird, raising his volume several decibels. Before I knew it, Katie came running back into the bedroom and right up to the bird's cage. She pulled at the sheet before tossing it to the floor.

"Good morning, Baxter," Katie said.

Baxter continued to bob his feathery head as he twisted it about, scanning the room beyond his wire-wrapped prison.

"*Squawk.* Morning."

Then, all of a sudden, the room became much more cramped as the rest of the family came rushing in.

"Hey, is Baxter talking?" asked Timmy.

"Yeah, he started it a few days ago," Katie said.

"*Squawk.* Talk."

Along with the presence of the entire family, the puppy followed. The moment he came in, he bolted right for me. This time, though, I was prepared. I was about to leave the godforsaken house for the morning anyway, and popped out just as the dog got near.

Chapter 4

I reappeared on my park bench. Thankful to be away from the sudden and unexpected madhouse, I leaned back and considered my situation. There was something about what Hauser had said earlier that continued to stay with me. *Other items*?

I pulled the rosary from my pocket to reexamine it and focused on each bead as I pulled it through my fingers. There had to be something about the chaplet that had helped Wilson along. Perhaps I needed to chant something. But what? Maybe some kind of prayer? I smirked. Perhaps I should have listened to my grandmother's urging and attended Sunday school after all.

Frustrated, I wound the beads tightly around my fingers until the tips turned white and the crucifix laid positioned toward me. I brought it to my mouth and gently placed my lips upon the cold metal.

"Uh, Father Almighty?" I began, remembering a few words that my grandmother would say when she prayed. "I, uh, believe . . . in God? Heaven on earth . . . uh, something about Jesus Christ, his one and only son . . ."

"You better release the tension there, buddy. You'll either cut the circulation off in your fingers or break the strand completely."

I leaped from the bench at the sound of Hauser's voice. "Jesus, Hauser!"

"No, but I've been mistaken for him at least once through my days as a soul collector."

"You nearly scared the shit right out of me. Can you please

155

give me some kind of warning next time? Seriously."

"Would you prefer I wear a bell around my neck?" Hauser grinned.

With my heart rate returning to normal, I sat back down next to Hauser. "Well, if you wouldn't mind, that would be great."

"Speaking of, try placing the rosary around your neck. That should get you a lot closer to figuring things out than where you were just heading."

Embarrassed, I fumbled around with the worn beads, avoiding Hauser's gaze. "Oh, I, uh . . . was just trying to remember the Apostles' Creed—"

"No need to explain. It's like I said earlier, though. Most items are earned, not taken. That was in Wilson's possession, am I correct?"

I couldn't bring myself to answer, so I just nodded my head.

"And did he give it to you, or did you take it from his person?"

"The cops were there, and if I didn't grab it, they would have certainly taken it," I explained.

"I see."

"And my penance?" I asked, keeping the religious theme rolling in the conversation. "Am I in trouble with the Sentinel, or whoever, for taking it?"

"No penance, Jack. I'm actually relieved that you took it before they moved his body off. You see, I gave that to him after his thirtieth collected soul."

"So there is a proverbial golden watch with each milestone."

"No, it was just that Wilson was . . . special. His thirtieth soul was more than just a regular milestone," Hauser said, his voice drifting off as he spoke. "It was more of breakthrough . . ."

"How so?" I asked.

"It's . . . difficult to explain," Hauser said.

Hauser looked off into the distance as we sat in silence for several minutes. It was quite apparent that there was more to the story.

"So around my neck then?" I asked.

Several moments passed before Hauser's attention returned to the present. He looked at me, smiled, and nodded. "Yep."

I unfastened the delicate metal clasp and brought it up to my chest, reattaching it behind my neck.

"Okay, now what?"

"No, no. You've got to do some of this work yourself. Like I said, you didn't rightfully earn this, so . . ."

"Ah, so there is contrition. Just in the form of limited information."

"Call it what you will, Jack. If you're going to make it as long as Wilson did, you're going to have to learn to think for yourself."

I nodded, and decided not to push the matter further. It was obvious that Hauser was not in the mood.

"Can you at least tell me what the rosary does?"

Hauser looked at me, his steely gaze lightening up momentarily. "It'll let you see into the future, but only for twenty-four hours, and it is not specific in nature."

"Twenty-four hours into the future, but not to any particular event?"

"Yes, that's right," Hauser said.

"So all this really does for me is, what? Gives me a day's head start?"

"Sometimes, Jack, an additional twenty-four hours means a great deal to how you cope with some of these deaths. Some are more gruesome than others, and how we handle each of them is key, emotionally speaking."

Listening to Hauser's words brought up another question that blurted from my mouth before I had a chance to stop it. "Is that why Wilson earned this after his thirtieth soul? Was that particular collection emotional for Wilson?"

Hauser bobbed his head slowly. "Something like that."

Silence enveloped us once again. Perhaps at some point I'd ask Hauser more, but for now I opted to focus at the task at hand. I lifted the crucifix from my chest and brought it to my lips. "Noah Clayton," I said softly.

Nothing happened.

"Show me Noah," I said, still holding the crucifix near my mouth.

Again, nothing happened. Hauser tilted his head, giving me a sideways glance. Then he smirked. "Boy, you're getting it all wrong. If I have to show you everything, you need to follow along with everything I say. Agreed?"

I nodded eagerly. "Agreed."

"First, posture is everything. You have to be standing for this to work."

Without hesitation, I stood and faced Hauser directly. "Next?"

"No, you're not quite right," Hauser said as he considered my stance. "Hold your head up higher, and straighten your back. Your shoulders are far too slouched for this to work properly."

I did as Hauser said and thrust my chest out, straightening my shoulders and back in the same motion. "Like this?"

"Yeah, kid, you're getting there. Now, place your right hand on your hip with your thumb to the back and your forefingers to the front."

I imagined the position in my mind before following Hauser's latest direction. "All right."

"Great. Getting close. Next, lift the crucifix with your left hand but only hold it away from your body with your pinky finger."

"Like this?" I asked. As ridiculous as I knew I looked, I could almost feel the future ready to surge through my mind, body, and soul.

"Great, kid. You're really outdoing yourself here. Now, this last step is tricky." Hauser smiled. "If you don't get it right, you're going to have to start all over, and let me tell you, you don't want to look like a fool two times in a row."

"Okay, I'm ready. What's the last step?"

"All right. Standing on your right foot only, lift your left foot into the air and whistle 'March from the River Kwai.'"

Without objecting, I lifted my leg and began to whistle the tune from the classic movie. With my lips pursed together, I made it through the entire first chorus before I noticed Hauser grinning cheek to cheek.

"What? Am I doing it wrong?"

Before Hauser could answer, he burst out laughing. I stood on my one leg for another few seconds before I concluded that he was having fun at my expense. Realizing at that moment that I'd not seen him laugh out loud since I'd known him, I began to laugh myself.

"Oh, God. Jack, I'm sorry, but that was so worth it. I really needed a good laugh right then."

As my chuckling subsided, I sat down next to Hauser. "I'm glad I could oblige."

Hauser continued laughing for a few more moments before he wiped the tears from his eyes and looked at me. "All right, Jack. I'll let you off the hook. You just have to be near your mark for the rosary to work."

"That's it? I just have to have the rosary with me and be near him?" I asked.

"No, you still have to have it around your neck, but just be near him and think of the future. Touching him, or her for that matter, helps, but it's not necessary."

"All right, then. I think I can handle that."

"One more thing, Jack. The rosary can be a curse at times, because of the horrific nature of our job. Sometimes it is really better to experience the death just once. Just think about that."

I nodded, understanding Hauser's advice completely.

"Thanks, Hauser. Now, if you don't mind, I'd like to go give this bird a whirl," I said as I twirled the rosary around my fingers.

"Knock yourself out, kid. We'll catch up later," Hauser said and then vanished. I straighten myself up and vanished a moment later.

Chapter 5

Back in Noah's apartment, the circus that I'd escaped from earlier had diminished, and the order of the house was much more akin to what I'd experienced over the previous three weeks. Ashley was reading, and the kids were playing in their rooms. Noah was on his computer, studying the screen intently. I scanned the room, looking for the Thing of Evil, a.k.a. the puppy, but he was nowhere in sight. Trusting that he was most likely in with the kids, I figured I'd better make my move quickly, before he noticed me here and began his howling tirade all over.

Stepping up to Noah, I briefly glanced at his computer screen. At first look he appeared to be on some kind of antigovernment website, but upon closer inspection, it looked to be some kind of weapons and ammo information site. Noah was a hunter? Who knew? Surprised at Noah's choice of hobbies, I shifted my focus to the task at hand. I straightened myself, checking that the rosary was securely suspended around my neck. I took a deep breath, then placed my hand firmly on Noah's head. The moment my fingers landed upon his tightly cut hair, a warming sensation shot up through my hand and into my body. A momentary instinct to release my grasp crossed my mind, but I held fast. I wanted to do this, needed to see for myself what lay ahead for Noah.

As I stood next to him, my hand melding with his soul, the room started to darken around me. I blinked several times, trying to determine whether it was my own vision faltering or if it was my surroundings changing abruptly. Looking about, I felt as if it were a combination of both, and there was no stopping it. I let it run its course, my hand firmly resting on Noah's head. Then, suddenly, Noah and I were ripped from the apartment and carried through time and space to what appeared to be an urban battleground.

I began to walk around, trying to discover exactly where we had gone. Unfortunately, nothing looked familiar. We were outside, and Noah wasn't alone. He was lying on the ground, holding some kind of foreign assault rifle. Well, it was foreign to me at least. He was dressed in army-green fatigues, as was his companion. The two lay behind some form of barricade, staring down the barrel of their weapons.

"Do you see Harvey? He should have made it to the safe zone by now," Noah said.

"Affirmative. He just entered the facility. Now we wait. We'll know if the trade was all worth it shortly," replied Noah's companion.

"All right. Hold this position while I work my way around their flank. If you see a shot, take it. Even if it means that Harvey is hit, it'll be collateral damage. We both know that their leader will never go for a fair exchange. If I'm on the other side when all hell breaks loose, I'll at least have a chance to grab the box in the confusion," Noah said as he rolled to his side and began a low crawl down the left side of the barricade.

As soon as Noah was out of sight, I tried to make sense of what the hell was happening. I'd have known if Noah was in some reserve division of the military by something around the apartment or by a conversation, but I recalled nothing. Maybe he was involved in some kind of militia, and this is where he'd lose his life. Intrigued, I chased after Noah with no concern for my own concealment.

Once around the side of the barricade, I was surprised to see that Noah had made it halfway down the outer edge of the surrounding field. His spiderlike moves were awe-inspiring. I trotted to catch up to him, and as I did, I could see the safe zone that he'd referred to earlier. It was a relatively small cube-shaped structure about twenty yards from our position. Around the base of the building was a four-foot perimeter marked in yellow paint on the ground. Outside that perimeter there was open ground for at least twenty feet in all directions. There was no sneaking up on the place. There was a single door on the adjacent wall, and it was closed. There were no windows that I could see.

Out of the corner of my eye, I saw movement on the opposite side of the safe house. It appeared to be another soldier dressed in brown camouflage-style clothing. He also wore a helmet and carried a rifle. I moved closer and saw that he wasn't alone. He was followed by at least three more brown-clothed troops.

"Shit!" I yelled. It was a trap. Had to be. I looked back at Noah, and just as I did, he rose up slightly to get a better view of the central safe house. Unfortunately for him, his low stance prohibited him from seeing the opposing forces working their way directly toward him.

Just then, his companion whistled a soft bird call. Noah nodded and motioned his buddy to move along the opposite side. They were going in. I knew I couldn't do a thing, so a leaned against a large tree trunk. As I did so, I noticed a green slime coating the entire tree base. I knew it was there and was most likely sticky, but I didn't move. I was in a future dream of some sort, and it wasn't real to me.

Refocusing my attention on Noah, I saw he'd moved an additional fifteen feet up the side flank and was about to make a huge mistake. I leaned forward anxiously as he rose up slightly. The enemy soldiers fired the first shot. It flew high and to the right, and Noah returned fire. Several shots perforated the shrubbery on the far side of the safe zone. With his finger off the trigger, he rose once more to see if he had actually hit any of the enemy. But just as his head peeked above his own foliage barricade, a single shot flew right toward him. It landed on its mark, directly in the center of Noah's forehead. If it hadn't been for the plastic face shield, Noah's face would have been completely covered in paintball goo.

Noah stood in protest and a barrage of shots flew in his direction, peppering his body with all shades of paint. Green, yellow, orange. I could hear Noah whimper slightly at the stings as he was decimated by the hits. So much for capturing his soul tomorrow, I thought.

Disappointed with the outcome of my first trip into the future, I decided to return to his apartment. I thought about my hand resting on Noah's head back in his apartment and envisioned me lifting it slightly. As I did so, I felt like I was being yanked backward, and before I could catch my balance, I blacked out momentarily.

When I came to, I was standing in Noah's apartment, alone. Noah was no longer at his desk, and the computer screen was now dark. I moved back into the living room and found Ashley fast asleep on the couch. Everyone else was gone, including the dog. I concluded that Noah and the kids must have taken him for a walk in the park. Knowing what the next twenty-four hours had in store, I didn't feel the need to follow along with Noah's every move, so I thought of my park bench and vanished.

Chapter 6

I wasn't terribly surprised to find Hauser sitting on the bench when I appeared. He was reading a book, and by his facial expressions it must have been some gripping tale. I sat quietly next to him, not wanting to interrupt his concentration, but when it appeared that he didn't even realize that I was back, I cleared my throat. His focus remained on the printed words, but he held up a solitary finger in my direction, asking for a moment. I gave him two.

"And, done!" Hauser declared as he snapped the book shut.

"What are you reading?" I asked.

"This, my friend, is *The Origin of Species*. Have you heard of it?"

"Um, yeah. I'm sure it was required reading back in college. Darwin, right?"

Hauser turned the book over and nodded. "What do you know? It is Darwin. Fantastically influential, wouldn't you say?"

I nodded, although it had been many years since I'd actually seen a copy. "Yeah, sure."

Hauser dropped the book on the bench between us and peered at me questioningly. "So? How'd it go?"

"Well, he's not going to die in the next twenty-four hours."

"No, what did you think of the adventure? Quite a ride, huh?"

I smiled and nodded. "Yeah, another new experience, that's for sure."

"That's it? Boy, you've just come closer to time travel than any of the living population would believe, and all you can say is, 'Yeah, sure'?"

"What do you want me to say? That it was a mind-blowing ride and that my life will be forever changed? Well, it was interesting jumping forward like that, but once we got to twenty-four hours ahead, things were just . . . weird. I could see Noah clearly, but everything else was kind of . . . kind of blurry. And all I could do was watch. I couldn't interact or change anything."

"Didn't you play around with the time tracking? Tell me you did something," Hauser said.

"Time what? I just thought it was a twenty-four hour advance glimpse and nothing more. You didn't mention anything about controls."

"Oh? It must have slipped my mind. Sorry 'bout that," Hauser said, dropping his chin slightly. "So, yeah. You can control a lot of what you see. You can only go forward twenty-four hours from your current time, but you can rewind and experience anything over again that is within the time window. I sometimes think of an hour ahead and then set it to a speed of five times normal. That way, I catch most everything that is happening, but I'm skipping most of the boring, monotonous stuff."

"Wait, how do I do that?"

"When you start, just think of the time of day and you're whisked off. Once there, just say or think the commands clearly. Like fast-forward or rewind. You can even pause it and move around a moment frozen in time."

"Okay, now I understand your excitement. If I'd had that information to begin with, I think I might have stayed there longer."

"Now you know. I'll bet your mind will be blown on your next trip."

I tilted my head from side to side but said nothing.

Hauser noticed, and asked, "What? Is all this boring you somehow? Wow, you're a hard man to please."

"No, I think you're right. It will certainly be an improvement. But why would I want to pause a moment in the future if it's always going to be just a blurred environment? Any way to clear that up?"

PAUL B. KOHLER

"I know what you're talking about. The future you are seeing is an estimation of projected occurrences. Even though the information you are experiencing is almost inevitable, sometimes things don't always occur as planned. So the images you see are a little fuzzy. The closer you get to the current time, the clearer everything will be. That is, unless there is an absolute certainty, you'll see the blur."

"So how does that work?" I asked. "Who is it that figures out what the window to the future entails?"

"Not sure. Don't care. Listen, Jack. The rosary is merely a tool. It's not a perfect tool, but it's there to give assistance in situations like this."

"But don't you ever wonder? How is it that all of these tools get made? Is there some kind of top-secret R&D division of the afterlife?"

Hauser shrugged, his eyes rolling back momentarily. "All right, Jack. Here's what I do know. There is somebody in the Sentinel that . . . creates these gadgets. How he does it is beyond me. I'm no scientist, and I'm not even sure science is what's used to make them. I'm just happy that we all get a new device every now and then."

"So you've met him? Or her?" I asked.

"Not formally. I was up . . . there for another matter and he was present. He's an older gentleman, long gray hair, silver eyes, reminded me of Gandalf"—Hauser chuckled—"and we didn't even speak. His stare was penetrating, and if it wasn't for his smile, I would've thought he was a curmudgeonly old coot that was the right hand of death."

I whistled quietly, feeling a little overwhelmed by the man's description. As I replayed Hauser's last words in my mind, something stood out.

"Up there?" I asked.

This time, Hauser's eyes rolled all the way back before he answered. "Okay, champ. Q&A is over. For now. I think you need to be on task and stay near Noah—"

"But he's not going to die right away, at least not in the next twenty-four hours."

"Just because you have this new tool doesn't mean that you

166

can get lazy. You should still be near him and glean as much knowledge from him as possible. You never know when you might need certain information to assist you in his transition."

"Like what he had for breakfast today? Or how long he was in the bathroom after breakfast?" I asked.

Clearly irritated at my sarcasm, Hauser stood up and shuffled from side to side as he appeared to be in deep contemplation.

"Hey, I'm sorry, I just don't get all of this."

"It's okay, Jack. If you can believe this, when I was being trained, I may have been even more of a pain in the ass about the whole situation than you're being now." He stopped pacing and stood directly in front of me. "Take Wilson, for example. He obviously had the rosary with him, but he still was with you for the majority of your day. He knew what you would be going through and was there in your moment of need. Regardless of your outcome, don't you think that his ability and knowledge of your past twenty-four hours would've helped your transition to the other side be more comfortable?"

Strangely, I hadn't given Wilson a whole lot of consideration over the past few weeks, and now that Hauser pointed out how genuinely dedicated he was, I felt somewhat embarrassed for my attitude.

"I really am sorry, Hauser. I'm on it. I'll stick with him and see this through."

"Apology accepted, champ. Just let me know if there's anything else I can do for you," Hauser said as he looked at his pocket watch.

"Wait! Before you go, what can you tell me about animals? Noah and his family apparently got a puppy, and he's able to see me. In fact he appears to have a strong dislike for my presence entirely."

"Ah, yes. Animals can see and interact with us. In fact, I have a goldfish back . . . Never mind. Yes, animals are a challenge for us. Perhaps you should get a hold of some dog treats before you head back. Make a friend. A few tender morsels and he'll certainly adjust his temperament toward you."

A moment later, Hauser vanished.

I sat for a few moments longer, deciding which pet store I

would visit before heading back to Noah's. Once I had my plan, I vanished.

Chapter 7

"Dad?"

"Yeah, kiddo," Noah replied.

"I miss Bailey already," Katie said before taking another lick of her melting ice cream cone.

"I know. I miss him too, but we'll be able to pick him up from the vet's office in an hour or so. He's just getting a . . . checkup," Noah said as he took a bite from his own ice cream.

"What's a checkup?" Katie asked.

"It's where the animal doctor checks to make sure that Bailey's health is okay. They give him shots that keep him from getting sick. They're also going to do a small operation on him . . . to make sure his insides are okay as well," Noah said.

Katie listened, holding her ice cream with one hand and deftly gripping a giant red balloon with her other. The balloon and ice cream were an attempt to preoccupy Katie's attention while her new puppy was getting fixed.

"Do all dogs have to get their insides looked at?" Katie asked.

Noah smiled. "Most of them do, here in the city. It's just the right thing to do if we want them to have a happy, healthy life."

Noah led Katie along the outskirts of the park, heading for their apartment. It was a very seasonal afternoon, with the temperature in the mid 80s. There wasn't a cloud in the sky. Ahead of them and to the right, several hundred geese foraged in an open field. It wasn't uncommon to see such a large gaggle at this time a year.

On the far side of the grazing flock, a man played fetch with a mature golden retriever. The man tossed the yellow tennis ball high into the air a dozen yards away. The retriever chased after it, catching the ball midflight before returning it back to his master. Noah and Katie watched with amusement as the game was repeated several times, until the man overthrew the ball slightly and the retriever missed the midair catch. The ball bounced on the ground, launching it toward the grazing flock of geese, and the retriever chased after it. On the second bounce, the ball struck a sprinkler head, launching it directly into the middle of the flock. The retriever barreled forward in chase. Katie began to giggle as the first few birds took flight. Within moments, however, she stopped laughing as the entire gaggle followed suit, rising up into the air and directly toward her and Noah.

The birds continued to rise, and some of them, lower than the others, nearly collided with her balloon. Katie screamed and ducked, dropping her ice cream and releasing the balloon at the same time.

"My balloon!" she yelled.

Noah ducked momentarily but looked up in time to reach out and grab at the string. Unfortunately his timing was a split second too late, and the balloon drifted farther from his reach. The downflow of air caused by the fleeing birds' wings caused the balloon to remain low. Noah lurched forward, trying to grasp at the fluttering string again, but his timing was off once again. It was clear that he'd get only one more chance at it before it was lost. He took a step off the curb in chase. As his fingers firmly closed on the string, he smiled toward Katie, only to see a look of terror fill her eyes. A second later, a city bus smashed into Noah, launching him several yards through the air. He landed so horrifically, the bus driver averted his eyes as the single red balloon drifted skyward.

"Rewind," I said, not believing my eyes.

The scene began to play forward again, starting at the moment Katie released the balloon.

"Rewind."

Life reversed further, and the dog had just burst into the flock of birds.

170

"Rewind."

Further back, and the retriever had just caught the ball. I continued to watch the entire scene play out again. The man throwing the ball. The high bounce. The first of the birds taking flight. The rest of the flock following. The balloon being released. Noah chasing after.

"Pause," I said as the bus was about to ram into Noah. I walked forward and noticed that the driver had been looking into his rearview mirror and not paying attention to the street ahead of him. That, in combination with Noah looking away from the flow of traffic, spelled a horrific outcome. And the worst part was that Katie, a mere ten feet away, had to witness the entire incident.

"Play."

The bus hit Noah with such force that his body flew forward nearly fifteen feet. He landed headfirst, driving his shoulder awkwardly sideways. His spine snapped over, his body folding backward unnaturally.

The grotesqueness made me cringe, and all I could think about was Katie. She stood at the edge of the curb as the bus driver slammed on his brakes, narrowly hitting the gnarled body of her dead father. She screamed at the top of her lungs but remained on the curb. The morbidly curious pedestrians neared the scene, and several bent over to retch. Within moments the crowd had grown large, and the well-meaning strangers moved forward to assist if they could, walking past Katie. Nobody paid any attention to the crying child as she remained at the edge of the sidewalk.

I let go of the rosary and was brought back to Noah's apartment. The moment I regained my bearings, I vanished back to my park bench.

Chapter 8

Images of Noah's body crashing into the pavement continued to replay in my mind, overwhelming me with emotion as I paced around. All I could think was how unfair life really was. I wished that I would've listened to Hauser's warning about not getting too attached. But I knew it was far too late for that. As I circled the park bench once more, I realized that it wasn't just Noah that I had become attached to but his entire family.

"Shit," I yelled.

I could feel my cheeks burn, anger fuming deep inside me. Poor Katie would forever live an altered life after witnessing the freak accident.

"But Katie hasn't witnessed anything yet," Hauser said, startling me back to the present.

"Sonofabitch," I exclaimed. "What?"

"I heard your thoughts, and you're only half right."

"What? I don't follow," I said, sitting down next to Hauser.

"Katie would have challenges coping with witnessing her father's death. You said . . . I mean, you thought that she would live an altered life after witnessing what she just did. But it hasn't happened yet."

"Semantics. You know what I meant," I snapped.

Hauser's eyes narrowed as he nodded slowly. "Suppose you're right. Want to tell me how it happened? I'm sorry, what *is going to* happen?

I exhaled and leaned back. "Yeah, sure. I went back to the

172

Claytons' apartment and jumped forward twenty-four hours. I was right at the edge of my limits, and Noah and Katie were walking by the park. They had just taken the dog in to the vet's office and Noah was treating Katie to a balloon and ice cream. As they walked along the sidewalk, a flock of birds startled Katie and she let go of her balloon. Noah chased after it, stepping into the street, directly in the path of a city bus."

Hauser winced at my description. "Well, if it's any consolation, it sounds like he didn't suffer. I'm sorry, at least he *won't* suffer."

"Yeah, I suppose. But the part that really got me was seeing the look of fear on Katie's face. No one should have to witness such a horrific accident so close, let alone one involving a parent." I leaned forward and rested my face in the palms of my hands. I wanted to undo what I had just seen.

Hauser looked at his watch. "You said you were at the outside limits?" he asked.

I lifted my face and peered at him. "Yeah. Why do you ask?"

Hauser stowed his watch and looked about the park. After a moment of silence, he said, "Oh, no reason, really."

"Jesus, Hauser, why is it that all of these good people die so helplessly? I mean Noah was a good person—"

"You mean *is* a good person?"

I nodded. "Okay, I get it. You don't have to continue to point out my tenses," I said. "He is a good father, a good husband, and he was just plain doing things right. How is it that his life can be taken away so easily while there are bad people that can continue living their bad lives at the same time?"

"So you're wondering why we don't have the ability to play God? Is that what you're asking?" Hauser said.

"Wait, what? No. I don't want to play God. I just think it's completely unfair that good people die when they shouldn't, while bad people continue to live."

"You want to play God. I get that," Hauser said.

I thought about his words for a moment. "Well? Is it that bad that I want to make positive changes?"

"No, it's not. And trust me, you're not the first one to have these thoughts. Every new collector has had similar reactions on the matter. And that's where I come in. I'm here to remind you that it's not our position, our duty, to dictate who lives and who dies. The balance of humanity is much larger than just you and I could ever imagine. Don't you remember just a few weeks ago when we were in the ghetto?" Hauser asked.

Somehow I knew he would bring up the gang fight. "Yeah, I remember."

"You see, not all bad people continue to live. There's a balance, and neither of us have *total* control over that. Besides, would you want the responsibility of judging who lives and who dies? Forever? For every soul you come into contact with? What if you made the wrong choice? Suppose you let a person live today, and somehow he changes two years, five years down the road? What if suddenly he snaps and becomes a serial killer? Would you blame yourself for letting this person live? Would you be willing to shoulder the burden of all the people that he'd kill?"

"Hey, slow down. I'm not saying I want total control. I'm just . . . venting, I guess."

"All right. I'll back off," Hauser said. "I just wanted you to see the alternative, is all."

"Thanks."

"So was this rosary experience any different than the one you had yesterday?"

I thought for a moment, trying to figure out where Hauser was going with this question. "I'm . . . not sure. Obviously it was in a different location."

"Not what I meant. What about the quality of your surroundings? Were they clear or were they still blurry? Like yesterday."

"Hmm. I guess a little of both. I remember the park was crystal clear, as was the bus. Noah and Katie were obviously clear, but the surrounding crowd was a little foggy," I said as I continued to replay the incident in my mind. "And I guess the geese were clear and blurry at the same time. Does that make sense?"

Hauser nodded. "Yeah. It was probably something to do with how they flew off into the air. Like I said, I'm not sure how it all works."

"The terrified look on Katie's face was the clearest of all," I said.

"Hey, don't beat yourself up too much," Hauser said as he stood and faced me. "Just remember, no one is dead yet." Then he winked and vanished.

Chapter 9

What the hell is that supposed to mean? I wondered. As I sat on the park bench, alone, I pondered Noah's impending death and its relation to the conversation I'd just had with Hauser. Here I was, a mere six weeks since my own suicide attempt, and I felt more confused and overwhelmed than ever. I'd gone from worrying about my own depression to contemplating playing God. What happened?

Just remember, no one is dead yet. There had to be a reason why Hauser had said that, and what was up with the wink afterward? Did he really just imply that he wanted me to actually attempt to intervene? To actually take on a God role in this particular soul collection? Was it even possible? Or was I reading too much into it?

I sat back and thought. If I could change the outcome, how would I go about it? I couldn't speak to Noah, to tell him that he needed to stay away from the park. I could only talk to Hauser and . . . and the animals. "Hey Bailey, do me a favor, would ya'? Bite your master so he can't walk in the park with Katie." Yeah, no. I didn't think that'd work.

What else? There was something else about the questions from Hauser that lingered in my mind. He'd asked about the scenery. The surroundings and whether they were clear or not. Why would any of that matter? That's when an idea began to form. I remembered another conversation with Hauser, when he'd said that the reason things were blurry or unclear was because those elements of the future were still uncertain. I tried to recall Noah's death again, but the imagery was already fading, drifting from my memory. I struggled at remembering what was real and what my mind was trying to convince me was real. No, I needed to see it all again. Regretfully, I needed to see Noah die all over.

I sprang from the park bench and vanished.

Chapter 10

Landing in the middle of the Claytons' apartment, I found the setting very much as I had left it not more than an hour earlier. I moved around the residence until I found Noah, slumped in an easy chair, reading a magazine. Wasting no time, I knelt down next to him and grasped the rosary. I touched his arm and within seconds was whisked away, back into Noah's future.

When my vision cleared, I stood on the sidewalk next to the park. In front of me, Noah's body lay awkwardly in the street. There were hordes of people surrounding the accident, but nobody moved. It was like the scene was frozen in time. It became clear to me that this must be the exact moment that Noah would die.

"Rewind. Rewind. Rewind," I said, wanting to go back far enough to get a feel of the entire incident once again. "Pause."

Noah and Katie stood in line at an ice cream vendor. The large open field with the gaggle of geese was just to my left. To my right was where Noah's crumpled body would lay shortly. With the environment frozen in time, I was able to move around and see everything from multiple perspectives. I walked toward Noah's position, studying everything as I went. As I weaved through the motionless pedestrians, I focused on the clarity of everything around me. Not surprisingly, things were somewhat clearer than they had been in my first review of Noah's future. I surmised that it was because I was now closer to his death.

When I approached the ice cream cart, the vendor was

holding an ice cream cone out to Katie, who had a cheerful smile on her face. I moved around all sides of the scene, looking for something, anything, that I could do to alter Noah's path. With all the people around me, I saw no way for me to do so.

"Fast-forward. Pause."

When the scene paused again, Noah and Katie were standing at the edge of the clearing, staring off into the distance. I walked up to where they stood and looked in the direction of their gaze. The man and his dog were still, lifeless, in the large grassy area. The man had just released the ball in the air and the dog had started his sprint in the direction of the throw. At that precise moment, I knew exactly what I needed to do. I ran toward the dog, my excitement building with each step. When I got to where the dog floated inches above the ground, I looked back toward Noah and Katie. Then I looked to where Katie would eventually release her balloon. I estimated that the distance would take them three to five minutes to walk. I knew that it was an exceedingly tight window in which to try to distract the dog long enough for them to pass that part of the park, but I had to make an effort.

"Play."

The dog in front of me continued charging forward and caught the ball. Without breaking stride, he returned to his master and dropped the tennis ball. Total round trip for the fetch was about sixty seconds. The dog's master picked up the ball again and tossed it through the air. The retriever missed catching the ball in midair but still continued the chase. The ball bounced high into the air and directly toward the birds. Thirty seconds. As the dog blasted through the outer edge of the flock, birds began to scatter into the air. Fifteen seconds. As the dog reached the tennis ball at the center of the flock, most of the birds were now flying away. Ten seconds. As the dog turned and ran toward his owner, I saw something.

"Pause."

I ran forward to where the flock had been just moments before. The golden retriever was in full stride back toward his owner, and when I got to his location, I noticed how blurry he and the ball were. I smiled, recalling once again what Hauser had said about the reasoning behind the blur. Sometimes things don't always occur as planned. That was it. I'd found it. I just had to distract the dog long enough.

"Play."

The scene continued as the blurry dog ran back toward his master. I turned to watch the birds fly toward Noah and Katie and noticed they continued to fluctuate between obscured blurs and crystal clear. I dismissed the vision as the red balloon began to flow through the air. As Noah took two steps into the street, I released the rosary from my grip.

I was back in Noah's apartment, kneeling next to his sleeping body. The magazine he had been reading just moments before was now lying across his chest. I stood and walked into the kitchen, looked at the clock on the microwave, and noted the time: 4:43 p.m.

I had about eighteen hours to kill before I put my plan in motion, which gave me plenty of time for a short visit to a sporting goods store and perhaps a brief rest until my next visit to the park.

A moment later I vanished from Noah's apartment.

Chapter 11

In all my life, I've never once stolen anything. I find it amusing that it took me until I was, for all intents and purposes, dead before I took up the knack. Just in the last twenty-four hours, I'd stolen animal treats, a tube of tennis balls, and a much-needed timepiece. All were justified acquisitions, so I didn't feel terribly bad for my sudden pilfering.

I slid my wrist out and admired the skeletonized face of my new Nixon Automatic. The time was 10:31 in the morning. I was nervous that my plan might not work at all, and I only had this one chance to make a difference. Therefore I had positioned myself in the park just out of sight of where the man would be playing fetch with the golden retriever. As I waited beneath the canopy of a mature elm tree, I popped open the can of fresh tennis balls and quickly brought it up to my nose. I inhaled deeply, enjoying a brief reflection of good times past. A memory from when Cyndi and I were first dating filled my mind. We had taken up tennis and even took a few lessons with a pro from the health club. Neither of us were very good at it, but it was quality time spent together, and that was all that mattered.

Reluctantly I pushed the memory away and focused on the task at hand. I needed to be ready for when the man and his dog first arrived at the park. I poured the first clean tennis ball out into my hand and gave it a tight squeeze. The texture of the ball against my skin gave me confidence somehow. I tossed the ball in the air a few times, catching it on the downfall. I was ready.

My plan was simple. I was going to wait until the dog trotted into view, and then I would throw the ball out from behind my hiding perch in an attempt to get the dog's attention. With any luck I could distract the dog long enough for Noah and Katie to pass the scene of the accident. It was a brilliant idea.

Five minutes later, I found myself staring out at the golden receiver being walked by his master. I waited until they were within throwing distance before I tossed the ball toward them. As the ball flew through the air, it flickered from a faded existence to a fully solid object. It bounced once, then twice before rolling gently across the dog's path. As expected, the dog bolted for the ball and scooped it up greedily in his mouth.

"Hey, Duke. What do you have there? That doesn't belong to you," said his master.

The dog pranced around, playing coy, and avoiding letting his master take his newfound ball away.

"Give it here. Drop? I'm sure someone will be looking for this," he said, glancing about the park. After several moments, he caved in. "All right, boy. I guess we can play until the owner comes to claim it."

Almost as if the dog understood what his master was saying, he quickly dropped the ball at his feet, anticipating the throw. The dog's wishes were quickly granted as the man picked up the ball and chucked it through the air. The retriever dashed after it, almost catching the ball in midair. After a short bounce, he caught it and quickly returned it to his master.

Wait, I thought. This isn't what I had planned. In fact, it appeared that I had just given the dog and his owner the very tool that would spell disaster for Noah in less than five minutes' time. I thought about tossing a few more balls out, but by the time the idea came to me, the dog and his master were several yards past me and were nearing the clearing with the birds.

"Shit!" I yelled.

I bolted from my hiding spot in an attempt to catch up to them. As I neared their position, I could see the silhouette of Noah and Katie walking down the sidewalk. I quickly revised my calculations and knew I had just minutes left to stop the birds from flying off, causing Katie to react.

I was nearly upon the man and his dog when a sudden idea shot through my mind like a freight train. Instead of slowing my pace to throw a new ball, I increased my speed and ran directly toward the geese. It was a huge gamble, but I felt I was correct in the assumption that if dogs could see me, so could a flock of wild birds.

I stole a final glance in the direction of Noah and his daughter. They were still several yards away from where the deadly accident would take place. Satisfied with their position, I dug deep and gave a final drive toward the center of the grazing birds. As I penetrated the outer perimeter of the gaggle, the birds merely parted around me, not flying away as I'd hoped. When my desired outcome didn't materialize, I stepped up my spectacle. I began to flap my arms wildly, screaming loudly as I continued to barrel through the flock.

"SQUAWK! SQUAWK! CUH-CAH!" I yelled. One by one, the birds began to take flight. I rushed forward with my lunacy and even began to jump up and down as I flapped away.

Within minutes most of the flock had flown off, with just a few stragglers hanging around on the far side of the clearing. I stopped my theatrics and dropped to my knees out of pure exhaustion. As I breathed deeply, I noticed Noah and his daughter quietly pass by the point of his uncertain death. A split second later, the city bus cruised by, the driver no wiser to the tragedy he was meant to be part of. Satisfied, I leaned back onto the grass and basked in my triumph. Within moments, I was startled by the wet tongue of the golden retriever. He assailed me with his kindness, and before his owner got curious about the situation, I thought about my park bench and vanished.

Chapter 12

Still exhausted from my magnificent performance, I collapsed on my park bench and let out a deep sigh. As I thought about the image of Noah and his daughter walking away from his own escapable death, I smiled widely. Within moments of experiencing the deep satisfaction that only hard work and determination can provide, Hauser appeared next to me. Hauser's sudden arrivals usually gave me a startle, but not this time. No way. I won— nothing was going to kill this high.

"So? How'd it go?" Hauser asked.

"Well, I think I might have a defective box," I smiled. "When I showed up at the scene of Noah's impending demise, things didn't quite play out as they had when I used the rosary." I looked straight ahead in an attempt to disguise the real truth from Hauser. My only problem: I was not that great at playing poker, and I sucked at bluffing.

"Jack?" Hauser said sternly.

I half smiled as I turned slightly in his direction. "Honest to God, Noah is alive," I said, holding back the rest of the story.

Hauser sighed deeply and looked away from me. "You know, sport, you're putting me in a tough position."

"How so?" I asked, almost certain I knew the reason.

"You went off and changed the course of his life. You played God." Hauser stared at me. "Tell me, Jack, how are we going to handle this?"

"But, I don't know—"

"Cut the crap, Jack. I knew the moment we had our last conversation that you were going to find a way."

I had been so happy just moments before, but now I could feel my cheeks reddening with embarrassment. "You can't tell me that you blame me for this. Noah is a good man. He has a loving family and—"

"Stop. I already know all that," Hauser said, holding his hand up to cut me off. After several moments of awkward silence, he continued. "Listen, Jack, I don't fault you for your reasons. I of all people would never question your moralistic fiber. I am disappointed that you actually followed through with it. And there will be consequences. Trust me, I know firsthand."

"Wait, you've done this before?"

Hauser nodded silently.

"Then what's the big deal? If you've done this, my punishment can't be too bad. You're my trainer, after all."

"My situation was a long time ago. My chastisement was quite severe at the time. Back then, the Sentinel was a lot different. They pulled me away from soul collection for almost a year, and that year was the hardest of my life."

"What made it so hard?" I asked.

Hauser shrugged. "My discipline is neither here nor there. I do know this: the Sentinel is very set in their ways today, and trust me when I tell you they won't be too happy to hear about your latest indiscretion."

Worry spread through my veins. Hauser was making it sound like I'd lose an arm or leg as penitence for my deed.

Hauser chuckled. "No, it's not going to be that bad."

"Been reading my thoughts much?"

Hauser winked.

We sat on the park bench and watched the random pedestrians walk up and down the sidewalk. Seconds turned to minutes. Minutes turned into hours. Before I realized it, the sun had gone down. Neither of us said a word. My own mind raced through numerous possible consequences for my actions. Hauser, who knows? He might have been thinking about feeding his goldfish for all I knew.

Hauser finally broke the silence. "It was shortly after my own training. I think it was around 1820, and I . . . was trying to atone for my past sins. The soul that I was sent to collect was that of a young girl, maybe thirteen or fourteen, I don't remember. Anyway, her father was killed in the war and her mother took any kind of job around the village that she could get so that she could feed her family. Because she was away so much, the little girl, I'll call her Alice, was in charge of her two younger sisters while their mother worked." Hauser paused but remained staring forward. "As you might imagine, back then there were fewer lawmen to keep the peace. With fewer police, the crime rate was a lot higher. I had just been given a device very similar to your rosary that allowed me to foresee the moment of death. Unfortunately, I didn't have twenty-four hours like you do now. I only had about an hour, maybe two."

"Why? Why are you telling me this now?" I asked.

"I've not told this to anybody, so take that for what it's worth. I just wanted you to know that you're not alone. Shall I continue?"

I nodded vehemently.

"When I used the device, I saw Alice and her two sisters being tortured, raped, and then killed. Two men were passing through town and had learned of the three girls being home alone when their mother inadvertently let it slip while working at a local pub."

"And you . . ."

"Yes, I saved all three girls that night. And at the same time I filled two boxes with the bad men."

"But how did you do it? I mean, I had to get creative with animal manipulation to save Noah. How did you save the three girls and kill the rapists at the same time?"

"That, my friend, is information that will never pass these lips. Let me just say that in this afterlife we live in, we have this . . . ability that even to this day, I don't know the full potential of."

I nodded, remembering something that Wilson had said before I took his soul. "Practical magic?" I asked.

"Yep. Wilson told you?"

"Yeah, but only briefly. I had asked him about his mind-reading ability and that's how he explained it."

"I'd imagine that you too will be developing that same ability anytime now. Maybe even before you collect your next soul."

"But what about my punishment? If you were pulled away for a year back then, what's going to happen to me now?"

"Well, I was . . . how can I say this? I was a special case."

"In what way?"

"My previous life was not filled with joys of spring, so to speak. I did some bad things, very bad. And to make up for those atrocities, I tried to save every soul that I could. It wasn't until those three girls that I finally got caught."

"Wow. What did you do? You know, before . . ."

Hauser's eyes were damp but the tears didn't fall. "I'd rather not. Not right now. I've already told you more than I've told anyone else."

I accepted Hauser's answer and didn't press. I already felt fortunate that he shared so much with me so soon after taking Wilson's position.

"So what do I do now?"

"Well, have you looked at your box since you freed your mark?"

"No. I don't mean that. What about me and the Sentinel? What are you going to tell them?"

"Don't worry about that, kid. I'm supposed to discourage your ability to alter reality. That's why I was so hard on you earlier. Everybody in our profession knows how much they can push the boundaries. I'll smooth it over with them and it'll be like nothing happened."

"I'm speechless, Hauser. Thank you."

"Don't mention it, kid. Now, where is your box?"

I pulled Noah Clayton's box from my pocket and held it in my hand. At the same time, Hauser pulled a glass vial from his own inside pocket.

"Go ahead and open it up," Hauser instructed.

I did so, curious as to what Hauser was up to. As I turned the open box toward him, he removed the rubber stopper from the end of the vial, and a very faint wisp of smoke floated out and into the box. The box closed and vanished.

"Don't I need to cleanse it first?"

"Nope. That was a clean, virgin soul. Hot off the presses, so to speak."

Curious, I asked, "And where exactly did you get a vial of a brand new soul?"

"Um, where is of no concern. The big guys upstairs know nothing about it, and I'd like to keep it that way."

"Mums the word," I said as a replacement box materialized in my hand.

"That's strange," I said as I turned the box over and over. "This box is like the last one. No name."

"Give it a minute. Sometimes they're a little slow to catch up."

Hauser and I sat on the bench, both intently focused on the box.

After what felt like an eternity, Hauser's eyes narrowed. He looked into my eyes and uttered two words.

"Oh, dear."

Book 5

NAPOLEON'S ASSASSIN

Chapter 1

Having maneuvered the endlessly stark hallways dozens of times over the past few months, I still couldn't get use to the stench. A sterile, antiseptic smell hung in the air like an arctic fogbank as I passed through the bleak corridors. Walking along, I could practically feel my energy being sapped from above. I knew it was a figment of my imagination, but I still found it oddly ironic that in place such as this, where life preservation was the standard, the harshness of the overhead lights seemed to counteract that exact intention. I wondered why it was different in other parts of the hospital; color and life were prevalent throughout the decor, but here in the Intensive Care Unit, white was the preferred palette.

Moving into the central core—the bullpen—I glanced at the personnel behind the counter. Having been a constant shadow in the ICU wing, I felt I knew the entire staff by name. When I saw a new male nurse standing near the coattails of one of the doctors, my interest was piqued. In all the time I'd spent searching for the owner of the soul I was there to collect, I had never once considered that it might actually be a doctor or a nurse, and not a dying patient.

I walked toward them in hopes of gleaning the new employee's name. As I stood near, listening to the doctor ramble on about the various patients' conditions, I looked over the nurse's uniform for any indication of his name. Unfortunately his ID badge had been flipped over, and I was unable to read the front side.

Finally, after several minutes of boring medical jargon, the doctor asked if Theo had any questions. After hearing his name, I didn't stick around a moment longer.

I walked out of the bullpen and headed directly to room 742. As I approached the opening, I glanced at the medical chart hanging just outside, where the name Alistair Hobbs was printed clearly. I smiled and walked in.

As I slid the door shut, Hobbs looked up at me from his bed and smiled. "Hey, Jack. What's the good word?"

"You know. Same shit, different day. How about you? Hanging in there I see?" I said.

"Well, I'm as surprised as you are. With the way these doctors and nurses prick and prod me, I feel like a human pincushion," Hobbs said as he adjusted the oxygen tubes near his nose. "Have any luck?" he asked.

"Unfortunately, no. I'm just starting my rounds for the day, but . . ."

"Hey, Jack. Keep your head up. I'm sure Calvin will present himself when it's time."

"I hope so, Alistair," I said, nodding. "Speaking of, did you by chance get any information out of the staff?"

Hobbs rolled his head from side to side as it rested on the pillow. "Sorry, pal, but as soon as I brought up another patient, they shut me down pretty quick, telling me that information was only released to family members. I couldn't even get anybody to confirm or deny that there was anyone named Calvin even admitted in the hospital." Hobbs closed his eyes and took in several deep breaths.

"You doing okay, Alistair?" I asked. "You look a little out of sorts."

"Hey, you know. One minute I feel like I'm doing better, then the next I feel like I might not make it to my afternoon sponge bath."

"And still no word? Your collector hasn't shown up yet?"

"Nope. The only ghost I can see or hear is you, my friend." Hobbs winked and smiled.

"Well, I'm sure that you're not in any rush to move on into the afterlife, but if I'm seeing you and talking to you, I'm sure your collector is on their way."

I felt awkward talking to Hobbs about his imminent death, but when I first met him two weeks ago, he had fully accepted the fact that he was going to die. In fact, he practically welcomed it with open arms.

"Is there a number you can call or something? You know, and request some assistance for me?" Hobbs asked with a grin.

"Ha ha. If there is one, my trainer didn't give it to me. But as soon as I see him, I'll ask him about the hold up. I'll make sure he comes to visit you right off. Deal?"

"Thank you, sir. It's not like I'm dying to get out of this world," he said with another wink and a chuckle, "but if it'll help with this pain, I'm ready to go now."

"Sounds good, Alistair. I'll keep you in the loop. But for now, I'm gonna go take a walk through the emergency room. With any luck, maybe my Calvin is just checking in. If I don't talk to you before, be sure to have a happy afterlife."

Hobbs nodded his head, then closed his eyes to sleep.

Stepping back into the nurse's galley, I decided to run by the patient board to see if any new names had been added. After a brief check, it appeared that someone had rewritten all the patients' names, eliminating all the first names from the list. All that was left was their first initial. I scanned through the names, arriving at a new patient's name that began with the letter *C*. A quick glance to the side and I found that he, or she, was in room 715. Without hesitation, I was off to look for Calvin.

"Please let it be," I said. I needed to move on from this soul and get out of this hospital.

As I sped through the stark hallways, I glanced at the room numbers as they decreased in count. Even numbers on the left, odd numbers on the right. Room 721. Room 719. Room 717. Room 715. I stopped in front of the door and took a deep breath before lifting the medical chart off the wall. It was clearly a new patient, as nobody had written in the patient's name on the board above the hook yet. As I flipped the aluminum cover open, my eyes darted to the top of the chart to the patient's name. Charles Grafton.

"Crap."

I slammed the medical chart shut and slapped it against the wall, barely catching the hook at the top. I felt like punching a wall.

"Dammit, Hauser. Why is this so difficult?" I said as I blasted out of the ICU wing and headed for the stairway.

"Hey, compadre. If you ask a question of me, you might want to stick around for the answer," Hauser called out from behind me.

Chapter 2

Hauser's voice halted my stride. I spun around and found him wearing a doctor's coat and a stethoscope around his neck. He was leaning casually against the side wall. I stared at him incredulously.

"What?" Hauser asked. "Didn't you just call out for me?"

Exasperated, I walked up to him, prepared to give him a piece of my mind. But before I could say a word, he threw his hands up in the air.

"Slow down there, Jack. You're the one that wanted to do this collection alone. I only gave you the space that you asked for. Am I wrong?" Hauser said.

"I . . . uh . . . yeah. I guess I did. I just thought that after—"

"Don't sweat it, kid. I get it. It's easy to feel the way you did after the successful sidestep of collecting your last soul. I guess I'd be feeling pretty invincible myself. But I don't think I would've handled it quite the same way as you."

"What? The same way as me? All I did was ask for some leeway on this new soul box."

"Yeah, I know. But it was the way that you asked for it. From the moment you got your new box, you started strutting around like you were omnipotent or something. I figured a little humble pie would do you well."

I could feel my heart beat faster but suppressed the building anger quickly. As much as I hated to admit it, Hauser was right.

"Well? Are you here to help or are you going to just continue to criticize me?"

"That's up to you, Jack. Do you want to carry on with training, like an adult, or do you want to hold on to your attitude?"

Goddammit, can't he just let it go?

"Careful, Jack. Your thoughts are louder than you might imagine," Hauser said.

Shit. "I mean, yes. I would like your help, and I will continue my training like an adult," I said, fighting back my temper.

"Great. Why don't you tell me what you've done up till now."

"Well, not a lot. I have the soul box with only a first name on it. It etched itself on the box shortly before you took off. But you already knew that. Unfortunately, the last name has yet to engrave itself, and for the life of me, I cannot find a soul bearer with the first name of Calvin in the entire hospital. Are you sure we're in the right place?"

Hauser's brow tightened as he listened to my update. He nodded his head. "Trust me, Jack. If I said you'd find him here, then he'll be here. Continue."

"Continue with what? That's it. I've been through the hospital more times than I can count, and I can't find a Calvin anywhere. That's what."

"Well, first off, I believe you're on the wrong floor."

"I only come down to the emergency wing thinking that Calvin might be coming in through an ambulance. I've spent the majority of my time up on the seventh floor. There's no Calvin there either. Trust me. I've looked."

"Relax, Jack. I know you're frustrated. I knew this would be a difficult collection from the very beginning."

Not exactly listening to Hauser, I continued. "I really thought with a unique name like Calvin, this collection would be so much simpler than how it has played out."

"Normally your process here would certainly produce desirable results. But for this soul, you might as well just throw all of that out the window."

"I don't follow," I said.

"What I mean is that tracking down a soul by only the first name might be successful if the soul you were here to collect was actually inside a living person. Jack, the soul you are here to collect has not even been born yet. We need to go up to the second floor, to the maternity ward."

"What the hell?" I snapped. "You knew this was going to be a newborn baby and you didn't say a word?"

"Well, you did say you wanted to collect the soul on your own," Hauser said with a smirk.

"Okay, okay. I get it. I messed up. I shouldn't have gotten cocky. But how did you know?"

Hauser began walking toward the stairwell. "I knew because I've collected souls from newborn babies numerous times over the years. I knew from the moment the blank box first arrived. Then, when the first name etched in, I figured I'd let you run with it. With the first name provided, it should have been a lot easier than how it was for me."

"Care to enlighten me?" I asked.

"The way I had it, I didn't get a name on my first newborn box. You see, the parents I had refused to name their child until the moment it was born. So I had to sit around for seventy-two hours until the box finally engraved. Once it did, it was a matter of deduction that led me to the dying child."

As we approached the stairwell door, we slowed our pace until the crowd around us dissipated. Once it was clear, Hauser blasted through the door and began the ascent to the second level.

"How'd you do that?" I asked. "Were you in a hospital? Or was this before hospitals were even invented?"

"Ha ha, smart ass. I'm old, but I'm not that old," Hauser said. "Yes, much like you, I maintained my presence in a local hospital. And because of where my location was then, there weren't very many births, so it was quite easy to locate."

As we stepped out into the second-floor hallway, I tried to imagine what Hauser's experience had been like.

"And that's it? You walk into the room and snatch the soul from a crying baby?"

"Taking a soul is never easy, Jack. You know that now, right? Just because the baby has no previous life experiences doesn't make it any easier."

Awkwardly, we stood in front of the glass wall surrounding the nursery in silence. We looked upon a dozen clear bassinets, with an infant wearing either a pink or baby-blue knitted cap inside each.

"Well, I guess we can at least eliminate any of the pink hats," I said. "But without a last name, how do we know which is the correct baby?"

Hauser pulled out his pocket watch and reviewed its face. A moment later he snapped it shut. "Well, none of these babies are your soul borrower. We're still early, and your child has yet to be born. Until that happens, we're going to have to do a little sleuthing in the matter."

"Sleuthing?" I asked.

"That's right, we're going to have to do a room-by-room search. See if we can find any clues on who our mother-to-be is."

"Don't you think that's what I've been doing for the last two weeks?"

"Obviously. But you were on the wrong floor entirely."

"Yeah, yeah. So you keep reminding me," I said. "So, wise sage, how do you propose that we proceed?"

"We'll just have to go into each birthing room and see if there's any indication on which mothers are having boys and then narrow it down from there. If there's conversation in the room, we'll listen for talk about baby names."

I sighed louder than I expected to. Hauser looked at me sideways, cocking his brow in question.

"Don't get me wrong, Hauser, but I almost prefer it to your old way.

"Boy, that's the lazy way. Whether you like it or not, we're going to do this. You need to learn to be proactive in these kinds of scenarios. And to make sure that you're not *phoning this in*, we're going to do this together."

"Oh, joy," I said as I pushed through the first door on my right.

Chapter 3

When I entered, I was surprised by the number of people that could actually fit in a room that was only fifteen foot square. Besides the mother-to-be, there must have been an additional dozen people waiting for the birth of the child. Fortunately, nobody paid any attention to me entering the room. Within seconds, Hauser materialized right next to me.

"You know, champ, you have certain skills that allow you to move about much more discreetly."

I nodded my head in agreement. "Yeah, I wasn't thinking when I pushed on the door. I'll be more cautious in the future . . . oh wise one."

Hauser winked and then moved through the crowd and stepped up to the bed. I followed, trying not to run into any of the people present.

"Well? Tell me what you see," Hauser said.

I surveyed the room, noticing a plethora of teddy bears and balloons scattered about—gifts from loving family members, no doubt. As I glanced down at the mother-to-be, I noted that she looked to be in good spirits but wore an air of tiredness. The man standing next to her, his hand woven into hers, was presumably her husband. He looked equally exhausted. The remaining people, all extended family, most likely, gave me no indication.

"I, uh, without looking at the medical charts, I . . . I'm out."

"What? You give up so easily?" Hauser said. "This one's an ace. Do you see all of the gifts?"

I looked around, taking in the deluge of gift-shop balloons and stuffed animals once again. I shrugged.

"Tell me, Jack. Were you color-blind before you became a soul collector, or is this a recent condition?"

The moment Hauser mentioned color, it hit me. All the balloons were pink. The couple were having a girl. I shook my head in disappointment and vanished.

I appeared outside the next room and waited for Hauser. Within seconds, he appeared next to me.

"There are signs everywhere, Jack. All you have to do is pay attention."

"Yeah, I'm not sure how I missed that one."

I stepped toward the door, and as I reached for the handle, Hauser gripped my shoulder and pulled me back.

"You know, we really don't have to go through each of these rooms when the medical chart is hanging right outside the door," Hauser said as he nodded to the familiar aluminum clipboard hanging next to the doorway.

Pulling the chart from the wall, I flipped it open and scanned through the pertinent information. Inside, there was the mother's and the father's names, along with their relevant medical histories. About midway down the page, there was a notation about the sex of the child. A capital F was present. Without wasting another moment, I flipped the chart closed and reattached it to the hook.

"Next," I said as I moved toward the next door.

Unfortunately, the next birthing room had no medical chart hanging outside, making our job slightly more difficult. I glanced at Hauser before raising my eyebrows and vanishing.

Popping into the room, we were met by a number of people. The pregnant woman in bed, her husband at her side, a slew of nurses, and a doctor sitting on a stool between the woman's legs.

Before I could comprehend the situation, the birth was already happening.

"Okay, Wilma. Are you ready?"

Wilma leaned forward slightly, her cheeks covered in tears. She nodded, then gripped her husband's hand. "I think so."

"It's time to push. Can you give me a solid effort?" asked the doctor.

In response, Wilma grunted and screamed as she pushed.

I glanced at Hauser, who was wide-eyed with anticipation. Personally, I had never witnessed a live birth in my life. And to tell the truth, the situation kind of gave me the willies. I thought back to my days in high school, when I'd freak out at the sight of blood. Now here I was at the precipice of life, and I wasn't sure how I would react.

I moved to the side of the bed, opposite of Wilma's husband, and looked toward the doctor. He was barely visible over the draped cloth covering Wilma's legs. Hauser, on the other hand, was completely visible. He stood directly behind the doctor, hunched over and looking up into the birth canal.

"Are you kidding me?" I asked.

"What? I find this all very exciting," he said.

"Okay then, any idea on the sex of this child? Is this something we really need to be sticking around for?" I pleaded.

"And miss the birth of a new life? No sir, I'm staying right here," he said, refocusing his attention between Wilma's legs.

I shook my head and looked around the room for any indication of gender. Unfortunately, the room was bare of any form of congratulatory paraphernalia. I did, however, locate the medical chart lying on the table next to the bed. I attempted to open it, at least to the first page, but as Wilma's husband continued to look in my direction, the chart wouldn't budge.

As I continued to search the room for a sign, any indication, the doctor continued to give instructions to Wilma and her husband. Hauser remained stationary behind the doctor. After surrendering to the fact that we would have to wait for the birth to occur, I moved to Hauser's side to see exactly what had captured his interest.

"Huh, this . . . isn't quite what I was expecting to see," I said as I peered over the doctor's shoulder.

"It's not like the doctor's performing some kind of a gruesome autopsy on the woman, Jack. He's helping her bring new life into this world. I think it's quite beautiful."

Within moments I could see the crown of the baby's head between Wilma's legs. Centimeter by centimeter, the newborn squeezed through the birth canal, and suddenly a brand-new baby boy was out and alive. The doctor expertly received the child and swiftly laid it atop the mother's stomach. Then, one of the nurses handed the doctor a number of medical instruments for him to clamp and sever the umbilical cord. A minute later another nurse scooped up the newborn and presented it to the parents.

"Congratulations, Mr. and Mrs. Coulter. I present you your son."

Wilma took the quietly crying baby from the nurse and gently laid it across her chest. Then she looked up at her husband and said, "My God, honey. Isn't he beautiful? What are we going to name him?"

The husband, who stood valiantly next to his wife, changed three shades of white. It was clear that he was overwhelmed with emotion.

"I think we should name him Neil, after your dad."

"Yes. I'd like that. I only wish he was here to see this," Wilma said between her own sobs of happiness.

Fighting back my own emotional outburst, I vanished from the room.

I popped back in the hallway right outside the most wonderful spectacle of life that I'd ever witnessed. I leaned against the wall and wiped my eyes dry before Hauser arrived.

"Wow. What a beautiful moment," Hauser said, leaning against the wall next to me.

"Yeah, it was quite something."

At that moment I knew, as sure as I've known anything else in my entire existence, I was not cut out for this job. How on earth was I going to be able to collect a soul from a newborn baby after witnessing that?

"I understand, kid, but it's not our choice," Hauser said, answering my thoughts.

"But how can you say that after what we just saw?" I asked, pushing myself away from the wall. I paced back and forth in front of Hauser before I continued. "I mean, that was . . . extraordinary."

"I agree, Jack, but some things are out of our control."

"Can't we save him? Like I did with Noah? And like you've

done numerous times in the past, on your own?"

Hauser fell into stride beside me and we continued walking down the hallway. "Listen, Jack. Just because you were able to make a change with Noah doesn't mean that you can make a change for everyone. Not all souls can be saved. And trust me when I tell you this, some souls are better off dying."

Hauser's words stung like a swarm of bees. "How can you say that? Isn't every life precious?"

"Well, according to you, only the good people should live and the bad people should die. Isn't that what you tried to tell me just a couple weeks ago?"

"Jesus, Hauser, why do you always have to throw that shit back in my face? You know what I mean here. This child, this Calvin, hasn't even had a chance to live and here we are, ready to take his soul without question. Don't you think there's something a little bit demented about that?"

"Relax, Jack. There are reasons why we do our job without question—"

"And I'm questioning it. I don't think this is right, to take this life away from loving parents. Losing a child at birth is going to decimate their lives. And I won't be any part of it."

"Come now. Be reasonable about this—"

"No. I am being reasonable. I refuse to collect the soul," I stated firmly and walked away. As I neared the adjacent corridor, I vanished.

Chapter 4

When I appeared at my bench, all I could think about was how unfair life really was. Over the years I'd heard from many people about the magic of childbirth. I'd heard about how wonderful and life-changing the event really was. But without ever experiencing it firsthand, I'd always assumed that those people were exaggerating greatly. Now, after witnessing just a single childbirth firsthand, I knew that assumption couldn't be further from the truth. For as long as Cyndi and I had wanted children, I'd never really considered what it really was that we desired. I'd assumed what we wanted was something to love and raise as our own. Throughout all of those conversations with Cyndi, never once had I given thought to what it really meant to bring life into the world. Witnessing that childbirth would forever stain my mind. My soul. And if the Sentinel expected anything different from me, we were going to have a problem.

As I sat alone, contemplating the situation, Hauser appeared in front of me. He stood, his feet shoulder width apart and his hands on his hips. He glared down at me as a disappointed father might. I stared back and uncontrollably rolled my eyes.

"What's going on, Jack?" Hauser asked. "One minute you're fine, and then the next you storm off like a child that didn't get his way."

"Well I guess I didn't really know what I was signing up for when I took Wilson's soul. I'm sorry, but I never really asked for this."

"No, I suppose you didn't. But the fact of the matter is, you accepted Wilson's offer, and according to the Sentinel you are expected to carry out that responsibility." Hauser's stare relented slightly as he sat down next to me. "What we have, Jack, is a responsibility. Yes, it's a difficult proposition, but it really is quite spectacular, what we do. We've been given the opportunity to maintain the balance of humankind. Whether you see it like that or not is totally up to you."

"But what about Noah? How was saving his soul even possible? How is that keeping the balance? You and I both know perfectly well that what I did there was the right thing to do."

"Jack, I don't know that. And how can you? For all we know, Noah might turn out to be wife-beating baby rapist—"

"Stop it. Just stop. Based on everything that we've witnessed so far in his life, I made the absolute right decision. And there's nothing you can do to take that away from me." I turned away from Hauser, hoping to screen my thoughts. Talking about Noah had brought up the thought of changing yet another soul's future.

"Jack, you can't. Just because you were able to save Noah does not entitle you to save every single soul that you come across. Sometimes, you just have to do your job—without question. You are not judge and jury, and neither am I. We cannot continue in this godlike way."

Why does he keep telling me I'm trying to play God when all I want to do is save a soul, I wondered.

Why can't he just get it through his thick head? This child's soul is not worth the agony and potential sacrifice of something far greater. If he could just only understand that—

"How can you say that, Hauser? How can you say that his soul is not worth a damn?"

Hauser's eyebrow arched slightly and he fidgeted nervously with his hands. "I'm sorry, Jack. I'm usually more in control of my thoughts. You were not meant to hear that. The good news is that it appears that you are developing your ability to read thoughts. Or is it all too late for that?"

"Hauser, there is no good news about this entire fucked-up situation. Having this new ability is not my consolation prize for having to take the soul of an innocent child."

"No, I never said it was."

"But you certainly implied it. And maybe it is too late. I'm not sure if I want to continue this . . . this heartless job."

"What are you saying, Jack? Are you gonna quit on me?"

I rose up from the bench and stood directly in front of Hauser. I looked down on him blankly. "Yeah, I guess I'm done. This isn't what I signed up for."

"Well, sport I have news for you: you just can't quit. You have an impending soul collection, and until that contract is filled, you're on the clock."

"Fine. If that's the way it is, then so be it. I will just give my soul in place of Calvin's. That way, everybody's happy. I've saved a child's soul, and I am no longer a pain in your side."

Hauser laughed. "Jack, you surprise me. One moment you show utter brilliance and then the next you spew out shit like that. Think about it, man. You can't give your soul away to an infant child that can't even walk or talk yet."

"Why does that matter? I'm allowing this baby to live."

"Don't be daft. You know very well that if you give your soul in his place, he will become the next soul collector. How can he do so if he can't communicate with the dying people that he's there to collect from? That's not an acceptable option. Try again."

"Well, then I guess we're at an impasse. I'm not going to take his soul, and there's nothing you can do to change my mind," I said, sliding my hand into my pocket and gripping Calvin's soul box firmly.

"Jack, I'm very disappointed in you. I had hoped that you would be able to see through this and move forward. But I see you're not leaving me, or the Sentinel, any choice. Hand over the box and I will collect the soul myself. Meanwhile, you will have to report to the Sentinel for disciplinary action." Hauser held his hand out expectantly.

I maintained the grip on my box and took a step backward. "There's not a chance in hell that I give you this box," I said.

Then I vanished.

Chapter 5

When I landed, I was not standing at the destination I had imagined. Instead I stood in a stairwell that twisted and curved up at a precarious angle. The passageway was tight, and the surface of the walls around me were equally bizarre. Having lived in New York for most of my life, it didn't take me long to realize exactly where I stood.

I began to climb the worn steel treads up to the observation platform inside the head of the Statue of Liberty. I wasn't too far off from where I'd imagined my destination to be. I'd initially thought about the immigration building on Ellis Island, which was a short five-minute ferry ride away. But as I weaved myself through the scattering of tourists trying to get a view of New York, I decided that this was actually a better destination after all.

As I leaned into the opening to catch a view of the city for myself, the voice behind me killed my buzz.

"You know, Jack, you can run, but you can't hide," Hauser said as he twirled his monocle around his finger.

"Jesus, Hauser. Why can't you just let me be? I've already given you my decision. I quit."

"That's fine, pal. Just hand over the box and you can go on your merry way. I'm sure with your current mindset, Enoch can guide you the rest of the way," Hauser blurted.

Startled at hearing the name from my dreams, I wondered what he meant by it.

"And like I said, nobody will be collecting Calvin's soul. Not if

I can stand it. Now, if you'll excuse me," I said before disappearing once again.

This time when I reappeared, I stood in front of one of the more than twenty entries leading into the grand bazaar in Istanbul, Turkey.

"Good luck finding me here, chump," I said aloud. I took a few steps through the first entryway before I vanished once again.

I continued to jump and land at another of the dozen or so entries, pausing just long enough to leave a faint trace before landing at the center of the site. Where I stood, several hallways met beneath a white domed ceiling. As I gazed down each passageway, determining my best route out of the bazaar, Hauser's familiar voice once again invaded my head.

"You know, I can do this all day long. Shall we just stop this nonsense?" he asked.

Overwhelmed with frustration, I squeezed my fists, driving my fingernails into the palms of my hands, before I vanished without another word.

I landed in the middle of the most tourist-laden place on earth—Times Square. From my vantage point, I could see no fewer than two Spidermen, one Batman, three Elmos, and one cowboy playing the guitar in his underwear. I smiled at the melting pot of oddity that was my hometown. Before Hauser could track my scent, I disappeared once again, and headed for another faraway land.

When I landed, I looked around at my surroundings, unsure of where I would be. I'd simply thought of an exotic location that I had not been to before. Who knew that the Parthenon in Athens, Greece, would be my destination? Without a second thought, I vanished from the base of the Parthenon and materialized at the tallest peak of the structure. I slowly eased myself down and sat with my legs dangling over the edge. From my new position, I could see the entire city of Athens, surrounded by water at the far reaches of my sight. As I took in the beautiful scenery, I wondered if Hauser would continue to follow me, and whether or not I would ever be able to escape his reach. As the seconds turned to minutes, I waited. I anticipated yet another interaction that I knew deep inside would be inevitable.

After fifteen minutes of solitude, I began to think that I might have actually done it. I'd finally gotten away from Hauser and his unreasonable expectations. Then, suddenly, I felt his presence.

"Are you kidding me?" I gasped.

Before Hauser had a chance to reply, I left Greece, my destination unknown.

I continued to jump and land at several nondescript locations in an effort to flee from Hauser's grasp. Each new location was far from the last in both position and scenery. A cornfield in Illinois, a mountainside in the Andes, a city park in Paris. On what I hoped would be one of my final transports, I landed in the midst of thin, wintry air. All around me were great plains of ice. I took a moment to consider my latest destination and realized I should've grabbed a jacket first. If I planned to be in the Antarctic for any period of time, I would certainly freeze to death.

Before I could let that thought sink in, I began to jump from ice cliff to ice cliff. With each new jump, I came closer to the frigid oceans surrounding my location. Feeling fairly confident that I had eluded Hauser for the time being, I quickly jumped back to New York and into a department store to grab a parka before returning to the exact spot on the ice shelf to wait. I donned the coat, lowered myself down, and sat in silence. I was amazed at just how quiet it really was. I'd always imagined that a place such as this would be bombarded with windstorms whistling across the frozen ground.

As I waited, my mind returned to the maternity ward at the hospital. Seeing the complete and utter joy that had spread across Wilma and her husband's faces would forever grip my soul. I knew it wasn't their child that I was there to take, but I was certain that I would be destroying another couple's happy future. I shook my head in disgust as the first bout of shivers rumbled through my body.

Then, suddenly, I was no longer alone. Feeling defeat once again, I looked over at Hauser. He sat next to me, also wearing a parka. How did he know he'd need a jacket?

"Just like you, kid, I landed and jumped back to grab a coat."

I stared into his eyes, fixing my gaze sternly. "Please don't make me do it, Hauser."

"I'm sorry, kid. It's out of my hands. If you just give me a moment to explain—"

"There are no words that you can say that will change my mind," I said.

"It doesn't have to be like that, Jack. If you would just come back to your senses, and away from this godforsaken wasteland, I'm sure that you'll understand everything. But you just have to let me explain."

I sat next to Hauser a moment longer before standing. I looked down at him, still sitting cross-legged at the edge of the cliff. "I don't think so. I believe this will be the last time that we'll talk for quite some time," I said.

"Dammit, Jack would you just grow up," Hauser said.

Without another word, I disappeared.

Chapter 6

Back in the city, I descended the grungy stairway into the subway. In all my years living here, I'd only used this form of public transportation a few times. Once, right after Cyndi and I moved into our first apartment, and I thought taking the subway to or from work made the most economical sense. Besides the overcrowded nature, it was the smell and the transient population that curbed my appeal.

The second adventure into the underground came after an out-of-control holiday office party, and was one of the most terrifying experiences of my life. Cyndi and I had been robbed at gunpoint at 1:30 in the morning. After making it out alive, we both vowed never to set foot in the godforsaken place ever again.

Now here I was, going against our agreement from years earlier. I smiled, feeling the irony of the situation. Cyndi and I had said that we'd never again venture into the subway as long as we both lived. Now she was dead and I was . . . sort of dead.

Hopping over the turnstile, I stepped up to the platform and waited patiently. Glancing at the train schedule as I passed through the entrance, I knew it wouldn't be long. Within moments I heard the metallic clanking sound to my right as the train came to a halt directly in front of me. I stepped into the first car and quickly turned toward the door. I expected to see Hauser materialize any second, but he was nowhere in sight.

A minute later, the doors closed and the train lurched forward, causing me to stumble back. After regaining my balance, my equilibrium quickly agreed with the forward momentum of the train and I relaxed for the next five minutes. When I felt that we had traveled about halfway toward the next station, I thought about my next destination. A moment later I vanished.

I popped back into reality at the mouth of King's Cross station. Having been to London numerous times, I was familiar with the tubes.

I rode down an exceedingly long escalator until I reached the landing below. I paused at a monitor displaying the route schedules and noted that a train would be arriving momentarily, but I'd have to hurry. I sprinted through the maze of tile-faced corridors until I arrived at my desired platform.

Having only briefly thought through my plan while I sat on that frigid ice shelf, I wondered if I was just wasting my time, or if jumping from a moving vehicle would actually help conceal my trail from Hauser's monocle. I remembered him mentioning something about being able to track other soul collectors by the scent they left behind.

The sound of the approaching train grabbed my attention, and within moments I was onboard and sitting next to a man dressed in a pinstripe suit, reading a newspaper. The train was hurtling toward the next station. Again, once we'd traveled through the tunnels for ten or fifteen minutes, a sudden inspiration hit me like the train that I was on. I smiled as my next destination formed in my mind. A moment later I vanished.

I popped directly onto the platform in St. Pancras International Terminal, which just so happened to be the boarding station for the Eurostar. I'd read numerous times about the train and the construction of the Chunnel and felt that this final adventure would be the perfect crescendo in my evasion of Hauser.

As I moved through the crowd along the platform, I had a heightened awareness for Hauser's presence. Realizing that spotting him in a crowd of so many people would be futile, I relaxed and stood alongside the multitude of people waiting to board the supersonic train to France.

Ten minutes later, boarding had completed and the train was about to depart. Not having a paid seat, I simply mingled about the cabin until all the passengers took their seats. As the train began to inch forward, I found a vacant seat on the aisle and sat down next to a woman, speaking what I believed to be French, on her cell phone.

As the time passed, so did the city. The congestion of row houses gave way to single, freestanding homes, which in turn gave way to farms and fields. An hour and a half later, the train dipped into the ground and began burrowing through the tunnel under the English Channel. After another thirty minutes, I felt confident that I had effectively eluded Hauser's trace. I had a final destination in mind, but I wasn't prepared to go there just yet. I had one last stop to make before I was confident that I'd avoided his monocle for good. A moment later I jumped from two hundred feet beneath the surface of the water to nearly a quarter mile above the city streets of New York.

I stood on the 102nd floor of the Empire State Building, the observation deck, and stepped outside. I'd visited the building numerous times through the years, having a great love of the height and view. I walked around the entire perimeter, pausing momentarily at each face to look out across the vast city. Even though I'd been up there a dozen times, the view from the top was still awe-inspiring.

After some time I found a vacant bench near the north entrance and sat. I wondered how long I should wait for Hauser before making my final move. Ten minutes? Half an hour? Longer? I had no idea. I waited until it felt right.

After nearly ninety minutes of people-watching, I was quite pleased that Hauser had not been able to follow me. I stood up and stretched before making one last lap around the observation deck. Satisfied that I wasn't followed, I jumped to what would hopefully be my last destination for the foreseeable future.

Chapter 7

Many years had passed since I'd last stepped foot into the long-forgotten mountain cabin. When I was growing up, my dad and grandpa would take me up there to camp and fish almost every summer. After Granddad passed away, Dad and I sort of just stopped coming. Then, after my own father passed on, I got word that he'd left the two-hundred-acre mountain property to some nature conservatory with the express consent that no commercial development would ever occur on the parcel. He wanted it left as pristine and unabused as he'd found it years earlier. That had been twelve years ago, and I'd only taken Cyndi up to the cabin once to share some of my history with her. Because of my family, the conservatory manager granted me use of the place anytime I wanted, and assured me that because of the remote location, it remained virtually unchanged, following my dad's request.

Now, as I stood on the front step, my heart pounded from the anxiety caused by the passage of time. Memories came flooding back as I lifted a rusted watering can from the windowsill and grabbed an old skeleton key. Sliding it into the keyhole, I hoped that the lock mechanism wasn't decayed. I twisted the key gently yet firm enough to throw the tumblers. A second later there was an audible click. I returned the key to the window ledge and stepped inside.

As I looked about the one-room cabin, memories continued to flow. Dust and cobwebs covered nearly every inch of the inside, but I didn't mind. I found a broom and dustpan in the pantry cabinet and got to work cleaning.

After an hour's effort, I had removed most of the visible grime from the walls and ceilings and dusted everything as best I could. In the process, I reminisced about the numerous days that I'd spent there in my youth.

With the sun quickly plunging behind the adjacent mountain range, I decided a fire was in order. Even though I was mostly dead, I still got the occasional chills.

With relatively little effort, I had a fire roaring in the open fireplace, thanks to the extremely dry kindling I found in the corner. As I kneeled on the floor in front of the heat, I felt the bulge of Calvin's soul box in my pocket. I withdrew it and turned the box over in my hands, wondering what I should do. The worst part about my decision was that I knew Hauser was right. I knew that neither he nor I had the right to decide who lives or who dies. I was playing God. But as these regretful thoughts spilled from my subconscious, images of the happy couple in the maternity ward crowded my mind's eye. Confusion quickly turned to anger, and I threw the soul box into the fireplace.

"There. I guess I've answered that question," I said as the flames flared high around the wooden box.

I moved away from the fire and settled into the dilapidated sofa at the side of the room. I extended my legs out to relax and stared at the amber glow. The longer I gazed at the dancing flames, the less aware I was of my surroundings. As time crawled along, so did the shadows across the floor. I retraced the events of my day, thinking about all the places that I'd visited in such haste. I quickly concluded that all of that jumping and landing really wore me out. Before I could stop myself, I was drifting to sleep.

The faint glow of the moonlight cast eerie shadows along the floor. I wondered how that could be as the room was fully lighted by multiple ceiling fixtures above.

"Quick, Jack. Take my hand," Cyndi demanded as she closed her eyes tightly and gritted her teeth.

"It's almost over, Cyn. Just another ten seconds," I assured her.

She squeezed my hand tightly, cutting off the circulation to my fingers. I remained strong for her support, but the pain was nearly enough to make me cry out as well. Finally, with the contraction subsiding, Cyndi released her death grip and opened her eyes.

"My God, that one was the worst," she said.

As if on cue, the doctor stepped into our birthing room and proceeded to hunker down between Cyndi's legs to perform a cervical exam. Peeking over the bed cloth, his piercing eyes looked at me first and then at Cyndi. A sudden sense of familiarity came over me, but I couldn't quite place where I had seen him before. Strangely, this was not our regular doctor, but I was not about to question it in the eleventh hour. I wanted the pain to go away for Cyndi. I wanted my new child.

"Your husband is quite right, Mrs. Duffy. It's almost time, and it'll be over quite soon, I assure you," said the doctor.

"Do you hear that, sweetheart? We're about ready," I said as I leaned in and kissed her forehead. "Now, take my hand again, and squeeze as hard as you want. I'll share your pain, because I love you."

Cyndi's weary eyes rolled back momentarily and she smiled. She took my hand and tugged on my arm slightly before replying, "I love you too, babe."

"Well then, shall we begin?" asked the doctor. "I need you to push, Cyndi. And when I tell you, I need you to push hard."

Cyndi pinched her eyes closed but nodded in agreement.

"Now, Cyndi, push for ten seconds."

With a guttural squeal emanating from her lips, Cyndi followed the doctor's instructions. After ten seconds, she released her downward pressure and breathed in and out, rhythmically, as we were taught in Lamaze class. After a short pause, the doctor spoke sternly.

"Push, Cyndi. Push now."

Cyndi squeezed my hand and cried out in pain. She pushed hard, and within seconds, she exhaled loudly.

"Good job, but we're not through yet. I need you to bear down once more, and push with all your might. I promise, Cyndi, this is it. The pain will be over shortly."

Cyndi took in several deep breaths and pushed our baby into

the world. Her final scream echoed through the room, then there was silence.

The silence was quickly replaced with the faint cries of the newborn baby in the doctor's hands.

"Congratulations, Cyndi and Jack, you have a healthy baby boy," the doctor said.

Tears of joy flowed from my eyes. I looked down at Cyndi. She cried as well, but for a much more painful reason.

"You did it, baby. You've given us a son," I said and kissed her warmly.

A moment later, the doctor interrupted our embrace.

"Jack, I need the box. Could you hand it to me?" asked the doctor.

"Box? What do you mean? Didn't you just tell me that he was healthy?"

The doctor sat up straight, still cradling our child in one arm, and removed a mask with his free hand. Instant recognition overcame me as I saw the face of Enoch Gant.

"What the hell?" I asked.

"I need your box, Jack. This soul needs to be collected, and a collection will be made."

"I will not. Just hand me my son, and you can go to hell," I said.

Enoch tilted his head back and laughed out loud. "The only way you'll hold your son is after I've removed his soul."

Cyndi's cries turned in to screams of fear. I released her hand and took a step toward Enoch and our newborn son.

"Give me my son, dammit," I demanded.

Enoch backed up slowly, turning our son toward us. Seeing him for the first time made my knees weak. I could see that he was warming up slowly, his flesh turning pink by the minute. He looked healthy. Normal. Then, he opened his eyes and stared directly at me. They were not baby blue as I expected, but were black, black as coal. A moment later the child smiled widely, opening his mouth and bearing a full rack of teeth, each one sharpened to a point. Suddenly the child began to giggle. Within seconds, the giggle turned into a full-on growling laugh. I jumped back, repulsed by what I saw. Enoch grinned at my reaction.

"You see, Jack, this baby is not yours. Never was. He's a product of the devil, and your only option in the matter is to release his soul to me." Then, both Enoch and the baby's cackling laughs joined in unison, causing Cyndi and me to scream in terror.

I lurched forward, raising my hands and aiming for Enoch's neck. Before I reached him, the room went dark.

I bolted upright, unaware of my surroundings. As my eyes focused on the slowly brightening room, I remembered that I was in the old family cabin. The fire had long since burned out, and the sun was peeking through the dirty windowpanes.

I stood and stretched for the ceiling, feeling the knots in my back groan in protest. Walking past the fireplace, I headed for the front door to introduce fresh air into the musty cabin. As my hand grasped the door handle, my mind slipped back to what I had just seen. I whipped around quickly and darted for the fireplace. Inside the burnt ash sat Calvin's soul box, completely intact. I grabbed it, noticing absolutely no blemishes on the surface of the collection chamber.

"Son of a bitch," I said. My mind raced at how else I could destroy the box. I rushed to the closet and rummaged through an old wooden toolbox until I found what I was looking for. I retrieved a five-pound sledgehammer from the very bottom of the box and grinned as I hoisted it from its resting place. Returning to the kitchen, I placed the soul box on the butcher-block counter and raised the sledge above my head. With all my might, I brought the head of the hammer down as hard as I could, driving it into the top of the soul box. The painful sensation that shot up through my arm and into my shoulder caused me to cry out.

"AHHH!"

As I regained my composure, I picked up the dropped hammer and laid it on the countertop next to the box. The undamaged box.

"Well, this might be more difficult than it seems," I said. At that moment, my next brilliant idea hit me like a ton of bricks. I returned to the closet and retrieved a spool of bailing wire. I rushed back to the counter and slowly, methodically, wrapped wire around the box and the handle of the sledge. Once that was complete, I gleefully grabbed the handle of the hammer and walked out the door.

Once outside, I headed around the cabin and ducked into the forest. A well-worn trail led from the clearing around the cabin, and if my memory served me well, would open up at Lake Sweeny, a small nature pond that was a long-lost secret in these parts.

The hike was just what I needed. I remembered the stroll through the forest taking ten or fifteen minutes in the past. But as the trail faded in and out from lack of use, I was led astray a number of times. Twenty minutes later, I finally found my destination.

The spring-fed lake was calm and still at this early morning hour. The occasional ripples caused by jumping fish in the distance were the only things that broke the mirrorlike finish of the surface. I contemplated dragging the old canoe from the shed but wasn't sure about its ability to float after so many years. I decided that I would rather test my arm strength than my sink rate.

I walked out onto the dock until I reached the edge. I stopped and looked around at the beautiful scenery. On all sides of the lake, dark green pine trees sprang from the edge, creating the perfect secluded fishing hole.

"Here goes nothing," I said. I began to swing the hammer like a pendulum, forward and backward then forward again. After a few practice swings, I released the hammer with the soul box tightly attached to it. It flew through the air gracefully.

Kerplunk! The water splashed several feet into the air, and then calm once again returned to the lake surface.

I turned and smiled. In fact, I smiled all the way back to the cabin.

Fifteen minutes later, I stepped out from the canopy cover of the surrounding forest. I paused momentarily as I noticed the old wood shed off to the side. Even though I didn't need to eat or drink, I had the sudden urge to fry up a beautiful lake trout for lunch. Stopping at the shed, I rummaged through the dozen or so fishing poles in the corner until I found my old favorite spinner reel. I grabbed the old tackle box and headed for the cabin to sort out the condition of the fishing gear inside.

As I stepped into the cabin, my eyes locked like a magnet onto the soul box sitting on the countertop.

"What the—" I blurted.

"You don't think you can shrug your responsibilities that easy, do you?" Hauser asked.

Chapter 8

"How'd you find me?" I asked, trying to hide my surprise.

Hauser smiled, then pulled out a pair of vintage wire-rimmed glasses and slid them on his face. "What do you think? Does it make me look . . . distinguished?" he asked.

I shrugged and avoided looking at him directly. I moved to the countertop and began untying Calvin's soul box from the sledgehammer.

"What? No comment about my new spectacles?"

"Okay, yes. You look very distinguished with your new glasses, Hauser," I said in a monotone voice. "I suppose you've had those this whole time."

"Nope. I actually have you to thank for these. If it wasn't for your little tantrum yesterday, I'm not sure when the Sentinel would've actually handed them out."

"Wait, what? You just got them?"

"Yep," Hauser said as he folded them and put them back in his pocket. "The latest and greatest from the masterful wizards that create useful things. They allow me, or whoever is wearing them, to see any active soul collector in the world. Pretty slick, huh?"

"Yeah, slick. So how does it work? You go up there, or wherever it is that you go to meet them, and tell them you have a problem, and they drop everything they're doing to create this new gizmo for you to, what? Become the bounty hunter of the afterworld?"

"No, not quite. I had this latest piece of hardware within an hour of you ditching me yesterday. I guess they'd had them ready for some time and were waiting for the right opportunity to release them into the collector circulation."

"I'm confused. Why'd it take you nearly a full day to come find me? If you've had a way to see where I was this whole time, why wait until today?"

"Well, buddy, after you lost me in the tubes of London—which I have to give you kudos for being very creative—I had a moment of clarity. I thought back to when I first became a collector, and how I struggled with the conflicting emotions battling inside me. I figured with the extraordinary training that you've already been through, you were bound to snap."

"Listen, I didn't snap," I argued. "I'm just not . . . willing to blindly collect random souls, when you and I both know that there is a better way."

Hauser nodded in agreement. "You're right. You're absolutely right, Jack. That's why I gave you some space. I needed you to find clarity on your own before I came to drag you back, kicking and screaming, if that's what it takes," Hauser winked.

"Why are you being so nice?" I asked. "You said it yourself that I've been a major pain in your ass through my entire training. And in your eyes, I threw this major tantrum, which we'll just have to agree to disagree about—"

"No, you threw a tantrum. There's no question," Hauser said with a smirk.

"Yeah, whatever. We all can't be as perfect as you at being an emotionless human, now can we?"

Hauser's winced slightly, then looked at his watch before stowing it back into his pocket. "Why don't you have a seat, champ. I see a lot of promise in you, and if sharing some of my past strengthens your ability, then I'm willing if you are."

Surprised at Hauser's sudden openness to share, I nodded and eased myself down into the lumpy couch.

Chapter 9

Hauser pulled up a wooden chair from the kitchen table and sat down across from me. He crossed one leg over the other and briefly fidgeted with his hands in his lap, clearly showing signs of trepidation. He stared off into space, as if looking for an invisible solution to his problem.

"You're only partly correct, Jack. I have far more emotion than I seem to let on. That's partly a carryover from my previous life." Hauser paused, folding his arms in front of his chest, then he looked directly at me.

"What I'm about to tell you is something that I am not at all proud of."

"If it's any consolation, I'm the last person in this world to judge," I said.

Hauser smiled. "Let's talk after you hear what I'm about to tell you. Before I became a collector, I was . . . a very bad man. I worked, if you would like to call it that, as an assassin . . . for Napoleon."

I inhaled sharply.

"See?" Hauser said. "It was shortly after the French Revolutionary Wars, and although a treaty was in place, the Napoleonic Wars were just getting started. I will not be in any history books. I was a . . . secret to Napoleon himself. At his charge I traveled through France, killing any and all British soldiers I came across, along with any French sympathizers for the British cause."

Hauser stopped and stood. He slowly paced around the small, musty cabin, almost as if he was looking for something. He opened all of the kitchen cabinets, finally reaching high on the top shelf and fumbling about with its contents. A moment later he withdrew a dingy bottle with a dark liquid inside. He removed the cork and brought the bottle to his lips. Tilting his head back, he poured half of the amber liquid down his throat.

"Whoa! That's got a kick," Hauser said as he offered the bottle of bourbon to me.

Nervously, I accepted the bottle and took a swallow. The phenolic sting glided down my throat and warmed me instantly. I handed the bottle back to Hauser, and he recorked it before returning to his chair.

"All in all, I killed nearly a thousand soldiers and innocent civilians between the years 1809 and 1811."

I gasped, much louder than I expected. I was speechless, but my mind was in overdrive, wondering what all that killing would do to a person's psyche. I couldn't imagine what Hauser had to cope with over the centuries, when here I was, unable to take a single soul from an unborn child.

"Sometime in the middle of 1811, Napoleon was beginning to lose his control. His victories in battle were becoming fewer and farther between. His defeats were increasing by the number. He began to lose focus at what he was fighting for, and I was eliminated."

"You mean, you were the reason for the decline of Napoleon?" I asked.

Hauser shrugged. "If you asked Napoleon at the time, that's precisely what he'd say. I was his scapegoat."

"So how did it happen?" I asked.

"How my life ended is not important. What came next is." Hauser remained seated as he uncorked the bottle and finished off the remaining bourbon in one long draw. "Sorry, kid. There's none left for you."

"No worries," I said. "I'm more of a Scotch guy anyway."

"Before I was killed, I suffered through four days of horrific torture at the hands of Napoleon himself. In between sessions I drifted in and out of consciousness. I struggled to maintain clarity on what was real and what were hallucinations. At one point, two men came into my cell and told me that they were there to collect my soul. I was sure at the time that they were simply hallucinations caused by the various concoctions given to me by Napoleon or his guards. I was further convinced they were hallucinations when they offered me to live beyond my death. They promised me a long life if I agreed to become a soul collector myself."

"So they recruited you?" I asked.

"Yep. After a few more encounters with the two gentlemen, it became clear that they in fact were real, and I wasn't conjuring them up as a form of mental escape. I listened to everything they had to say and figured that I had nothing to lose."

"If you've committed all of those murders, why did the Sentinel want you? Wouldn't they want to cleanse your soul of all its evil?"

"It was precisely because of all of those murders that they wanted me. They saw me as an emotionless individual and felt that having the ability to collect a soul regardless of how I felt about human life was an attribute they desired."

I was beginning to understand more about life and death and everything in between. "Then I might be a liability to the Sentinel."

Hauser nodded. "You might be, Jack. But a man can change."

"But I don't want to change, Hauser. I like caring for humankind. I can't become like you, an emotionless killer.

Hauser nodded. "Toward the end of my tenure as Napoleon's personal assassin, I began to grow a conscience. Something happened in the last year of my life that I can't quite put a finger on. I began to feel. I started letting people go that I was sent to kill. The feeling that flowed inside of me with each life that I saved was far more rewarding than that when I took a life. When the two collectors were sent for my soul, I knew I had an opportunity for redemption."

"So why did they send two collectors for you? Were they afraid that you might not come quietly?" I asked

Hauser chuckled. "No, not quite. One of the two collectors was retiring, and the other man would became my trainer."

I wasn't sure if it was the shot of bourbon that I had taken or if it was hearing everything that Hauser had just revealed, but I began to feel lightheaded.

"I know exactly how you feel, buddy," Hauser said, tossing the empty bottle into the fireplace, the glass exploding upon impact.

For several moments Hauser and I stared at the settling ash in silence.

"So is your trainer still around?"

Hauser's hands returned to his lap, once again fidgeting nervously. "Yes, and no."

"I don't understand. Do you know or not?"

"The man who trained me was Enoch Gant."

Chapter 10

"Holy shit," I exclaimed. "The same Enoch from my dreams?"

"The very one," Hauser said. "At the time, Enoch was the Sentinel's head trainer. He was the best at what he did, and he knew more about our line of work than anyone else . . . including most of the Sentinel's council. He, like myself, was quite young when the Sentinel brought him on. Also, like myself at the time, he had been a cold-blooded killer. Then, a few months after my training was complete, Enoch went rogue."

"Rogue? You mean he quit? Like me?"

"Not at all the same, Jack. The reasons for your resignation were righteous. Enoch became power hungry. He saw the potential in life, and death, and took it upon himself to live a different path on the run."

"And the Sentinel can't locate him? Maybe he died."

"He's believed to be alive, but unfortunately, the Sentinel has no way of locating him."

"What about your new spectacles? You were able to find me pretty easily."

"It's ironic that you bring up the glasses. You see, the Sentinel has been trying to develop an item that might have the ability to locate Enoch Gant. In fact, that whole R&D department, as you appropriately coined it earlier, was established with the sole purpose of locating Enoch. This latest item," Hauser said as he tapped his pocket where the glasses resided, "tracks any soul box. But Enoch is without a box in his possession."

"How did he—I mean, how did he—"

"Exactly. We don't know how he eliminated his last soul collection chamber. It happened so long ago that we don't even know where to look."

"Wow. You're really blowing my mind, Hauser. First you tell me you were a mass killer, and now you tell me that Enoch Gant, a man from my dreams, is real and is a wanted felon in the afterlife. What next? Are you going to tell me that God isn't real?"

"First off, God is in all of us. He is as real as the day is long."

"So God is a he, then?" I asked.

Hauser chuckled again. "God is neither he nor she. And both at the same time. He, or she, just is."

"Wow, thanks. Thanks for clearing that up for me," I smiled.

"As for my regrettable past, I continue, every day, to try to right the wrongs that I've done."

"Then why not let me save Calvin? He's an innocent child that could have a bright future."

"Like I said, Jack, not all souls can be saved."

"So you keep saying. Why is it that we can't save Calvin?"

"Because, Calvin will be born with a disease that will take him moments after birth. There is no cure for what he'll have, and if we were to allow him to live, his burden would far outweigh the sacrifice."

"My God, I had no idea. Why didn't you—hold on . . . wait a minute. How did you know, and why didn't you tell me?"

"Because you're in training, and I was trying to teach you patience and self-reliance. Also, the Sentinel believes that limited knowledge is best, in most circumstances. The council knows nearly every specific detail of literally every impending death in the pipeline."

"Then why not let us soul collectors in on that knowledge? It would make this whole job a lot easier, right?"

"One would think, champ. All I know is that the Sentinel has their reasons. I learned a long time ago to not question a lot of their mysterious ways. It's taken me centuries to gain their trust, and that means something."

"Well, I do apologize. You have certainly taught me a little humility after all."

"And for what it's worth, I was going to let you know earlier on, but then you threw your little hissy fit and didn't give me a chance."

"Yeah, I'm sorry about all that too," I said, dipping my head low to hide my embarrassment.

"So, are you ready to return to your obligation now?" Hauser asked.

"I am. But I have one more question first."

"Just one? Shoot."

"How is it that Enoch continues to invade my dreams?"

"Have you had another dream?" Hauser asked, clearly disappointed at my choice of sleeping again.

"Yeah, after all of that jumping around yesterday, I fell asleep in front of the fire," I said apologetically.

"Understandable," Hauser said. "When Enoch disappeared, he took with him all of the tools of the trade that he had with him. There was one item in particular that the Sentinel wants back like no other. It is a device that allows him to enter the mind of anyone that he chooses. Alive or dying. That's how he's able to exist in your dreams."

"Oh my. And there's no way to turn it off, or deactivate the device?"

"The powers that be are working on that very thing. But they've had no luck. So we're all encouraged not to sleep until Enoch is captured and the device is returned or destroyed."

A moment later, Hauser stood and returned his chair to the kitchen table. When he turned toward me, he glanced around and said, "You know, this place is very similar to my own humble abode. I'll have to show it to you sometime. I think you'd like it."

A moment later we vanished from the cabin.

Chapter 11

Hauser and I arrived in the maternity ward, very near where we'd last visited.

"You know, we still have the problem of only having a first name," I said.

"Well, Jack, we never really had a problem with that. I have a . . . gadget—"

"Of course you do. And where was this gadget earlier?" I asked.

"Training, compadre. I had to make you work for some of this. But now we might be cutting it close." Hauser pulled out his pocket watch and flipped open the cover. He held it out in front of us. On the face were several lighted dots. Some were brighter than others, while some flashed on and off.

"Okay, what does this do?"

"Each dot represents an impending collection. The brighter the dot is, the closer to its collection event. The closer the dot is to the center of the dial, the nearer we are in proximity to that soul," Hauser explained.

I pointed at one of the flashing dots. "And what about the dots that won't stay lit?" I asked.

"Those souls are still in flux. Those are . . . how can I say this? They still have options at life."

"What? So not every soul will be collected?"

Hauser cringed at my question. "Yeah, I knew this would come up at some point. Besides our own ability to deviate from filling individual boxes, with extreme prejudice I might add, some souls might continue living their lives."

"And who makes that determination?" I asked.

"Neither you nor I have any control of those souls. They are simply undecided—a decision based on the individual at the time of death, or impending death, rather. Take your soul, for example. If I'd been your soul collector, your soul would have flashed the majority of the day leading up to your collection. Suicide is the biggest unknown in our profession."

Being reminded of my selfish act once again, I lowered my head in disgrace. "Yeah, I guess that makes sense."

Wanting to change the subject, I took Hauser's watch and held it at arm's length as I slowly spun around. "It looks like there is a soul that is bright and close to the center," I said. I turned toward the long hallway. "And it appears to be just up ahead." I handed the pocket watch back to Hauser, who verified my assumption.

"Lead the way, Skipper," Hauser said, handing the watch back to me once again.

I walked down the hallway slowly, holding the open pocket watch out in front of us. Like Hauser said, the closer we got to the soul, the brighter the dot became, and all the other souls on the dial began to slide off the edge. It was as if the radar was zooming in to the soul the closer we got to it. When the soul was practically at the center of the dial, we stopped. I gradually swung my arm around in an arc. As I did so, the dot near the center circled around the dial, returning back to the center as I faced room 228.

"I think he's in here," I said.

I stepped toward the door and reviewed the medical chart hanging just outside. The name on the chart was Penelope Rose, and the baby's gender was male. I sighed and stepped into the room.

Once inside, it was clear that we were not in an ordinary birthing room. It was far more sterile and bland compared to the soothing colors and comfort level of the previous birthing rooms. Besides Hauser and me, the mother, Penelope, was alone. As we neared the edge of the bed, her face came into view. It was contorted, as if she'd been suffering the pains of contractions. Her eyes were closed and her entire face perspired.

"Well, no birth yet," I said to Hauser.

A second later Penelope opened her eyes and stared directly at me. "What, what did you just say?" she asked.

I was shocked to hear her address me and quickly glanced at Hauser for direction. He promptly pulled out his pocket watch to review, then shrugged but said nothing.

"I am . . . sorry, but you can hear me?"

"Of course I can fucking hear you. You're standing right next to me," she snapped angrily.

"I . . . I'm sorry, I thought I was . . . speaking in a quieter tone," I lied.

"Well, either speak up or get out!" she bellowed.

"I apologize," Hauser said. "We're just making rounds, and my colleague here was expecting a birth in this room any moment."

"Well, do you see a goddamn baby?"

"No, you're quite right. Please forgive the intrusion," Hauser said as he tugged on my arm to retreat.

As we approached the door, a doctor and several nurses walked in. One of the nurses stepped up to Penelope's bedside and began to review her vital statistics. Meanwhile, the doctor wheeled up a small stool at the foot of the bed.

"And how are we doing today, Penelope?" The doctor asked.

"How the hell do you think I'm doing?" she barked. "I'm nine months pregnant and in pain."

The doctor smiled briefly before continuing. "Well, let's see if we can fix that, shall we? Let me check your dilation and see where we stand." The doctor lifted the end of the bedsheet and slid his gloved hand beneath. As he reached deep under the covers, Penelope squirmed uncomfortably. A moment later the doctor withdrew.

"Well, unfortunately, your dilation has stalled. Right now our only viable option is to perform a Cesarean section. Are you familiar with the procedure?"

Hauser and I remained at the edge of the room, just out of Penelope's sight. Hauser withdrew his pocket watch and reviewed its face. A look of confusion filled his eyes as he tilted the dial to me. At the center of the watch, there were two distinct glowing dots. One burned solid, while the other flashed on and off. I looked at Hauser and raised an eyebrow. He returned my quizzical look and repocketed his watch.

As the doctor explained the surgical procedure to Penelope, she began to cry. He tried to soothe her, assuring her that although it was not common practice, it does happen in about thirty percent of all childbirths, and that she would be awake for the entire procedure. Penelope nodded slowly.

"If you'd like, your spouse can still be in the operating room for the birth," said the doctor.

"No. There is no father. It's just me," Penelope said softly.

"All right then. Nurse Perry here will prep you, then wheel you down to the OR." Hauser and I jumped into the corridor before the doctor made his exit.

"Well, how fortunate for us," Hauser said.

"How do you mean?"

"The C-section will make this soul collection much easier on everyone. Because Penelope will be on some fairly heavy anesthesia, she'll be slower to react to the death of her child than if she gave birth naturally."

"That makes sense, but how does that make it easier on us? We're still collecting the soul from a newborn baby."

"Unfortunately, that's unavoidable, but it will make it easier on us not having to witness the mom react as emotionally, otherwise."

I nodded. "I guess you have a point there."

"Now let's go find some scrubs so we can blend in while in the operating room. If Penelope is in flux, we don't necessarily want to alarm her by being the only two plainclothed men in the OR."

Chapter 12

We had little difficulty finding the supply room, but the procedure was still halfway done by the time Hauser and I entered the operating room. Penelope lay with her head away from the door, an anesthesiologist right next to her ear. Penelope's arm was extended out to the side and was strapped to a padded board. Multiple IVs were taped along her arm. She was awake but groggy.

On either side of her abdomen stood a doctor and a nurse. As Hauser and I approached, I mistakenly glanced down at the point of incision and nearly lost my lunch. Sitting on top of her chest were half of Penelope's internal organs. Having never witnessed an open operation before, I felt a little light headed. Instinctively, I turned my back to the doctor and focused on Penelope's face. Otherwise I was certain to pass out.

If it wasn't for the mask covering Hauser's face, I would have sworn he was grinning at my wooziness.

I looked down at Penelope, and she returned my gaze. She blinked her eyes slowly then shifted her focus to Hauser before returning them back to me. I nodded reassuringly, and she smiled. Quite the contrast to her behavior earlier.

Moments later, the doctor spoke. "Penelope? Can you hear me?"

"Yyyess," she slurred.

"Congratulations, Penelope, you have a son. Have you selected a name yet?" asked the doctor.

Maintaining my focus on Penelope, she nodded her head

almost imperceptibly. "B-B-Blake," Penelope stuttered.

As the nurse took the baby to the cleanup station at the side of the room, panic engulfed me. I quickly withdrew the soul box to read the name. Blake was not on the box. Calvin still was engraved clearly. As I showed the box to Hauser, he once again retrieved his pocket watch, flipping it open for both of us to see. It was apparent that the soul to be collected just moved to the far side of the room. A dot still flashed at Penelope's location.

"W-wait," she protested. "C-Calvin. Don't take my Calvin away," she cried, looking me in the face.

Hauser motioned me toward the faintly crying baby with his eyes. He nodded, then stepped between Penelope and the warming table, blocking her view.

As I approached the nurse attending to the newborn, I saw that she'd already cleaned the birth residue from his body. As he lay there, he squirmed slightly but was quite lethargic. A moment later, his body stopped moving completely, as his pink skin began to fade. The nurse began several resuscitation procedures, but there was no change. Calvin was unresponsive.

"Doctor? We have a problem. He's stopped breathing," the nurse said calmly.

The doctor rushed over and tried to revive the baby. After several minutes attempting to bring life back to the newborn, he dropped his head low and shook it. "Dammit," he cried.

A moment later a faint wisp exited the baby's mouth. I quickly retrieved my soul box and captured Calvin's soul. Forgoing the cleanse for the moment, I slipped the box back into my pocket.

When I returned to Penelope's side, Hauser looked at me expectantly. I nodded and patted my pocket. I then looked down at Penelope's tear-streaked face with a heavy heart. She was still groggy, but she was very aware of our presence.

"I am so sorry for your loss. I wish there was another way," I said.

Penelope nodded almost imperceptibly then closed her eyes tightly and sobbed.

Hauser and I disappeared a moment later.

Chapter 13

Back at my park bench, Hauser and I stood in silence for a moment.

"What the hell?" I asked.

"My sentiments exactly," Hauser replied.

"What just happened? I mean, we're not supposed to be able to be seen or heard by anyone living, right?" I asked.

"Yes, that's right. Unless the soul is in flux. But usually those situations act more like a living being than one that is about to die. They still shouldn't be able to see us until death is absolute or imminent." Hauser scratched his head in contemplation. Then his eyes brightened up instantly. "Quickly, Jack. Cleanse the soul and get your new box. Maybe Penelope's soul will be next."

I brought the box to my lips and inhaled sharply. A second later the box disappeared. Then, surprising both Hauser and me, two boxes appeared in its place. I looked at Hauser, whose eyebrows raised nearly off his head.

"Well, champ. It looks like you've graduated. You've got your first double collection from the Sentinel."

"But wasn't Abigail and Raymond a double collection?" I asked.

"Not exactly. Yes, they happened in quick succession, but were two separate collections. Usually when there is a double collection like you have now, the circumstances are quite different. The deaths will be nearly instantaneous."

"Like from an accident?"

"Typically, yes. That's how most multiple deaths occur," Hauser said slowly. "Unless . . . unless it is—well, never mind."

"Go on?" I urged.

"Unless there's some kind of catastrophe that causes multiple deaths instantaneously. Tell me, Jack, who are the two names on your boxes?"

I twisted the boxes in my hands until the names were clear to me. "Luke Holloway and Meghan Sharp."

"Well, neither of them are the baby's mother, so I'm not sure what that's about. Why don't you start tracking down your new marks, and I'll go find out what's up with Penelope's fluxing soul."

"Yeah, sure. But, before you go, what about—"

"Don't worry about it, kid. Your little temper tantrum earlier is water under the bridge. If the Sentinel really accepted your resignation, they would not have given you another soul box, let alone two at the same time. Let's just try and stay on target from here on out, agreed?"

Strangely, a wave of relief overpowered me. Part of me really wanted to be done with this godforsaken job. But at the same time, I felt at home. I felt right, like I was in the right place at the right time, doing the right thing.

"Sounds good, Hauser. I'll try and do my best."

"I know you will," Hauser said. "Now, if you'll excuse me, I need to—"

"Wait! I almost forgot."

"I know, kid. Alistair Hobbs. I've got somebody working on him as we speak. Remember," Hauser said as he dangled his pocket watch between his fingers, "I'm all knowing." Then he winked, turned, and vanished.

I leaned back on the bench that had been my safety zone for the past six months. Although the location was centrally located, I realized that in order for me to truly move on, I'd have to leave the city entirely. And walking away from the park bench was the first step.

I stood up and took in the cozy park and its unassuming surroundings one last time. "Good-bye, Wilson," I said, wondering if he could hear me from wherever he was now. "Thanks for . . . everything, I guess. But I think I'm going to find my own way now."

I turned and walked down the sidewalk, trying to decide whether to begin tracking down the borrowers of my next two souls, or jump to my cabin in the woods. My home.

A moment later, I vanished.

BOOK 6

CHAOTIC DUPLICITY

Chapter 1

A faint autumn breeze filtered through the partly open drapes in Luke Holloway's apartment, causing goose bumps to spread across Meghan's bare skin. She had just stepped out of the shower and paraded through the bedroom to her overnight bag for a clean pair of panties. Rummaging through her bag, she withdrew a pair of pink lacy boy shorts and quickly slipped them on. Next, she picked out a clean skirt and top before returning to the bathroom.

"You know, you don't have to get dressed on my account," Luke said.

Meghan smiled as she leaned her head back into the bedroom. "But if I walk out in public naked, people will point and laugh."

"The fact that people will point is a given. However, they will not be laughing. They'll be admiring your sheer sexual appeal," Luke said, tossing the bedsheets to the side.

Meghan giggled girlishly before ducking back into the bathroom to finish dressing.

Luke moved to the window and closed it to within an inch of the bottom. He parted the drapes fully and peered out. Both sides of the street were lined with townhomes similar to his own. The sun shone brightly, causing him to squint momentarily. He reclosed the drapes, then pulled on a pair of gym shorts before joining Meghan in the bathroom.

"You know, it's still pretty early. Are you sure you have to go?"

241

Meghan was standing at the mirror, applying mascara to her already long lashes. "I know, babe. I wish I could. But we've had a wonderful three days together, and Dana is expecting me back around lunchtime."

Luke stepped up behind Meghan, wrapped his arms around her and gently kissed the nape of her neck.

"Luke?" Meghan pleaded.

"What? I was just . . . hoping to convince you to stay."

Meghan lunged her elbow backward sharply, forcing Luke to retreat.

"Oww," he gasped.

"Oh, stop, you big baby. We'll see each other again soon enough," Meghan said, then returned to the mirror to finish her makeup.

Luke rubbed his ribs soothingly as he moved into the living room. He sat on the sofa and thumbed through an irrelevant magazine while he patiently waited for Meghan to finish getting herself ready. Fifteen minutes later she walked out, dressed and looking vibrant. She looked around the living room, picking up the remnants of last night's undressing, tossing them into her bag as she went. Luke sat quietly, watching her every move. As she made a second pass, Luke began to smile widely. Finally, Meghan noticed.

"What are you smiling at, you goof?" she asked.

"Oh, nothing. Just formulating a bribe is all," Luke said.

"Oh yeah? What kind of bribe are we talking about?"

"You know. It's one of those 'makes one take notice of the situation' kind of enticements. Hard to resist."

"Okay. I'm intrigued."

Luke sprang from the couch and met Meghan in the middle of the living room. He kissed her lips, gently. She returned his affection but held her position.

"First, Meg, my dear, you have to close your eyes."

Meghan did so as a smile crept across her mouth. A moment later Luke slipped his hand into hers and led her through his apartment.

As they neared the bedroom door, Meghan said, "If your bribe is sex, you're out of luck. I've already tasted that morsel and—"

"Hush now," Luke said, guiding her through the door and up to the bureau next to the bed. "Okay, you can open them."

Meghan opened her eyes, and her confusion showed plainly on her face. "Oh, sweetie. How'd you know I wanted . . . furniture?" she said playfully.

"Okay, you. Now, open the top drawer," Luke said.

Meghan nodded and followed his instruction. The only thing inside was a set of black silk bra and panties. Matching, of course.

"Um, thank you?" Meghan said as she lifted the elegant lingerie from the drawer. "Oh look, and you even got my size right."

"Well, those are really for me . . . but, the drawer? It's all yours."

"Luke Holloway, you devil," Meghan said as she flung her arms around him, kissing him passionately. "I love it, I absolutely love it."

"Well, I figured that we've been spending more time together, and there's no reason for you to pack a bag every time you stay over," Luke began. "And . . . you can come by anytime you want."

"This is perfect! It's been a long time since someone has given me something so heartfelt."

"So you're not freaked out?"

"Not at all. I really do like this, you, everything. This is absolutely perfect," she said.

"Wow, that's a relief. I was worried that it was too soon."

Meghan weaved her hands through Luke's arms and hugged him warmly. With her lips brushing up against his ear, she whispered, "You did good. Consider the bribe a success."

A moment later, their lips met in an impassioned kiss. Then, Meghan pushed Luke away and held up the new lingerie.

"Now, seeing as this was for you," she said, smirking, "let's see how you look in it."

Chapter 2

The aroma of freshly pressed panini sandwiches wafted through the gourmet kitchen. Luke expertly worked the sandwich press while Meghan finished redressing.

"Soup's on," Luke said as he plated up two turkey and Swiss on herb-crusted focaccia sandwiches and set them on the kitchen table.

Moments later, Meghan walked in, having freshened up after just being ravaged. She dropped her overnight bag next to the door and joined Luke at the kitchen table.

"This smells wonderful," Meghan said as she sat across from Luke.

"What, this? It's nothing, really. It's just a product of my latest kitchen gadget, the Presto Sandwich Maker 2000," Luke said proudly.

Meghan smiled as she took a bite of her sandwich and glanced at her watch distractedly.

"Hey, I want to apologize if I've made you late," Luke said, noticing the action. "I didn't think my coercion would be so successful." He winked.

"Don't apologize," Meghan said, wiping her lips. "I'm the one that made you actually model my new underwear. If I hadn't taken the time to rip them off you and jump your bones, you'd just look silly walking around in them all day long," she joked.

Luke smiled, blushing at the embarrassment of actually wearing women's lingerie. "Well, I really am sorry, and to make it up to you, here's a small token as a peace offering." He slid a shiny brass key across the table.

"Oh. My. God," Meghan gasped. "I don't know what to say. Is that what I think it is?"

"Yeah. I was going to give it to you inside your new dresser drawer, but the sexy black skivvies won out."

Meghan slid her plate to the side and continued to stare at the key. She reached out for it, but paused before touching it.

"Go ahead. It won't bite," Luke said. "I want you to have it, and I'd like to remind you that you're more than welcome to use it anytime you want."

Meghan picked up the key and closed her hands around it. "Thank you, Luke. I . . . really am speechless." Meghan looked at her watch, and frown lines spread across her forehead. "I only wish that you'd have given this to me sooner so that I might have been able to thank you properly."

Luke blushed again. "Oh, I don't know. I'm not sure I'm man enough to handle you three times in a row, all before lunch," he joked.

Meghan moved around the table and dropped herself into Luke's lap. "Oh, I think you'd do fine. I would've done most of the work anyway," she said before kissing him deeply.

After several minutes of the passionate embrace, Luke pulled away and said, "Well, I guess I'm willing to give it a try if you are."

Meghan pecked the tip of his nose before standing up. She looked at him, her smile waning. "But there's no time. I've already called for a cab, and the driver will probably be here any minute."

"That's okay. Just call and cancel. I'll have my driver take you anywhere you need to go," Luke offered.

Meghan began to clear the table and said, "I don't know. I feel weird imposing on a US Congressman's son like that."

"There's no imposition about it. He's my personal driver, and he'll do whatever I ask of him," Luke said, rising up to distract Meghan.

Before Meghan could consider his offer, the sound of a honking horn echoed up and through the open window. Meghan peeked through the drapes and saw a yellow cab double-parked in the street, right in front of the townhome.

"Well, it's too late now. You'll just have to wait for your reward until the next time we get together." Meghan walked around the kitchen island and stopped in front of Luke. She leaned in for a final kiss good-bye. Their embrace would have lasted longer if the cabbie hadn't honked again. Finally, she pulled herself away and headed for the door. She lifted her overnight bag and paused before stepping outside, then turned toward Luke and smiled. "Thank you again for the drawer. I left you a little surprise inside, until next time."

A moment later, she was gone. Luke stood in the middle of the entryway, looking like a lost puppy.

"I give you an *E* for effort, my friend," I said, standing next to Luke. "But to me, it felt like that cat couldn't leave fast enough."

Oblivious to my presence, Luke rushed in to the bedroom and opened the top drawer. Inside sat the very same silky lingerie that he'd worn not more than an hour earlier. He smiled fondly.

"Well, sorry chap, but I have to go. If it hadn't taken me more than a week to track you down, I'd have more time to sit here and get to know your life better. But I have to follow your girlfriend and see what she's all about first," I said, standing next to Luke.

A moment later I vanished from his townhome.

Chapter 3

I popped back into reality in the backseat of the cab, right next to Meghan. The taxi driver was waiting patiently for a destination.

"It's 155 West 84th Street," Meghan said.

Without another word, the taxi sped off down the street. Visualizing the map of the city in my mind, I anticipated no less than a fifteen-minute drive. Seeing as it was the middle of a Sunday, traffic might be a bit lighter. But then again, this was New York. There was no such thing as light traffic.

Refocusing my attention on Meghan, I studied her persona. She wasn't much older than me, possibly in her mid-thirties. Having just recently seen her completely naked, it was quite apparent that she was a fan of exercise. And from the brief time that I'd been around her, she flaunted it proudly.

As the driver merged into traffic on the next street, Meghan pulled her smart phone from her purse. A quick finger swipe and her screen was unlocked. Seconds later she'd brought up her messaging app. As her fingers danced across the screen, I leaned in close to see who she was texting.

There were no recent text conversations to continue from, so she began tapping a few letters until her contact list populated. She typed *D-A-N*, and the first contact up was Dana. She picked the name and tapped out the message, *On my way. Got delayed,* then hit send.

She rested the phone in her lap and looked out the side window of the cab, blankly. A few minutes later, her phone came to life.

Ding.

Great. I'm starved. Waited for lunch till you got home. Chinese?

She smiled briefly, then tapped in a reply: *Yes, please. Sriracha Beef for me. You know I like it hot.*

Seconds later, Dana replied: *Ordering now.*

Meghan once again rested the phone in her lap as a look of deep concentration passed over her face.

After a few moments, she lit up her phone again and tapped in a new contact, *J-E-N-N*. When Jennifer appeared, she selected the contact and tapped out a message, grinning from ear to ear as she went. *OMG! Luke gave me a key!*

As Meghan waited for Jennifer's response, she beamed continuously, like a giddy school girl. Ah, young love.

Ding.

R U 4 REAL?

I snorted out loud at reading the abbreviated text acronyms. Before she could reply, her phone dinged again.

I miss you already, read the text. There was no personal name associated with the message, just the word *OFFICE* along the top.

As a heart attack! She tapped to Jennifer. *And aww! He's so sweet. He just txtd that he misses me.*

After a few more girl talk messages back and forth, Meghan replied to Luke that she missed him too. I assumed that *OFFICE* was her nickname for him. I wondered if it had anything to do with him being the Congressman's son.

As the texting conversation began to slow, I started to recognize our surroundings and knew we were moments away from our destination. Eager to find out more about Meghan's life and clear up some of the confusion I was having from reading her texts, I fidgeted in my seat like an impatient child on a long road trip.

When the driver turned onto 84th Street, I noticed Meghan quickly clear her texting history. Her motions were well rehearsed, and witnessing the deceptive task deepened my confusion.

Once the cab stopped, I vanished from the backseat, popped onto the front step of Meghan's apartment, and waited. She paid the driver and climbed out of the backseat, her overnight bag trailing behind. Within moments she stood next to me at the front door of her apartment. Interestingly, she rang the doorbell instead of simply walking in. A moment later though, she twisted the door handle and stepped across the threshold.

"Chinese delivery," she announced in a playful tone.

I stepped through the door after her and moved to the side of the entryway. I scanned the foyer and saw that it led toward the back, most likely to a kitchen and family room. To the left was a dining room, and to the right appeared to be a study. There was a narrow stairway ascending to the upper levels of the residence.

Meghan dropped her bag and purse at the base of the stairs and walked into the study.

"You're not the Chinese delivery person," a man said as he sat at a desk covered in paperwork.

Meghan smiled and walked up to him, then leaned in and kissed him on the lips. "No, but we can only hope that it gets here soon. I'm famished."

"I'd imagine so. How was the flight in?" he asked.

What the hell is going on here, I wondered.

"Oh, the usual. Getting a cab at JFK is continuing to prove more of a challenge than you might imagine," Meghan said as she began to retreat from the study.

"Hey, missy. Not so fast," he said latching on to her arm and pulling her into his lap. "I've missed you, baby."

"But the conference was only three days long—"

The man interrupted her pleas with another kiss on her mouth. "You taste salty, with a hint of basil?" he said

Meghan smiled nervously. "Oh, it must have been from the seasoning on the trail mix they had on the flight," she lied.

"Whatever it is, I like it," he said.

"You do, huh? Well, there's plenty more where that came from for you later."

"What's this about later?" he said. "You really have no idea how much I've missed you," he said, inching his hand beneath Meghan's skirt.

"Hey now, mister. Just because you're my husband doesn't mean you can have your way with me any time you like," Meghan teased. "Besides, isn't the Chinese food going to get here at any moment?"

"Husband? You two-timing cow!" I blurted.

Dana smiled coyly. "Your assumption would be correct if I'd actually ordered when we talked. I only got off the phone with them moments before you walked in."

"You sly dog. Were you planning this all along?" she asked.

Suddenly and without warning, Dana hoisted Meghan onto his desk and stood in front of her. "Maybe I was, maybe I wasn't. You'll never get the truth from me," Dana said dramatically, his hands continuing to caress the exposed skin of Meghan's legs.

"But if we do it right here, won't your paperwork get all messy?" she asked.

"Not to worry. I can print fresh ones," he said. Dana lowered himself back into his chair, with Meghan's legs straddling him. Slowly yet methodically, Dana slid his hands beneath Meghan's skirt before he tugged the pink lacy boy shorts from beneath. He dropped the panties to the floor and began kissing Meghan's knees, slowly inching forward.

Overcome with passion, Meghan moaned softly and lay back across the desk. A moment later, Dana's head disappeared beneath her skirt.

"Are you fucking kidding me?" I blurted. "Hauser! Where the hell are you? Did you know this about my new souls?"

Meghan's moaning stopped suddenly, and she pulled herself upright. A look of confusion spread across her face.

"What's wrong, baby?" Dana asked.

"I don't know. Did you hear something?"

Dana retracted his smiling face from between Meghan's legs and looked about the room. "I don't know, like what?"

"Voices maybe? I could've sworn that I heard . . . someone call out a name."

"The only name I would be calling out is yours, baby," Dana said with a cheesy wink. "But my tongue has been . . . preoccupied."

"No, I'm serious. I think the name was . . . oh, never mind. Now, where were we?"

Dana stood and quickly dropped his trousers. "Let me introduce you to my little friend," he said as he leaned into

Meghan.

I stood next to them, blown away by the deception. My first thought about the sudden, not to mention completely revolting, revelation was that Hauser may have been incorrect. Maybe my training wasn't over, and this current collection, so closely linked to my own past, was yet another lesson to be learned.

Thoroughly disgusted by the duplicity of the situation, I vanished from the study.

Chapter 4

When I'd felt enough time had passed so that I didn't have to witness Meghan's deceit in its full, carnal extent, I returned to them just as Dana had finished the last few morsels of his moo shu pork and began to eye Meghan's untouched egg roll.

"Are you going to finish that?" he asked.

"No, go ahead. I can't eat another bite. I'm stuffed."

Dana scooped up the eggroll and promptly dipped it into his sweet-and-sour sauce before taking a bite. As he chewed, he continued to stare at Meghan from across the table. He swallowed and washed it down with a long pull from his Heineken.

"So, tell me about your conference. How'd it go?" he asked.

Meghan pushed her half-eaten lunch away and leaned back in her chair. "You know, as good as a conference over a weekend can go, I guess. It was really kind of a nonevent to tell the truth."

Dana bobbed his head as he listened, maintaining eye contact with her.

"And the flight? Did you get an aisle seat or did you get stuck with the window?"

"Aisle," replied Meghan promptly.

A few moments later, Dana continued his barrage of questioning. "I forget, didn't you tell me that you stayed at the same hotel that we did last spring, before we were married?"

Meghan leaned forward, crossing her arms on the table in front of her. "No. I stayed at the Gerard this time."

"But wasn't the conference at that other hotel? The Radisson, was it? Wouldn't it have been easier just to stay there instead of spending half your time driving back and forth?"

"You'd think, but the Gerard's rates were almost half of what they were at the Radisson," Meghan said as her eyes flickered around the room.

"Huh. You don't say. You'd think that—"

"What's with the third degree?" Meghan asked. "You've never been this interested in my weekend conferences before."

"I don't know, Meg, you tell me. It's just that things don't quite add up lately."

"Don't tell me you're going to start that again," Meghan snapped.

"Well, can you blame me? You leave here every other weekend for some new conference or seminar, and when you return you clam up about everything that happened while you were there. I just don't know what to believe."

"For heaven's sake. For the hundredth time, I'm not having an affair. I am fully committed to you and this marriage."

"I really want that to be true, Meg, but didn't it take you four long months to even put in it for a name change at the DMV? It was like you were waiting as long as possible before you were willing to accept Sharp as your surname."

"That's not true. You know the hoops I had to jump through to get all that paperwork just right. I can't help it if they lost the same form several times."

"Tell me, Meg: Do you think we'll even make it to our one-year anniversary?"

"Where the hell is that coming from? Have I ever given you any sign of leaving you? Dana, you're not even thinking straight," Meghan said.

Dana leaned forward, crossing his arms on the table, mirroring Meghan's posture. "But you have, Meg. You leave me every couple weeks. That's how it feels to me, at least."

"That's not fair. You know how much I love you. You are my rock. If you'd rather me not work, I'd be all for that. But until the pet store can support our household expenses, I don't see any other choice but to continue on like we are now. And for me to work, I can't control when the company sends me out of town."

A moment later, she stood and circled around to Dana's side of the table. She wrapped her arms around his neck and kissed him on the side of his cheek. "I love you, baby. You can trust me."

Dana sat motionless for a few moments. Finally he reached up and caressed her arm and leaned into her cheek.

"All right, my pet. I'm sorry. I just get so jealous when I'm alone for too long. Between that and being at the pet store nearly full time, my mind really does wander."

"What? You're gonna believe this tramp?" I said from my seat on the countertop. "Don't trust a thing she says. She's just a cheating whore."

"Speaking of, how is the hunt going for your first employee? Have you found anyone worthy to hire?" Meghan asked as she returned to her seat.

"As a matter of fact, I did. It's been a hellish several weeks, interviewing practically nonstop. Finally, I hired a girl and she started on Friday. We went through the basics of the store Friday and Saturday, and she seems pretty quick at picking things up."

"That's fantastic, honey. Who is she?"

"Her name's Maxine. Yeah, I think she'll do okay. But still, it's just so difficult letting go of certain aspects of the business. You just don't know who you can and cannot trust in this world."

"Hey, buddy. I think you need a lesson or two in life lessons on how to read people," I said, not believing what I was hearing from this guy.

Dana leaned forward, staring into Meghan's eyes. "So, are we okay? Do you forgive my jealous tendencies?"

Meghan reached out, stroked his face, and smiled. "Sure thing, sweetheart. And I do apologize for being away so often. It really does take it out of me too, you know?"

"That I do," Dana said.

"Well, then if you don't mind, I think I might go up and take a quick catnap," Meghan said as she began to rise from the table.

"Sure thing, Meg. Why don't you do that and I'll take care of this lunch mess."

A moment later, Meg disappeared around the corner. The creaking sound of her climbing the stairway could be heard throughout the apartment.

Chapter 5

As soon as the sound of Meghan's exit faded, Dana sprang from his chair, rushed into the foyer, and grabbed Meghan's purse. Moments later, he returned to the kitchen and instantly began rummaging through the various zippered compartments. He finally found what he was looking for and withdrew Meghan's cell phone. Unlocking the screen, he went directly to her messaging app and started it up.

"Sorry, bro, but you're wasting your time," I said. "She already deleted everything."

A moment later, Dana discovered that very thing and sighed deeply.

Dana replaced Meghan's cell phone exactly where he'd found it, minding to return everything to its original condition prior to his search, then took the purse back into the entryway. When he returned to the kitchen to clean up, I decided to jump upstairs and find out if Meghan and Luke's well-earned demise was imminent. A moment later, I vanished.

I landed in the master bedroom and found Meghan already in bed. Her eyes were closed, but her breathing was still shallow; she wasn't asleep yet. I knelt down next to her and slipped the rosary over my head. Lightly grasping the crucifix, I touched the back of her hand gently and thought of a point twenty-four hours ahead.

Within seconds, I was standing back downstairs in the kitchen, and Meghan sat at the kitchen table, her eyes brimming with tears.

"I don't know, Meg. You say one thing but somehow mean something completely different," Dana said, leaning against the kitchen countertop, his arms crossed in front of him.

"I've already told you. I was at the conference. Why don't you believe me?" Meghan cried.

"You see, that's the thing. I wanted to believe you, but there was just something . . . something that wasn't settling with me. When I got to work this morning, my curiosity got the better of me. I called the Radisson, and guess what they told me?"

Meghan's eyes locked on to Dana's and her tears slowed. "You what? You checked up on me?"

"I did. And it was a good thing, too, because they told me there was no conference there this weekend. Tell me, my faithful wife, if you were not at the conference this weekend, where the hell were you?"

Tears returned to Meghan's eyes in full force. "I swear, Dana. I was there. I don't know who you talked to, but there was a conference and I was there. It was mandatory for all of the employees to go."

"Okay. Let's say I believe you. What do you have from the conference that you can show me?" Dana asked. "Hotel bill? Airline ticket stub?"

"Are you kidding me? Yesterday you tell me you're okay with everything, and now you're calling to check up on me? To track me down, to find out every movement I make?" Meghan stood up abruptly and stormed out of the kitchen. A moment later, Dana and I followed.

Dana caught up to Meghan in the foyer. "You know, this whole thing could all go away if you just show me something, anything that you took away from your 'conference,'" Dana said, throwing up air quotes in a dramatic fashion.

"Well, to hell with you. I'm not about to start justifying my every move for you. Not now, not ever," Meghan said as she slung her purse over her arm.

"So, what? You're just going to run away? Is that it? You're going to run away from this adult conversation we're having?" Dana asked.

"No, I'm walking away. From you. I need a break, and so do you. I'll be back later. And hopefully by then you'll have had some time to realize just how much of an asshole you're being about this entire situation." Then she walked out the door.

I released the rosary and was brought back to the present.

When my vision cleared, I was sitting on the floor and Meghan was fast asleep on the bed next to me.

"I don't know how you can do this," I said. "How can you sleep so peacefully with all of that deceit flowing through your veins?"

I stood and hovered over Meghan for several minutes as I contemplated my next move. My emotions were running high, and I needed an escape. Not an escape like Meghan, but I certainly needed a mental break from the adulterous situation. From what I'd learned in the flash-forward, I knew I had at least twenty-four hours before anything would happen. I formulated a destination in my mind, and a moment later I vanished from Meghan's bedside.

Chapter 6

When I reappeared, I stood in a cavernous warehouse filled with aisles of metal shelving stacked to the ceiling. As I made my way through the maze of storage shelves, I hoped that my stash of goods hadn't been relocated. A third of the way down the aisle, I arrived at a grouping of shelves that were host to several boxes with the name *Duffy* plastered on their sides. After shuffling around the first few empty boxes, I came to one that was full and quite heavy. I tipped the lid off and quickly filled each arm with volumes of my own books. I scooped up as many as I could carry, emptying the entire box. With my elbow, I nudged the lid back over the box and then promptly disappeared.

Landing in the middle of my new domicile, I moved to the side of the fireplace and began placing my prized book collection on the rustic bookshelves that I'd fabricated from reclaimed barn wood taken from the shed a week earlier.

One by one, I placed the books on the shelf, reciting each of the titles as I did so. About halfway through the second armful, a plain white envelope slipped out of one of the books. I sat the remaining books down before picking up the fallen envelope. I turned it over in my hand, but there were no visible words on either side. I didn't recall placing it in any of my books before, so I was at a loss as to where it might have come from.

Turning it back over, I flipped open the rear flap and looked inside. What I saw caused my heart to skip a beat.

"My God, I haven't seen this in ages," I breathed.

I backed up and lowered myself into my lumpy couch before sliding the envelope's contents out. I held a copy of Cyndi's and my marriage license, accompanied by several aged photos from our wedding day. From what I could remember, we had received the photos a few months after our wedding from one of our friends. Because they were so candid and unplanned, both Cyndi and I cherished them greatly.

As I flipped through the stack of photos, memories of our wedding came rushing back. I could remember nearly every moment of that day vividly, because it was the most cherished moment of my existence. I remembered having lunch with Cyndi that day at the restaurant where we had had our first date. We'd had the same meals on both occasions—a lasagna roll for me and fettuccine Alfredo for Cyndi. And just like our first date, Cyndi had barely touched her meal.

Fast forward a few hours, and I remembered standing on a raised brick platform surrounded by half a dozen bridesmaids and groomsmen. And then it had happened. I saw my beautiful bride-to-be being led down the aisle by her father, and my emotions would not stay in check. My eyes had filled with tears, but I had smiled from ear to ear. When I saw the pure joy in Cyndi's face as she approached, I had cried openly.

I shuffled through a few more photographs, occasionally wiping my eyes. When I reached the end of the stack, I slipped them back into the envelope and returned them to the bookshelf.

I rambled aimlessly about the cabin for hours, contemplating the similarities between Cyndi and me, and Meghan and Dana. I tried to figure out exactly what caused infidelity. Was it boredom? Was it weakness? Something else? I had no answers, but I did know one thing: I knew, as sure as I knew anything in this world, Cyndi had in fact been my soulmate. If that woman could continue to haunt my soul several months after her own death, I knew there was a connection. I just wondered if there was a similar connection between Dana and Meghan.

Having lost track of time, I decided it was time to get back to my responsibilities. I wondered if Meghan had returned home to work things out with Dana or if she had run off to be with Luke.

A moment later, I disappeared from the cabin to get caught up on my marks' locations.

Chapter 7

When I arrived at Luke's apartment, it was late morning and Luke was just sitting down for lunch. As I sat across from him, I wondered whether he was aware that Meghan was married, or if she was being equally deceitful with him. Hoping to glean something relevant from Luke's future, I quickly donned the rosary. I thought ahead twenty-four hours, and a moment later the room around me faded to black.

When my vision returned, I stood at Luke's bedside. I looked down at him and Meghan, their naked bodies intertwined, then glanced at the alarm clock next to the bed. It was almost noon. Having discovered that they were both still alive, I was about to release the rosary to avoid witnessing any more of their adulterous ways when Meghan spoke.

"Are you sure?" she said.

"Absolutely. It's like I said last night, I've never felt for anyone else the way I feel about you right now. I love you, Meg, and I hope you feel the same."

Meghan didn't reply right away. She lay next to Luke, her head on his chest, and from where I stood, I could see tears beginning to fall across her cheek.

"I'm not sure what to think. When I'm with you, all I can think about is being with you. When I'm away from you, all I can think about is wanting to get back to you."

"Meg, you've just described my world for the past month."

"But is that really love? I remember those same feelings when Dana and I first met. Sure, they weren't as deep as they are with you, but I still had them. They were real feelings for him, early on. But somehow, what you and I have is—"

"Different? I don't know, Meg, but I think you might be my . . . my soulmate. I've never had such feelings for anyone else in my entire life."

Meghan dried her eyes before she looked up at Luke. "How can you tell?"

"I don't know, it just . . . feels right. It's like I ache when you're not around, and when you are here, I ache at the thought of you having to leave."

"I don't want you to ache," Meghan said as she leaned in and kissed Luke's chin, inching up to his lips.

Suddenly, a loud commotion echoed in from somewhere else in Luke's apartment. Before either Meghan or Luke could move, a tall man burst through the bedroom door.

Meghan looked up and screamed in horror at the sight of her husband. He was holding his vintage Colt revolver, pointing it in their direction.

Luke moved toward the edge of the bed, but Dana pulled back the hammer of his pistol. "Don't you move an inch," he said sternly.

Luke froze, then slowly leaned back against the headboard.

"Dana, I can explain," Meghan said. "I was going to tell you today."

Dana's eyes blazed red with anger as he pointed his pistol at Luke.

"Wait! It's not his fault," Meghan pleaded. "I was the—"

Bang, roared the gun.

"DANA! What've you done," Meghan screamed as Luke's body went limp.

"I'm ending this," Dana said calmly.

"By k-k-killing him?" Meghan asked as she began to sob.

"Meghan, baby, you were supposed to be mine, and mine only."

"But is that a reason t-to k-kill someone?" Meghan pleaded.

"Shut up! Just stop it. You are tainted now, and you mean

nothing to me," Dana said as he pulled the hammer back on his pistol and fired it at Meghan.

As if in slow motion, the bullet crawled through the air, spinning slightly, before penetrating Meghan's bare chest, blood splattering across the sheets.

A split second later, Dana cocked his pistol again and pointed it at the side of his own head. I saw him squeeze the trigger, but then everything froze. There was no more gunfire, no more blood, no more death. Everything around me paused eternally. I released my grip on the rosary and was brought back to the present.

I still sat at the kitchen table, but Luke had moved into the living room and was napping on the couch. I looked at my watch and saw that it was just about two in the afternoon. Remembering my last trip ahead with the rosary, I figured that Meghan and Dana were just about to have their fight.

"You better wake up, buddy. Your girlfriend is going to be on her way shortly and she is going to be needing you, of that I am certain."

Luke continued to slumber, not hearing my words.

Feeling overwhelmed with emotion, I needed time to think. I had about twenty-four hours to kill before it was time, and sticking around there served no purpose. A moment later I vanished.

Chapter
8

I leaned back on my couch, propping my feet up on the armrest. The sun had just set, and the flicker of the fire caused shadows to dance across the floor. Coping with this latest soul collection had left me mentally exhausted and wanting to escape my own past once again. As I lay still and silent, I could feel my eyelids drooping, almost as if they were being pulled down by some unnatural force. But I resisted the temptation to sleep. Visions of Enoch Gant and his evil ways flashed through my mind. I would not give him the satisfaction of another mind-altering dream. I recalled Hauser's advice and knew that just by relaxing quietly for a few hours, I could refresh my soul.

As I glanced at the stack of faded photographs on the coffee table, I had a sudden and strong desire to talk to Cyndi. Just one more time. It had been several months since I had caught her cheating, and I was still filled with more questions than answers. After collecting her soul, I'd thought I was ready to move on. Now I wasn't so sure. Dealing with Meghan and Luke, I began to wonder if Cyndi was in fact my soulmate. Just yesterday my mind had been set on it. But now I wasn't so sure.

"Where did we go wrong?" I asked aloud, hoping Cyndi could hear me, wherever she was in her afterlife. "Was it me? You?" I was pretty sure it wasn't us, because when we were together it felt like we were best friends. If I just had something, anything to tell me what had gone wrong, I might be able to make changes. Changes for others.

And where the hell was Hauser? I looked around the small cabin, as if by that act I could make him appear. Since the day I had collected Calvin's soul, I'd not seen hide nor hair of him, and that just wasn't like him.

"Hauser? If you're hiding behind the bookcase, listening to me ramble, I need your help. I . . ." I paused, wondering how I should phrase my mental state. "I'm lost and confused. I really have no reason to object to this current collection, but I'm having second thoughts, again. I see the love between Meghan and Luke, and I'm torn. I know that what Meghan is doing to Dana is wrong, but after seeing the ugly side of him, it really burns me up to see them get slaughtered like that. So carelessly. If I could just get them to . . . move on in life, nobody would have to die so, so tragically. I could really use your help and guidance on this one. Hell, I'm not even sure a change can be made, but—"

My pleas for help were interrupted by a screeching howl that echoed through the woods just outside the cabin door. As I craned my neck to peek out the front window, I heard a loud thump from the back of the cabin.

"Hauser?" I asked, eager to have another person to actually talk to.

Bump, bump. The sound continued rhythmically.

I jumped from the couch and went out to investigate, only to find a fallen branch that was brushing up against the rear wall of the cabin. Disappointed at finding myself still alone, I returned to the couch next to the fireplace. I lay back down, propped my feet up again, and returned to the previous realm of thoughts.

Since becoming a soul collector, I'd been conflicted with nearly every soul collection that had passed through my hands. Why had it taken me so long—until entering the afterlife—before I actually gave a shit about life and for the living? Deep inside, I hated to see anyone die. But it was only through Hauser's—or was it the Sentinel's?—training regimen that clarity was being brought forth in my own soul. I truly wanted to save everyone, and I was fairly confident that that realization was not what the training was intended for.

With no real sign or indication to do otherwise, I decided a change was going to be made. Not being a God-fearing man, I prayed regardless. I prayed that the Sentinel wouldn't come down on me too hard for what I was about to do. Tomorrow morning, with any luck, three lives would be forever altered.

Chapter 9

As I walked in the front door of Hero's Pet World at just after ten in the morning, I passed by the front-window display cages that housed the puppies and kittens. I continued walking through the store, down aisles stocked full of nearly every pet care item the mind could conceive. Having never been a pet owner myself, it boggled my mind at just how much money the average American spent on their pets. I had no doubt that Dana's business would be a gold mine.

Nearing the sales counter at the back of the store, I came upon a woman I assumed was Maxine. The store had just opened moments earlier, and I was surprised that Dana wasn't in control of his retail world. At least momentarily, that is, until he decided to go kill his wife and her lover.

I walked by Maxine and stepped into the back hallway, passing by a series of animal cages housing various older cats and dogs. As I did so, each of them sensed my presence, barking or hissing as I passed by. At the end of the hallway, I came to a closed door labeled PRIVATE and promptly jumped to the other side of the wall, unnoticed.

Once inside the manager's office, I found Dana sitting at his desk talking on the phone.

" . . . and you're sure that it's her? . . . Yes, I know that's what I paid you for, but I need to be positive about this. . . . Okay, and is she alone or is she with someone? . . . Duke, no Luke? Holloway. . . . No, it doesn't ring a bell. . . . Okay, I'll take your word for it. . . . What's the address again? . . . Got it. Okay, thanks. Send me your bill and I'll pay it promptly."

Dana hung up the phone with what I assumed was a private detective. I looked over his shoulder as he rewrote the address on a new sheet of paper and tucked it into his shirt pocket. I recognized it as the address of Luke's apartment.

Shit. Things were already in motion. I looked at my watch. Had an hour actually passed since I first came into the store? No, it couldn't have. I wondered if my mind was slipping or if it was something else. Was something in the afterlife being altered?

As I contemplated the time differences between regular life and the afterlife, Dana slid open his desk drawer and withdrew a Colt revolver. It appeared to be the same one I'd seen him wield in Luke's flash-forward. Dana's hand trembled as he ejected the six-round chamber and fumbled with loading its bullets. It was clear that he was nervous about what his next move might be.

"Just stop, buddy. There's other ways to handle this. Killing your wife is not the answer. No matter how torn up you feel inside. Trust me, I know."

It was clear that Dana couldn't hear me as he finished loading his gun. Once the last bullet slid into its chamber, he closed the revolver and spun it, just like I'd seen in the movies hundreds of times. Then he unzipped the bank bag sitting on the corner of the desk and dumped all of the cash into the desk drawer. With the bank bag empty, he slid the loaded revolver inside and zipped it closed. A moment later he rose from his desk and walked out the door.

Shit. What could I do?

I followed Dana out into the store, walking by the barking dogs once more.

"Hush up, guys," I said. "I'll be gone in a moment, I promise."

Dana stopped at the front counter and talked to Maxine. "How's it going out here?" he asked.

"It's all good," she replied. "The store is open and I've stocked the shelves like you've asked me to. No customers yet."

"And you think you'll be okay for a while? Alone?" he asked.

"Sure thing. If it's anything like Saturday was, I should be fine on my own for a few hours."

"Great. I just have a few errands to run, and I need to stop by the bank," Dana held up the bank bag, "but I should be back by the end of the day. If not, you do have your key, right?"

"I do. Everything is going to be fine, Mr. Sharp."

"Okay, then. Don't forget to feed all of the animals before you leave as well," he reminded her.

The animals! That's it. But how—

Just then, a brilliant idea came to me. I jumped from standing next to Dana and Maxine and landed at the front of the store, just out of their eyesight. I leaned down to the puppy cage and unlatched the door, instantly releasing all the puppies into the store. A second later, I jumped to the other side of the entry and did the same to the kitten cage. "Go. Be free," I said.

The puppies wasted no time exiting the cage, but the kittens were much more passive about venturing out into the store. My plan wasn't exactly panning out as I had hoped, as the puppies only circled around my ankles.

"Scat! Go play!" I demanded, but none of them obeyed. So I began to jump around the store, landing first by the food and then by the toys, leading the puppies as I went. Finally, both the puppies and the kittens were wondering about the store aimlessly, and then it happened.

"Who let the dogs out?" Dana said in a panic. "And the kittens!"

"I . . . I don't know," Maxine responded, rushing out onto the sales floor.

Within moments, both Dana and Maxine had gathered up nearly all of the kittens and a few of the puppies. I suddenly knew that the distraction was not enough to cause him to miss his appointment with doom. That's when I remembered the adult dogs and cats at the back of the store, and jumped to their cages. A moment later, real chaos ensued.

I opened every cage, releasing more than a dozen full-size dogs and several cats out into the store. I again jumped from spot to spot in the store. The adult cats were much more brazen than the kittens and exited their cages far more eagerly. With the cats on the prowl, the dogs began to chase. Hissing and growling and barking and more hissing ensued, causing quite a scene.

As I jumped forward in the store, Dana caught sight of the debacle happening at the rear of the store and screamed at Maxine to close the front door. Within seconds, Maxine sprang to action. She unlatched the hold-open on the door and it began to close slowly. Just as the latch clicked, a number of wandering dogs charged in that direction.

I continued jumping from spot to spot throughout the store, keeping an eye on my watch. The double murder was to take place just after lunch, and Luke's apartment was a good forty-minute taxi ride away. It was 11:20 a.m. according to my watch. I just had to keep the chaos going on little longer to prevent Dana from leaving.

I jumped to the front of the store while Maxine and Dana were at the back. I once again unlatched the puppy cages, releasing them back into the store. Then, suddenly, a customer opened the front door.

As the middle-aged woman walked in, she was nearly assaulted by an adult Doberman pinscher, launching its open jaws toward her face. She screamed in horror, bringing her arms up in defense. Dana heard the commotion and bolted toward the new catastrophe, making it to the front of the store just as the Doberman was about to land on the cowering woman. He grabbed the dog's collar and yanked him back just in the nick of time.

"I'm so sorry, ma'am. We're not sure what's going on this morning. It appears all of our pet cages won't remain shut." Just then, he noticed the puppies scouring about the store again.

I jumped once more, finally landing on top of the sales counter to watch. Maxine was attempting to herd the cats back into their cages while also trying to keep the dogs from chasing them. Dana was at the front of the store apologizing profusely to the female customer. I glanced at my watch and saw that it was now just past one in the afternoon. I concluded that it would be difficult for Dana to make it to Luke's apartment in time to kill them at the time I witnessed earlier. Still, I remained on the sales counter for another thirty minutes, enjoying the spectacle in front of me.

At a quarter till two, I felt confident that I had once again changed fate, and Meghan and Luke would continue on living. I smiled as Dana and Maxine captured the last few fleeing animals in the store. A moment later, I vanished.

Chapter 10

When I arrived at Luke's apartment, I was surprised at myself for actually being happy to see both him and Meghan alive. They were in the kitchen, about to have a late lunch.

"I have to say, Meg, if you're going to be around here more often, constantly building up my appetite, we're going to have to switch to low-fat food. Otherwise, I'm going to gain like twenty-five pounds before you know it," Luke teased.

"Don't put the blame on me, mister. You're the one that has the grabby hands and the irresistible moves. I guess we'll just have to increase our sexual activities to keep the weight gain at bay."

"That would just create a vicious circle," Luke said, brushing up against her. "But I'm not going to complain,"

"It's nice that you two finally get out of bed," I said, moving from the living room into the kitchen.

Meghan looked at me, let out a slight scream, and dropped the glass she was holding. Luke, who was equally startled, jumped at my voice and turned in my direction.

"Who the hell are you? And how'd you get into my apartment?"

I was at a complete loss for words. I hadn't expected them to be able to see or hear me.

"I, uh, I'm here to . . . warn you that Dana knows everything," I said slowly. "In fact, he may very well be on his way here right now."

Meghan gasped in horror.

"You're lying," Luke protested. "Just because I'm the Congressman's son doesn't give you the right to follow me around, perpetuating lies for your own personal gain."

"Believe what you want, buddy, but it's the truth. I'm . . . the PI that he hired to follow you two around. He knows everything, and to say that he's pissed would be an understatement."

"Then if he hired you, why are you telling us? Isn't that some kind of conflict of interest in some private detective code of conduct, or something?" Luke asked, clearly still skeptical.

I looked at Meghan. Fear was clearly present on her face. She obviously knew what Dana was capable of.

"If you don't believe me, just ask your little girlfriend here and she'll verify just how much of a lunatic Dana Sharp really is."

Luke looked at Meghan as she started to cry. She began to hyperventilate and could only nod in agreement.

"See?" I said. "I suggest you two end this now before someone gets hurt—and I mean really hurt. Or, Meghan, you need to end it with Dana before he does something drastic." As I talked, I tried to figure out why these two could see and hear me. If I'd made the change, their deaths would no longer be imminent, therefore they should be as oblivious to my presence as Dana was earlier. Had a change actually been made, or had I only succeeded in delaying their deaths? Only time would tell now, unless . . . unless I could get them to make the change for themselves.

"Suppose we believe you," Luke said. "You seem to have more information that you're withholding. What are you not telling us?"

I threw my hands up. "Hey, I'm just the messenger. Dana hired me to follow you two and confirm his suspicions. After I gave him this address, my contract with him was over."

"So you do want money, then," Luke demanded.

"Nope. None whatsoever. This is a friendly warning and nothing more."

"If that's true, then who's the guy behind you? Is he your muscle? The wrench to squeeze the money from my pocket?" Luke asked.

I spun around, expecting to see Dana walking in holding the gun. But to my surprise, I saw someone that I had never expected to see in person.

Enoch Gant stood by the front door.

Chapter 11

"I bet you're surprised to see me," Enoch said, tipping his bowler hat slightly.

"What? What, what are you doing here?" I asked.

"I'm here to lend you a hand, obviously," Enoch said, coming to stand next to me in the kitchen.

"So you do know him," Luke said.

"Actually, Mr. Holloway, Jack and I have not been formally introduced. We're kind of coworkers in an estranged sort of way, isn't that right, Jack?" Enoch said.

Ignoring Enoch's question, I said, "There's nothing left here to handle. You're wasting your time and you should leave."

"Oh, sure there is, Jack. You haven't yet fulfilled your obligation to the Sentinel."

"Is the Sentinel the name of the PI firm you two work for?" Luke asked.

"Shut up, Luke," I snapped.

"Why so short-tempered, Jack?" Enoch asked.

"Because I know what kind of person you are and these two do not."

"You guys are really kinda freaking me out. I'm going to have to ask you to leave," Luke said.

"Shut up, Luke," Enoch said.

Luke gasped then went for his cell phone sitting on the corner of the countertop. "If you don't leave, I'm going to call the police."

Suddenly Enoch withdrew a Colt revolver from his inside suit pocket. It was amazingly similar to the revolver that Dana had not more than an hour ago.

At the sight of the gun, Meghan shrieked and grabbed on to Luke. They both stepped away from the countertop.

"Hey, now. We don't want any trouble. I'm just asking if you two would leave. I won't call the police if you guys leave right now."

"Well, would you look at that? Jack, I see why you saved these two souls. They have such . . . intelligence. Seems such a shame that they have to die anyway."

"What are you talking about?" I asked. "Their event has come and passed, and—"

"And what? Why exactly are you here, then?" Enoch asked.

"I just came by to see that they were, in fact, still alive."

At that moment Enoch raised the revolver and pointed it at Meghan. Before I could protest, he pulled the trigger, shooting her in the head.

"Well it looks like you were wrong. One is alive and one is dead. I'd say plot twist, but then you'd just ignore my humorous jabs?"

Luke held Meghan's limp body for a few seconds longer before he reluctantly let her fall to the floor. "You sonofabitch. You killed her!" he screamed.

With Enoch's attention on Luke, I lunged for the gun in Enoch's hand, but before I could grab it, Enoch vanished and reappeared two feet behind me.

"What the hell just happened?" Luke asked.

"Shut up, Luke," Enoch and I said in unison.

"You see, Jack, sometimes you can't actually change fate. Luke and Meghan were supposed to die, and dammit, I'm gonna make sure that happens."

"What does it matter to you if they live or die?" I demanded.

"Honestly, it really doesn't matter one iota. I just saw an opportunity here, and I decided to take it."

"What opportunity is that?" I asked, stepping toward Enoch discreetly.

"Back off, Jack. You don't want to end up like Meghan here, do you?" Enoch asked.

I froze. Out of the corner of my eye I noticed Luke once again inching toward his cell phone.

I raised my hands up in surrender. "Hey, it's no sweat off my brow either, buddy," I said as I took two steps back, hoping to keep Enoch's attention away from Luke.

Enoch raised an eyebrow. "You surprise me, Jack. I thought you were all about saving lives. Why the sudden change of heart?"

"No reason, really," I said, taking another step back.

Enoch instinctively glanced toward Luke, grasping his cell phone in his hand. Without another word, Enoch squeezed the trigger, placing a bullet in the side of Luke's temple. He dropped to the floor next to Meghan's dead body.

"Nice try, Jack. But what do you think him calling the police would've done for your cause? I'll tell you, absolutely nothing."

I rushed into the kitchen, knelt down next to the bodies, and felt for a pulse. There was none, on either of them. Instinctively, I withdrew their soul boxes from my pocket.

"Not so fast, Jack," Enoch said as he leveled the revolver in my direction. "I need you to back up, and I mean right now."

I saw the revolver cocked and loaded, and obeyed Enoch's command, stepping away from the dead bodies. I wasn't entirely sure whether or not I could be killed again, seeing as I was, for all intents and purposes, dead already. Regardless, I wasn't about to tempt that particular fate.

A moment later, Enoch withdrew a cylindrical copper tube no longer than a medicine bottle. He unfastened the lid, and an instant later Luke and Meghan's souls shot directly into the opening. Enoch reattached the lid and slipped it back into his pocket.

"What, you did this just so you can collect their souls on your own?" I asked.

"I have my reasons, and none of them are of any of your concern." Enoch continued to point his pistol in my direction. We stood, facing each other in silence. Slowly, Enoch began to move toward the entry door of the apartment, shuffling his feet backward, blindly.

Suddenly, Hauser appeared next to me in the kitchen.

"Oh, I was wondering when you would show up," Enoch said, now pointing the pistol at Hauser.

The look of surprise on Hauser's face spoke volumes. Without a single word, he smiled, then vanished just as suddenly as he'd appeared.

Enoch blinked rapidly as he swung the pistol in an arc around the room, expecting Hauser to reappear just as randomly. Thinking along the same lines, I also disappeared, jumping into the bedroom momentarily before returning to the living room. Enoch's back was toward me, but he sensed me almost instantly. He repointed the pistol at me, but before he could pull the trigger, I vanished again. I continued to jump in and out of the bedroom and various parts of the living room and kitchen until Enoch clearly became bored with the game. He stopped pointing his gun at me at every reappearance.

Then, Hauser reappeared right behind him. He reached out to grasp Enoch's shoulder, but before he could get a grip, Enoch vanished himself. He rematerialized near the apartment door.

"If you want to catch me, old man, you're going to have to get up a little earlier in the morning," Enoch said. He no longer pointed the gun at either of us but just stood there, waiting for something.

As if on cue, the apartment door opened and in stepped Dana Holloway.

Enoch looked in our direction one last time, then winked. He handed the revolver to Dana and vanished.

Dana looked at the gun in his hand quizzically before looking up at Hauser and me. "What . . . what's going on here?" he asked.

Curious, I wondered how Dana could see any of us. Was he still destined to die? In Luke's flash-forward, Dana had taken his own life after he'd killed Meghan and Luke. Now I wondered if he would do the same once he discovered that they were both already dead in the kitchen.

Before Hauser or I could answer, we heard the sound of police sirens out front, and then the screech of tires echoing between the buildings. I looked at Hauser, who nodded his head slowly and then flipped his thumb up and over his shoulder. It was time to go. We vanished from Luke's apartment.

Chapter 12

"What the hell was that all about," I asked as I paced around my cabin.

Hauser stood at the center of the room, his eyes staring off into space, as if trying to focus on a distant star. "I don't know. I haven't actually seen Enoch in person for—"

"No, not that. What was up with him killing Luke and Meghan?" I asked.

"I'm sorry, what?" Hauser asked.

"Didn't you see them dead? Haven't you been following me around, silently, letting me stumble and fall?"

"No. I've been . . . busy. You say *he* killed them?"

"Yeah, kind of like that dream I had a few months ago. He kind of just showed up, and when I wasn't willing to take their souls, he killed them both."

"Wait, slow down. I need you to tell me everything," Hauser demanded.

I recapped my search for Meghan and Luke, my dismay at their infidelity, and my decision to intervene once again in my soul collection, pacing around the cabin as I spoke. When I finished catching him up, I sat heavily on the couch. "You're telling me you really didn't know anything I was doing?" I asked.

"No, nothing whatsoever."

"Well, after deciding to save their two souls, I jumped back to Luke's apartment to make sure that they were okay, and that's when Enoch showed up and killed them both. Your timing couldn't have been worse. He fired the gun just seconds before you arrived."

"My God, so it's true."

"What's true? That Enoch is a psychopath? I thought we knew that already."

"No, that he is in fact interfering with the collection of other souls."

"Well, I believe that's the understatement of the century," I said, then wondered if my own interference would be equally feared by the Sentinel. Granted, my own changes in fate were far less violent than Enoch's, but still, I was changing fate just the same.

As Hauser and I contemplated the situation, I began to worry that things might be far worse than I'd imagined. Hauser's was not his usual jovial self, and a worried look was plastered across his face.

"Anything else?" he asked.

"Well, after he killed them, I attempted to collect their souls. But before I could do so, he pulled out some kind of collection chamber of his own and took both of the souls instantaneously."

Hauser stopped pacing and stared at me. "Was it a copper tube, and about yea big?" he asked, holding his fingers a few inches apart.

"Yeah, that's about it. What's this all about?" I asked.

"I . . . I have no words. I had always thought that it was a rumor. What you just described is what we've coined a soul magnet. It is believed to have been created centuries ago for the mass collection of souls without the need of cleansing. The way that it was rumored to work was that you opened the vessel and any free soul present with a hundred-meter radius would shoot into the tube."

"You say rumored. Has the Sentinel not told you anything about it?"

Hauser shook his head. "No, the Sentinel even withholds information from me from time to time."

"Well, then what's our next step? I still have their soul boxes," I said, pulling them from my pocket.

Hauser took them from me and held them out in front of us

so that we could see the names. Luke Holloway and Meghan Sharp still was etched on each of the boxes.

"Curious. I would've thought that once the soul magnet took their souls, your boxes would re-etch with new names."

"Well, it doesn't appear to have happened that way. Can't you use one of your devices and go after Enoch? Maybe we can still get those souls from his soul magnet thingy."

"No, I've chased after him in the past, and he's wise to the maneuver. He instinctively jumps to locations that would leave a follower in a precarious situation. There have been a number of times that I nearly died following him. So, no, we can't go after him. Not now."

"So, we can die again?" I asked, fearing for my own mortality.

"In an abstract sense, yes. We really never actually died, you see. We just left the life of the living, breathing population. So, yes, you should fear for your own mortality, because it is still just as fragile."

"Then what's next?"

"Well, my friend, I think we have no other choice than to finally introduce you to the Sentinel. Maybe they can give us some kind insight on the situation."

"Oh. Oh my. I . . . I'm not sure how I feel about that. Won't they be a little upset with me for avoiding the collection of these two, especially after my previous indiscretions?"

"You can't worry about that, Jack. There are far more important things that are on their minds, I'm sure."

"You're the boss," I said nervously. "Lead the way."

Hauser stepped to my side and held his arm out level with the ground. "Take my arm, Jack. Take my arm, and clear your mind of all thoughts. You're just along for the ride."

I did as he said, forcing every possible thought away. When all that was left was Hauser and me, we vanished

BOOK 7

The SURROGATE SOUL

Chapter 1

I was enveloped in total blackness. A shade so dark that only moments before I didn't even know existed. It was calming and disturbing at the same time. In the far distance, I heard a faint hum. It was almost imperceptible. But, as the hum got louder, so did my senses sharpen. Before I knew it, the hum had developed into a full blown shriek. The blaring of a car horn woke me from my deep unconscious sleep, causing my heart rate to increase rapidly. I sprang to my feet and rubbed the blurriness from my eyes.

As I stood, dizziness instantly overwhelmed me and I nearly fell backward. I grabbed at the back of the bench to steady myself. I looked around. I focused on the park bench for which gave me stability and expected to find the surroundings of my old park bench in New York. But, I recognized nothing. I stood in the middle of a large cobblestone pavilion, pedestrians milling about all around me. The two drive lanes to my left and right were vacant, save for a white bus that was driving away from me in the far distance. Taking in the building façade surrounding the plaza, I tried to remember if I'd seen any of it before. Unfortunately, nothing looked remotely familiar.

"Where the hell am I?" I mumbled to myself.

I looked at my watch but the second hand had stopped. I shook my wrist a few times to activate the automatic winder, and the seconds once more began to tick away. As I watched the rhythmic mechanical movement, I remembered that automatic watches such as mine would stop ticking after twenty-four to thirty-six hours of inactivity. Had I actually been unconscious for more than a day, on a bench in an unknown city?

I tried to recall my last clear memory. Hauser and I had been about to leave my cabin. Enoch had just killed the last two souls I'd been assigned to collect. I remember Hauser telling me that it was time to . . . to do something. I just couldn't remember what.

A sudden pressure assaulted my inner ears. It felt as if my head would explode. I shut my eyes tightly and rubbed the sides of my temples to help soothe the pain. *When was the last time that I had actually had a headache?* I couldn't remember having one since I'd entered the afterlife.

As the throbbing pain slowly ebbed, I opened my eyes, but the wooziness remained. I scratched at the back of my head absently as another sharp pain shot through my body. I pulled my hand away, and the tips of my fingers were covered with some kind of red residue.

"Holy shit," I gasped. Gingerly, I touched the spot on my head and found an enormous knot—my hair crusted over with blood.

I decided to do a quick check of my own mental facilities.

Who am I? I'm Jack Duffy.

What do I do? I'm a soul collector in the afterlife.

How did I become a soul collector? I tried to kill myself and only moderately succeeded.

Do I have any family or friends? My parents had passed away years ago. My wife died shortly after I left the living. As for friends, I had only one true friend. Hauser. Hauser . . . what? Did Hauser have a last name?

Where are you? I'm not sure.

Why are you here? I don't know that either.

An old Camus quote came to mind. It went something like this: *To know oneself, one should assert oneself.*

So, action it was. I began to walk through the unknown place. *Is this just another part of my hometown?* Possibly, but the architecture was different, and the smell was unique. I could smell fresh air like I'd not experienced in quite some time. No, I was not in New York. I was someplace . . . different.

I thought about jumping to my cabin, to a place that was

familiar to me, but decided against it. What if I was supposed to be here? What if Hauser was nearby and I left without saying a word? Wherever I was, there must have been a reason for me being here. I decided to continue walking through the pavilion with hopes that I might figure out where I was.

As I neared the end of the block, I found myself standing at the corner of Sixteenth Street and Champa Street. *Champa doesn't sound remotely familiar.*

I stopped at the corner, looking up and down the cross street, and saw mountains near the horizon. *My God, where the hell am I?*

Ding, ding. Ding, ding.

The sound echoed between the buildings. Startled, I looked over my shoulder and saw another white bus with the words *The Ride, Denver's Free Shuttle* plastered along the side.

"Huh, so I'm in Denver," I said.

"That's very astute, Jack," came a voice from behind me. A voice that I instantly recognized and one that I would never forget. I spun around and found Wilson Oliver smiling at me.

Chapter 2

It took me nearly a full minute of staring into Wilson's seasoned eyes to realize that he was in fact standing in front of me. "My God, Wilson. Is it really you?" I asked.

He bobbed his head slowly, maintaining eye contact. "It is I, but honestly, Jack, it hasn't been that long since we last spoke."

"Sure it has. It's been what? Almost six months?" I asked.

"Funny thing, time. For some it passes at a snail's pace, while for others . . . well, let's just say that I remember seeing you as if it were just days ago," Wilson said.

Hearing the old man speak was music to my ears. After so many months of limited company—listening to Hauser's satirical comments and bravado or the occasional deathbed conversation with the souls that I was there to collect—actually being in Wilson's presence was just what I needed.

"But how is this possible? How is it that you're alive? You are alive, right?"

"Ah, yes very much so."

"But how? I took your soul. I . . . I visited your dead body on that park bench for many days after your . . . death."

"Well, Jack, turns out that having been a successful soul collector for as many years as I was has its privileges," Wilson said proudly. "You see, after my soul was delivered to the Sentinel, I was given the option to either be reincarnated into a new being or to reclaim my old body and take a seat on the high council, with the Sentinel."

"Wow, and I thought that you would've taken reincarnation. Have the chance at a new body?"

"Trust me, Jack, the thought did cross my mind. But I've become quite accustomed to this old bag of bones, and the opportunity to be on the council was really something I'd never imagined possible for myself. But that's enough about me. How about you? It appears that you're in a bit of a pickle once again."

I nodded in agreement. "Yeah, you could say that. I seem to have lost time . . . again. I think it has something to do with this bump on the back of my head." I bowed my head down to give Wilson a look.

"Ouch, that certainly looks like it smarts. What is the last thing you remember?" he asked.

A sudden recollection flooded my mind. "Well, as irony has it, Hauser and I were about to come visit the Sentinel, I think. There was a . . . complication with my last collection, and Hauser thought it was imperative that we seek advice from the Sentinel. My last clear memory was grabbing a hold of Hauser's arm and darkness came over me. Beyond that, I can't remember a thing. I can see visions of scenes—almost as if a film projector is out of focus—but I just can't make anything out. Does that make sense?"

"I understand. As a matter of fact, the event you speak of occurred almost three days ago. I imagine there's a logical explanation for the memory loss."

"Three days? Are you shitting me? How can I have lost three days?"

Wilson contemplated the situation for several moments. "I think you might be right, Jack—perhaps the bump on the back of your head is your problem. Thankfully, you and I have the ability to re-experience your past. You do still have the coin, don't you? Are you a willing to take another trip down memory lane?"

I began to turn out my pockets, emptying everything that I had on my person. First out was the rosary, which I handed to Wilson. Next I pulled out two soul boxes. One had my name on it—the very box that Wilson gave me when I took his soul all those months ago. The other box had a name that I also recognized. The name of Calvin's mother—Penelope Rose. Lastly, I pulled out the coin.

"That's strange. The last two boxes I remember having were for Luke and Meghan. I don't remember getting Penelope's box," I said.

"Is there anything else?" asked Wilson.

"Nope. That's everything I have." I handed him the coin and took back the rosary and the two soul boxes.

"All right, then. I suggest we find a place to sit and get started."

Wilson turned and headed down the pavilion toward a grouping of vacant patio chairs beneath a large oak tree. As we neared the seating area, more flashes were coming back to me from my lost time. I had a sudden sense of recognition as I eased myself down into the chair.

"It's strange, Wilson, but there's something about this area— I don't know, it just feels familiar."

"That's good, isn't it? What is it that makes you feel that way?"

"I don't know, I can't quite put my finger on it, but . . . there's something about the buildings, maybe, that is remarkable. Almost as if I'd been here before."

Wilson smiled and sat in the chair across from me. "Well then, Jack, how about we see what happened with your past seventy-two hours."

Taking the coin from Wilson and turning it over in my hand launched me into the past, just as it had done numerous times before. A sense of contentment overwhelmed me, and despite the peculiar situation I was in, I felt like things would be okay.

Chapter 2.5

Darkness turned to light as the soles of my feet slammed to the ground, the momentum forcing me to my knees. Dizziness and nausea overwhelmed me and I uncontrollably hurled. Thankfully I hadn't eaten or consumed any liquids in quite a few weeks, and I only dry heaved.

"And after all this time, I thought you would've mastered the ability to move around in the afterworld," Hauser said, standing above me.

I wiped the spittle from my mouth and leaned back on my haunches. "Yeah, me too. I haven't had a bout like that since, I don't know, maybe the second or third jump?"

Hauser held his hand out and helped me up. "To be fair, transporting is quite a bit different when there's multiple people involved. Until now you've only traveled by yourself."

"But that's not so," I protested. "You and I have both traveled at the same time."

"Yes, but we did so on our own volition. We always had the same destination in mind and just transported simultaneously. This time you had no idea where we were going, as I was in the driver's seat. You were just along for the ride, so the effects of the jump are much more intense."

"I'd say," I said as I looked around at my surroundings. We stood on a relatively nondescript city sidewalk, surrounded by a few pedestrians. The cloudless sky above was the deepest blue I'd ever seen, and the air was thin and fresh. "So where is this place?

Is this the Sentinel? Heaven or hell?"

Hauser chuckled. "None of the above, compadre. This is Denver, Colorado. Some people have said this is the closest to heaven that they've come, but I tend to disagree. Denver's nice and all, but it's a little too uppity for my taste."

"Then I'm confused. I thought you said we were off to meet the Sentinel. Why take me to Denver first?"

"Because to get to the Sentinel, we have to go through Denver. You see, there's only one way in and out of the Sentinel, and that's through the Daniels and Fisher tower." Hauser directed my view to the slender high-rise a block ahead of us.

The building was not very large—maybe thirty feet square—but shot up around twenty floors. Near the top, a large clock face was situated on each of the four building sides. The roof was steeply inclined to a cupola at the very peak. The entire building façade was constructed from blonde-colored brick. It very much reminded me of the St. Marks bell tower in Venice.

As we walked the final block toward the building, Hauser explained its history.

"This building, this clock tower, was the tallest building this side of the Mississippi in . . . 1910, I think, but only held on to that designation for a short period before the Smith Tower in Seattle claimed the moniker."

"That's great, Hauser, but what does that have to do with the Sentinel?"

"Patience, Jack. I'm getting there. You see, when this building was completed, the Sentinel needed a new headquarters. Things were really on the move back then, and at the time, the Sentinel had their base of operation in a location that was too close to the public eye. They chose Daniels and Fisher tower for two reasons: because of its modest style and because it was quite removed from the hustle and bustle of the rapidly growing coasts of the country."

Hauser and I had stopped at the base of the building. I looked up at the façade in awe. "Who knew? Those that control the fate of every living soul in the world are located in a Renaissance-style building in Denver, Colorado," I said.

"Well, that's not exactly true. The Sentinel is not really inside the building. We can only access their location through here."

I shook my head in utter confusion. "You know, Hauser . . . just lead the way. I shouldn't be surprised about anything that you tell me on how things work in the afterlife."

"That's the spirit, my boy."

Hauser and I walked up to the glass entry doors and stepped through. Once inside the lobby, my initial sense of the building's demure size was compounded. Straight ahead of the doors we'd just walked through were another pair of glass doors exiting the opposite side of the lobby. To the left was the bank of elevators—correction, *the* elevator. The building was small enough that only one lift was provided. There were two doors on either side of the elevator, most likely stairwell access points. To the right was yet another pair of glass doors exiting back outside. On each side of the doors were two small offices.

Considering that this was the entry point to the headquarters of the afterlife, I truly expected to see gold-encrusted chandeliers and imported Italian marble floors. Instead, the floor had some kind of 60s-era linoleum finish, and the walls had a wainscoting of faded cream-colored beadboard with a hideous lavender wallpaper above. The light fixtures were simple, clear glass luminaires.

"I like it," I said. "Not at all pretentious."

Hauser chuckled as he pressed the call button for the elevator. A moment later a mechanical bell rang as the tarnished brass door opened.

"After you, sport," Hauser said, motioning me into the lift.

I stepped past him into the elevator and was confronted with the splendor that I had expected in the lobby. The walls were lined with pearl-essence panels, and every exposed screw or fastener appeared to be gold-plated. On the ceiling of the elevator was an extravagant chandelier, with hundreds of crystal prisms reflecting the light magnificently in the compact space. I laughed out loud.

Hauser joined in my laughter. "I tell you, boy, you should see the look on your face."

As our laughter subsided, the elevator door closed. Hauser and I stood next to each other quietly. On the elevator panel were buttons for every floor from the lobby up to the twentieth floor. There were also two additional buttons: basement one and basement two.

After an uncomfortably long pause, I looked over at Hauser. He stood silently, as if waiting for something to happen.

"So are we going to actually push a button?" I asked.

Hauser held a solitary finger up as he continued to contemplate something. After a few more moments he nodded his head, then reached out and simultaneously pushed the seven and thirteen buttons. As he did so, a scattering of other buttons lit up, but not the seven or the thirteen.

"Is that some kind of a surreptitious access code?" I asked sarcastically.

"The Sentinel is nothing without its obscure security protocols. They change the sequence every so often, and it's linked to the moon phase and the current month. I was trying to figure out the exact combination. Thankfully, today was an easy one. I've had to enter the elevator before when the combination was ten buttons. And you have to press them all at the exact same moment."

"And what if you get it wrong?" I asked.

Hauser whistled and arched his eyebrow. "Well, I've only heard stories . . ."

Before he could continue, the lighted buttons began to blink out one by one. Twenty-three. Nineteen. Seventeen. Eleven. Five. Three. Two. One.

"Is there any coincidence that including the two buttons you pressed, all of the lighted buttons were prime numbers?" I asked.

"I tell you, Jack. You are one sharp wit. They actually had to draw me a diagram about it all when I first came in here."

A moment later the elevator door opened, and I suddenly realized that the elevator had not moved an inch the whole time. Surprisingly, though, the lobby was not the same lobby that we had just been in. The decor of this lobby mimicked that of the elevator car.

Hauser stepped out first and I followed. As soon as we were both off the lift, the door closed then vanished. I nearly jumped out of my skin. In its place stood a man with his back toward us. He wore a tan suit and a white fedora.

Hauser cleared his throat.

The man before us turned sharply and the sudden recognition sent chills throughout every point of my body. It was Wilson Oliver.

Chapter 3

I released the coin, and was back on the pavilions in Denver. Wilson sat across from me, smiling.

"Why didn't you tell me that we've already been reintroduced?" I asked.

"Well, I wasn't sure how much memory loss you'd actually suffered. I didn't want to startle you too much with the state of the situation," Wilson said, avoiding eye contact.

What is he hiding? I wondered.

Wilson brought his eyes up and met mine. "I see Hauser hasn't taught you how to control your mind quite yet," he said.

Shit. "I mean, yeah, not so much. I've only just recently been able to hear the occasional thought from someone else, and Hauser is the proverbial blank slate when it comes to his thoughts."

"Hauser is one of the best at controlling what can be heard from deep within his mind. It's almost as if he has the ability to . . . tick off a list of what he'll allow out and what he keeps private. Personally, I hold everything in and don't allow a single thought to leak away. It's easier that way."

"Then I'm confused. I thought that my training was complete. Is that not so?" I asked.

"I think it best that we reenter your past," Wilson said, avoiding answering the question. "I think you would do much better learning about the status of things all on your own. What do you say we give the coin another flip?"

I exhaled deeply, feeling my frustration build. My earlier restful senses were quickly being replaced with feelings of disdain. Regardless of my reservations, I picked up the coin and flipped it over.

Chapter 3.5

I was speechless. I stole a quick look at Hauser, who just grinned smugly. I returned my unbelieving gaze toward Wilson.

"Ah, Mr. Duffy," Wilson said. "It's great to see you again. Aside from the recent . . . complications, how has the afterlife been treating you?"

I tried to hide the shock—seeing my first collected soul standing right in front of me, in person, just as he'd looked all those months ago—but I failed miserably. "I, um . . ."

Wilson and Hauser both laughed at my sudden inability to speak coherently. I knew they weren't laughing at me, but most likely at the odd situation that we were all in. "Odd indeed," Wilson said. "And I'd imagine that you are full of questions right about now. As much as I would like to sit down with you and explain everything, we have more pressing matters to attend to."

I nodded. "Yeah, maybe later?"

"I'm not sure if we have time on this trip, compadre," said Hauser. "Perhaps if the meeting with the council doesn't go too long, Wilson here can fill you in briefly."

"Yes, yes. If this session is as expeditious as I'm hoping, we should have a few moments." Wilson turned and began to walk down the corridor. "If you would follow me, council is already in session, and they're waiting for us."

Oh great. We come up here, wherever this is, and we get thrown right to the wolves.

"Please, Jack. Try your best to silence your thoughts. Once

we're inside the council, it would be best to speak only when you're spoken to, and really try to focus on the conversation at hand. We don't necessarily want to let on anything that is . . . questionable?" Hauser said.

I caught his drift instantly. I forced my recent deviances from my mind, and nodded.

Hauser and I fell into stride with Wilson. We walked down the polished marble corridor. It didn't take long for me to realize that we really weren't in the same building. The compact floor plan of the building we'd entered moments before couldn't have been more than three or four office-sized rooms wide and deep. But the corridor we walked down had to have been at least a full city block long in each direction.

After some twenty feet down the hallway, a room opened up on the left, encompassed by windows. I tried to take in a glimpse of the view, but Wilson and Hauser continued on in the opposite direction, turning away from the glass. As we entered the new corridor, it carried on dozens of yards as well.

"Is this place real?" I asked.

"Yes, and no," Hauser said. "Everything that you can see and feel is as real as if it were in your own home. As for the location, I'm not sure if I'm qualified to answer that. It exists, but not in the sense of space that you and I are used to. It just is."

"Well thanks for clearing that up for me," I remarked, showing only a hint of the sarcasm that I truly wanted to convey.

A moment later we came to the end of the corridor, and a pair of hand-carved wooden doors. Wilson paused momentarily before gripping the polished-brass door handles and pushing in.

Wilson and I followed, walking into a large gathering room. The sudden change in décor made it feel like we'd just stepped into the past. The walls were lined with faux-wood paneling, and the floor was covered with green shaggy carpet. The low ceiling was textured with acoustical popcorn. Along the far wall a series of glass windows looked outside. At the center of the room, a number of Naugahyde-covered chairs were arranged in a full circle. Most of them were already occupied.

Stepping forward, Wilson sat in the last armed chair in the circle, while Hauser led us to the remaining two armless chairs.

As I sat, I glanced around at the members of the council and was dumbfounded. I recognized Martin Luther King, Steve Jobs, and, if I remembered my history lessons correctly, I thought I saw Winston Churchill in the group. A woman sitting directly across from Hauser and I had an appealing appearance, albeit masculine. Her mysterious yet highly publicized disappearance in the late thirties made her practically immortal, if in name only. It was Amelia Earhart.

To her right sat an elderly gentleman with a beard down nearly to his lap. He had bushy grey eyebrows and if he'd been wearing a white tunic, I'd imagine this would be the Gandalf character that Hauser had mentioned back when he was explaining the origination of the mystical gadgets that he possessed. Just as those thoughts coursed through my mind, the older man looked up at me, winked one of his silvery-grey eyes, and smirked.

Oh shit, I thought. *Control. Control. Control.*

I quickly shifted my focus to the other members of the council and was continually surprised at the recognizable faces. I continued to look around the room until I arrived back at Earhart staring right at me. A moment later, I released the coin.

Chapter 4

"Did I really just see Amelia Earhart?" I asked.

Wilson chuckled. "Yeah, Amelia was a direct recruit. She came onto the council reluctantly."

"You mean the Sentinel targeted her directly? How is it that the council is made up?"

"The high council is mostly formed by past soul collectors. Hence, my appointment. There are, however, a number of non-soul collector folk in place. In addition to Earhart, I gather that you noticed other familiar faces, correct?"

I nodded. "Yeah, I did, but I couldn't put names to a few of the people."

"Yes, the high council of the Sentinel is diverse to a fault. It consists of twelve men and women from virtually all times and locations from earth's history. Each council member is given the opportunity to serve as long as they wish, but as far as I'm aware, most of the past members have limited their stay. As a matter of fact, Florence Nightingale was the member that I recently replaced."

"Are you serious? Did you get to meet her before she . . . what? Moved on to the other side?"

"I did meet her briefly, but we only exchanged short pleasantries."

"Wow. What was she like?" I asked, completely enamored.

"She was actually a very attractive woman. But she seemed . . . I don't know, worn down, maybe?"

"Wilson, you sly dog. She had to have been, what, a hundred and something? I don't even know."

"You see, when you become a member of the Sentinel, you get to choose the physical representation to carry on in the afterlife. She chose herself when she was in her mid- to late-thirties. And I have to say, it was a fine choice," Wilson said with a wink.

"So if she was in her thirties when she joined the Sentinel, did she continue to age?"

"No, it's quite a bit different from being a soul collector. Once you join the Sentinel, you cease to age, and rarely do environmental changes affect you."

Trying to wrap my mind around this new information made my head spin. I was having trouble thinking straight. As much as I'd wanted to get back all of my lost memories, I was feeling severely inadequate. Here I was, the most recent recruit to the soul collecting ranks of the afterlife, being thrust into the presence of some truly great people. Despite their historically benevolent natures, I was unsure just how compassionate they'd be if they fully realized my most recent past. Just being in the presence of all those that ruled in the afterlife made me terribly edgy.

"It's all right to be nervous, Jack. Regardless of their current status, those people were just as normal as you and I were at one point in time."

I shrugged. "I suppose, but you're not as normal as I am, and I'm not as normal as I once was."

"It's all relative, Jack. They're good people, now and before. Besides, your hesitation now is unwarranted. You've already been through all of this. You're now just reliving what has already occurred."

As Wilson explained this, I rubbed the back of my neck until there was an audible crack. I tilted my head back to the right and it popped again. "I suppose you're right."

"Then are you ready to continue?" Wilson asked.

"Yeah, I suppose," I said reluctantly. I picked up the coin and flipped it over in my hand.

Chapter 4.5

As Earhart continued to stare at me, I felt as if she was staring into my soul. I shifted my eyes to the Gandalf character, who I decided to coin Mr. Wizard. He was staring off into the distance and appeared deep in thought. As I continued to look around the circle of council members, each of the faces looked wise beyond their years. Each one held a certain level of confidence that was comforting, yet at the same time moderately intimidating.

"Thank you, all, for agreeing to grant us audience," Hauser began. "We realize that your time is valuable, and we're honored—"

"Let's forgo all the formalities, Mr. Hauser," said Earhart. "Tell us what you know."

Mr. Hauser? Is that his last name? If that's true, then what's his first name? I wondered. I made a mental note to ask him about it later.

Hauser cleared his throat. "It appears that Enoch Gant has taken an interest in my latest protégé, Jack Duffy. He's been visiting Mr. Duffy's dreams on and off over the past few months. Then, in an unprecedented event, he arrived at the scene of Mr. Duffy's latest collection assignment and seized the souls before Jack had an opportunity to do so. From what Jack tells me, Enoch possesses a soul magnet."

There were gasps from a number of the council members, while others in the gathering remained completely emotionless.

"Silence, silence," said Earhart. "Mr. Hauser, is this just

hearsay, or is this a witnessed event?"

Am I chopped liver? I thought. *I'm sitting right here. Can't you just ask me?*

Careful, Jack. If I can hear you, they most likely can hear you as well, Hauser's words echoed inside my mind.

"Yes, Amelia. Jack witnessed the soul acquisition from Enoch just hours ago. He described the collection chamber precisely: a small copper tube, three inches long. It's unmistakable."

"Granted, this is disturbing news about Mr. Gant, but I am not sure it warrants a knee-jerk reaction from the Sentinel," King said.

"It's not just Jack's eyewitness that prompted this gathering," Hauser said. "I've heard from a half a dozen other collectors in the past few months, relaying similar situations where Enoch has attempted to interfere. Fortunately, none of those have developed to the extent of Jack's latest encounter."

As a number of the council members broke off into smaller, individual conversations, Hauser and I sat in silence.

"There's one more thing," Hauser said, bringing the attention back to us. "Enoch has not only taken these two souls, but he's also threatened our lives."

"How so?" Earhart asked.

"Moments before he vanished, he threatened to kill Jack and me with a gun. This all took place just minutes after he shot and killed Jack's two marks."

A new round of shocked outbursts filled the room.

"Silence. Silence," Earhart demanded. Turning back to Hauser, she asked, "Do you expect us to believe that Enoch Gant is capable of murder? To take the word of an inexperienced soul collector trainee?"

"I do," Hauser said firmly. "If Jack tells me that's what happened, I believe him completely. Regardless of Jack's experience level, why would he lie about this? He has nothing to gain from it. Besides, it's common knowledge that Enoch Gant has been actively pursued by me and by others in the council."

As isolated conversations ensued, I watched Earhart and Mr. Wizard lean in toward one another, whispering discreetly into each other's ear. After several moments, Earhart returned order to the gathering.

"Attention please. We've all known that Enoch Gant had the potential to be a loose cannon, and this recent incident is further proof of that. However, we feel that this may very well be an isolated incident, and maintaining the status quo is the prudent thing to do."

What does she mean, status quo? I thought.

Not now, Jack, Hauser thought back.

"Amelia, I don't think these are isolated incidents," Hauser said. "Yes, this is the first physical interaction with him, but he's been tampering with many soul collectors' minds over the past several months."

"Then enforcing the current sleep ordinance should alleviate that, Mr. Hauser. None of the soul collectors should be sleeping anyway. That was a directive handed down more than two years ago, but it continues to happen."

"Sleep aversion is not the answer here," Hauser said. "It's just a stopgap. It's clear that Enoch is getting more brazen by the day and who knows how far he'll go—"

Earhart nodded her head. "I happen to agree, Mr. Hauser, but we can only react to what we know. And right now all we know for certain is that he's invaded the dreams—"

"And so much more," Hauser snapped. "He's killed two living souls and threatened our lives."

"He's *allegedly* threatened your lives," Earhart shot back. "I've just spoken with Mr. Whitman, who will begin working on a personal protection device. He believes that he should be able to create something that will protect the lives of all our soul collectors."

"Well, that's a start. But how long before this device can be ready?" Hauser asked, looking at Whitman.

Whitman did not reply, but just stared at Hauser.

After a long moment of silence, Earhart spoke. "I believe that will conclude our meeting today. Mr. Hauser, I trust that you will relay the council directive, expressing the urgent nature of foregoing sleep to all active soul collectors?"

"Yes, Ms. Earhart—"

"What? That's it?" I blurted. "I think you're missing an

incredible opportunity here!"

"What exactly do you mean, Mr. Duffy?" Steve Jobs asked impatiently.

"It's my understanding that none of you know where Enoch is. From what Hauser tells me, he cannot be traced because he no longer possesses a soul box, am I correct?" I said.

A number of council members around the room nodded their heads, a look of irritation on each of their faces.

"He's obviously honed in on me," I said. "Isn't there some way that we can possibly trap him?"

"I don't think one chance meeting with you would necessarily qualify for him honing in on you," Jobs snapped.

"That may be, but he has invaded my dreams on virtually every collection that I've been assigned. I'm not sure if that's a regular occurrence or not, but I think that you all should be taking advantage of that somehow. Can't Mr. Wizard there create some kind of a device that can capture him next time he comes at me, or interferes with my next collection?" I asked.

"What makes you think that Enoch will attempt to interfere with your next collection?" Earhart asked, cutting off Jobs in the meantime.

"Isn't it obvious? I've tried to save the last several souls that I've been sent to collect. Quite successfully I might add," I said, ignoring the gasping outbursts from the council. "And I believe that my doing so has somehow triggered something in Enoch's mind, driving him to come and physically interact with me."

The council once again dispersed into individual discussions of shock and surprise at hearing my recent soul collection activities.

"And what gives you the right to save souls?" Churchill demanded. "Explain yourself!"

Be careful, Jack, Hauser thought to me. *The high council here does not know everything that has occurred down there.*

Terror filled my mind as visions of poking an angry bear filled my mind. A moment later I released my coin.

Chapter 5

I leaned back in my chair and looked at Wilson, who had a disapproving look on his face. I momentarily shifted my gaze elsewhere.

"So, obviously, none of this is new to you," I said.

"No, Jack. If I was present in your memories, I have already experienced this. However, we're not reliving these memories for my benefit but for yours. You need to figure out where you've been to discover where you're going."

"Where exactly am I going?" I asked.

"In due time. There is much to be reviewed prior to you learning about your ultimate destination," Wilson said, continuing to hold my deviating gaze.

I nodded. "I suppose you're right." I said. "Tell me, Wilson, why isn't the Sentinel taking the situation with Enoch Gant more seriously?"

"Trust me, Jack, they are. What you've experienced in open council may not show that, but you can take my word for it. Mr. Gant is a high priority."

"All right. You've not steered me wrong so far. It's just so . . ."

"Political? There is far more going on behind the curtains of the Sentinel. Between Walt Whitman and Amelia Earhart—"

"That's who that is? That's Walt Whitman?"

Wilson smiled. "Not at all what you expected, right?"

"Not in the least. And what is up between him and Hauser? The tension between them seemed pretty severe."

"Walt and Hauser have a strained history, which dates back to Walt's father's death back in 1855. Hauser was there to collect the soul, and somehow, Walt was able to witness the collection."

I leaned forward, my interest brimming about the famous poet. "How was that possible?"

"It's never been positively determined, but it was assumed that Walt was possibly depressed at that point in his life and was considering suicide. He was an emotional mess, having just published *Leaves of Grass* a few days before his father's death."

"I get that Walt was probably upset at the time, witnessing a strange man taking his father's soul, but hasn't he forgiven Hauser for it by now?"

"Oh, he has. It's actually Hauser that has held the grudge after all this time. That's how Walt tells it, at least. If you ask me, I think the both of them are being quite childish about the whole ordeal," Wilson said, wiping his brow with his sleeve.

I nodded as the latest information about Hauser sunk in. His psyche was deeper than I had ever imagined.

"I couldn't ask while in the council, so I'll ask you now: What exactly were you thinking when you tried to save those souls?" Wilson asked.

Here it comes. Go ahead and give me the same verbal reprimand that Hauser did.

"Don't get me wrong, Jack. What you did is neither here nor there. I'm just curious what inspired you to try and change the life direction of those souls. I want to know . . . for myself."

"Are you telling me that you've never altered fate, not even once? You've collected every single soul that was assigned to you?" I asked. "How'd you do it so . . . so absentmindedly, when there were so many good people—great people—dying for no good reason?"

It was Wilson's turn to avert his eyes. "Jack, I've never been a rule breaker. Yes, I've thought about making a change a time or two but I just couldn't follow through with it. I didn't find it appropriate in the least."

"Well, I think that's what makes you and me different. I understand your stance on the *rules*. In my past life, I was the proverbial brownnoser at work. In corporate America, it's a form of survival. If you don't follow along and do as you're told, you are promptly eliminated and replaced with a yes-man," I said. "Since taking over for you, a bit of clarity has come over me and I've realized that changes can and, right or not, should be made. I respect your decision to have followed the rules for so long, but it's not my approach."

Wilson nodded but continued to avoid eye contact. "Wait a minute, come to think of it, I haven't collected every soul that was sent for. I didn't collect your soul," Wilson said excitedly.

"But weren't you allowed to let me keep mine?" I asked.

Wilson smiled. "Yes, that's right. You were destined to enter the afterlife with your soul intact."

"Hmm. That brings up another question: Was I recruited or was this your idea to let me continue on in the afterlife?"

"Well, it was a little bit of both. After sixty years, I really was tiring of my duties. But as for you, yes, you were a targeted interest."

"Was it because of my work history?" I asked.

"No, not entirely. Although that did have a part to play in your recruitment. They were more interested in the fact that you had no living family members to speak of. Both of your parents had passed on years ago and you were an only child. Aunts and uncles?" Wilson asked.

I shook my head. "No. I think there might have been some distant relatives that I'd never met, but none within the state."

"You see, the Sentinel targets people that have no reason to make life-altering changes for their loved ones. Fate already had it that Cyndi was going to die within days of your own death. She would have been a deal breaker if she would have lived on. But because her accident and injuries were so severe, there was really no way for her to continue on. You were an easy pick as my replacement."

Thinking back to Cyndi's terrible fall down the stairwell made me shudder. Until Wilson brought up that horrific accident, I had been doing a decent job forgetting it. But now sorrow began to set in all over again.

"That's all water under the bridge, Jack. You can't go back and save her now. I think you've been procrastinating long enough. Let's flip the coin and catch up to where you are now."

I nodded my head in agreement and turned the coin over.

Chapter 5.5

Suddenly Hauser stood and moved to the center of the circle. He slowly walked around, looking each of the council members in the face.

"Before we jump to any disciplinary conclusions, I think what Jack says has a lot of merit."

"Proceed," Earhart said.

"Perhaps trying to capture Enoch the next time he shows up is aiming a bit too high. Perhaps approaching this from a different angle might be more appropriate. If Walt can create something, some kind of marker that we can tag Enoch with the next time he comes around, perhaps we might then be able to track him back to where he hides out."

As Hauser continued his slow, concentric path at the center of the gathering, I noticed a number of the council members begin to nod their heads. When I glanced at Whitman, he was looking right back at me. He smiled briefly. Nervously, I returned his smile and refocused my attention on Hauser.

"Despite Jack's indiscretions with his duties, I think we should encourage him to save yet another soul. I think we should give him a new soul box and allow him to once again try and change fate," Hauser said, holding a hand up to the oncoming challenges from the various council members. "We allow Jack to continue the farce long enough to coax Enoch to him. I'll be there throughout the entire process. Either he or I should be able to attach whatever Walt can come up with to Enoch's body. Once he's been tagged, our battle is half over."

Hauser retook his seat and we both looked around the gathering. The temperament had certainly changed and I was very thankful for Hauser's interference.

You're welcome, buddy. You owe me one.

The gathering room filled with murmurs of the possibilities of potentially apprehending Enoch. Hauser and I sat silently as the council discussed all aspects of the proposal. After nearly an hour of planning and negotiating, Earhart spoke.

"It is the ruling of the council that Jack Duffy will maintain his soul collection abilities for the time being. There will, however, be a full review of his work history upon the completion of his next soul collection. In addition, Jack will be given an additional ability to aid him with this task. Do you accept these conditions, Mr. Duffy?"

"I do," I said without hesitation. "But what additional abilities could you possibly give me that I don't already possess?"

"You will be given the ability to converse with the living. For all intents and purposes, you will be a living, breathing person. You will be able to be seen and heard by everyone around you. We feel that this enhancement, albeit temporary, will give you the edge you may need to help achieve your goal."

"And you feel this way because . . ." I urged for more information.

"Because, Mr. Duffy, the next soul that will be assigned to you will be for Miss Penelope Rose," Earhart said. "Because of your previous interactions with her, we feel that having the ability to be seen and heard by everyone should improve the likelihood of achieving your objective without raising too much suspicion."

My God, not Penelope. Hasn't that woman suffered enough, losing her own son?

Careful, Jack, Hauser thought to me.

"Yes, Miss Rose will attempt suicide. And it seems to be an unavoidable fate. But with your own personal history on the matter," Earhart said, "you might be able to convince her otherwise."

My head began to spin as comprehension set in. I tried not to think about the ramifications of the plan until we were away from the Sentinel, but I failed miserably. Having the chance to right the wrongs that I'd done to myself was more than I could ever ask for. I was beyond excited to get started immediately.

"Mr. Duffy," Earhart said, "do keep in mind that this is only a luring tactic. If you and Mr. Hauser are successful, Miss Rose's soul will still be collected, as originally foretold. You have to *think* that saving her soul is the ultimate goal, in the off chance that Enoch is invading your thoughts. But do realize that in the end her collection shall be made."

"I understand," I said, forcing a mental block on my thoughts.

"One more thing, Mr. Duffy. It is blaringly clear that you have absolutely no control of your inner thoughts. It is imperative that you not *think* about the plan without some self-control. Enoch seems to have mastered the technique, and a great deal of practice on your part is in order if we want this plan to succeed."

"Yes, ma'am. I will do my best," I said, embarrassed.

"Well then, if you two would like to stop by Mr. Whitman's lab before picking up your new soul box, I pronounce this gathering concluded."

I released the coin and was brought back to Wilson in the park.

Chapter
6

"Tell me, Wilson. What's going to happen to me after I complete this ruse?"

"I don't know, Jack. Up until the point that you left the council chamber, I was aware of your entire past. From that point forward, I'm in the dark just as much as you are."

"Haven't you been able to use the rosary and see ahead?" I asked.

"Unfortunately, no. You have my rosary in your possession. I've had no need for it. And until just recently, the Sentinel has had no idea if the plan has been proceeding accordingly. Besides, not all devices work on both the living and those in the afterlife. Using the coin was a calculated attempt, and I'm thankful that it has played out for us. I have severe doubts that the rosary would work in the same fashion."

I pulled the rosary from my pocket and handed it to Wilson. "Well, care to give it a try?" I asked.

Wilson slipped the rosary around his neck and held the crucifix between his fingers. He closed his eyes and placed his free hand on my arm. Having not experienced this from this side of the rosary, I was unsure if Wilson ventured ahead in my future or if he was simply concentrating silently. After several moments, Wilson let go and withdrew the rosary before handing it back to me.

"Just as I expected. The rosary would not take me forward. Nice thought though, Jack."

I slipped the rosary back into my pocket and looked back at Wilson. "So we're back at square one."

"More importantly, Jack, neither of us knows what happened to you from the moment you left the Sentinel until now. I think that is more important to discover. And until you flip the coin over again, neither of us will know what to do next. I suggest that you turn the coin and proceed."

I nodded in agreement and twisted the coin between my fingers.

Chapter 6.5

After many hours of tedious mental training to help me control my thoughts, we were finally able to leave the Sentinel. With my new soul box in pocket, we stepped back into the thin air of the streets of Denver.

"Well, Jack, do you feel any different?" Hauser asked.

I breathed in deeply and exhaled a moment later. I looked around at the various pedestrians on the sidewalk. Nobody paid me any attention. It was as if I was invisible.

"No, not really. Should I?"

"Don't know. I've never been given the opportunity that you have," Hauser said.

If I didn't know any better, I'd think Hauser was envious by the tone he used in his question. He looked at me sideways, waiting for my response. Maybe I was reading too much into his actions.

"Well, unless you want to have people stare at you for talking to yourself in the middle of the street, I suggest we go someplace a little more private to prepare our plan," Hauser said.

"Lead the way," I said. "Just tell me where we're going and I'll meet you there."

"Actually, I have something else in mind. If you don't mind, how about you let me drive once more. It'll be a new location for you," Hauser said, holding his arm out to my side.

I placed my hand on his arm and a moment later we vanished.

As my vision cleared, I felt much better than the last time I'd let Hauser transport us without my control. Despite the faint dizziness, I began to walk around our destination. We were in a large, cavernous room, approximately the size of two basketball courts side by side. The floor was distressed concrete, and the four outside walls were made of glass, albeit covered with grime. The ceiling, which rose up nearly twenty feet, had been painted white at one time, but was now water stained from years of neglect. At the center of the large room was a freestanding wood structure, no more than eight or nine feet tall and quite ominous. Hauser was already walking toward the single door on the structure.

"This way, champ. Welcome to my humble abode," Hauser said as he walked through the door.

I caught up and entered behind him, unsure of what to expect. Once inside, the interior of the space more resembled a studio apartment than an abandoned warehouse.

"You live here?" I asked.

"Yep. We're in the outskirts of Detroit, and as most of the town's been abandoned, nobody even knows I'm here."

"The fact that nobody can see you probably helps a little bit too," I said sarcastically.

"True, they can't see me, but they certainly could see any of my possessions that I've collected over the years. Hence, the apartment built inside an open warehouse."

"I'm sorry, what did you just say?" I asked, seizing the opportunity to razz my mentor. "What's this about possessions? Didn't you tell me all those months ago that I had to, how did you put it, forget about everything I'd ever owned?"

Hauser winced, then turned his frown into a smile. "Come now, Jack. You do realize that you were in training, right? There are certain things that you needed to learn so you wouldn't continue to dwell upon your past. I had to get you and your mind away from Cyndi. Look around. None of these possessions were from my previous life. They're all things that I've collected through the years, and they're not even mementos or keepsakes whatsoever. They're just . . . things that spoke to me. They called out to me. Does that make sense?"

I shook my head. "Not in the slightest," I said as I moved

around Hauser's hideout.

The space was fairly modern in its decor, and included a kitchen and bath, along with a sleeping area as part of the living room. Besides the bath and a wardrobe closet, everything was in a large room. There were no windows, but there were pieces of art hung around the perimeter.

"Why did we come here and not Penelope's apartment?" I asked.

"Considering your new ability, we couldn't very well just pop into her apartment, now could we? She would be able to see you instantly, regardless of her impending death. Seeing as she is still in flux," Hauser said, patting his pocket watch, "I felt it best that we go someplace more private to work out the details of the plan. And besides, I've got a head start on all things Enoch." Hauser nodded his head in the direction of the dining area.

I walked up to the large wall behind the dining table, which was plastered with news clippings and photographs.

"I've been tracking Enoch Gant for years now," Hauser explained. "Everything you see on the wall is mysterious reports that I've linked to Enoch himself."

I scanned the headlines, which sounded somewhat familiar. A number of them spoke about eyewitnesses of a man in a blue suit with matching hat, in relation to various mysterious deaths. But many of the clippings were from foreign newspapers. "I can only read half of these, Hauser. What do they all say?"

"They're all pretty much the same. Just different locations. Our man Enoch has been a busy boy. Until recently I wasn't completely sold on the idea that he was in fact murdering innocent people. But after your last soul collection, all bets are off."

"If I am the first soul collector to have the ability to be seen and heard by those still living, how are the reports of Enoch being seen even possible?" I asked.

"That's the question of the century, Jack. I've been told that Whitman's lab had been working on the enhanced abilities that you have now for quite some time. It was my understanding that they were still a good deal away from completing their objective. The only thing that we can surmise is that Enoch himself has been working on the same technology, or he has someone on the inside helping him out."

"A mole?" I gasped. "I'd never imagined there would be so much cloak and dagger going on in the afterlife."

"Yeah, well, the Sentinel completely missed the character markers with Enoch. They usually do a much better job at recruiting."

"So what have you learned from all of this?" I gestured at the news printings.

"With each new sighting, I would jump to the location and do my own research. Obviously, by the time each of these made print, I was far too late to attempt a capture of Enoch. But I still went to each one. There were a few times though that Enoch stuck around to watch the reactions of the public. And on more than one occasion, I was able to chase after him. I was close enough to catch his scent, but he was far too clever. He would lead me into hazardous locations, catching me off guard. If I wasn't quick enough to transport away in time, I would've died a long time ago. After one too many close calls, it was decided that a direct pursuit of Enoch was forbidden until we had a better plan worked out."

"And now we do," I said, taking a seat on Hauser's sofa.

Hauser sat across from me and looked at me thoughtfully. "So how are we going to save Penelope's soul?"

"Well, I suppose we should first start by getting close to her, finding out what it is that makes her who she is. Find out what is triggering her suicidal tendencies."

"That might be easier said than done," Hauser said. "Despite what the Sentinel thinks, your new abilities may prove to be more of a hindrance than anything else. I think we're going to have to do a tag-team reconnaissance on this one, and limit you to personal interaction only."

I sat up. "We're going to split up? Is that wise with Enoch on the prowl?"

"I don't expect Enoch to be knocking on Penelope's door anytime soon. For all we know, he has no idea that you have a new soul to collect. Also, at this point there are only the two of us, and the Sentinel, that know we will even attempt to save her soul. It might be a number of weeks before he comes out of the woodwork, but—"

319

"But he also might have that mole in the Sentinel that you mentioned. He might be at her place right now."

Hauser nodded thoughtfully. "Precisely why we need to split up. But first, I think we need to talk about the injectors that Whitman gave us," Hauser said as he pulled two cylindrical devices from his inside pocket. "I'm actually surprised he was able to create something so quickly."

Hauser handed me one of the pen-shaped devices. "It looks like one of those epinephrine pens that are used for asthma attacks or allergic reactions."

"That's precisely what it is. While you were visiting the mind control specialist, Walt told me that in the rush we were in, he had to use an actual EpiPen and modify it for our purposes." Hauser removed the cap to demonstrate its use. "All we have to do is stab the black end of the pen somewhere on his body. It will inject some microscopic tracking dots into his body. It'll be impossible for him to hide after that."

"And Walt was able to devise these . . . nanites that quickly?" I asked, skeptical.

"He has a number of science geeks working with him, and they can sometimes pull off miracles," Hauser said as he recapped his pen. "Now, let's go over everything once again, and then I'll go track down Penny."

Chapter 7.5

When we arrived back in New York, Hauser dropped us in a dingy alleyway just off of Forty-Third Street.

"With your new ability of being visible, I think it best that we only travel to and from vacant areas," Hauser said as he began to move toward the end of the alley.

I fell into stride next to him, ignoring the putrid smell emanating from the nearby dumpsters. "That makes sense. Where is it that we're going, though?"

"It's a community center about a block away. After I tracked down where Penelope lives—incidentally, she goes by Penny—I was able to utilize Wilson's, er, I mean your rosary, to see ahead to this point."

"Does she work at the community center, maybe as a volunteer?" I asked.

"Not exactly," Hauser said, shaking his head. Penny is . . . confused. She's here at a support group for depression."

"That makes sense. I would probably be a little depressed as well if I had recently lost a newborn."

"So this doesn't bother you?" Hauser asked.

"No, should it?"

"Well, considering how you left your life, I would assume that . . ."

"Are you sure that she's going to try to kill herself?" I asked.

"All of the signs say yes. No, I haven't seen her death, yet. But in addition to her depression, her soul has been in flux from the moment I found her in her apartment. Much like it was at the hospital, when she lost her child."

"Calvin. Don't remind me," I said.

"Well? Are you going to be okay?"

I sighed. "Don't you think it's a little late for that?" I said. "Besides, I'm here to convince her *not* to die. I'm here to help her continue living. That is something I can be on board with."

"Just remember, sport, Penny here is purely bait. Your intentions, no matter how sincere, are only present to lure Enoch out into the open. You're not actually going to be able to save her," Hauser said, stopping at the end of the alley to look me in the eye.

"Yeah, okay. I got it. I'm not gonna save her soul," I said in a monotone.

"All right. I think we're ready to go in, then."

We stepped from the alley and onto the open sidewalk. Hauser was walking a little faster than normal, and I increased my speed in an attempt to match his pace. Before I knew it, I walked right into the back of another pedestrian. The collision nearly knocked me to the ground.

"Hey, buddy, why don't you watch where you're going," said the stranger before stomping off down the street.

After regaining my composure, I looked up and found Hauser staring back at me, smiling ear to ear. "Wow, having to relearn how to interact with society has to be a real bitch," he said.

I chuckled, trying to hide my embarrassment. I was actually surprised how quickly I'd lost the ability to interact with other people. Since entering the afterlife all those months ago, I rarely gave it a second thought when walking around or through the living.

"I guess I need to regain some manners," I said.

"At the very least," Hauser said. "This way, compadre."

Hauser looked both ways before crossing into the street. I followed in his footsteps, verifying that he wasn't foolishly luring me into a dangerous situation. He glanced back at me just as I looked up and down the street, and then chuckled. "What? You think I would actually put you in harm's way?" he asked.

I shrugged as I passed him and stepped onto the sidewalk.

"So what's our play? Do I just to go up to her and start

chatting with her?" I asked.

"Well, maybe something not so direct, but yeah."

"And you're sure she's in there?" I asked.

Hauser pulled out his pocket watch and flipped it open for us both to see. As we stood right outside the community center, the only dot on the face of the dial flashed slowly.

"Yep. She's here. And from the speed of the flashing, it looks like whatever they're talking about in there is doing her good."

I leaned around the edge of the building and peered inside the glass storefront. From where I stood, I could see close to a dozen people sitting in plastic chairs arranged in a circle. I held my position for a few moments, studying the group.

"I don't know, Hauser. I think your pocket watch might be broke. I don't see her in there."

"Trust me, she's in there. She may look a little different from the last time you saw her, but she's there."

I peeked around the corner again, scanning the group. As I did, individuals in the group began to stand up and mingle around, a few of them refilling their drinks from a buffet table at the side of the room.

"And you're sure that Enoch will pick up on our activities?" I asked nervously.

"What's going on, Jack? You obviously want to save all of the souls, so what's causing the blockage right now?"

Hauser was right. There was something blocking my confidence, but I couldn't quite put my finger on it.

"I don't know. It's just that . . . I guess I've just gotten use to not interacting with people, formally. I've never really been socially awkward or anything, but I'm having some strange feelings of inadequacy right now."

"Nobody said this was going to be a walk in the park, Jack. Just do your best and I'm sure you'll do fine."

I took a deep breath, then walked around the corner and opened the front door.

Chapter 8.5

When I stepped into the Forty-Second Street community center, several small independent groups murmured quietly around the room. As I walked farther into the gathering, I casually looked around at all of the female guests trying to find Penny.

"Welcome," a woman said from the center of the room.

I smiled and walked up to her. "Hello," I said nervously. "Uh, a friend of mine said there was some kind of group that I could, um . . ." I held the pause to exaggerate the awkwardness of the situation. "A place that I could come to if I was depressed."

"Your friend is correct. I am Alisha. I'm a support counselor here, and our door is always open. If you ever want to talk, there will always be somebody here to listen." She smiled. "We have weekly gatherings where you can come and participate in group sessions. There's one going on right now, but we're just on a little bit of a break."

"Oh, thank you. I'm not sure if I'm quite ready to jump right into a group environment . . ."

"That's quite all right, Mr. . . . ?"

"Uh," I stammered.

"I'm sorry, you don't have to tell me your last name. First names are fine."

"I, um, I'm Jack."

"Welcome, Jack. You're more than welcome to participate today if you'd like, but you could also just observe today if that makes you feel more comfortable."

"Thank you. I'd like that. I'll just hang out if that's okay?"

"Absolutely. Help yourself to refreshments, too. There's snacks and punch at the back."

I smiled and nodded, then shuffled through the crowd, trying to be aware of my surroundings as to not run into anyone. When I reached the back table, I filled a cup with punch and picked up a chocolate chip cookie. As I turned back to face the room, I saw her. Penny was sitting alone and looked far worse for the wear than I'd anticipated. Her eyes were ringed in pink and swollen, and her hair looked as if it hadn't been combed in quite some time. Her shirt appeared inside out, and her jeans were stained with grime.

There she is, I thought to Hauser.

"See? I told you so," Hauser said from beside me. "Now, it's all up to you."

"Oh great. Way to put the pressure on me," I said as I fidgeted nervously.

"Relax, Jack. It's not like you're going up to ask her out on a date or anything. You're just here to . . . talk to her, get to know her, and find out how close she is to killing herself."

Hearing Hauser talk about committing suicide as if it were just another daily occurrence bothered me. Having mostly come to terms with my own fatal decision helped soften the impact, but the entire situation disturbed me just the same. Then a thought crossed my mind.

"Wait a minute. Won't she recognize me from the hospital?"

"Well, I wasn't going to bring it up, buddy, but she might very well remember you. Before she went in for the C-section, she was on no medication or drugs whatsoever. We just have to hope that enough time has passed that you're just another stranger to her. Now go. You're not getting any younger," Hauser smirked. "And be cautious when speaking to me in public. You do realize other people can hear you talking, right? It looks like you are having a deep conversation with yourself."

Got it. I forgot there for a minute, I thought.

As I walked toward Penny, I brought the cup of punch to my lips to take a drink. Just as the sugary sweetness reached my tongue, my elbow struck someone's back, causing me to spill red liquid down my chin and all over my chest.

"Son of a—" I exclaimed as I stepped around the perturbed man frowning awkwardly at me. "I mean, sorry about that," I said.

Brushing the liquid from my shirt, I walked over to Penny's chair. "Hi. Is anybody sitting here?" I asked.

Penny barely acknowledged me and shook her head.

I lowered myself into the chair next to her and continued to dab awkwardly at the fruit punch soaking through my shirt. "I don't suppose you have an extra napkin on you?" I said.

"No, sorry," she said, standing up to leave.

"I'm sorry, miss. I didn't mean to intrude. It's just that . . . I'm new here and I'm a little nervous."

She looked at me and tilted her head slightly. "You're new?" she asked. "I think I've seen you in here before."

Oh crap. She does remember me, I thought to Hauser.

"Keep going, buddy," Hauser said from behind me. "If she'd remembered you from the hospital, do you think she'd still be standing here, waiting for your response?"

"Yeah, I suppose you're right," I said aloud.

"So you're not new?" Penny asked.

"Um, what I meant to say . . . was that you're right. I have been in here before, but I haven't participated in any of the sessions. I've been sort of a shadow really, just staying on the fringes of the room."

"Nice recovery, ace," Hauser said.

"If I make you uncomfortable, I can leave," I said.

"No, it's all right," Penny said as she retook her seat. "We're supposed to talk about our feelings anyway. Isn't that why we're all here?"

I nodded. "Yeah, I suppose so. I've just never been that big of a sharer, if you know what I mean."

"Totally," Penny said as she continued to stare at me awkwardly.

"So have you been coming here long?" I asked, fidgeting with my sleeve again.

"Seriously, Jack. You're not trying to pick her up. You're acting as nervous and awkward as a high school boy at cheerleader tryouts."

"I mean, have you been attending these sessions long? Have they helped you at all?" I said, wondering why this was so difficult.

Penny shrugged and rolled her eyes. "Yeah, I guess."

"Have any pointers for a newbie?"

"I don't know. I guess just try not to dwell on the past. At least that's what the counselors keeps telling me."

"You don't sound too convinced," I said.

Penny stared straight ahead. "I don't know. It just seems that all of this is bullshit anyway. First they tell you to forget about the past, then in the next breath they tell you to look deeper at what's causing the depression. Most of the time that *is* the past. So I guess I don't have anything worth saying," Penny said.

"Careful, Jack. Penny's soul is beginning to flash faster. Try to calm her down," Hauser said.

"I feel the same way. I'm Jack, by the way."

"Penny."

"A friend of mine has told me to let bygones be bygones and all that, but, I don't know, I do sometimes feel better when I talk about what happened."

Penny tilted her head in my direction. "And what's that?"

"It's still a little difficult to talk about, but . . . my wife committed suicide about six months ago," I said, the words out of my mouth before I could take them back.

"Jesus, Jack. Are you trying to convince her to kill herself?" Hauser asked.

Penny's eyes widened and she turned her body toward me, her interest piqued. "How did she . . . I mean I'm sorry for your loss. How did she do it?"

"Whatever you do, Jack, do not tell her how to kill herself," Hauser snapped.

"I'd rather not talk about the details if that's all right," I said. "It's still pretty painful."

"Oh, I'm so sorry," Penny said, her voice cracking slightly.

"It's okay, you didn't know. Maybe in time it'll be easier to talk about," I said, hanging my head low, enjoying the false sympathy. "What about you? What's your story?"

"I'm lonely, I guess. I don't have any family, and I had a pretty traumatic event a few months ago."

"Do you want to talk about it?" I asked, pivoting toward her.

Penny breathed in deeply and exhaled slowly. "I lost a child at birth," she said, tears welling up in her eyes.

"Oh, how tragic," I said, placing my hand on her shoulder.

Back off, you creep, Penny thought. *I'm not a piece of meat, old man.*

Old man? I thought.

"Jack, she does have a point. You are coming off a little desperate. Now would be a good time to extricate your hand from her shoulder," Hauser said.

I casually dropped my hand to the side. "I . . . know what you're feeling."

"How could you? Have you recently popped a child out of your vagina?" she asked angrily.

I turned away quickly, hoping to come across less threatening. "No, that's not what I meant. I mean, I understand what it's like losing something or someone. After my wife died, I constantly asked myself, why me. She left me on this earth alone, and all I can think about is why me." I lowered my eyes and hoped that I didn't look too pathetic.

Penny sighed heavily. "Exactly. I've lost the only thing important to me, and I don't know why I feel so . . . abandoned. Sometimes I just don't want to continue," she said as tears streaked down her face.

"Hey, hey. Don't think like that. Your life means so much more than you could ever imagine. Life has two rules: One, never quit. And two, always remember rule number one. You'll get through this, I promise."

How the hell can you promise something like that, Penny thought. *I just met you, and . . .*

"I can because I'm living proof," I said.

"Watch it, Jack. You're answering her thoughts with your own words," Hauser said.

"How did you—" Penny began.

"I guess I just knew what you were thinking because I've been there. Granted, it's taken me six months to get past everything, and I'm now starting to see the light at the end of the tunnel. I know that's so cliché, but suicide is not your answer."

"To hell with you, buddy. You just met me and you're telling me what's right for me?" Penny yelled and stood up so fast her chair slid halfway across the room.

"Penelope, please," I begged. "I didn't mean to—"

"I never told you my full name. Who are you? Wait a minute, never mind. Fuck you," Penny said as she stormed out.

Shit, I thought.

"That's an understatement, buddy. I'd point out just how horrible that went, but I assume you realize that all on your own," Hauser said.

"Well, now what? Did I completely screw the pooch on this one?"

"I don't know, Jack. Time will tell. I suggest you make a discreet exit and then we can regroup back at your place."

I nodded and made for the exit, avoiding eye contact with anyone in the room. As soon as I was out of sight, I vanished.

Chapter 9.5

As I stood on the rooftop of Cornwell Tower on Forty-Eighth Street, I hoped I was in the right place. Having just walked through Penny's future using the rosary, I could only recognize certain aspects of the environment before coming here in person. I was nearly certain that this was the very rooftop from which she would take her life.

I moved to the edge and looked down. Even though I'd never really experienced a fear of heights, standing more than fifty floors above the earth made my knees weak. Nervously, I inched away from the edge and turned toward the stairway door. I waited.

Thankfully, my wait was brief as Penny blasted through the door right on time. She wasted no time and marched directly toward me and the edge of the roof. I'd hoped that she might take her time, convincing herself that this was her only way out as opposed to taking the bull by the horns and advancing toward her death so quickly.

"Penny, wait," I said. "You don't want to do this."

Penny continued her march, walking past me and right up to the edge. She paused and looked down just as I had done moments before.

Nervously, I moved to her side. "Penny, why do you want to kill yourself? I'm here to tell you that whatever the reason is, it's no good reason at all. Trust me when I tell you this. I'm speaking from personal experience."

Penny raised her head up and looked toward the sky. She

took in several deep breaths before hanging her head low once again. As she stood there, silently, her toes inching forward and over the edge of the roof, she swayed back and forth, tempting gravity to take over.

"I don't understand, Penny. Why are you ignoring me?" I said, hoping to distract her for even just a moment.

Penny continued her silence as she inched even closer toward her death. Finally, when I felt she had reached the point of no return, I reached out to pull her back from the edge.

"You can't keep ignoring me," I yelled, just as my fingers touched her warm skin. Or so I thought. I had expected my hand to wrap around her arm, but my hand passed right through her body. *What the hell?*

Just then, I heard a loud voice across the vast rooftop.

"What the hell are you doing? Do not interfere! Haven't you meddled in the lives of other people enough?"

A man in a blue suit with a matching bowler hat was running at full sprint in our direction. It was Enoch Gant.

"Penny! Quick, get away from the edge," I pleaded.

Penny continued to ignore me, but she turned to the sound of Enoch's voice.

As he neared our position, his speed increased exponentially. He was going to plow into the both of us, carrying us all over the edge.

"Stop, you lunatic! What the hell are you doing?" I demanded.

He was getting closer by the second, his face intense and manic. If I hadn't known any better, I would certainly classify it as suicidal. He was going to kill himself, along with Penny and me.

I tried once more to grab Penny, but again my hand passed through her as if I didn't exist. It became obvious to me that she could not see or hear me.

Suddenly, Enoch was upon us. He spread his arms wide and wrapped them around Penny and me as he launched over the edge of the building. Strangely, I was not transparent to him but only to Penny, as the sharp pain in my ribs forced me to gasp out loud. Enoch drove us over and toward our death.

"Why are you doing this, you son of a bitch?" I screamed as I sat up.

"Easy there, partner. I'm only here to help you. You know that, right?" Hauser said, sitting next to me on my couch.

I opened my eyes and rubbed the sleep away. As my surroundings became clear, I realized that it was all a dream. "Jesus, Hauser. How long was I out?" I asked.

"Not sure, champ. I've only just arrived a few moments ago," Hauser said, lifting himself up from the lumpy couch. "I see that you've taken the warnings to not sleep to heart." He winked.

"It's not like that. I had a plan."

"I'm sure you did, but you know what the Sentinel said."

"I do, but I figured that if I could dream about saving Penny, that would help our efforts in luring Enoch out."

"And? Did it work?"

"Well, sort of. He was in the dream, and I was trying to save Penny, but he ended up killing all three of us by pushing us over the edge."

Hauser looked at me thoughtfully. "Hmm. I suppose that makes sense. So you actually died in your dream?"

"Well, no. Not exactly. Enoch did push us all over the edge, but I woke up, here, before we reached the ground."

"Well that's a relief. You know what they say, if you die in your dream you die in real life."

"I've never heard that before. Yanking my chain?" I asked.

"I don't know, sport. It must be something that I read on the Internet somewhere."

"Wait, what? The Internet wasn't even around when you became a soul collector."

Hauser winked. "Let's get back on topic shall we?"

I nodded. "All right. What did you find out?"

"I spent the greater part of the last day with Penny at her apartment. She is pretty messed up. She is as alone as she said, and I'm not sure if she can actually be saved, Jack."

"Shit. So I did mess up, didn't I?"

"Well, not so fast. Yes, you spooked the crap out of her at the community center, but at the same time she has been continuing to think about what you said to her."

"Really?" I said eagerly.

"Besides the fact that she still thinks that you're an old

pervert, she's been contemplating the value of life. I think that might be your saving grace."

Relief spread through my veins. I suddenly felt euphoric, like a load had been lifted from my shoulders. "That's fantastic, Hauser."

"Not so fast, champ. You still have a lot of work ahead of you," Hauser said as he reached out and twisted my arm so he could read my watch. "And there's not a moment to waste. You need to be at the bookstore in thirty minutes."

"What happens in thirty minutes?" I asked.

"Penny will be there, and it will be an excellent opportunity for you to make amends."

"What exactly do I have to do? You used the rosary, obviously."

"What I saw is not important, Jack. What is important is you arriving at the bookstore early, and then you need to knock your coffee over."

"That's it? That's your big plan to make everything right?"

Hauser shook his head. "Just trust me, won't you?"

I sensed something more, something he was withholding. "What aren't you telling me, Hauser?"

He sighed. "There is . . . an incident. And if you just follow along with my instruction, we can minimize the ramifications. I don't have time to go into it further, you just have to trust me. Can you do that?"

"So I just have to spill my coffee? Will I know when and where to pull off such an ingenious plan?"

"Don't worry, buddy. I'll be there with you and will walk you through everything step by step."

"All right, let's get a move on, then. Where is this bookstore that you speak of?"

"Great! It's just a few blocks from Penny's apartment. I think you'll like it. You collect books, right?"

Chapter 10.5

When I walked into the Dreamcatcher Book Emporium, I was momentarily breathless. In all my years of living in the city, I found it odd that I'd never been to this particular bookstore. I thought I'd known where every one was throughout the city.

The store occupied the first two floors of an old brick warehouse. The interior walls were exposed brick, giving it a loft-style environment. The bookshelves stood away from the walls, creating a sort of racetrack feel all around the store. At the second level, open rails overlooked the central coffee bar.

As we moved into the coffee shop, I could see more aisles and rows of bookshelves retreating back from the second floor balconies. It was all very chic in a shabby kind of way.

"Okay, now what?" I asked. "Do I just stand here and wait, or should I go grab a book to read until she comes in?"

"First off, you should probably go get yourself a cup of coffee with the money I gave you. Then you need to take a seat there," Hauser said, pointing to a table at the perimeter of the small café, "and sit with your back toward the door."

"You're so very precise, Hauser. How long did it take you to calculate every action and setting? I feel so very much like a marionette," I said sarcastically.

"Just get the coffee, bub. I'll wait here."

Feeling more comfortable with public interactions by the minute, I bought my coffee and sat at the table with my back to the door. "Okay. Am I sitting properly? Should I cross my leg? Or should I sit here with my head on the table?"

"That's enough, smart-ass. Just sit and wait. You should also take the lid off of your coffee," Hauser said.

I removed the lid and took a small sip of the steaming liquid. It had been quite some time since I'd had any caffeine whatsoever, and if I didn't know any better, I'd swear I could practically feel the liquid adrenaline pulsing into my veins.

As the minutes passed, I continued to take small sips of the coffee. Hauser stood next to me, scanning the bookstore, looking for Penny's arrival.

"Okay, you're on champ."

I instinctively straightened my posture and adjusted the collar of my shirt.

"Now, when I tell you, I want you to spill your coffee."

"Just pour it out, or do I—"

"Just knock the damn thing over," Hauser snapped. "Now."

I swung my arm to the side, tipping the nearly full coffee cup over. The liquid quickly spread across the table and dripped into my lap.

"Holy shit," I exclaimed. "That's fucking hot."

"Well if you weren't such a klutz, you'd stop spilling liquid all over yourself," Penny said, standing next to me.

I sprang from my chair and reflexively swiped the steaming liquid off my pants. "I'm sorry. I don't know what just came over me. I went to look at my watch and just knocked my coffee cup right on over."

"Are you going to be all right, or do you need me to call somebody to take care of those burns?" Penny asked.

"I think I'll be okay. It doesn't hurt too bad . . . but if you have a couple of napkins, that might help with this mess."

Penny walked up to the counter and returned with a handful of small cocktail napkins to dab up the remaining coffee from the table.

"Thanks," I said. "I'm actually kind of surprised that you'd even talk to me again."

"Yeah, about that. I'm sorry I stormed off. You probably understand. I'm an emotional mess most of the time, and that day was not particularly good for me," Penny said.

As I finished cleaning up the spilled coffee, I retook my seat and motioned for Penny to join me. "That's understandable, Penny. I remember experiencing days just like that after my wife . . . you know."

Penny accepted the offer to join me and smiled discreetly. "So, do you live around here or are you stalking me?" she asked.

"Neither. I collect books. It's a crazy, expensive addiction. A friend of mine told me about this place, and I figured I couldn't pass it up."

Penny smiled again and looked at me with a strange, sideways glance. "You know, it's funny. I know you said that you've been to the community center before, but I just . . . I don't know. I think we've seen each other someplace else. I just can't put my finger on it."

Panicked, I said, "That doesn't surprise me. I'm told that I have a very recognizable face. You would not believe how often people tell me that they remember seeing me from someplace else."

"Nice cover, Jack," Hauser said. "Now, change the subject before she thinks about it more. Buy her a cup of coffee."

"I'm sorry, where are my manners? Can I get you something? Maybe a cup of coffee . . . that's not spilled all over my lap?" I asked.

Penny giggled. "That would be great, thanks. House coffee with cream, please."

I excused myself and bought two more coffees quickly. I sat down again, and we both sipped awkwardly at our hot drinks.

"So, Penny, seeing as I was here first, I think it's you that is stalking me," I said teasingly.

"Don't you wish, perv," Penny said dryly. "Actually, I live nearby and coming here takes my mind off of . . . things."

"This place certainly is wonderful," I said. "What with the vast book selection in all genres."

Penny nodded. "Yeah, there's that. But then when I get to the family and parenting section, I usually lose it."

"Yikes, I'm sorry. Change of subject?" I asked.

"No, it's all right. Like we said the other day, it's sometimes good to talk about things."

"Okay then, tell me about yourself."

"What do you want to know? Am I single? Do I enjoy long walks on the beach? Do I like the sound of rain?" she said sarcastically.

"No, nothing like that. Tell me about your family, about your parents. Do you have sisters or brothers?"

"I had a brother, but he died a few years ago," Penny said, her voice dropping. "I don't know my real parents. I've been in foster homes for as long as I can remember," she said, her mood dropping even further.

Well, crap, I thought.

"Have you tried to track down your real parents?" I asked.

"I tried several months ago, right after I got pregnant. But it was a lost cause. Nobody had any paperwork on how I even entered the foster care system."

"I really don't mean to sound like a broken record, but I'm sorry, Penny."

"It's all right. It's not your fault. I just seem to have been dealt an unlucky hand in life, or so it seems sometimes."

"Can I ask about the father of your child? Is he around?"

"Ha, funny story," Penny said sardonically. "The father of my child was my very last foster father."

"Holy hell, Jack. Change the subject quick," Hauser said.

Ignoring Hauser momentarily, I pushed further. "I'm curious. Did you still live with your foster parents when that happened?"

"No, I thought they were actually good people all along. I'd been living on my own for a few years by then, but I still stayed in contact with them. Having dinner with them occasionally, holidays and weekends and such. Then something changed. Theodore, my foster father, just snapped one day and forced himself on me, and there wasn't anything I could do about it."

"Oh, Penny. Did you report him to the police?"

"No. He told me if I said anything he would hunt me down and kill me."

My blood began to boil with each additional detail Penny told me, thinking about the injustices of collecting the good souls while assholes like Theodore continued to live.

"You know, the police could have protected you," I said,

walking gingerly through the conversation, remembering how volatile her personality was from our last meeting.

"Yeah, I know that now, but back then I was pretty scared. Now I don't really care what happens to my life."

"Penny, all life is precious. You're a very special young woman, and you have a lot to offer this world."

"Is that your expert opinion? After what? Having a few brief conversations with me?" she asked angrily.

Drastically wanting to lighten the mood, I felt a joke here would help. "I don't know, Penny. If you weren't here, who would help me every time I spilled something on myself?"

Penny gave me a ghost of a smile. "I don't know; I think you'd manage okay."

I leaned back and looked around the coffee shop as I tried to think of another humorous anecdote, when Hauser spoke up.

"Look up now, Jack. Enoch is standing at the second-floor balcony!"

"I see him," I said, raising my sight, focusing on Enoch's face just as Hauser spoke.

"I'm sorry, what?" Penny said. "You see who?"

Crap, I thought. "I, um, was just visualizing myself spilling my next hot beverage," I said.

"Excuse yourself, Jack. We need to move on this, and I mean now," Hauser said as he disappeared from my side.

Suddenly, my vision blurred. The entire room faded in and out of darkness. An uncontrollable whirling sensation overcame me, and I felt as if the room was about to turn on its side. Just as panic was about to take over, all of my senses returned just as quickly as they'd begun to skew.

"I'm sorry, Penny, but I need to go the men's room and check my . . . legs. I may have actually burned myself with that coffee spill," I said, standing and walking toward the back of the bookstore until I was out of sight. The moment I was clear I vanished from the main floor and reappeared on the second floor right next to Enoch Gant.

Chapter 11

I dropped my coin into my lap and was brought back to the present. Wilson was staring at me expectantly.

"Why did you stop?" he asked. "Is there something wrong?"

"No, I just . . . wanted to see if that dizziness was part of the flash back or if it might somehow be connected with my injury," I said as I caressed the tender mass on the back of my head.

"I'm not sure what you're talking about, Jack. I didn't experience any unsteadiness from my point of view. Can you explain it?" Wilson said, worry lines spreading across his face. He leaned forward.

"I don't know. It felt kind of like when we travel and everything blacks out. But it was different somehow. It almost felt as if I'd had too much to drink and was about to pass out."

Wilson leaned back in his chair and seemed to contemplate something as I explained the account. "I suppose it might be a carryover from the effects of caffeine on your system."

"But you said you didn't notice it from your point of view. Aren't you seeing things as I am? I've only used the coin a few times since getting it from you."

"You're partly correct, Jack. I am seeing what you see, but not to the full extent. Because these are your memories and feelings, not everything translates the same way to me," Wilson said. "It's either that or your head trauma is causing interference somehow. Do you feel dizzy right now?"

I took in a deep breath and exhaled slowly. I stood and walked around for a few moments. "No, I feel surprisingly well. My headache is even gone," I said, delighted.

"Just to be safe, I think we should give your mind a short break before going back in. Just try and remember where you were when you left."

I nodded and retook my seat. "I was standing next to Enoch on the balcony."

"Precisely."

I continued to breathe in the fresh mile-high air as a number of thoughts crossed my mind. "Tell me, Wilson. Do you have any regrets?"

"Such as?" he asked.

"I don't know. Like do you wish you had just died back then? Do you wish that you would have just passed on becoming a soul collector altogether?"

"I think there was an immediate sense of regret early on. But the longer I did the job, the easier everything became," Wilson said, looking at me suspiciously. "No lasting regrets."

"I see," I said, as I formulated my next question. I didn't want to let out anything that might jeopardize my own personal agenda on Penny's collection. "Wilson, can you . . . hear my thoughts while you're experiencing my memories with me?"

"I don't follow what you mean," Wilson said, a quizzical look crossing his face.

"I mean, can you hear my internal thinking? When I think words to Hauser, I assume that those are in my own head."

"No, no. Those are not just your own. I can hear all of your conversations just as clear as if you were speaking them out loud."

"What about my personal thoughts? Can you hear those as well?" I asked, hoping to maintain at least a sliver of my deeper plan.

"You mean inconsequential thinking? Can you give me an example?" Wilson asked.

"For instance, when I had a sip of the coffee, I thought about the nutty, burnt flavor, and how much I missed drinking it every morning," I said, hoping to steer the conversation in a safe direction.

"No, I'm sorry Jack, but I did not get any of that from your shared memories. Needless to say, it appears you are still privy to your own thoughts. Either that or you've learned to control your thoughts more efficiently since your training with the Sentinel."

I nodded, thankful that not everything was being shared with Wilson. I wasn't entirely ready to disclose my personal feelings regarding the afterlife, so I was relieved that I didn't have to explain anything further.

"All right, then. Let's get back to this," I said, picking up the coin and flipping it in my hand.

Chapter 11.5

I stood to the right and slightly behind Enoch. I waited a few moments, trying to figure out the best way to administer the injection before he could jump. As I replayed our plan in my mind, Enoch suddenly turned to face me.

"So you think you can track me?"

Crap, I thought.

"And you think that the Sentinel would actually just sit back and do nothing?" I asked.

"No. Quite the opposite. I fully expected the Sentinel to react, but what surprises me is that they sent you, all on your own. You are alone, aren't you?" Enoch asked as he looked around our immediate vicinity.

"Yes, it's just me, and you'd be a fool to underestimate my capabilities," I said, thankful that I hadn't betrayed any more of our plan.

"Well? Give me everything you've got," Enoch said, holding his hands in the air, tempting me to try and apprehend him.

I gripped the injector in the palm of my hand, but hesitated. "No, not quite yet," I said. "I'd like to know why first. Why are you doing all of this?"

Enoch dropped his hands into his pockets and swayed, casually shifting his weight from foot to foot. "Why am I taking your souls? Or why am I focusing on you?"

"Both."

"They sort of go hand in hand, wouldn't you say? You are the newest soul collector that the Sentinel has, and you are weak, man. You're an easy target for me, and it gives me the ability to take the souls that you're sent to collect without resistance. How does that make you feel? Does that upset you?"

Don't let him get in your head, Jack, Hauser thought to me. *Keep him talking and I'll try and sneak up behind him.*

"No, it doesn't. Honestly, I have far thicker skin than you might imagine. As well as a stronger passion for life salvation than you will ever have."

"Ah, so there it is. You are in the Sentinel on false pretenses. Do they know that you're reluctant to take *all* the souls that you've been tasked with?"

"They do. That is a benefit—"

"Cut the crap, Jack. I'd imagine that the Sentinel is quite disappointed in you. Tell me, was it Wilson that picked you out, or was it somebody else higher up the chain?"

I could feel my anger building, and it boggled my mind that Enoch knew more about me than I did. "That doesn't really matter here, now does it? I'm here, and there's nothing you can do to change that." I caught a slight movement over Enoch's shoulder as Hauser, popping in and out of reality, got closer and closer to Enoch.

I smiled, ignoring the verbal jabs. "All I know is, you should just move on and forget about interfering with my current collection."

"Where's the fun in that, Jack? I've been following along with you and Penny, and she seems just about prime for the picking."

"I said back the hell off! Seriously, can't you just go fetch your own souls? Why just prey on the ones I'm supposed to collect?"

"If you must know, I've been able to take a random person's soul many times, but somehow I've lost the ability to do so. Something happened to me some time ago that only permits me to take the soul from someone that the Sentinel has already deemed close to the end of their fate. I can't actually kill anyone anymore, and I have to say, it's quite disheartening."

Relieved at hearing this, I took a step closer.

"Back off, Jack. I said that I could no longer kill, but that only applies to those that are fated to continue living. You, on the other hand, are fair game. I could kill you right now and take your soul without breaking a sweat."

I froze. Was he telling the truth? I contemplated asking Hauser through my thoughts, but did not want to give Enoch any more knowledge of our plan. I held my hands up in the air and took two steps back. "All right, all right. If you have the ability to kill me and take my soul, why haven't you done it already?"

"Isn't it obvious?" Enoch asked. "It's because you are my pipeline. Your weak mind is all I need to continue my personal agenda. And neither you," Enoch paused, "or Hauser, who is making his way up behind me now, can do a thing to stop me."

Before I could ask more about his personal agenda, Hauser materialized right behind Enoch. But as he raised his hand with the auto injector, Enoch vanished then reappeared on the balcony just across the way.

"You two think you're so sly. Did you think I'd actually let you mark me somehow with whatever that device is? And truly, Hauser, I would've expected more from you."

Hauser vanished and reappeared on the far balcony, right next to Enoch. A moment later I followed. Unfortunately, as I reappeared, Enoch vanished again, followed by Hauser. I stood and looked around the second floor of the bookstore before I noticed Enoch standing right behind Penny.

"Penny!" I shouted.

She looked up at me quizzically, but did not say anything. Hauser appeared next to Enoch and reached out with the injector pen, but he narrowly missed his mark as Enoch vanished once again, reappearing right next to me.

"Well, Jack, it appears that you've been holding out on me. It looks like you have a new ability, and I want it. Whatever it is that the Sentinel has given you, I suggest you hand it over," Enoch said, pulling out a gun and pointing it at my chest.

"Sorry, Enoch, but whatever they've done to give me this temporary life interaction, it's nothing that I have and can hold. It's something that they control from above, and there's no way for you to get it," I said smugly.

"I think you're lying." Enoch pulled back the hammer on his gun. I glanced at Penny, who was staring right at me. I was in quite the predicament. If I stood there any longer, there was a good chance that Enoch would actually pull the trigger. If I vanished, Penny would see, and I wasn't sure how she would react.

On the count of three, Jack, I need you to jump right here to Penny, Hauser thought to me. *At that same moment, I will jump up and tag Enoch. Nod if you understand.*

I nodded then looked into Enoch's eyes. "Okay, you got me. I do have a device and it's in my pocket. Let me grab it."

"Not so fast. I'll get it myself," Enoch said, reaching into my inside pocket. As he began to feel around, I heard Hauser's thoughts.

Jump now!

A split second later I shoved Enoch backward and vanished. I appeared next to Penny at the same time Hauser appeared on the balcony, his injector at the ready. Unfortunately, Enoch was prepared. He fired his pistol right at Hauser, and they both vanished.

Chapter 12.5

When I appeared next to Penny in the café, she was still staring up at where I'd stood just seconds before. Her eyes were wide with shock at seeing me disappear. When she finally sensed my presence and turned to look at me, the shock turned to fear.

"What the hell are you?" she asked, recoiling from my presence.

"It's going to be okay, Penny. I'm not here to hurt you," I said, hoping to calm her reaction.

Suddenly Penny's expressions changed again, fear being replaced with recognition. "Wait a minute. I know where I've seen you before. You were at the hospital," she said.

I exhaled slowly as I sat across from her. "Yes, that's right. I was there the day that you gave birth to your son," I said.

"So are you magic or are you a ghost? I don't even know what to think."

"I can imagine the confusion that you're experiencing right now, but if you'd give me a chance to explain—"

"How can you even begin to comprehend what I'm experiencing?" she snapped.

"Because, Penny, I've been in your exact same situation, and it wasn't all that long ago."

"Who are you?" Penny began to cry.

"My name really is Jack, but I am not who you think I am. I have been sent here to . . . to collect your soul. Just as I was sent to collect Calvin's soul a few months ago."

"What? Like a grim reaper?"

"No, what I do is more civilized than that. Once a person dies, whether through their own volition or by some natural or accidental occurrence, their soul is released. I capture that soul and cleanse it before it goes to another person," I said. "The grim reaper mythology is such that they take your soul by force occasionally, and with malice regularly."

"So I am going to die, then," Penny said, more of statement than a question.

Before I could reply, Hauser reappeared. I looked him over and saw no signs of blood. *Great, you weren't shot.* With a huge sigh of relief, I looked at him expectantly. *Well?*

He shook his head. "No dice. He was able to get away from me. But I think our mission is almost complete, and I'd expect Enoch to return sooner than later. How's it going here?" he asked.

Well, the cat's out of the bag, so to speak, I thought to Hauser. *Penny saw me disappear from the balcony.*

"Well that complicates things. What have you told her? And can she see me?"

"Penny, do you see anyone else with us right now?" I asked.

She glanced around our immediate vicinity, looking through Hauser. "What is it you want with me? Are you fucking with me?"

"No, not at all. I was just curious if you were aware of anything else out of the ordinary."

"Beside you disappearing from the balcony up there and reappearing a split second later? No, everything is just peachy," she said, her voice beginning to crack.

I sensed Penny's frustration building and wanted to stop any overreaction before it occurred. "How much should I tell her?" I asked Hauser.

"In for a penny, in for a pound," Hauser said with a chuckle.

"Penny, ever since you lost your son at childbirth, you've been depressed, isn't that right?"

Penny nodded.

"And I gather from these depressed feelings that you've considered suicide?"

Again Penny nodded, her eyes widening with surprise.

"First, let me tell you that you should reconsider."

347

"What are you doing, Jack?" Hauser asked. "The plan is nearly a success. Enoch is on task. We both know what the end game is going to be here. You're just going to make it more difficult."

"Are you sure?" I asked.

"Am I sure, what?" asked Penny.

"Come on, Jack. Use your head. It's obvious that she can't see or hear our conversation. You're now just mentally torturing her."

I shook my head out of frustration. "I'm sorry, Penny, but there is another person here who you cannot see or hear, and he's not happy with me right now."

"That's an understatement," Hauser said.

"How can I believe anything that you're saying? As far as I know, you're just an old guy playing a mean trick on me, and none of this is real."

"Be careful, Jack. You're just going to make this that much more difficult when it comes time to—"

Relax, I have a plan, I thought to Hauser. *If we're going to end up taking her soul anyway, what does it matter what we tell her? And besides, if Enoch is going to continue to pursue her, wouldn't it be better if she was prepared? And I think it's also better that we remove her from the public eye.*

I looked up at Hauser as he contemplated what I was saying. After a few moments, he nodded. "Okay, Jack. Proceed. Maybe you should take her to your cabin. At least that way we can control the outcome of the situation."

"I'm sorry, Penny, but I was just having a brief conversation with my partner. If proof is what you're looking for, I think I have a way to provide that."

Penny stared at me skeptically. "All right. If you are who you say you are, why can't you show me your imaginary friend here?"

"Well, you'll see him sooner or later, that I can guarantee. But how about for starters, I take you on a little trip?"

"What, like in a car or on a bus? A plane or a train?" she asked, sounding like a Dr. Seuss book.

"Not at all. I have the ability to travel from place to place instantly. You obviously saw me disappear from upstairs and reappear down here. What if I were able to take you to a different place in the same fashion? Would you be willing to give it a try?"

Surprising both Hauser and me, Penny nodded her head vehemently.

"I hope to hell that you know what you're doing, Jack," Hauser said.

Chapter 13.5

We landed in the middle of my cabin. First Penny and me, then a few moments later, Hauser popped in next to the fireplace.

"Holy shit! What a mind fuck," Penny stated emphatically. Then she slowly began to walk around the rustic cabin.

"Penny, how do you feel? Are you dizzy? Do you feel like you might be ill?" I asked.

"No, not at all. I actually feel pretty good, considering."

"That's good. My first experience was . . ." I looked at Hauser, my eyebrow twisting up questioningly. *Why is it that she is able to transport on her first try without feeling the side effects?*

"I don't know, champ. Some people just react differently to the experience. Some of the collectors in the past have been affected much the same way that you have, while others have only experienced only light cases of dizziness. Looks like Penny here is a natural when it comes to travel in the afterlife."

"Was what?" Penny asked, settling down on the lumpy couch.

I grinned at Hauser's last comment before answering Penny. "Much to the chagrin of my partner here, I threw up a little on my first trip."

"Get out!" Penny said, more vibrant than I'd ever seen her before.

"So, anyway, this is my . . . home? Right now we're deep in the woods of upstate New York. Is that enough proof for you?" I asked.

"It's a start. Assuming that this really is where you say it is and not some kind of a mind trick that you're playing on me," Penny said, far less skeptical than she had been at the bookstore. "Let's say I believe you. How does this all work? You're here to take my soul?"

"That's pretty much it," I said. "That is, assuming that you follow through with your suicidal thoughts."

"Watch it, Jack," Hauser said. "Her soul is still in play. As long as Enoch is on our trail, I think it best that we don't detract her too much."

"Well, I'm not gonna lie. After losing Calvin, I've pretty much given up on everything."

"I'm no shrink, but I am probably the perfect person to talk to about this."

"Why, because your wife killed herself?"

Hearing Penny talk so casually about suicide made my heart ache. "No, that was . . . kind of a fib. I needed to talk to you, get to know you. You see, I took my own life about six months ago."

"What? You lied to me?" Penny said, her anger causing her complexion to turn amber.

"Stop right now, Jack. Do not tell her anything about Enoch. She doesn't need to know about our plan," Hauser said.

"I, um, wanted to talk to you about it to make sure that is really what you wanted to do. Personally, I've regretted it every day since."

"Then if you're dead, how are you even talking to me?" she asked.

"Wait, slow down a minute. We can talk more about me later. I would like to talk about you and your own personal reasons."

"Whatever, man. You're the one that brought yourself up," Penny said, rolling her eyes just like a teenager. "Like I said, it was real rough after Calvin died. I've already told you about my foster parents and all of that. I'm just so alone and I feel worthless to the world. That's it. There's nothing more to say."

"Okay, good, Jack," Hauser said. "Her influx dot is flashing a little faster than before. Try and keep her mind in that phase."

Penny sprang from the couch and spun around toward the fireplace. "Who the hell are you?" she asked, staring right at Hauser.

"Never mind him, Penny. He's just my—"

"Hi, there. My name is Hauser. I'm Jack's trainer in the afterlife. It's a pleasure to meet you," Hauser said, cutting me off.

"You two are really fucking with my mind right now," Penny said, lowering herself back down onto the edge of the couch.

"I know what you're going through, Penny. I really do. But regardless of what Hauser says, just because you're lonely and you've had a loss in your life is no reason at all to kill yourself. You are a vibrant young woman, and trust me when I tell you this, you will make friends. You will mean something," I said with as much passion as I could muster.

Wow, that was quite poetic, Jack, Hauser thought to me. *One thing I've learned in all the years of being a soul collector: It's always the broken souls that are trying fix others. But in this case, I suggest you tread lightly.*

Before I had a chance to respond, I suddenly heard a slow, deliberate clap echo from the kitchen. I whipped my head around to see Enoch leaning against the countertop.

"How the hell did you find us?" I asked, standing up between him and Penny. A moment later, Hauser stepped in beside me.

"I'm sorry, I didn't know this was a private party. Besides, do you think Hauser is the only guy in the afterlife that gets a bag of tricks all for himself?" Enoch held open his blue blazer, displaying a number of gadgets hooked to the inside of his jacket. I instantly recognized the soul magnet, along with his own pocket watch and rosary.

Shit, Hauser, I thought. *What do we do now?*

"Don't worry, Jack," Enoch said. "This will all be over momentarily. Then you can go on with your own miserable afterlife. I just need you two to step aside."

"Sorry, old friend, but that's not going to happen," Hauser said.

Suddenly Penny squeezed herself between Hauser and me and stepped forward. "You three guys are really freaking me out. Who are you?" she asked Enoch.

Enoch smiled but didn't say anything. He slipped his right hand into the left inside jacket pocket and withdrew a sawed-off shotgun—the same shotgun that he'd used in my dream with

Noah Clayton. He raised the barrel up and pointed it directly at her head. "I'm here to do what neither of these two clowns have the balls to do."

Faster than I've ever seen a person move before, Hauser charged Enoch, dislodging the gun from his hand, causing it to fly across the room and clatter beneath the couch.

"Jack. Go, now. Take Penny to your last safe place," Hauser said as he whipped out his injector pen and thrust it toward Enoch.

I turned toward Penny, but before I could grasp her arm, she bolted out the door. Shocked at her sudden self-preservation response, I stumbled after her. As I reached the cabin door, I glanced back just as Enoch kicked Hauser in the shin, forcing him to drop the Epipen to the floor. It clambered across the floor and disappeared beneath the couch, right next to Enoch's shotgun.

Chapter 14.5

As I burst through the door and headed toward the wooded surroundings, I caught a glimpse of Penny charging onto the trail that led toward the lake. Knowing the exact path, I disappeared from the porch and reappeared several yards into the woods, just on the edge of the trail, and waited. Within moments, Penny came into view, panting heavily. I stepped on the trail, startling her to a halt.

"Penny, stop. Let me get you out of here. Let me take you someplace safe."

"Who is that lunatic? And why was he trying to kill me?"

"In a minute. Let's just get out of here." I reached out and gripped her arm firmly before vanishing.

Seconds later, we appeared at my old park bench in the city.

"I know you're not gonna want to hear this, but I need to leave you here," I said.

"Wait. You gotta tell me something. Anything. I mean, I just don't know what to think about any of this," Penny said as tears welled up in her eyes.

"Hey, hey," I said, easing her down onto the bench. "That man, the man in the strange blue suit, is your mythical grim reaper. His name is not important, but let's just say that he's not exactly right in the mind."

Penny brought her hands to her face and massaged her cheeks. "I, uh, I'm scared, Jack. First you tell me that you're here to collect my soul. Strangely, I was okay with that. Then you really prove to me that you are who you say you are by magically taking me someplace that I've never been. All the while, you're telling me that killing myself is not an option. I just don't know what to believe. Tell me, Jack, what does all this mean? I just need something. I need the truth."

"I have to say, none of this has gone as I'd anticipated. For that I am sorry," I said. "The truth. I became a soul collector shortly after I tried to kill myself. Since that time I've found a way to help certain people continue living instead of collecting their souls. Enoch, the man in the blue suit, somehow—and for some unknown demented reason—has taken it upon himself to start killing the souls that I'm trying to save. I wanted to save your soul in order to capture Enoch."

"You son of a bitch. You . . . you used me as bait?"

I nodded slowly, feeling Penny's piercing eyes upon me. "I am sorry, Penny. I really did want to save your soul. But my superiors agreed that capturing Enoch was a priority, and when I suggested this plan—"

"This was all your harebrained idea?"

I nodded again. "With any luck, Hauser has Enoch tagged as we speak."

"Then what? Are you still going to take my soul? What if I don't want to kill myself after all?"

"Penny, that's wonderful to hear. I'll do everything in my power to save you, but right now I have to go."

"So, what? Do I just sit here and wait?" Penny asked.

"Yes. I don't think Enoch knows about this place, and this park doesn't get a lot of visitors. You should be safe here until I return."

I stood to leave, but Penny launched herself from the bench and hugged me tightly. "Please. Don't go. I'm so scared," she said, trembling in my arms.

"I promise, Penny. I'll be right back. I just need to go help Hauser for a bit," I said, patting her back. "The sooner I go, the sooner I'll be back. Then we'll figure out how you can be saved."

Penny released her hug and slunk back to the bench. "Please hurry."

Strangely, I landed back in the forest, right where Penny and I had left just moments before, and not at all where I'd thought—at the cabin. Frustrated at the confusion, I ran toward my cabin. Just as I broke through the canopy, I heard the first of several gunshots, firing in quick succession.

I ran faster. As I leaped onto the porch of the cabin, I saw the silhouettes of two men struggling just inside the window. Then a blinding flash of light shot out through the windows, followed by a blast so strong my body flew backward through the air a dozen yards.

My cabin exploded into flames, burning timbers flying in all directions. My body and soul stopped suddenly as my head cracked on a boulder protruding from the ground. I tried to stand, to save Hauser, but my vision blurred and darkness fell upon me.

Chapter 15

I removed the coin from my hand and slipped it into my pocket. When I looked up at Wilson's troubled eyes, fear and confusion danced freely in the blue-grey of his irises.

"I . . . I just don't know what to say," Wilson said. "I had no idea Enoch was so dangerous."

"So you knew of none of that?" I asked.

"No, not entirely. We were only aware of some of the incidents that have occurred. Our only way to truly find out what had happened was to find you, and re-experience your last forty-eight hours."

"If you knew some of what happened, why be so coy? Why didn't you tell me about any of this?"

"Well, Jack, we wanted to have you experience everything as fresh as possible. This really isn't an exact science, and we were unsure whether or not your mind could influence your own past experiences."

"Regardless of what we just witnessed, I'm still filled with questions."

"As are we, Jack," Wilson said. "You are not alone."

"What about Hauser? Enoch? Did either of them make it out of my cabin before it . . . exploded?" I asked, replaying that horrific catastrophe over in my mind.

"Nobody at the Sentinel has heard from either of them, although we have reason to believe that Hauser may have survived."

"What makes you think that?" I asked. "Is there a way to track him?"

"Unfortunately, no, not at this moment. When the two of you came to the Sentinel to report Enoch's situation, we removed his current soul collection chamber from his possession so that he could devote 100 percent of his time to aid in capturing Enoch. And I'm not sure if you know how it all works yet, but we can only track the collection chamber and not the collector. Right now, he's lost in the wind."

"Then why do you think he's alive?"

"Because, Jack, you are here, and you are alive."

"Of course I am. We just witnessed me not being blown to bits along with my cabin."

"Yes, but when you blacked out, you were in the clearing in front of your cabin. Did you wake yourself up and bring yourself to that bench in Denver? No, that wasn't present in your memories. We assume that Hauser brought you here."

"Okay, I'll go along with that. Then if Hauser is alive, what's our next step?" I asked.

"Slow down, Jack. Let's not get ahead of ourselves. For all we know they both might have succumbed to the fire in the cabin, and you got here some other way entirely. It is only an assumption that Hauser made it out. At this point, that's just a theory."

"That's easy. Let's go take a look at the cabin site right now. Maybe we can find a body or two, or none at all."

"Several members of the high council have already been to the site—"

"So you did know about this?" I demanded.

"Relax, Jack. As soon as Hauser failed to make his scheduled check-in, we sent several collectors to New York to track the two of you down. We found Penny wandering through the city alone. We were able to determine that neither of you were in her vicinity. Then we began to track down your soul box. That's when we found you here in Denver. Before that point, the Sentinel members visited your cabin and investigated the debris. The site was so severely burned they couldn't determine whether human remains were inside."

"But, like you said, how else could I have gotten here? It had to have been Hauser. I'm willing to stake my life on it."

"That's neither here nor there, Jack. Right now the Sentinel has ruled that the crisis is over and you will return to your soul collection abilities, with your last assignment still a priority. You need to collect Penelope's soul."

Chapter 16

"I'm sorry, but I think I just heard you say that I still need to collect Penny's soul?" I said.

"That's right, Jack. Penny's fate is sealed. You must follow through with your initial order. We know that you still have her soul box, and your last known location of her was on the very same park bench where I gave you this incredible opportunity. I believe, however, that she has moved on from that location."

"You can't be serious," I said angrily. "They want me to forget everything that we've been through? Forget about Hauser? They just want me to take Penny's soul after everything that she's just gone through? Don't you think they could cut her a little slack, give her a second chance or something? Consider it reparation for being our bait?"

"The decision is not up to me, Jack. Believe it or not, I'm on your side on this. I lobbied for operational forgiveness on your behalf, but a number of the council members did not see the hardship as I did."

"But that's not fair," I protested. "You all agreed that I should persuade her not to kill herself, and that's exactly what I've done. Talk about bait and switch."

"There's no arguing that fact, Jack. That was the plan, and you seem to have executed it wonderfully. And this wouldn't be such a difficult situation if you hadn't divulged so much information about the Sentinel and the afterlife."

As we sat staring silently at one another, I tried to think of a scenario where everyone could win. Obviously the Sentinel was unwavering in their demands to collect her soul. I, on the other hand, wanted to save her, but at what cost? If Hauser were only here, maybe he would have some words of advice.

Then it hit me—*my God, I can't believe Hauser is gone.* I started to wonder if this was the Sentinel's plan all along, to distract me from Hauser's death with the unrealistic demand that I take Penny's soul anyway. After everything that I'd been through in this godforsaken afterlife, I truly did not know what to do.

"Jack, please remember that when I sacrificed my soul for the sake of you living on, you accepted that responsibility to the Sentinel. And they will hold you to it. I'm sure Hauser has expressed that before."

I nodded but bit my tongue to keep from saying something I might regret.

"All I'm asking is for you to complete this assignment and move on to the next. I promise you this, your next assignment will not be as difficult."

"How can you promise that?" I asked, doing my best to corral my venomous tone.

"Because, Jack, I am going to be your new trainer. And as such—"

"Wait, what? My trainer? Hauser isn't even gone for a single day and they appoint you to be my new trainer? And I thought my training was over. At least that's what Hauser said."

Wilson nodded in agreement. "Yes, that's correct. Hauser did submit that your training had been completed in an acceptable fashion. But with the recent events, namely you divulging that you've avoided a number of assignments, the Sentinel feels it best that your training be extended indefinitely."

"I can't believe this, Wilson. Don't they know what it's like? Have any of those yahoos up there—which I don't entirely understand where *up there* is, ever had to collect the soul from an infant child? From an innocent man on a walk through the park with his daughter? From a girl that's so depressed that she feels that she needs to take her own life? I'm really starting to believe that nobody on this high council has a soul of their own."

"I understand that you're upset, Jack, but we feel that this is the best solution at the moment. I will continue to urge them to suspend your training, but you have to meet me halfway. Let's get through this next collection first, and then we'll see. Can you do that for me? Can you just get through this next step?"

By this point in the conversation, I was listening to Wilson talk but couldn't hear a word he said. I'd made my decision, and my soul be damned for my efforts.

"Okay, Wilson. I'll do it. Can I at least get a few days to track her and try to unexplain some of the things that I've already told her?"

"I think you'll be pleasantly surprised at the ease of this particular collection, Jack. First of all, she is most likely back at her apartment by now, and as for timing, please do take as much time as you need. I will personally cover for you with the Sentinel. You may think that they're a bunch of soulless overlords, but they do have compassion deep down."

"So, that's it? Just get back to work? Will you be accompanying me on this collection?"

"No, I am not going to be in the field as often as Hauser was. For the most part, you'll be on your own, but I will be in to check up on you from time to time."

Hearing that news was the brightest part of the conversation, and I thanked God for small miracles.

"One more thing, Jack. Your ability to interact with the living has been revoked as well. It was temporary, so that should come as no surprise," Wilson said.

"Oh well, it was nice while it lasted," I said.

"Yes. I suppose it was." Wilson stood to leave. "Anyway, Jack, I wish you luck with Penelope. And try not to dwell on the loss of Hauser. It will lead you nowhere."

Chapter 17

From my seat in the pavilion, I watched Wilson casually amble down the sidewalk and enter the main floor lobby of Daniels and Fisher tower. Sounds of the afternoon traffic echoed between the various mile-high city buildings. As I sat alone, I contemplated everything that had happened since my first fateful conversation with Wilson all those months ago. It felt as if I'd lived a lifetime in those six months. And now, the distinct possibility that Hauser, the one person that I'd come to trust and care for deeply, was dead or missing did not settle well with my thoughts of the future.

"Hauser, my friend, I hope that you are in a better place now," I mumbled aloud. "I can only imagine living as long as you have, suffering through the internal torment that you've had to deal with, must have been tough. I hope now you are in a place that you can now breathe freely."

Not wanting to get too wrapped up in sentimental bullshit, I sighed and thought about Penny and her impending soul collection. As much as I was not looking forward to what needed to be done, I stood defiantly. I took in one final view of the Denver skyline, backdropped by the Rocky Mountains. Then I vanished.

Recalling Penny's personal information from an earlier conversation with Hauser, I was able to land at her apartment door. The central hallway that fed a half dozen flats was dingy and unremarkable. A stark white piece of paper was taped to her door, covering her apartment number. "NOTICE OF EVICTION" was printed in bold black letters.

"Oh shit," I mumbled. If Penny wasn't depressed already, she certainly would be after seeing that.

I knocked on the door and waited a few moments. Even though she knew who I was and what I was there for, it didn't feel right just jumping into the middle of her apartment. But when several minutes passed with no answer, I vanished from the hallway, landing on the opposite side of her door.

Her apartment was a small studio unit, with a pullout sofa to the left and a compact, utilitarian kitchen to the right. Protruding from the end of the kitchen was a small dining alcove with a café style dining table at the center. As I walked through the small space, it was clear that Penny wasn't home.

What was equally clear was the sense of surrender flowing freely in the apartment. Dishes were piled high in the sink, and a mound of overdue bills were stacked on the countertop. In the living room, outdated magazines and newspapers were piled nearly two feet high. The only thing that seemed out of place in the chaos was the kitchen table. It was clean and clear of everything, save for a pad of paper and a pen. Lowering myself down into a chair, I read what was written:

You cops will want to know why I did it. Well, let's just say that I know what I'm doing and it'll be better this way for everyone.

So, yeah. I killed myself. I could no longer cope with the betrayal that life has given me. I have always felt that the grim reaper was just around the corner, waiting. And it turns out that he was. He arrived here today and I knew it was the right thing to do. So yeah.

Please tell my brother that I love him, and that he means the world to me. I think he's in some cabin upstate somewhere. He'll understand, I hope.

Good-bye world, it's been real.

My first thought was that I'd failed. After everything she'd been through, I'd failed to save her soul. But on my second read through, I realized that, while the suicide note was written by Penny, these were not her words. Why would she want to apologize to her brother, whom she told me specifically had died years ago?

And that reference about the grim reaper . . .

Suddenly, I heard the sound of splashing water coming from behind a door that I'd overlooked before. It must be the bathroom, and maybe she was taking a bath or a shower. Then I realized that she could be in there right now trying to kill herself.

I rushed to the bathroom door and twisted the handle. It wouldn't budge. The door was locked from the other side. I pounded on the door. "Penny, it's Jack. I'm here to . . ." What was I really there for? I wondered. Was I going to follow through with the Sentinel's plan? Or was I to make yet another fateful decision, a godlike decision, to save her soul?

"I'm here to help you get through this. Penny? Can you hear me?"

She didn't respond, but more vigorous splashing could be heard from the other side of the door.

"Penny, I'm coming in. I don't want you to do something that you'll regret," I said before jumping to the other side of the bathroom door.

I was instantly filled with rage by who stood before me. It was Enoch Gant, holding Penny's head beneath the water in a nearly full tub.

"Penny!" I said as I rushed forward. Her lifeless eyes looked up at me through the water, unaware.

"You bastard!" I screamed, launching myself into Enoch's torso. The force driving him backward, causing him to lose his balance. As we dropped to the floor, the momentum drove our bodies toward the commode. I saw the impending collision and rolled to the side. Enoch, however, slid right into the base of the toilet, his head firmly connecting with the porcelain.

Slowly, I pulled myself up to my knees and rested on my haunches. Enoch was out cold. Blood began to trickle from his temple.

"Take that, you fuck," I said, then rushed to Penny and pulled her out of the water. I laid her dead body on the floor and tilted her head back. I tried to recall the company-sponsored CPR training that I'd reluctantly gone through several years before.

I pinched her nose and blew deeply into her mouth, watching her chest rise. Next I placed my hand over my fist and began to rhythmically pump her chest at a pace I hoped was correct. I alternated the procedures for several minutes, praying to God that I could save her fragile life. I was about to concede defeat when I heard a voice from behind me.

"Jack! Look out!" Hauser yelled from just outside the now open bathroom door. I whipped my head around in Enoch's direction just as he pointed his shotgun right at my head. Instinctively I dropped to the ground, landing directly on Penny's chest, just as Enoch fired. The buckshot flew over my head, and the report of the gun caused my ears to ring loudly. I knew I only had seconds before Enoch would reload to shoot again.

I pushed myself off of Penny and noticed that she had begun to convulse, spewing water from her mouth and nose. I rolled her over on her side before I attempted to disarm Enoch.

A guardian angel must have been looking over me, because Enoch's gun jammed. He continued to point it at me, constantly trying to squeeze the trigger to get it to fire. I knew I only had one shot at disarming him as I dove for the gun. I knocked it from his hands as he attempted to clear the chamber.

As Enoch and I thrashed about on the floor next to Penny in the compact bathroom, I called out to Hauser. "Quick! Throw me the injector."

Hauser slid the device across the bathroom floor. As Enoch rolled to his side in chase of his gun, I scooped up the pen and jabbed it in the side of his neck, injecting its contents into his system.

Hauser squeezed into the small bathroom, straddling Enoch and I on the floor. By then, Penny had sat up and was coughing uncontrollably. Hauser placed his foot on Enoch's hand, before leaning over to grab his gun.

Suddenly Enoch launched his body up with great force, driving both Hauser and me back into the tub. In all the commotion, Hauser dropped Enoch's gun in the water.

"I'm not sure what you just shot me up with, but let me tell you, this isn't over. You've not seen the last of me," Enoch stated, then vanished.

Chapter 18

As soon as Enoch was gone, Hauser and I stepped out of the tub and tended to Penny. "Are you okay?" I asked as I knelt down beside her.

Her eyes were bloodshot, and the side of her face was bruised. She nodded in between coughing fits.

"Can you move?" I asked.

Penny rolled to her side and tried to stand, but fell back against the wall. Hauser and I lifted her and carried her into the living room. We laid her down on the sofa, propping her head up with a seat cushion.

"Why don't you rest for a bit?" I said. "I think you're out of danger for the moment. Either way, I'll be here to protect you if Enoch returns."

She tried to speak, but it only induced more coughing.

"It's okay, Penny. You can trust me," I said as I stroked the hair away from her eyes.

Hauser motioned for me to join him in the kitchen, just out of Penny's earshot. I nodded, then said to Penny, "I'm just going to be right over there. If you need anything, just . . . throw something my way." I winked.

Joining Hauser in the kitchen, I had a million questions, but first I gave him a big hug. "Hauser, you're alive."

"Yep. I seemed to have dodged yet another bullet," he said, patting me on the back. "Although it was touch and go there for a while."

"What happened? I brought Penny to the city, but when I got back to the cabin, I heard gunshots and then the entire place exploded."

"Sorry about that, champ. It looks like your homestead is in need of a bit of repair. After you two left, Enoch and I had a fairly drawn-out battle. We each went for the gun and the auto-injector, but thankfully I was able to secure them before he had a chance to. Unfortunately, though, he threw a gas lantern across the room at me, spreading fuel throughout the cabin. As I tried to maneuver closer to him, he continued to throw crap across the room at me. We both jumped in and out of space, trying to get the upper hand on one another. Finally, I'd had enough and decided to take a shot at him with his own shotgun. It was all so fast, I don't really know what happened. The gas fumes must have ignited or Enoch had a stick of dynamite. As soon as I pulled the trigger, the cabin exploded, and Enoch and I both jumped out of there."

"Then where'd you go? If he wasn't tagged yet, how were you able to follow him?"

"Well I've been trying to narrow down where he stays, as you've seen from all the news reports and research that I've done at my place. So I had a pretty good idea of the region. As we jumped out of the cabin, I was able to follow him a number of jumps before he lost me. Finally, I called off the hunt. It would be just a matter of time before he jumped in the middle of a volcano or something and bye-bye, Hauser. Then I came back and found you lying unconscious on the ground and figured the best bet would be to put you as close to the Sentinel as possible before I went back out after Enoch."

"That is how I got there, then," I said. "Just so you know, Wilson and the Sentinel believe that you and Enoch are both dead. With no contact from you, they don't know what to think. They've made some changes, and—"

"Jesus, I wasn't gone for that long. Just a few days really," Hauser said, shaking his head.

"Well? What did you expect? Anyway, they've made Wilson my new trainer and sent me here to finish Penny's soul collection," I said, nodding in her direction on the couch.

"Well I'll stop by the Sentinel and straighten them out before

I go on the hunt. A hunt that was only made possible by you, Jack. We would not have been able to get this far without your help."

"You mean you're going to go after him yourself?"

"Yep. I wouldn't miss this opportunity for the world. That bastard has been a thorn in my side ever since he went AWOL."

Hauser then looked at Penny resting on the couch not ten feet from us. "And whatever your play is here with Penny, I will back you up. Whatever it takes," Hauser said as he slyly slipped a glass vial from his pocket and handed it to me.

I held the vial up to the light and, seeing a faint silvery mist inside, knew instantly what it was.

"Use your imagination, kid," Hauser said, nodding in Penny's direction. "Now, if you'll pardon me, I need to go catch me an Enoch."

I stashed the vile in my inside pocket and nodded. "Thanks for everything, Hauser. You've done so much for me in the past six months, and I don't know how I would've made it without you. You really are a good person, and it's been a real pleasure to have known you," I said, hugging him again.

"Hey, relax, buddy, I'm coming back. Between me and any number of other Sentinel members, we'll be able to bag Enoch with ease. Of that I am certain," Hauser said.

"Just be careful, then," I said, stepping back into the living room. "Wait, before you go, Hauser, you never told me your last name. What is it?"

Hauser smiled widely. "It's Teufel. It's German for the devil. It was agreed upon that I would not use it in the afterlife."

"Ah, wise choice," I said.

Hauser winked, then he vanished.

Chapter 19

I stood by for several minutes, wishing I had said more to Hauser before he left. Now, he'd never know really how much he truly meant to me.

I returned to the living room and found Penny staring up at the ceiling, looking lost.

"How are you feeling, champ?" I asked, borrowing a moniker from Hauser's vocabulary.

She blinked her thoughts away and looked up at me, then smiled. "I'm . . . I'm feeling okay, but I've been better," she said, her voice a little rough.

"I'd imagine so. You nearly died."

Penny sat up and leaned awkwardly against the back of the couch. "No, there was no *almost* about it. I did die. I was dead, Jack."

"Ah, technicalities. At least you're here now, right?" I said, hoping her suicidal tendencies had passed.

"I suppose, but I would liked to have stayed dead just a little longer."

Surprised by her answer, I asked, "Why is that? Does that mean that you're still wanting to give up?"

Penny shrugged. "I—I'm not sure yet. When I was . . . there, I saw my brother. I would've liked to talk to him, but there wasn't enough time. One minute I was walking toward him and he smiled at me. Then a moment later I was pulled away. It was so brief."

"I don't know what to say, Penny. I didn't know what you just described was even possible. I thought that once a soul was collected, it was reincarnated into another living being. What you just described certainly gives me hope," I said, trying to maintain my composure until my final plan was put into motion.

"Yeah, me neither. At least I was able to see him for a moment, and he looked happy. And that makes me happy."

"That's great, Penny," I said. "But where does that leave you and your situation? Are you still feeling depressed? Are you still contemplating suicide?"

"I don't know, Jack. I don't know what to think. With everything that I've witnessed since first meeting you, I'm confused more than anything else. Nothing can change the fact that I am alone on this earth. And before you go on telling me that I can make friends, let me just say that being alone is not a terribly bad situation for me. I have been alone for so long, I've learned to crave the solitude."

I raised my eyebrows at that.

"But at the end of the day, I don't think I'm ready to turn in my soul."

"Well then, I think today is your lucky day," I said as I sat next to her on the couch. I reached in my pocket and pulled out my coin and my rosary before setting them both on the couch between us.

Penny sat up and looked down at the two items. "What are those?"

"Those are tools of the trade, so to speak. One can take you into the past, and one can take you into the future."

Then I removed the glass vial that Hauser had given me and set it on the couch next to the other items. Finally, I removed the two soul boxes and held them in my hands.

"This is everything I have in my possession, Penny. And I want you to have it all."

"But won't you need them? You know, for your job and all?"

"That's the thing, Penny. I want you to have it all because I think you should take my soul so you can continue living in the afterlife."

Chapter 20

"So you're just going to quit?" Penny asked.

"Well it's not like I've just right now made this decision. I've thought about this for a while now, and as time has gone along, I've felt more and more out of place in the afterlife than I ever did in my past life," I said.

"It's your life, man. But what makes you think that I'll be any better at this job than you?"

"The last six months have been the most difficult of my life. It's hard to explain. I think for starters I miss the personal interaction. I thought I'd be able to get by in the solitude, but in the end, that wasn't so much the truth. Secondly, I seem to want to save every soul I come across. I wanted to save you well before it was a plan to do so. I did in fact save the two souls right before yours, but Enoch put an end to that. I could go on and on, but I think you get the point."

"And you think by dying you'll suddenly get to walk and talk with everyone, just like before?" Penny asked.

"Listen, I'm not sure what the right answer is here. I really don't know what to expect after you take my soul. All I know is that being a collector is not for me."

"And you think it is for me?"

"From everything you've told me, you'd be a perfect fit for this."

"I don't know, Jack. I wouldn't even know where to start," Penny said, eyeing all of the trinkets sitting between us.

"Well that's the glory of this. Hauser will no doubt be your trainer, just as he's been my trainer, and probably the trainer of most of the soul collectors in the last century and a half."

Penny's eyes widened. "Damn, how old is he?"

"I don't recall offhand, but I think he said that he died somewhere around 1810? Don't quote me on that. I'll let him tell you about his own life at his own pace."

"And how about you? How old are you?"

"Me? I'm not that old at all. I was thirty-five when I killed myself, and I've only been here in the afterlife for six months, like I said. You see, things are different here. You continue to age, but at an eighth of the pace that the rest of the world does. There's some strange things that happen with time and how it passes, which I haven't quite figured out. Maybe that's the first thing you should talk to Hauser about."

"Slow down, man. I haven't agreed to any of this yet, and you are continuing to talk to me like I have."

"I'm confident that you, being a youthful person, will be able to cope with the demands of being a soul collector much easier than I have."

"What kind of demands are there?"

"Well, Penny, I'm not gonna sugarcoat it for you. You have to take the souls of people that are dying. The Sentinel, which at some point you will probably meet, will demand that you take each soul that comes into your trust, without question. That is the single most difficult part of this job. That and the loneliness, for me."

"I think that part I would thrive on," Penny said.

"You will have some perks as well. Namely, you can travel by thought. You think of a location or a destination and within moments you are there. Quite handy when you really want to get away from it all," I said jokingly.

"And what about all this stuff?" Penny asked, motioning to the items between us.

"Well, the coin will allow the holder to review parts of their life. For example, if you were to pick up the coin and turn it over in your hand, you could think back to a place or a time and relive that moment. I, as your soul collector, would also live through that moment with you. It also can be used, has been used on me a number of times, to recall past memories that have been forgotten."

"Wicked."

"And this," I said, picking up the rosary, "will allow you to go forward in time, up to twenty-four hours, and witness anticipated events."

"Anticipated?" Penny asked.

"Yes. Not everything you see in that future will absolutely happen. It is an anticipated future that has a high probability of happening. I don't think I'm qualified to tell you much more than that, so I'll leave that up to Hauser to cover in your training."

Penny nodded, then picked up the vial. "What does this do?" she asked, clearly intrigued by the silvery liquid contents.

"That is something that is quite precious. That is a virgin soul. In the event that you come across a soul that you feel deserves to continue living, once a change is made in their fate, you can use this soul as its replacement."

"What do you mean 'virgin'?"

"I know this is a lot of information to take in, and I'm really doing you a favor by telling you this all now. It took me six months to get all of this information myself. That being said, there are old souls and new souls. This is a new one, whereas old souls are reclaimed. That is what our job is, to collect souls. None of us own our souls—we only borrow them."

"Wow, this is all really freakin' blowing my mind," Penny said, staring at the two soul boxes in my hands.

"These are what you collect the souls into. Each soul box has a name, and once you collect the soul, the box vanishes and is replaced with a new one. It's all kinds of magical, but the intrigue will wear off I'm sure."

"Wow, this is really a lot of information to take in. How long will I have to decide?"

"Well you've already died, so your soul is officially no longer yours. I either have to collect it now or you collect mine. In that event, you will become the new soul collector."

"And that's it? I take your soul, then I have the job? No interview or anything?"

I smiled. "Honestly, Penny, I'm not exactly sure how the Sentinel will react to this. When Wilson surrendered his soul in place of my own, my position in the afterlife had already been vetted by the high council, which is just a bunch of guys and gals up someplace making all the life-altering decisions. I'm certain this will blow their minds as soon as you show up for your next collection."

"So you're really just throwing me under the bus so you can get out?"

"Not entirely. Being a soul collector is a thankless job, but it really does have to be done. I do get that, but I just don't think I'm cut out for it. I'm a pretty good judge of character, and I believe that you are."

Penny and I sat in silence for several minutes. Finally, she reached into my hands and took the two soul boxes. She looked at the box with her name first, then the box with mine.

"Okay. What do I do?" Penny asked, her eyes bright and eager.

"Are you sure?" I asked. "Once you take this on, Hauser and the Sentinel will expect a lot from you."

"Like you said, I've already died, right? What's my other choice? You take my soul and be rushed off to the great unknown? I think I'd like to give this a try at least," Penny said. "Besides, if I end up not liking it, I'll just follow in your footsteps. Who knows. Maybe we'll see each other again sooner than you think. Yeah, I'm ready."

"All right. I'm not exactly sure how this works on my end, but once you open a box, if there is a soul present, it will find its way in."

"And you're sure?" she asked. "You're ready to end it all? No going back, right?"

I nodded and took a deep breath. I was more certain about this than I'd been about anything else since I died on that New York bus. Now as I sat next to Penny, my entire fate resting in the palms of her hands, I could only think about Cyndi. Would I see her again? Lord, I certainly hoped so.

"Well, Jack it was nice knowing you, as brief as it was," she said and opened my soul box. When she turned it toward me, I exhaled uncontrollably. I felt as if I were in the vacuum of space as my last, dying breath was extricated from my body.

As the wisp of smoke exited my mouth, I began to re-experience my entire life in reverse. Images of every person I'd ever met flashed through my mind. No matter their impact on my soul, I recognized each and every one. As the years slipped by, the memories began to move increasingly faster. I re-experienced my parents' funeral, but before any emotions could come, I witnessed them alive and full of vigor.

Then Cyndi came. I saw her images the most, and it pained me to see those memories fly by so quickly. I was able to see how happy we were together early on. Then our wedding. She was such a beautiful bride. Our courtship lasted mere seconds, while in life we'd dated for several years before even getting engaged. Finally, the day we met. That magical moment where she won my heart thankfully slowed down, even if minutely.

I relived my entire college days in a matter of moments. The late night study sessions, the frat parties, the binge drinking—all without any fanfare.

Then I was back in high school, middle school, elementary, and then preschool. All passing by in the blink of an eye. I watched myself take my first steps as a child, a smile as wide as the world is large.

At the end of my thirty-five yearlong replay, I looked at Penny one last time. Then the lights dimmed, fading out like the flame of a candle.

Epilogue

No sight—no sound—no smell. The darkness that enveloped me was total. I was weightless and free. Then, I noticed something in the distance . . . glowing faintly. The glimmer was small, but it began to build in size, practically imperceptible to the naked eye. Moment by moment, the light intensified and became more pronounced. If it hadn't been for that strange brilliance, I would have been sure that I no longer existed.

The silence became overpowering when I realized that I could no longer hear my own heartbeat. The pulsing whump-whump in my inner ear was alarmingly silent. The unexpected tranquility was surprisingly disturbing.

This is what it's like to be dead? I wondered. My mind was still present, but nearly every other one of my senses appeared to be absent. I'd try to reach out and feel something, but there was nothing near me to touch. Then again, if I could pick something up, how could I bring it to my mouth to taste? To my nose to smell? I couldn't feel my hands.

As I continued to focus on the growing light, I waited. I waited for what I'd hoped was some kind of resolution to my life. I'd existed for thirty-five years among the living, and even more time in the afterlife. Now, here I was, at the precipice of something . . . I don't know, something completely unknown, but entirely anticipated nonetheless. I had hope for only one thing—one particular soul to meet me in the end, and I feared that it would not come. I feared a tremendous disappointment in my uncharted future.

With the radiance ever expanding, I tried to look away. I tried to look down or around, but my vision was fixed. I could only focus on the growing light before me. I had no idea of the completeness of my existence. Did I have a body? Arms, legs? Anything? All I could do was stare forward, unaware of anything else.

Then, finally with the light source large enough to cast shadows, I saw a shape at the center of the expanding intensity. It began as a vertical line emanating from the bottom of the bloom. Slowly, it began to grow as the light itself did. Within moments, the sliver of darkness developed into a somewhat more pronounced shape.

The line began to spread at the base, and thicken as it rose up from the bottom edge. Near the top of its existence, it narrowed again, sharply. The outside edge became more apparent and I could begin to make out the hazy outline of what I'd guess was a person. Still, whatever was causing the shadow was a great deal away.

I tried to move again, but no matter my will of efforts, I remained fixed in my position. I couldn't maneuver an inch. All I could do was wait . . . for what I'd hoped was worth surrendering everything.

A sudden realization hit me—a new sense. I had the sense of regret. Was that an actual sense? Maybe it was an extended form of feeling, but just not in the sense of touch. I could *feel* the wants and desires of life, but in a completely different aspect. Here I was—not alive in the aspect that I'd experienced for my entire existence in the world, but I still felt emotion. I wanted to . . . no, needed to see who was approaching slowly, coming in from the light.

Then, for the first time since entering the darkness, I felt movement. I wasn't sure if it was my mind playing tricks on me, or if I was actually moving forward. I felt the undeniable momentum of advancement toward the light. Toward the entity ahead of me.

Was it God or was it something entirely different?

With my forward migration clearly advancing, coupled with the expanding light source, it didn't take long to reach equilibrium. I was now surrounded equally by light and dark—though the darkness shrank more quickly by the moment.

Could a new sense be returning to me? The sense of time passing? I shrugged, or at least, I thought I did. In my mind, I visualized my shoulders rise marginally.

Was all this in my mind? I wondered. If I closed my eyes, would I still see the light continue to expand? Would the darkness continue to flee from existence? I tried to shut my eyes, but I was unable to. I had no control of my vision. I continued to stare straight ahead at the approaching shadow.

Was it male or female? Adult or child? I couldn't tell yet.

"Hello?" I said. Or at least, I thought I did. I couldn't feel my tongue or my mouth. I could only feel a ghost of my own existence. I was there, but I wasn't. It was the strangest sensation.

Finally, with the surrounding darkness almost completely eliminated, the person that was approaching me become clearer. I could see movement in their body. I began to see arms and legs sway in motion as they moved ever closer to me. Whoever it was, they were close enough that I should have been able to make out some kind of recognizable detail about their being. But, all I could see was a hazy outline.

He or she was nearly upon me now, and I could barely control my anticipation. Would I recognize the person or would they be foreign to me? Not ever being a spiritual man, I wondered if God were to approach me like this, would I know who it was? I shrugged my nonexistent shoulders once again.

At last, the shadowy figure stopped right in front of me, and I could just make out long, flowing hair in the outline. Or was that my own craving desires taking over?

"Is it you?" I asked.

"It is me," came the familiar voice.

It was Cyndi, and she suddenly appeared in my vision completely. She wore a pale white sun dress with a crimson ribbon around her waist. She was barefoot and wore no makeup. Her hair was shoulder length and held no style in the modern sense. She looked completely natural and radiant.

I tried to reach for her, but I had no arms to do so. I tried to smell her near me, but there was no scent in the air. All I could do was see her standing in front of me.

"Is this real?" I asked.

"It is if you wish it," Cyndi said, her eyes focused on my own.

"I don't know. I seem to be missing several of my senses. I only wish to touch you once again."

Cyndi reached out and caressed my cheek. Then, I felt her touch my neck, my arm, my chest. As the seconds passed, I could feel her touch over my entire existence, all at the same time. The warmth of her contact with my skin felt real.

"Will this do?" she asked, lovingly.

"It's a start," I said, as I was completely enveloped by her embrace.

I felt wanted. I felt loved. I felt at home.

ABOUT THE AUTHOR

When not practicing architecture, Paul works on his writing. He lives in Littleton, Colorado, with his wife and daughter.

To learn more about him and his books, visit www.Paul-Kohler.net